GLUCK

AN EIGHTEENTH-CENTURY PORTRAIT IN LETTERS AND DOCUMENTS

Patricia Howard

CLARENDON PRESS · OXFORD

1995

Oxford University Press, Walton Street, Oxford OX2 6DP

Oxford New York
Athens Auckland Bangkok Bombay
Calcutta Cape Town Dar es Salaam Delhi
Florence Hong Kong Istanbul Karachi
Kuala Lumpur Madras Madrid Melbourne
Mexico City Nairobi Paris Singapore
Taipei Tokyo Toronto
and associated companies in
Berlin Ibadan

Oxford is a trade mark of Oxford University Press

Published in the United States
by Oxford University Press Inc., New York

© Patricia Howard 1995

British Library Cataloguing in Publication Data
Data available
ISBN 0–19–816385–1

Library of Congress Cataloging in Publication Data
Howard, Patricia.
Gluck: an eighteenth-century portrait in letters and documents /
Patricia Howard.
p. cm.
Includes bibliographical references.
1. Gluck, Christoph Willibald, Ritter von, 1714–1787.
2. Music—18th century—History and criticism—Sources.
I. Gluck, Christoph Willibald, Ritter von, 1714–1787.
Correspondence. English. II. Title
ML410.G5H668 1995 782.1'092—dc20 95–17332
ISBN 0–19–816385–1

1 3 5 7 9 10 8 6 4 2

Set by Hope Services (Abingdon) Ltd.
Printed in Great Britain
on acid-free paper by
Biddles Ltd.
Guildford & King's Lynn

For Alexander

INTRODUCTION

GLUCK left no coherent collection of letters to a single correspondent that shed the same degree of light on a significant period of his life as do, for example, Mozart's letters to his father in the early 1780s, or Elgar's letters to Jaeger in the first years of the twentieth century. The longest sequence of letters is addressed to the Austrian diplomat Kruthoffer, but Gluck wrote these mostly during periods of inaction, precisely because he was away from Paris, the focus of activity in his last creative decade: 'Send us all the theatre news' is a recurrent plea. Unlike Verdi, Gluck left few letters illuminating the collaboration between composer and librettist—though the surviving correspondence addressed to Du Roullet and Guillard is of unparalleled interest in documenting his creative process. Unlike Tchaikovsky, he wrote virtually no letters to his immediate family (Mme Gluck rarely left his side), and the only extant one is a curiously cold homily to a brother-in-law (16 January 1769) who is never heard of again. There are, of course, the famous manifestos: although Gluck almost certainly had Calzabigi's help in writing the dedications to *Alceste* and *Paride*, he was articulate in defending his aims, and the same phrases are echoed when he expounded his artistic principles to Wieland (7 August 1776), Klopstock (10 May 1780), and Valentin (17 April 1782), and appear in ironic inversion in the cunning riposte to his critic La Harpe (October 1777). I have included all Gluck's letters extant at the time of writing. They do not offer easy access to a portrait of the composer. The jigsaw is incomplete and some vital pieces are missing. Such material as exists evokes a complex personality, extrovert, gregarious, uxorious, and massively energetic, while at the same time careless, avaricious, gluttonous, and totally self-centred.

The sources consulted—autograph, facsimile, transcription, and published—are listed in the notes. There is at present no readily available edition of even a portion of the letters in their original languages, though Tiersot's publication of much of the autograph holdings in the Bibliothèque nationale, Paris ('Pour le centenaire de Gluck', *Le Ménestrel*, 1914)[1] and Kinsky's admirably annotated edition of the correspondence between Gluck and Kruthoffer (*Glucks Briefe an Franz Kruthoffer*, Vienna, Prague,

---

[1] The Bibliothèque nationale, Paris, is referred to throughout this book by the siglum F-Pn.

and Leipzig, 1927) are starting-points. Further discoveries by Alcari, Hortschansky, Komorn, and Spulak show that the field is still open.

While the prime aim of this book is to publish the letters in readable translations, there are many other source materials which can contribute to a portrait of the composer. Gluck features in many personal records of the period: in private diaries (such as Zinzendorf's), in journals circulated in manuscript (Mannlich's 'Histoire de ma vie', Grimm's *Correspondance littéraire*), in published memoirs (Amélie Suard's *Essais de mémoires sur M. Suard*), in colleagues' reminiscences (Dittersdorf, Salieri, Kelly), and increasingly, as he acquired celebrity, in travellers' tales (Burney, Sonnenfels, Nicolai, Kraus). These offer an abundance of colourful narrations, and pose an obvious problem of authenticity. There is, in principle, no reason to believe every word of them, but then there is no very good reason to disbelieve them, either. Gluck's larger-than-life personality lent itself to vivid anecdotes, but the agreement between the accounts serves, cumulatively, to substantiate them. Gluck's after-dinner behaviour, for example (often at the keyboard, acting, singing, emotionally roused, and casting a powerful spell over his audience) is consistently attested over a twenty-one-year period from 1762 (Zinzendorf on the *Orfeo* previews) to 1783 (visits by Kraus and Reichardt). His despotic conduct of rehearsals appears to have been remarkably similar in the very different conditions in Vienna and Paris, whether inferred from words attributed to him by Burney, or in Mannlich's detailed description; moreover, as Klopstock told Cramer, it was imitated in miniature on an occasion when the composer instructed his niece in public (Karlsruhe, winter 1774). Mannlich described his greed at table in 1774, Reichardt confirmed its continuance till at least 1783. Calzabigi, who had an axe to grind, insisted on Gluck's faulty command of languages, but D'Escherny and Salieri, who had not, confirmed the charge. All in all, the anecdotes stand up well to probing.

There is a special case among them which repays closer examination. Five years after the composer's death, Reichardt, in the course of correcting Gerber's dictionary article on Gluck, published a 'French manuscript from the hand of a gentleman in Vienna', containing nine anecdotes which range across the whole of Gluck's professional life, from the occasion of his first opera *Artaserse* in 1741 to a visit to him in 1786.[2] These anecdotes

---

[2] The anonymous 'French manuscript' is no longer extant, and can be read only in Reichardt's French translation, quoted in full in his 'Fortsetzung der Berichtigungen und Zusätze zum Gerberschen Lexicon der Tonkünstler' and published in the periodical he edited, *Musikalische Monatschrift*, 3 (Sept. 1792), 72–4. In my paper 'Anecdotal Evidence: Reichardt's *französisches Manuscript*' (paper read to the Open University Postgraduate Research Day, London, 19 Nov. 1994) I have argued that the content of the MS, though not the authorship, can be attributed to Gluck himself.

have puzzled Gluck's biographers. Is it conceivable that in the course of his very first opera, Gluck departed from the 'superficial' style of his mentor Sammartini, and first shocked then captivated the Milanese with his more vigorous music, pointing up the difference by including a single aria in Sammartini's 'insipid' manner? The other stories attribute a similar boldness to the composer, with seven of the nine episodes taking the same format, opening with a challenging situation, proceeding to tell of an act of artistic, social, or physical daring by the composer, and ending with a happy outcome.

Putting aside for the moment question of the truth of the anecdotes, it is useful to ask who originated them. The narrative structures of the episodes are so similar that they strongly suggest a single author (there are many other anecdotes told about Gluck which take a different structure). If, as fact or fiction, they stem from a single narrator, the period of time over which they took place becomes interesting. Only one person was able to tell stories about the whole period covered by the manuscript—Gluck himself. In support of this inference, we note that the stories are all very much to Gluck's credit, and that no one would have had a greater interest in disseminating them than he. Further, they are all highly dramatic; the fundamental structure is almost a three-act opera of crisis, action, *lieto fine*. There is at least a strong possibility that Reichardt's manuscript authentically reconstructs Gluck's conversation, faithfully recorded by someone who visited him as late as 1786, the date of the last episode.

It would, of course, be interesting to know how far the tales are true. Some are self-evidently so (the award of the Golden Spur and Gluck's pride in using the title), others are backed up by objective sources (the *Mémoires secrets* confirmed his refusal to accept an understudy for one of the principal roles at the première of *Iphigénie en Aulide*). Most focus on his high-handed treatment of those who might be thought to be his superiors—Caffarelli, Millico, Durante, and Metastasio. The remainder illustrate his intense involvement in his art. With the exception of an episode from the last year of his life, which clearly arose from direct observation, it is safest to understand these scenes as showing what Gluck chose to remember as the truth, a fact in itself sufficiently revealing to justify their inclusion in this 'portrait'.

We are on securer, if duller, ground with the more official records, among them the court diary of Khevenhüller-Metsch in Vienna and the literary chronicle of the *Mémoires secrets* in Paris. The particular value of these sources is that they tell very precisely how things appeared at the time. Described on a daily basis, public opinion is represented in all its fluctuating nuances. The authors, particularly of the *Mémoires*, are often taken by surprise, for example at the reception of *Cythère assiégée*, which the *Mémoires* expected to repeat the success of *Iphigénie*; their reluctant acknowledgement of its failure guarantees the unmanipulated truth of their reporting. The *Mémoires secrets* may have had an extra role in shaping some of the diary accounts written, or at least polished, long after the event: there are sufficient verbal parallels between Mannlich's 'Histoire' and the *Mémoires* to suggest that Mannlich used the contemporary record when polishing his account some two decades later.

This is not a biography. My aim has been to assemble a selection of the material on which a biography might be based, and to structure it as a series of episodes in a life. I have excluded discussion of the music, other than sketching in its immediate reception. This treatment mirrors the nature of Gluck's reputation in the two hundred years since his death; interest in the man and his historical significance has, sadly, far outweighed knowledge of his œuvre, and since it does not lie in my hands to remedy the imbalance, I hope to have helped ensure at least that the enduring fascination of this remarkable character is soundly based.

When, in the autumn of 1775, Gluck was lying gravely ill, his wife intercepted a letter from Kruthoffer describing the failure of *Cythère assiégée*. She had it translated from German into French, and sent it to Du Roullet for comment. Chided by Du Roullet for his lack of tact towards the invalid, Kruthoffer replied that the damage lay in the translation, which was 'more literal than faithful'. A weighty responsibility rests upon the translator of a complete volume of material, of which no more than a few pages originate in the English language. To the French, German, and Italian writers, there is a duty to render their thoughts accurately. There is also an obligation to provide English-speaking readers with prose which does not offer constant reminders of the fact that it is a translation—such literal treatment, indispensable in making individual documents available to professional scholars, becomes intolerable in a continuous narrative. My translations have aimed at fidelity to meaning and tone rather than literal correspondence with the original wording, and although there are a handful of obscure passages where I have had to confess to puzzlement (Dittersdorf on the scenery for *Le cinesi* for example), I have found that by far the hardest task has been to render easily understood terms into English equivalents—for example the French *spectacle*. The presence of German, French, and Italian languages, appearing not only cheek by jowl in consecutive letters, but jumbled together in a single document according to Viennese eighteenth-century usage, brings about a disconcerting mix of Herr and monsieur, Ritter, chevalier and cavaliere, and so on. I have been guided by OUP house style for the translation of titles, and have corrected the spelling of all proper names other than for Gluck himself, where the variants are often instructive in revealing how his ambiguous nationality was interpreted at any time. On the translation of the obscurer passages and historical usages I have been advised by many colleagues and friends including Lia Bodenham, Stephanie Clennell, Charlotte Goddard, Sara Marani, Doreen Murray, and Hildegard Wright.

Many librarians and archivists have helped me to research the primary sources. In particular I should like to thank staff at the Open University Library, the British Library, the New York Public Library, the Bibliothèque nationale and the Archive de l'Opéra in Paris, the Steiermärkisches Landesarchiv in Graz, the Bayerische Staatsbibliothek in Munich, the Hauptstaatsarchiv in Stuttgart, the Herzogin Anna Amalia Bibliothek in Weimar, and the Österreichische Nationalbibliothek and the Haus-, Hof-, und Staatarchiv in Vienna. The following individuals have been of particular assistance in enabling me to locate documents: Dr Gabriele Buschmeier, Dr Walter Henn, Dr Edward Olleson, Dr Vera Sustikova, and Dr J. Rigbie Turner. The responsibility for the selection is my own, constrained chiefly by length—it is worth recording the fact that the book could have been twice as long and still not have contained all the available and relevant sources from the Paris years. I owe a very great debt to colleagues who have read and commented on different parts of the typescript, particularly Dr Donald Burrows, Professor Bruce Alan Brown, and Professor Julian Rushton. Finally I must thank my family for thoughtfully keeping their crises at bay while work was in progress.

CONTENTS

Contents

LIST OF PLATES

between pp. 112 and 113

1

A BOHEMIAN CHILDHOOD
(1714–1734)

CHRISTOPH WILLIBALD GLUCK was born on 2 July 1714 in the small village of Erasbach in the Upper Palatinate, now northern Bavaria.[1] His baptism, two days later, was recorded in the shared parish register for the parishes of Weidenwang and Erasbach. The officiating priest was Simon Papst, the godfather Christoph Fleischmann.[2]

Little it known of his mother, Anna Walburga. Her maiden name and the date of her marriage to Alexander Johannes Gluck are lost. Christoph Gluck was her oldest surviving child; she had four further sons and two daughters.

The baptismal register gives Gluck's father's occupation as 'venator', huntsman. At least three generations of Glucks had been foresters, huntsmen, and gamekeepers, and Gluck's early life was shaped by his father's career. The mayoral archives of Erasbach show that a forester's dwelling was built in the village for Alexander Johannes Gluck in 1713.[3] On becoming forest-master to the Duchess Anna Maria of Tuscany, in October 1717, he moved with his family to Reichstadt (now Liberec) in Bohemia; in 1722 Alexander took up a similar position with Count Philipp Joseph von Kinsky in Böhmisch-Kamnitz (Česká Kamenice), his family occupying the forester's house in the village of Kreibitz (Chřibská); in 1727 he moved to Eisenberg (Jezeři), near Komotau (Chomutov), to take up his last post as head forester to Prince Philipp Hyazinth von Lobkowitz.

---

[1] At different times, Gluck himself referred to his place of birth variously as Erasbach (on entering the Univ. of Prague; see below) and as the nearby town of Neumarkt, some 20 km. to the north (on his marriage certificate; see Ch. 5 below).

[2] The entry in the baptismal register is reproduced in *La Revue musicale*, 10 (1914), second plate (unnumbered) between pp. 2–3. Fleischmann also stood as godfather to Gluck's younger brother, Christoph Anton, in 1716, when he was identified as a miller in Weidenwang.

[3] Joseph Schmitt, 'Zur Familiengeschichte des berühmten Oberpfälzers Christoph Willibald Ritter von Gluck', *Verhandlung des historischen Vereins für Oberpfalz und Regensburg*, 95 (1954), 217.

Gluck's early travels later gave rise to debate as to whether he was a German or Bohemian composer. From the age of 3, he spent his childhood in Bohemian villages. The earliest account of his childhood can scarcely be reckoned a reliable document. In 1774, at the start of his busy and successful Paris years, Gluck reminisced about his Bohemian childhood to his self-appointed biographer, the painter Johann Christian von Mannlich, who retold the account as follows:

Mme Gluck invited me to dinner in the park at Saint-Cloud, Our provisions were laid out on a cloth on the ground and we all sat around it. Fontenet[4] had brought us some fine fruit and I, for my part, had put a bottle of old Rhine wine in my pocket for Papa Gluck (as all followed the example of Millico[5] in giving him this name). He was in the best of moods, and drank and ate with a good appetite. 'Long live the simple life,' he told us, 'the life that is independent, free from all bother, worry and prudence. I've always sought it, and in the whole of my long career I've only enjoyed it for a fortnight. I shall never forget those days. . . .

'My father was water bailiff and forester at N. in Bohemia, and he had planned that I should one day succeed him in his post. In my country, everyone is a musician. Music is taught in school, and in even the smallest villages the country people sing and play a variety of instruments in church during high mass. Since I was fascinated by this art, I made rapid progress. I played several instruments, and the master, singling me out from the other pupils, gave me lessons in his own home in his spare time. I thought and dreamt of nothing but music, and I neglected the art of forestry. That wasn't what my father had planned. He doubled my workload and insisted on its completion in order to divert me (as he put it) from a career which would never equip me to earn my bread. No longer free to practise by day, I sought to do so by night, but that disturbed my father's sleep and that of the other occupants of the household. My instruments were locked away. Unable to resist my passion for music, I took up the jew's harp, and soon became adept at this new, less penetrating instrument.[6] In church on Sundays I had nothing more to wish for. At last, consumed with the desire to dedicate myself entirely to my passion, I begged my father to send me to Vienna[7] and to have me study music there. He was adamant and drove me to despair. One fine day, having only a very little money in my pocket, I left

[4] Pierre Fontenet, musician and fellow courtier with Mannlich to Duke Christian IV.

[5] Guiseppe Millico, castrato and intimate friend of the Gluck family; see Ch. 11. Mannlich writes 'Milico': the spelling of proper names has been corrected throughout, except in the case of Gluck, where variant spellings sometimes reveal how his ambiguous nationality was interpreted.

[6] Mannlich, whose French is often faulty, writes 'pur brouillant', presumably for 'peu bruyant' meaning 'not very noisy'. In the German text, *Ein deutscher Maler und Hofmann* (Berlin, 1910), however, the phrase is mistranslated, and the instrument described as 'lärmenden', noisy.

[7] Mannlich writes 'Vienna' as the destination of Gluck's ambition. It is possible that this was Gluck's goal, but as his first student travels took him to Prague, this is likelier.

my father's home, and, in order not to be caught, I avoided taking the shortest route to Vienna. Wanting to husband the little wealth I had, I approached a rustic cottage where the family were sitting down to eat. I took my jew's harp from my pocket and treated them to a few tunes. Seeing that I was decently dressed, they bade me enter and made room for me at their table. When night fell, I found myself in another village, where my jew's harp earned me eggs, bread, and cheese, which were given me at the windows of houses where I made myself heard. At the last house I asked for accommodation, and it was gladly given, and what is more, on handing over my eggs, my bread, and my cheese, I was given a good supper. My hostesses cared for me as if I were a member of the family, so greatly had my instrument and my songs endeared me to them. The following day, after a good breakfast I continued blithely on my way. And that was how, thanks to my portable instrument and my voice, confident of a good reception wherever I offered myself, I moved happily towards the capital, without a worry in the world. On Sundays and feast-days, I would play sometimes one instrument, sometimes another, in the village churches. There I was taken for a virtuoso, and the priest would welcome me and would usually put me up in his house. These worthy pastors were all musical, and would sometimes detain me for several days in their homes.

'There, making music all day, well esteemed, well provided-for, free, and independent, I was the happiest of lads.

'As I travelled in this way towards Vienna, the last priest, in whom I had partly confided, gave me a letter for one of his friends in the capital.

'On arrival there, I confidently introduced myself to him; he received me kindly, but did not hide from me the fact that in Vienna there were thousands of virtuosos of my rank, and that with my abilities I would run the risk of starving to death if no one afforded me the opportunity to make progress in my art. I had to tell him who I was and where I had come from. He took an interest in me, wrote to my father, and persuaded him give up his opposition to my wishes. Eventually [my father] gave way and assisted me.

'If on the one hand I lost the independence, the freedom, and the delights of a carefree vagabond existence, I could, on the other hand, abandon myself to my passion without reserve, play and compose music from morning to night.

'This is how I came to be what I am today, always nostalgic for the two weeks spent in freedom with the single resource of my jew's harp.'[8]

This picaresque account poses several problems. If it were a true record of an episode in the composer's life, it would be crucial to know whether it referred to Gluck's bid for freedom which resulted in his admission to the

[8] 'Histoire de ma vie', excerpted in Henriette Weiss von Trostprugg (ed.), 'Mémoires sur la musique à Paris à la fin du règne de Louis XV', *La Revue musicale*, 15 (1934), 260–1. I have retained the unconventional paragraphing to facilitate comparison with the original.

University of Prague in 1731, or whether, if the references to Vienna were correct, it described his arrival in the imperial capital in 1734 or 1735. The whole anecdote could have been inflated from a brief childhood escapade. There is an air of romance about it, but then Gluck's fondness for travel and his uninhibited delight in unconventional instruments were traits which remained with him throughout his life. Conformation of the narrative appears in Anton Schmid's biography, which is based on family reminiscences. Schmid plausibly locates Gluck's adventures in his university vacations, when he would 'wander from village to village . . . entertaining the inhabitants by playing and singing, and often gaining from his village performances nothing but eggs, which he elsewhere exchanged for bread.'[9] If, however, the entire episode is fictitious, a possible source of inspiration is not hard to trace. We know that Gluck was an enthusiastic reader of English novels in translation, and that Goldsmith's _The Vicar of Wakefield_ was a particular favourite.[10] In chapter 20 of that novel, George Primrose relates how he undertook a similar journey: 'I had some knowledge of music, with a tolerable voice, and now turned what was once my amusement into a present means of subsistence. . . . Whenever I approached a peasant's house towards night-fall, I played one of my most merry tunes, and that procured me not only a lodging, but subsistence for the next day.' Primrose's journey may, in its turn, have been created from Goldsmith's own continental travels, which he pursued on foot, earning food and accommodation by playing his flute.

One reason for accepting Mannlich's anecdote as genuine is that it is consistent with other accounts of musical education in Bohemia. It is worth looking briefly at two such sources, since both authors were known to Gluck, and the first account was written immediately after its author had visited Gluck in Vienna. The historian Charles Burney, on his tour of 1772 to investigate the 'present state of music in Germany, the Netherlands, and United Provinces', set out to discover the truth of what he had 'frequently been told' (by Gluck?) 'that the Bohemians were the most musical people of Germany, or perhaps of all Europe':[11]

I crossed the whole kingdom of Bohemia, from south to north; and being very assiduous in my enquiries, how the common people learned music, I found out

---

[9] _Christoph Willibald Ritter von Gluck_ (Leipzig, 1854), 22. Schmid claimed to have taken information from Tomaschek, who had known Gluck's brother Franz Anton Ludwig; Schmid also collected reminiscences from Gluck's nephew and niece, children of another brother, Karl (ibid. 12).

[10] See Ch. 20 below.

[11] _The Present State of Music in Germany, the Netherlands, and United Provinces_, 2nd edn. (London, 1775, repr. New York, 1957), ii. 3.

at length, that, not only in every large town, but in all villages, where there is a reading and writing school, children of both sexes are taught music. . . .

I went into the school, which was full of little children of both sexes, from six to ten or eleven years old, who were reading, writing, playing on violins, hautbois, bassoons, and other instruments. The organist had in a small room of his house four clavichords, with little boys practising on them all. . . .

These schools clearly prove that it is not from a partially in *nature* that Bohemia abounds so much with musicians; for *cultivation* contributes greatly towards rendering the love and knowledge of music general in this country: and the Bohemians may as well be called a *learned* people because they can read, as superior musicians because they can play upon instruments, since the study of both are equally made by them essential parts of common education.[12]

A few years later, Johann Friedrich Reichardt, minor composer and major music historian of the later eighteenth century, expanded upon Burney's observations. The further reasons he offers to account for Bohemian musicianship are consistent with Gluck's reminiscences:

Burney found the sole cause [of Bohemian musicality] to lie in the singing schools, which are found in Bohemian towns and villages. But there are also singing schools in Moravia and Austria, and yet their inhabitants are not nearly so musical. The chief causes are to be sought elsewhere.

A notable fact which I must mention first is that in the country schools, not only is singing taught, but also instruments, though both only for the unpolished performance of the easiest church music. And so in almost every village and on nearly every holy day, a band of villagers can be found, who honour their God and their saints, and edify their fellows, by playing the violin, flute, trombone, and trumpet until the very graves and vaults resound. But can this instruction alone produce the skilful Bohemian virtuosos who are found in almost all European orchestras? We must investigate further. . . .

The majority of these people are tradesmen, who ply their trade in linen and glass throughout Europe. . . . But before a father sends his son out on business, he sends him to the schoolmaster or the choirmaster, who has already taught him to sing and play while at school, for advanced instruction on one instrument, so that if he should find himself in a distant land . . . and if his trade should not prosper there, he will be able to support himself with his music.

The second cause is that almost every Bohemian gentleman has some of his servants taught by skilled masters, so that he can easily acquire his own orchestra.

But the third cause, almost as important as the first, is the University in

---

[12] Ibid. ii. 4–25 *passim*.

Prague. Every ordinary [trades]man in comfortable circumstances will send one of his sons to study in Prague, but will give him a little less than he needs to support himself; so the son has to earn part of the income he needs through his music. . . . He is soon playing more than he studies, and ends up altogether a musician.[13]

Is this not exactly what happened to Gluck? 'Gluck Christophorus, a Palatine from Erasbach' matriculated in the Faculty of Philosophy at the University of Prague in 1731,[14] and left there perhaps some three years later, 'altogether a musician'. Reichardt outlines the kind of musical experiences Gluck may have enjoyed:

Daily in the churches, [the student] plays the finest compositions; he attends all public concerts given by travelling virtuosos, and has the opportunity to learn from them. He may well also attend the Italian opera buffa, and hear a variety of good things there, and soon develops into a skilful man. For a while he will remain in Prague in these circumstances, till he eventually sees that too many around him are striving for the same goal; then he will move away and seek his fortune further afield.[15]

What little is known of Gluck's time in Prague agrees well with Reichardt's account. Gluck played the organ at the Týn church; he also sang and played the violin and cello, perhaps taking part in the Italian oratorios given in the church of St František. He would surely have attended the operas given by the company under the direction of Antonio Denzio. Although presented in the private theatre of Count Franz Anton von Sporck, the opera was advertised as open to the public. In the 1730s, though, the repertory was dominated by opera seria; not until 1738 or 1739 was a new theatre, the Teatro nuovo or Comoedia-Haus, opened at Kotce as a venue for touring companies, mostly presenting opera buffa. In Gluck's first year in Prague, performances included operas by two Venetian composers, Albinoni (*Didone*) and Vivaldi (*Alvilda, Regina dei Goti*); also an opera by the Viennese Caldara (*La pravità castigata*). He

---

[13] *Briefe eines aufmerksamen Reisenden die Musik betreffend* (Frankfurt and Leipzig, 1774–6), ii. 123–34.

[14] The University of Prague was later called the Charles-Ferdinand University, after its founder Charles IV. The record of Gluck's matriculation, in which he is assigned to classes in logic and mathematics, is reproduced in Hans Joachim Moser, *Christoph Willibald Gluck: Die Leistung, der Mann, das Vermächtnis* (Stuttgart, 1940), 24. The mention of Gluck as 'a Palatine from Erasbach' recalls Moser's hidden agenda to claim Gluck as a German composer: I have not been able to trace the archival entries he cited.

[15] *Briefe*, ii. 131.

⟩

could also have heard settings of texts which he later set himself, including Costantini's *Ipermestra* (1731) and Lucchini's *Issipile* (1734).[16]

[16] Herbert Seifert, 'Der junge Gluck: Das musikdramatische Umfeld', *Gluck in Wien: Kongressbericht Wien 1987*, ed. Gerhard Croll and Monika Woitas (Kassel, 1989), 21–30; see also Jitka Ludvová, 'Prague', *The New Grove Dictionary of Opera*, ed. Stanley Sadie (London, 1992), iii. 1082–3.

2

AN ITALIAN APPRENTICESHIP
(1734–1745)

FROM the record of his matriculation at Prague University in 1731 until his arrival in Milan in 1737, Gluck's activities are undocumented. He is presumed to have remained in Prague for three years, moving to Vienna towards the end of 1734.

There are strong grounds for believing that, on arrival in Vienna, he was taken into the Lobkowitz household, in the old palace in the Minoritenplatz.[1] Retelling information derived from Gluck's relatives, Schmid records that 'among the greater and lesser music-loving Bohemian nobles, Gluck gained many patrons who, as he could scarcely too often declare, supported him munificently, namely the princely family of Lobkowitz, to whose service in the noble arts of forestry and gamekeeping many of his ancestors had dedicated their lives'.[2] At the presumed time of Gluck's move to Vienna, his father was in the service of the ageing Prince Philipp Hyazinth (who died on 21 December 1734). Independent of this connection, there were links between Gluck and three other Lobkowitzes. Philipp's successor, his brother Georg Christian, was probably the composer's employer in Vienna in 1735–6, and, as governor of Milan from 1743 to 1746, was certainly a patron of Gluck and the dedicatee of two of his operas. Gluck may have travelled with Georg's son, Joseph Maria Karl, to Frankfurt in September 1745 for the coronation of Emperor Francis I. Another Lobkowitz, Ferdinand Philipp (son of Philipp Hyazinth), was in London at the time of Gluck's visit in 1745–6. If, however, in the mid-1730s Gluck was a member of the Lobkowitz musical establishment, his precise

---

[1] Walther Brauneis, 'Gluck in Wien: Seine Gedenkstätten, Wohnungen und Aufführungsorte', *Gluck in Wien*, ed. Croll and Woitas, 42.

[2] *Gluck*, 22. A less attractive account of Gluck's later relationship with the Lobkowitzes is cited in Ch. 18 below.

employment there, whether as a singer or an instrumentalist (and on which instrument), is not recorded.

Some notable new appointments were made in Vienna at this time. In 1730 Metastasio became court poet, a year later writing the poem *Artaserse*, which was eventually to be the text for Gluck's first opera. In 1731 Karl Georg Reutter became court composer; he could be tenuously linked to Gluck through the subject-matter of his opera *Il sacrifizio in Aulide* (1735). Gluck might have had the opportunity to see two operas whose texts he was later to set for himself: Caldara's *La clemenza di Tito* in 1734, and the original version of *Le cinesi* in 1735.

Gluck's first known patron was the Milanese Prince Antonio Maria Melzi. It is likely that the prince came to know Gluck through the Lobkowitz family, and engaged him to play in his orchestra at his residence in Milan. The 65-year-old prince married the 16-year-old Maria Renata Harrach on 3 January 1737, and returned with Gluck to Milan soon afterwards.

After his arrival in Milan, another four-year silence obscures Gluck's activities. A pertinent issue is his precise relationship with Giovanni Battista Sammartini. Sammartini was certainly the city's leading musician throughout the 1730s and 1740s. Already described as 'very famous' in 1726, he taught at the Collegio de' Nobili from 1730, and adjudicated at the trials for cathedral posts from 1733.[3] Burney, who met him in 1770, describes him as then being 'maestro di cappella to more than half the churches in the city'.[4] Was Gluck formally his pupil 'for several years', as Giuseppe Carpani suggests?[5] That Gluck regarded himself as Sammartini's pupil for the whole eight-year period he spent in Italy is unlikely. Carpani is more persuasive on the obvious stylistic influences: 'It is only necessary to compare Gluck's instrumental music with that of the master to grasp how much he owed him.'[6] Gluck not only produced during these years work which is clearly characteristic of the Milan instrumental style (the Six Sonatas published in London in 1746), but also later made adaptations of Sammartini's music (the first movement of the overture to *Le nozze d'Ercole*, 1747).[7] It is unlikely that Sammartini afforded an operatic model. When Gluck arrived in Milan, Sammartini had written only two operas (*Memet*, 1732, and *L'ambitione superata*, 1734); his remaining

[3] Bathia Churgin and Newell Jenkins, 'Sammartini', *The New Grove Dictionary of Music and Musicians*, ed. Stanley Sadie (London, 1980), xvi. 452–7.

[4] *A General History of Music* (London, 1786–9); ed. Frank Mercer (London and New York, 1935, repr. New York, 1957), ii. 454.

[5] *Le Haydine* (Milan, 1812), 59.   [6] Ibid. 60.

[7] Bathia Churgin, 'Alterations in Gluck's Borrowings from Sammartini', *Studies in Music*, 9 (1980), 117–34.

work (*L'Agrippina*, 1743) might well have been influenced by Gluck's early successes, the pupil turning master. More practical theatrical advice could have been forthcoming from Lampugnani, who used Gluck's music in his pasticcios, and who may have forged a link in the chain of contacts and recommendations which eventually led Gluck to London. Lampugnani, however, produced no operas in Milan during the years of Gluck's stay.

At some point in the years 1737–41, Gluck's activities moved from Melzi's household to the theatre. His first opera, *Artaserse*, was given at the Teatro Regio Ducal on 26 December 1741 for the reopening after the mourning for Emperor Charles VI. The occasion is described in Reichardt's 'French manuscript':[8]

Gluck, who was engaged in the year 1738 as musician in the household of Prince Melzi, and had already given various proofs of his musical genius, was invited to compose a grand opera for the theatre in Milan. Gluck accepted this invitation, and in the course of abandoning himself to the inspiration of his genius, he departed from the usual run of other compositions of the age, and wrote really expressive music—a style in which he later excelled and which he could be said to have created. The occasion gave rise to the following anecdote. Gluck was an intimate friend of Sammartini, who lived in Milan and was famous in those days. [Gluck], however, undertook his new task without taking advice from anyone, and finished the opera apart from one aria needing different words, and which therefore remained to be composed. The first rehearsal of Gluck's opera was held in the theatre, and it drew a crowd, curious and impatient to judge the first attempt of a new composer. The ears of the audience were not accustomed to this style of music, and they mocked the young composer, making him the butt of their comments. Gluck observed this, said nothing, and remained true to his instincts. He composed the previously unwritten aria, however, in a completely different manner, trying only to charm the ears with it, regardless of any other consideration. It was wholly to the taste of the Italians, who love this [style], since they look only for a superficial entertainment in the theatre, without involving themselves in the work, and having scant regard for its unity. The dress rehearsal attracted an even greater crowd, and as soon as the audience heard the new, pleasing aria, they broke into loud applause, and whispered to each other that the aria must be by Sammartini. Gluck saw all, heard all, and remained silent. At the first performance of his opera, this is what happened: the music was a complete success (for truth will out). The aria which differed so greatly from all the

[8] Reichardt's MS is discussed in the Introduction. See also Max Arend, 'Glucks erste Oper *Artaxerxes*', *Neue Zeitschrift für Musik*, 82 (1915), 201–2. The article includes, between pp. 208 and 209, a transcript of one of the two surviving arias from this opera.

others was found to be insipid, and so inconsistent with the rest, that the cry went up that it spoilt the opera. Now Gluck had his revenge and confirmed the over-hasty public in their belief that the aria was truly by Sammartini.[9]

It is highly unlikely that this account, written half a century after the event, contains more than a fragment of truth—though an additional aria, 'Da te s'io cerco amore', was inserted into Metastasio's libretto.[10] If, as I have argued, the anecdote arose from the composer's own reminiscences, it may preserve Gluck's distant memory of genuine tensions between himself and Sammartini. *Artaserse* brought Gluck into collaboration with two singers important to the interpretation of his early operas: the soprano Caterina Aschieri contributed significantly to the popularity of the operas in Milan, and the castrato Giuseppe Jozzi was to sing in Gluck's first London opera, *La caduta de' giganti*.

There can at least be little doubt about the success of *Artaserse*: the commission to write an opera for the feast of the Ascension in Venice must have followed immediately, for *Demetrio* was premièred on 2 May 1742 at the Teatro Grimani di San Samuele, with the Viennese castrato Felice Salimbeni in the title role. At the end of the same year, another opera was announced in Milan, with Gluck mentioned as 'the noted *Maestro di Cappella*'.[11] *Demofoonte* was given on 6 January 1743, and elicited the first authentic review of a Gluck opera:

Last Sunday the drama entitled *Demofoonte* was performed for the first time in the Teatro Regio Ducal, and received, as expected, widespread satisfaction and applause. It has attracted, moreover, each evening, a good number of spectators, who praised the ability of the cast, among which they especially admired the exceptional ability in singing and acting of the famous Sig. Giovanni Carestini. No less applause was evoked by the vivacity and caprice of the dancing, the charm of the most imposing decorations, superbly painted by the celebrated Galeari brothers, and the magnificent ensemble of the costumes, to all of which is added the noble entertainment of the players engaged at the said Teatro Regio Ducal, which was completely delightful, drawing an ever more numerous gathering of citizens.[12]

The presence of Carestini, one of the most celebrated castrati of the age, guaranteed the success of this opera, which was performed the same year

[9] 'Fortsetzung', 72.

[10] Alfred Wotquenne, *Chr. W. v. Gluck: Thematisches Verzeichnis seiner Werke*, tr. Josef Liebeskind (Leipzig, 1904), 4.

[11] Klaus Hortschansky, 'Gluck nella *Gazetta di Milano* 1742–1745', *Nuova rivista musicale italiana*, 6 (1972), 512.

[12] *Gazetta di Milano*, 9 Jan. 1743, cited in Hortschansky, '*Gazetta di Milano*', 514.

in Reggio, Florence, and Bologna, repeated in Ferrara in 1745, and revived in Milan in 1747 and in Florence in 1749.[13]

Gluck's next commission, *Tigrane*, was given in Crema on 26 September 1743. In 1744, three operas were produced: *Sofonisba* in Milan on 18 January, *Ipermestra* in Venice on 21 November, and *Poro* in Turin on 26 December. Additional evidence of Gluck's growing popularity may be inferred from the inclusion of his arias in two pasticcios: Lampugnani's *Arsace* in Milan on 26 December 1743 and Giacomo Maccari's *La finta schiava* in Venice on 13 May 1744.[14]

The last opera from this Italian period, *Ippolito*, was given in Milan on 31 January 1745. The extraordinary success of this production, again due rather to a singer than to the composer, nevertheless brought Gluck his first 'publication':

Here on Saturday [6 March], the end of Carnival climaxed in the last performance of the advertised drama in the Teatro Regio Ducal. Like all the previous performances, it drew a great crowd of visitors and locals, the like of which had not been seen for many years, as could be seen from the fact that with the vast parterre full to capacity, being packed from side to side, it was necessary to open up access to the stage, to admit the impatient spectators who completely filled the boxes. The most noble Signora Caterina Aschieri Romana shone as always. On this last evening, the sweetness of her singing and her lively and appropriate acting, which have earned her the highest praise and applause, were commemorated with the distribution of the finest of copper engravings, similar to those issued several days previously, as proof of the universal acclaim in which, more than ever before, she is held and celebrated.[15]

Two different commemorative engravings have been found. One includes a portrait of the singer, a representation of part of the stage and orchestra, and seventy-six bars of the second-act aria 'Non sò placar'.[16] The second engraving also contains a portrait and a scene from the opera, together with thirty-five bars of the florid aria which closes Act I, 'Agitata non trovo riposo'.[17]

After the decided success of this spell in Italy, we lose sight of Gluck

[13] Alfred Loewenberg, *Annals of Opera*, 3rd edn. (London, 1978), 199.

[14] Klaus Hortschansky, 'Gluck und Lampugnani in Italien: Zum Pasticcio *Arsace*', *Analecta musicologica*, 3 (1966), 49–64; id., *Parodie und Entlehnung im Schaffen Christoph Willibald Glucks* (Cologne, 1973), 264–6.

[15] *Gazetta di Milano*, 10 Mar. 1745, cited in Hortschansky, '*Gazetta di Milano*', 518.

[16] This engraving is described, and the aria reproduced, in Hermann Abert, 'Zu Glucks *Ippolito*', *Gluck-Jahrbuch*, ed. H. Abert, 1 (1913), 47–53.

[17] This engraving is reproduced in Hortschansky, '*Gazetta di Milano*', facing p. 514.

until he emerges in London towards the end of the year. It is usually presumed that he journeyed to England via Frankfurt, where, in common with travellers from all parts of Europe, he attended the festivities surrounding the coronation of Emperor Francis I on 28 September 1745. Such an event afforded opportunities to many musicians, in particular itinerant opera companies. The suggestion that Gluck might have been in Frankfurt is supported by the presence there of one such troupe, directed by Pietro Mingotti, and the fact that within two years, Gluck had joined this troupe.[18]

[18] Erich Hermann Müller von Asow, *Angelo und Pietro Mingotti* (Dresden, 1917), 41.

3

GLUCK IN LONDON
(1746)

W HEN did Gluck come to London? There is no mention of him in the press until the announcements of the forthcoming *La caduta de' giganti* in the *General Advertiser* of 4 January 1746. The commission to write this particular opera is unlikely to have been given before the second week of December 1745. The King's Theatre was closed for most of 1745 'on account of the [Jacobite] rebellion, and popular prejudice against the performers, who, being foreigners, were chiefly Roman Catholics'.[1] *La caduta* was seen to address both the rebellion and the prejudice:

a splendid Drama is prepared in Honour of his Majesty, of the Nation and of our Arms; the sincere Attachment of the Managers of the Opera to the present happy Establishment (spite of the very idle Suggestions of Malice) being well known; not to mention that the Performers were born among our Friends and Allies, and not amidst our Enemies as some have falsely insinuated.[2]

Subtitled *La ribellione punita*, the theme of Gluck's opera anticipates the English defeat of the revolt, which was signalled by the retreat of Bonnie Prince Charlie from Derby on 6 December 1745, though not completed till the Battle of Culloden on 16 April 1746.

Why Gluck came to London at such an unpropitious time is equally obscure. His appointment as house composer at the King's Theatre would have been in the gift of Lord Middlesex, who headed the committee in charge of the theatre, but no record of such a commission exists. A powerful incentive for Gluck's visit might have come from Prince Ferdinand

---

[1] Burney, *General History*, ii. 844.
[2] *General Advertiser*, 4 Mar. 1746, fo. 1ᵛ. Members of the Roman Catholic Arne family, notably Mrs Cibber, were among the musicians accused of disaffection. 'Popular prejudice' seems not to have affected the engagement of Jozzi and Monticelli.

Philipp Lobkowitz, who had arrived in London earlier in 1745, but again, evidence of such an invitation is missing. Several of Gluck's Milan friends could have recommended the enterprise to him: Lampugnani might have boasted of his success in London in 1743 with his opera *Roxana*; Sammartini's brother, Giuseppe Sammartini, could have told an equally optimistic tale, having been established in London as oboist and composer since 1723. The most likely agent was Abate Francesco Vanneschi. His tour of Italy to recruit singers for London resulted in the engagement of the castratos Jozzi and Monticelli, creators of the title roles in *Artaserse* and *Ippolito* respectively, and the soprano Teresa Pompeati (née Imer), who had sung in *Demetrio* in Venice. Vanneschi, who was to be the librettist of Gluck's two London operas, was likely to have met Gluck in the course of poaching his singers, and must have heard him praised.

The first document is an announcement of *La caduta*:

HAY-MARKET. AT the KING'S THEATRE in the HAY-MARKET, on Tuesday next, will be perform'd a MUSICAL DRAMA, in Two Parts, call'd LA CADUTA DE' GIGANTI, The FALL of the GIANTS. With DANCES and other Decorations Entirely New. Pit and Boxes to be put together, and no Persons to be admitted without Tickets, which will be delivered that Day at the Opera-Office in the Hay-Market, at Half a Guinea each. Gallery 5s. The Gallery to be open'd at Four o'Clock. Pit and Boxes at Five. To begin at Six o'Clock.[3]

Burney is a major source for Gluck's brief visit. Brought to London as apprentice to Thomas Arne in 1744, he soon embedded himself in the musical life of the capital as Arne's copyist, occasional composer, and freelance violinist and harpsichordist, while keeping detailed notes on concerts and performers, which formed the basis of the later chapters of his *General History*. His account of *La caduta* combines memory with hindsight. The first part of his notice may have been compiled from notes made at the time of performance, but his comments on specific musical numbers deal only with the six 'Favourite Songs' published by Walsh in the same year[4] and are clearly prompted by the score:

There was no opera attempted in the great theatre in the Hay-market till January 7th, when LA CADUTA DE' GIGANTI, set by Gluck, was performed before the Duke of Cumberland, in compliment to whom the whole was written and composed. The singers were Monticelli, Jozzi, and Ciacchi; with Signor[e] Imer, Pompeati, afterwards better known by the name of Madame

[3] *General Advertiser*, 4 Jan. 1746, fo. 2ʳ.
[4] *The Favourite SONGS in the OPERA Call'd LA CADUTA de' GIGANTI* (London, 1746).

Cornelie, and Frasi. The first woman, Imer, never surpassed mediocrity in voice, taste, or action; and the Pompeati, though nominally second woman, had such a masculine and violent manner of singing, that few female symptoms were perceptible. The new dances by Auretti,⁵ and the charming Violetta, afterwards Mrs Garrick, were much more applauded than the songs, which, however, for the time, had considerable merit. The first air in G minor is of an original cast, but monotonous. The second air has genius and design in it. There is a duet, in which he hazarded many new passages and effects. The following air, for Monticelli, is very original in symphony and accompaniments, which a little disturbed the voice-part in performance, I well remember, and Monticelli called it *aria tedesca*. His cotemporaries in Italy, at this time, seemed too much filed down; and he wanted the file, which when used afterwards in that country, made him one of the greatest composers of his time. The next air printed, is in a very peculiar measure, and like no other that I remember: it has great merit of novelty and accompaniment; the voice-part wants only a little more grace and quiet. The following song, set for JOZZI, a good musician with little voice, is full of new and ingenious passages and effects; I should like much to hear this air well performed at the opera; it is kept alive from beginning to end. Something might be expected from a young man able to produce this opera, imperfect as it was. It had, however, but [6] representations.⁶

Two months later, Gluck's second opera in England was given:

HAY-MARKET. At the KING'S THEATRE in the HAY-MARKET, this Day, will be perform'd a New OPERA, call'd ARTAMENE. With DANCES and other DECORATIONS, Entirely New. Pit and Boxes to be put together, and no Persons to be admitted without Tickets, which will be delivered this Day, at the Opera Office in the Hay-Market, at Half a Guinea each. Gallery 5s. By HIS MAJESTY'S COMMAND, No Persons whatsoever to be admitted behind the scenes. The Gallery to be open'd at Four o'clock. Pit and Boxes at Five. To begin at Six o'Clock.⁷

Burney's memory of the occasion again seems prompted by the published extracts:⁸

March 4th, was first performed, ARTAMENE, set by Gluck, in which Monticelli was every night encored in *Rasserena il mesto ciglio*. The motivo of this air is grateful to every ear; but it is too often repeated, being introduced seven

---

⁵ The dances occur not in *La caduta* but in *Artamene*. See *General Advertiser*, 11 Mar. 1746, fo. 1ᵛ: 'Madem. Violetta, a new dancer from Vienna, will perform this Day, for the first time.'

⁶ *General History*, ii. 844. 'Signora Imer' is Marianna Imer, elder sister of Teresa Pompeati. Burney records only five performances.

⁷ *General Advertiser*, 4 Mar. 1746, fo 1ᵛ.

⁸ *The Favourite SONGS in the OPERA Call'd ARTAMENE* (London, 1746).

times, which, there being a *Da Capo*, is multiplied to fourteen. The second part is good for nothing. Indeed no other air in this opera, that has been printed, furnished a single portent of the great genius this composer afterward manifested. This opera ran, however, ten nights.[9]

The most lasting result of Gluck's London visit must surely have been his intimate acquaintance with and lifelong appreciation of Handel's music. The relationship of the two composers is tantalizingly undocumented. On the evidence of the music which has survived from this London visit—the six 'Favourite Songs' from each of the two operas, and six trio sonatas[10]—the judgement attributed by Burney to Handel is not unreasonable:

When Gluck came first into England, in 1745, he was neither so great a composer, nor so high in reputation, as he afterwards mounted; and I remember when Mrs Cibber, in my hearing, asked HANDEL what sort of a composer he was; his answer, prefaced by an oath—was, 'he knows no more of contrapunto, as mein cook, Waltz.[11]

This anecdote circulated widely, turning up in the earliest dictionary article on Gluck, where Gluck's reputation is defended.[12] In his additions and corrections to Gerber's *Lexicon*, Reichardt adds another Gluck–Handel anecdote before responding to the slur on Gluck's contrapuntal ability:

Gluck's first [London] opera did not please at the first performance, and Gluck bewailed the fact to Handel, showing him the score. Handel answered him saying, 'You have taken too much trouble with the opera, but that is not needed here. For the English, you must have something striking, which has its effect directly on the eardrums, and your opera will then be sure to please.' This advice gave Gluck the idea of adding trombones to the choruses in the opera, in consequence of which the opera was extraordinarily successful. I tell this anecdote as it was told to me. But Handel's harsh judgement on Gluck as contrapuntist is also no more than hearsay, and is less probable. One can, however, accept both anecdotes as true, and that Handel, being one of the greatest contrapuntists of his time, should compare Gluck as contrapuntist with himself, and find him to be no contrapuntist at all, is no criticism of the great expressive dramatic composer [i.e. Gluck].[13]

---

[9] Burney, *General History*, ii. 845.

[10] *SIX Sonatas for two Violins & a Thorough Bass* (London, 1746).

[11] *An Account of the Musical Performances in Westminster Abbey and the Pantheon . . . in Commemoration of Handel* (London, 1785), 33.

[12] Ernst Ludwig Gerber, 'Christoph von Gluck', *Historisch-biographisches Lexicon der Tonkünstler* (Leipzig, 1790–2), i. 516–17.

[13] 'Fortsetzung', 74.

Gluck himself disseminated the substance of this reported conversation with Handel in his verdict on England, told to Burney and cited at the end of this chapter.

The relationship between the composers must have been sufficiently warm to have resulted in the joint charity concert in March, its honours almost equally divided between Gluck, Handel, and Galuppi (whose pasticcio *It trionfo della continenza* had opened at the King's Theatre on 28 January 1746). The programme ran as follows:

PART I

Overture *La caduta de' giganti*, by Gluck
Air 'care pupille' from *La caduta de' giganti*, sung by Sig. Jozzi
Air 'Son prigioniero' from *Il trionfo della continenza*, by Galuppi, sung by Sig.ra Pompeati
Air 'Bella, consola' from *Il trionfo*, sung by Sig. Ciacchi
Air 'Men fedele' from *Alessandro*, by Handel, sung by Sig. Monticelli
Air 'La sorte mia tiranna' from *Il trionfo*, sung by Sig.ra Imer.

PART II

[?Flute] Concerto by Weideman
Air 'Return, O God of Hosts' from *Samson*, by Handel, sung by Sig.ra Frasi
Air 'Il cor mio' from *Alessandro*, by Handel, sung by Sig. Monticelli
Air 'Pensa che il cielo trema' from *La caduta*, sung by Sig. Ciacchi
Air 'Mai l'amor mio verace' from *La caduta*, sung by Sig.ra Imer
[?Violin] Concerto by Carbonelli.
Air 'O da pastor' by Lampugnani, sung by Sig. Monticelli.

PART III

[?Bassoon] Concerto by Miller.
Air 'Per pietà' from *Il trionfo*, sung by Sig. Jozzi.
Air 'Volgo dubbioso' from *La caduta*, sung by Sig.ra Pompeati
Air 'The prince unable to conceal his pain' from *Alexander's Feast*, by Handel, sung by Sig.ra Frasi.
[?Oboe] Concerto by Vincent.
Duetto from *Il trionfo*, sung by Sig. Monticelli and Sig.ra Imer.
A Grand Concerto by Handel[14]

Whatever the success of his operas, or his standing with the leading composer of the day, a certain thread of cheerful opportunism, already evi-

[14] *General Advertiser*, 25 Mar. 1746 fo. 1ᵛ. Of the items from *La caduta*, only 'Care pupille' (taken from *Tigrane*) exists in Walsh's collection (see n. 4 above). 'Mai l'amor mio verace' was taken from *Ipermestra*. Charles Frederick Weideman, Giovanni Stefano Carbonelli, (?Edward) Miller, and Thomas Vincent probably played concertos of their own composition for their principal instruments.

dent in Gluck's Bohemian wanderings with his jew's harp nearly twenty years earlier, surfaces in his exploitation of the London taste for novelties. Horace Walpole noted the occasion: 'The operas flourish more than in any latter years; the composer is Gluck, a German: he is to have a benefit, at which he is to play on a set of drinking glasses, which he modulates with water.'[15] Gluck gave two such concerts in London, and later revived the novelty in Copenhagen in 1749, and in Naples in 1752. Sources from Naples reveal that he played the glasses by striking them with rods (see Chapter 6 below). The two advertisements give some clues to the mixed programme content:

AT Mr Hickford's Great Room in Brewer's-street on Monday, April 14, Signor GLUCK, Composer of the Operas, will exhibit a CONCERT of MUSICK By the best Performers from the Opera-House. Particularly, he will play a Concerto upon Twenty-six Drinking Glasses, tuned with Spring-Water, accompanied with the whole Band, being a new instrument of his own invention; upon which he performs whatever may be done on a Violin or Harpsichord; and therefore hopes to satisfy the Curious as well as the Lovers of Musick. To begin at Half an Hour after Six. Tickets Half a Guinea each. Tickets to be had at the Orange Coffee-house in the Haymarket; at Mr Walsh's in Katherine-street in the Strand; and at the Place of Performance.[16]

At the Desire of several Persons of Quality, At the New Theatre in the Haymarket, this day, will be performed, a concert of vocal and Instrumental MUSICK By the principal performers from the Opera, particularly Signor GLUCK, Composer of the Opera, will play a concerto, and a Song to be sung by Signora FRAZI upon a new instrument of 26 Glasses and therefore hopes to satisfy the Curious, as well as all Lovers of Musick. Pit and Boxes to be put together at Half a Guinea each. Gallery 5s. To begin at Half an Hour after Six. Tickets to be had at the Prince of Orange Coffee-house in the Haymarket.[17]

Gluck apparently left England shortly after the second of these concerts and never returned. In retrospect, he attributed a valuable formative role to his experiences, hinting to Burney the advice that Reichardt claimed Gluck had received from Handel. Recording a conversation held on 2 September 1772, Burney wrote:

---

[15] Letter to Horace Mann, 28 Mar. 1746, in *Letters of Horace Walpole to Sir Horace Mann*, ed. Lord Dover (London, 1833) ii. 138–9. The instrument retained a curious celebrity in London. The 'talk of high life' in Oliver Goldsmith's *The Vicar of Wakefield* (London, 1766) was of 'pictures, taste, Shakespear and the musical glasses.'

[16] *General Advertiser*, 31 Mar. 1746, fo. 2ʳ.   [17] *General Advertiser*, 23 Apr. 1746, fo. 1ᵛ.

I reminded M. Gluck of his air, *Rasserena il Mesto Ciglio*, which was in such great favour in England, so long ago as the year 174[6]; and prevailed upon him, not only to sing that, but several others of his first and most favourite airs. He told me that he owed entirely to England the study of nature in his dramatic compositions: he went thither at a very disadvantageous period; Handel was then so high in fame, that no one would willingly listen to any other than to his compositions. The rebellion broke out; all foreigners were regarded as dangerous to the state; the opera-house was shut up by order of the Lord Chamberlain, and it was with great difficulty and address that Lord Middlesex obtained permission to open it again, with a temporary and political performance, *La caduta de' giganti*. This *Gluck* worked upon with fear and trembling, not only on account of the few friends he had in England, but from an apprehension of riot and popular fury, at the opening of the theatre, in which none but foreigners and papists were employed.

He then studied the English taste; remarked particularly what the audience seemed most to feel; and finding that plainness and simplicity had the greatest effect upon them, he has, ever since that time, endeavoured to write for the voice, more in the natural tones of the human affections and passions, than to flatter the lovers of deep science or difficult execution.[18]

---

[18] *Present State ... Germany*, i. 267–8. Burney's comment on the popularity of the aria 'Rasserena il mesto ciglio' is confirmed by a notice in the *General Advertiser* of 12 Apr. 1746, fo. 1ʳ, in which it is sung by Mrs Arne at her husband's benefit night, 'being particularly desired by several ladies of quality.' The aria enjoyed renewed popularity in London when introduced into the pasticcio *Silla* by Pasquale Anfossi in 1783, and pub. as 'The Favourite Song sung by Sigʳ Pacchierotti in the Opera of Silla' (London, 1783). Gluck included it in his next opera, *Le nozze d'Ercole e d'Ebe*.

4

THE ITINERANT MUSICIAN

(1746–1750)

FOR more than a year following his two London concerts in April 1746, Gluck again disappears from view. The pasticcio devised by Maccari for Venice in 1744 enjoyed a new lease of life: *La finta schiava*, containing at least two arias by Gluck, was performed by Angelo Mingotti's travelling opera company in Graz during the Carnival season of 1746, in Prague later in the same spring, and in Leipzig on 11 May 1746, but we cannot assume that Gluck was present at any of these performances.[1] He may have journeyed directly from London to Hamburg and there joined the company of Angelo's brother Pietro Mingotti, whose troupe he could have encountered at the coronation of Francis I in Frankfurt the previous September.[2] Although there is no evidence to show where and when he met Pietro Mingotti, Gluck must have joined the troupe sooner or later during the twelve months after leaving London, since his next documented activity is the performance of *Le nozze d'Ercole e d'Ebe* by Mingotti's company in Dresden on 29 June 1747. The possibility exists that music by Gluck was performed at a concert, involving members of both Mingotti troupes, in Leipzig on 15 May 1747, at which 'arias by a great master from Italy' were sung by the tenor Settimo Canini and the contralto Giacinta Forcellini, 'to great applause.'[3] Canini had sung in both *Tigrane* and *Sofonisba*, and both he and Forcellini were to sing the following month in *Le nozze d'Ercole e d'Ebe*.

The occasional serenata, *Le nozze*, formed part of the celebrations of a double royal wedding which united Maria Anna of Saxony with Maximilian Joseph of Bavaria, and Maria Antonia Walburga of Bavaria[4] with Friedrich Christian of Saxony. The celebrations lasted for more than

---

[1] Müller von Asow, *Mingotti*, 46–51.   [2] Ibid. 41.   [3] Ibid. 67.
[4] A singer and composer in her own right, Maria Antonia composed two operas, *Il trionfo della fedeltà*, 1754, and *Talestri, regina delle Amazoni*, 1760.

three weeks, and included (besides two works by Mingotti's principal director, Paolo Scalabrini) an opera by the Dresden Kapellmeister, Johann Adolf Hasse, *La spartana generosa*, whose cast of famous dancers included Jean-Georges Noverre, who was to cross Gluck's path twenty years later.[5]

Le nozze was the second of two entertainments given in the open-air theatre in the gardens of Schloss Pillnitz. Whether through lack of time, or in an attempt to re-establish the success he won in Italy, or because of a loss of confidence bred during his fallow year, Gluck adapted earlier music for seven of the thirteen numbers: one aria was taken from *Sofonisba* and one from *Ippolito*, four were from *Artamene*, including 'Rasserena il mesto ciglio' which had proved so popular in London, and the first movement of the overture was adapted from a movement by Sammartini.[6] The young soprano Regina Mingotti (Pietro's wife) took the leading role of Hercules;[7] Canini sang Jove, and Forcellini, Juno. It is not known whether Gluck or Scalabrini conducted. *Le nozze* was given only one performance: the following day the court moved back to town.[8] Gluck's other activities in the troupe remain obscure. A receipt shows that on leaving the company on 15 September 1747, he was paid 412 thaler 12 groschen.[9] Designated in the official records as 'singer', he is unlikely ever to have fulfilled this role.[10] It is usually assumed that Gluck left the company to return to the family home at Hammer bei Brüx (Most), in order to sell property he had inherited. His father had died in 1743, his mother in 1740.

Gluck's next opera took him back to Vienna. *La Semiramide riconosciuta* was commissioned for the reopening of the Burgtheater in Vienna on 14 May 1748. The occasion is noted in the diary of the court official Count Johann Joseph Khevenhüller-Metsch. Khevenhüller's record is of limited value in constructing a portrait of Gluck. He confirms dates and gives some indication of the reception of works, but his diary focuses on the social circumstances of the performances (who attended and where they sat), often to the exclusion of any mention of the music; it is many years until he mentions Gluck by name:

---

[5] See Ch. 10.

[6] Churgin, 'Alterations in Gluck's Borrowings', 119–24.

[7] Burney gives a racy sketch of her life in *Present State . . . Germany*, i. 152–63.

[8] Moritz Fürstenau, *Zur Geschichte der Musik und des Theaters am Hofe der Kurfürsten von Sachsen und Königen von Polen* (Dresden, 1861–2), ii. 248–50.

[9] Facsimile of the receipt in Müller von Asow, *Mingotti*, 70.

[10] From the several descriptions of Gluck's voice later in life, it seems unlikely that he earned his living in this way, though its expressive quality was remarked on whenever he gave informal performances of his operas in private circumstances. Bruce Alan Brown points out (private communication) that Gluck did sing from the wings when a singer became ill during a performance of *L'Arbre enchanté* in 1761.

On the 14th, the court came into town for the reopening of the old opera house, originally a tennis-court, now magnificently extended and renovated by the new management. [The reopening] celebrated yesterday's royal birthday with the performance of a drama by Abate Metastasio called *La Semiramide riconosciuta*. The opera had been carefully chosen for the exceptional magnificence of the spectacle and the decorations. The management wanted to make its mark right away, consequently the best voices that could be found were assembled, including, from the court at Dresden, the famous tenor [Angelo] Amorevoli, the soprano Venturini [Ventura Rocchetti], and the dancers Sig. Lenzi and Mlle Tagliavini, both of them excellent (he distinguished himself with a particularly high and nimble cabriolet). In addition the Florentine Tesi [Vittoria Tesi-Tramontini], very celebrated for her acting, was brought from Italy, together with several orchestral virtuosi mentioned elsewhere.[11]

Khevenhüller added the fact that the opera maintained its popularity for the next two months; it received twenty-seven performances, closing on 11 July.

Why was Gluck, at that time little known in Vienna, given this important commission ahead of the obvious candidate Hasse, or the local up-and-coming Wagenseil? The likeliest explanation, supported by the engagement of singers and dancers from Dresden, is that the single performance of *Le nozze* had impressed Prince Nikolaus Esterházy, the Austrian ambassador to the Saxon court in Dresden. It was a commission worth winning. The occasion was not merely another royal birthday, nor yet a landmark in the development of the Burgtheater,[12] but a political event, affirming Maria Theresia's right to rule. The first woman Habsburg to inherit the imperial throne (in 1740), the empress was crowned in 1743 but had to face continuous challenges to her inheritance (the War of the Austrian Succession) which were not quelled until the Treaty of Aix-la-Chapelle in October 1748. The choice of subject, in which Queen Semiramis of Assyria secures her succession by reigning in male disguise, was patently influenced by this episode of dynastic history. A setting of the same Metastasian libretto (probably by Hasse) had been given to celebrate her coronation. The opera's long-running success is confirmed in a letter from the librettist himself:

---

[11] *Aus der Zeit Maria Theresias: Tagebuch* (Vienna, 1907–25 and 1972), 1745–9, 224. The new management was directed by Baron Rocco Lopresti, who raised a subscription among the Viennese nobility to underwrite the rebuilding.

[12] The renovation of the Burgtheater is described in detail in Daniel Heartz, 'Nicolas Jadot and the Building of the Burgtheater', *Musical Quarterly*, 68 (1982), 1–31.

Learn that *Semiramide* is lauded to the skies, thanks to the excellence of the company and the magnificence of the decorations, despite the ultra-barbaric and intolerable music.[13] Tesi declaimed in a manner which surprised not only me but the whole people of Vienna of both sexes. Venturino [Rocchetti] and Amorevoli enchanted. Monticelli was admired. Lenzi and Tagliavini defied credulity. In all, it was one of the most magnificent spectacles that could be offered to a sovereign. The most frequent and enthusiastic spectators are the most unbending matrons, and the ministers and clergy most burdened with years and merit.[14]

Gluck had already set six librettos all or partly by Metastasio, and was to set thirteen more, including his next nine operas. There is, however, no record of any actual collaboration between the men at this period, and Gluck probably made his adjustments to Metastasio's poem (for example setting some of the simple recitative in Act III as arioso) without consulting the author. This letter contains the first indication of Metastasio's opinion of Gluck. Although the court poet was to warm slightly towards the composer in future years, there was little sympathy, personal or artistic, between them.[15]

We next hear of Gluck in Hamburg, where by September 1748 he had rejoined Pietro Mingotti's troupe, with enhanced status. Scalabrini had succeeded Johann Adolf Scheibe as Kapellmeister to the Danish court on 11 February 1748, leaving the post of director free for Gluck to assume as soon as his Viennese undertaking had concluded. It may have been the offer of this post which drew Gluck away from Vienna so soon after the successful run of *Semiramide*.

The main source for the following months is an exchange of letters between the singer Marianne Pirker and her violinist husband Franz. Both had been employed in the King's Theatre, London, in 1747, but were working separately and corresponding frequently during 1748–9, Franz remaining in London, Marianne having joined the Mingotti troupe in Hamburg in August 1748.[16] The first mention of Gluck as musical director of the troupe comes in a brief sentence from Franz Pirker, dated 10 September, in the midst of words of professional advice to his wife: 'I

[13] 'una musica arcivandalica insopportabile'.

[14] Metastasio to Giovanni Claudio Pasquini, Vienna, 29 June 1748, in Metastasio, *Tutte le opere*, ed. Bruno Brunelli (Milan, 1947–54), iii. 354.

[15] See Ch. 6 below.

[16] The autographs of the letters between the Pirkers are contained in Stuttgart, Hauptstaats-archiv, A202 Bü 2839–42. The correspondence is discussed, and the references to Gluck transcribed and excerpted, in Roswitha Spulak, 'Ein unbekanntes Schriftstück Christoph Willibald Glucks', *Die Musikforschung*, 40 (1987), 345–9. Quotations from the Pirker correspondence are all translated from this source unless otherwise indicated.

send my compliments to Mr Gluck; tell him what you want and he will soon bring the orchestra to reason.' Confirmation of Gluck's promotion comes in a newspaper cutting dated 3 October 1748: 'The celebrated musician Herr Gluck is now Kapellmeister instead of Herr Scalabrini, who has entered the service of the King of Denmark.'[17]

The Pirker correspondence now centres on a commission from Gluck to Franz Pirker for the purchase of two watches. Gluck's request was enclosed in a letter from Marianne Pirker, dated 24 September 1748. (References in the letters of both Pirkers indicate that several messages from Gluck had been transmitted earlier that autumn.) It is not unfitting that the first, almost illegible words we read from Gluck's own hand concern such a worldly matter:

My dear Pirker,

I ask you to be so good as to bring me a silver watch with diamonds by Poi [Godfrey Poy]; it will cost about eight *Pfund*. Do not tell him you are my agent. I also want a good [watch] in pinchbeck from another maker, at about three and a half *Pfund*. In addition three or four dozen fine, women's scissors at about one or one-and-a-half schillings each. As soon as you get here I shall gratefully repay what you have spent. Adieu.

Gluck.[18]

Pirker appears to have acted immediately on Gluck's request. In a letter to Marianne dated 7 October, he presents his compliments to Gluck and assures him that Poy has begun work on the watch. There is some suggestion that the Pirkers considered making a little commission on the watches, but were deterred because 'Gluck knows to a whisker what they cost here' (Franz Pirker, 3 October).

Gluck was clearly doing business on his own account: the forty-eight pairs of scissors might have been requested by friends, but if he intended selling them on, it would be consistent with what we know of his character. (Compare one of Haydn's shopping lists, compiled with individual needs in mind, recorded in his notebook for 1792, which included 'Knitting needles, scissors and a little knife for Frau von Keess. For Biswanger,

---

[17] The document is reproduced in Müller von Asow, *Mingotti*, 87, and Roland Tenschert, *Christoph Willibald Gluck: Der grosse Reformator der Oper* (Olten and Freiburg, 1951), 171. Müller von Asow states that it is a newspaper cutting pasted into Mattheson's MS supplement to *Der musikalische Patriot* (Hamburg, 1728). I have not been able to trace the original.

[18] Hamburg, 24 Sept. 1748: autograph in Stuttgart, Hauptstaatsarchiv A202 Bü 2840; facsimile and transcription in Spulak, 'Ein unbekanntes Schriftstück', 346–7. Pinchbeck, named after its inventor, Christopher Pinchbeck (1670–1732), is an alloy of copper and zinc, giving the effect of gold.

spectacles for someone between 50 and 60 years of age. For Hamburger, nail-scissors and a larger pair. A woman's watchchain.'[19])

Later letters from Pirker include frequent requests for payment in advance: 'If Gluck wants to have his watches, he must send me the money' (28 October). Eventually Gluck reduced his order to one cheaper watch, made in pinchbeck, and devised a way to send Pirker the money through the agency of John Wyche, an English diplomat in Hamburg, who returned to London towards the end of 1748:

My dear Pirker,

You will receive twenty ducats from M. Waich [Wyche], which Mlle Bec[c]heroni has given him; please be so good as to buy the watch with it. But have it made in pinchbeck, with Poy's name on the watchcase, and it must have a diamond movement. Deal prudently in the matter so that of the twenty ducats enough remains for a fine steel chain and perhaps a gold [seal?]. You must not tell M. Wyche what the money is for, only that it was given by his wife to Mlle Beccheroni. Farewell, my dear Pirker; forgive me for troubling you.[20]

Gaspera Beccheroni was Wyche's mistress, and also Gluck's—to his cost, as will shortly emerge. Gluck's change of order, from the pair of watches to the single cheaper model, must have exasperated Pirker, who wrote to his wife on 31 January 1749: 'The silver watch which [Gluck] ordered in the first place is ready. He can also have one in pinchbeck, as he desires, but the payment must be arranged in a better way than hitherto.' Orders and counter-orders, difficulties over money (which was not forthcoming from Wyche), and the style of the watch continue for the best part of a year. The final mention occurs in a letter from Pirker to his wife dated 5 September 1749, written in Italian: 'I have had something of an argument with Poy, which, because he wanted to be paid for Gluck's watches, came near to preventing me from making my journey. If Gluck had not told me the facts, and if I had not kept a cool head, there would have been considerable trouble.' We do not discover if and how Poy was paid, nor whether Gluck ever received his watches.

Meanwhile, the Mingotti troupe, with Gluck as its new musical director, had travelled to Copenhagen, arriving at the end of November 1748. On 3 December, Marianne Pirker gave her husband the news that Gluck 'had other things to think about than spending money'; he was 'very ill, infected

[19] Quoted in H. C. Robbins Landon, *Haydn: Chronicle and Works* (London, 1976–80), iii. 129.

[20] Hamburg, Jan. 1749: autograph in Stuttgart, Hauptstaatsarchiv, A202 Bü 2841; facsimile in Müller von Asow, *Mingotti*, 93, and transcription in Spulak, 'Ein unbekanntes Schriftstück', 348. Some words remain illegible.

by our buffa' [Beccheroni]. Gluck's illness, presumably syphilis, is usually cited to explain his childlessness. Marianne calls Beccheroni a 'sow', and swears to avenge Gluck by letting Wyche know of the incident, but she is at the same time anxious that Wyche should not hear of the affair from her husband.[21] It is worth noting that this is the only occasion in his long career in the theatre on which any scandal is known to have touched Gluck's relationships with his singers.

By February Gluck was well enough to have written and begun to rehearse *La contesa de' numi*, an occasional *festa teatrale* to celebrate the birth of an heir to the Danish throne. In the circumstances, it is surprising that only two of the arias were taken over from earlier works, though the striking G minor introduction to Act II was adapted from Sammartini.[22] The fact that Gluck and Scheibe (the court Kapellmeister whom Scalabrini replaced) were in Copenhagen at the same time has given rise to the speculation that Scheibe may have discussed his dramatic theories with Gluck. No record of any such meeting survives, but Gluck could have had access to Scheibe's theories (advocating simplicity of texture, the primacy of melody, and a return to nature) through the preface to his opera *Thusnelde*, published in the same year as *La contesa*.[23] Gluck's opera was premièred on 9 April, in the Schloss Charlottenborg. We have no account of its reception or even the cast list. While in the Danish capital, Gluck gave more recitals on his glass-harmonica: in a letter dated 15 April, Marianne Pirker mentions two such concerts.[24] An announcement for one of them survives:

On Saturday 19 April in the Italian theatre in the royal Schloss Charlottenburg, Herr Kapellmeister Gluck will give a very fine and appealing concert of vocal and instrumental music, in which, as a special attraction to the audience, he will play on an instrument made of glass never before known here As there will be only one performance, he hopes that gracious music-lovers will have all the more pleasure in attending. The concert will begin at half past six.[25]

The Mingotti troupe left Copenhagen on 23 April.

[21] This further part of Marianne's letter of 3 Dec. is transcribed in Müller von Asow, *Mingotti*, 91.

[22] Churgin, 'Alterations in Gluck's Borrowings', 124–31.

[23] *Thusnelde* was probably never performed in Scheibe's lifetime, and the music is now lost. Gerhard Croll, 'Gluck', *New Grove*, viii. 457, suggests that Gluck did become acquainted with Scheibe's theories, and that this knowledge is shown in the opening of the piece, where the stormy D minor overture leads directly into a powerful accompanied recitative. Neither in 1749 nor later in Gluck's life, however, was this early 'reform' the subject of any surviving comment.

[24] Müller von Asow, *Mingotti*, 96.

[25] *Postrytten*, Apr. 1749, quoted in Angul Hammerich, 'Gluck und Scheibe in Kopenhagen', *Festschrift: Hermann Kretzschmar zum 70. Geburtstag*, ed. Max Friedlander *et al.* (Leipzig, 1918), 47.

Gluck again disappears from view until the performance of his new opera, *Ezio*, at the Teatro nuovo in Prague in the carnival season of 1749–50, the première probably on 26 December 1749. The production was by the touring company managed by Giovanni Battista Locatelli. Locatelli, who had begun his career as a member of Pietro Mingotti's troupe, signed a contract to take over the Teatro nuovo from March 1749. Thereafter he alternated between spending carnival in Prague and the summer season in Dresden. There must have been considerable rivalry between the troupes; on this occasion, Locatelli succeeded in detaching from Mingotti's company not only Gluck but also the experienced Gluckist tenor Canini. Gluck gave Canini the outstanding lyrical metaphor-aria 'Se povero il ruscello', which, several transformations later, was to become 'Che puro ciel' in *Orfeo* (1762). When Locatelli took *Ezio* to Leipzig in 1751, he included two additional arias by other, unnamed composers—a sure sign that Gluck was not present on that occasion.

5

MARRIAGE
(1750)

AFTER the performances of *Ezio* during the carnival season of 1749–50, Gluck's activities are again uncharted. At least a portion of the summer months of 1750 would have been devoted to preparing for his wedding. Exactly when Gluck met his future wife, Maria Anna Bergin (or Pergin), is not known. Such a meeting may have occurred as early as 1748. Schmid handed down a family tradition that Gluck did indeed meet Marianne (as she is always known) in this or the following year, but that the marriage was forbidden by her ambitious father, the wealthy merchant Joseph Bergin, on whose death Gluck 'flew on the wings of love' to Vienna to claim his bride.[1] More recent research has shown that if opposition there was, it must have come from Marianne's guardian, Joseph Salliet, since Joseph Bergin died in 1738.[2] If Gluck did have to endure a prolonged, secret betrothal, it might have arisen from the disparity in ages: in July 1750 he was 36 years old, Marianne was 18. Such a discrepancy was common-place in aristocratic marriages (for example that of Gluck's patron Prince Melzi)[3] but less common in middle-class couples.

The marriage contract is a typically eighteenth-century betrothal document, severely practical in all its clauses. Gluck was considerably the gainer.

In the name of the Most Holy Trinity, God the Father, Son,
and Holy Ghost, Amen.

This day, on the date stated below, between on the one part the nobly born Herr Christoph Gluckh,[4] bridegroom, and on the other part the noble

---

[1] Schmid, *Gluck*, 46–7.

[2] Max Kratochwill, 'Christoph Willibald Glucks Heiratskontrakt', *Jahrbuch des Vereins für Geschichte der Stadt Wien*, 10 (1952–3), 234–9.

[3] See Ch. 2.

[4] In both the contract and the certificate, all participants are refered to as 'wohl edel geboren'—nobly born. This polite fiction was in common use.

spinster Maria Anna Bergin, bride, in the presence of the bride's mother, the legally appointed guardian Joseph Salliet, and of the invited witnesses, the following marriage contract on behalf of the bride was agreed, authorized, and irrevocably concluded, namely:

Firstly, after the aforementioned Herr Christoph Gluckh had, with the consent of her mother and guardian, sought from the said spinster the promise to be his future wife, and after both marriage partners had confirmed the betrothal by word of mouth, by clasping of hands, by exchange of rings, and with a priestly blessing, the following worldly provisions were made

Next, the said bride has promised to endow the bridegroom from her own means with a true and legitimate dowry of 500 Rheinish gulden, after the wedding-day and on production of a receipt, to which the aforementioned bridegroom makes a settlement of 1,000 Rhenish gulden, so that the dowry and the settlement together shall comprise provision for the survivor of 1,500 gulden.

Thirdly, after the wedding-night, out of the deep affection he bears his beloved bride, the said bridegroom has promised to pay fifty gold ducats,[5] furthermore

Fourthly, both parties are agreed that the residue of the bride's current fortune of 4,000 gulden, that is 4,000 florins, is to be prudently invested ['ad fructificandum'], the certified yearly interest accruing thereto—apart from 100 gulden which have been expressly reserved for the bride's own personal expenditure—is to be used for the benefit of the joint household expenses; whereas

Fifthly, whatever is, by the gracious providence of God, received, earned or inherited during the period of the marriage, shall be the property of both.

Sixthly, as a token of her fondest maternal love, the bride's mother promises to provide appropriate and adequate furnishings and fittings, concerning which

Seventhly, all the goods brought to the marriage and acquired during it shall remain the property of the surviving partner, with the proviso that

Eighthly, should there be no issue, at the death of one partner, one half of his possessions at the time of death shall be transferred to the survivor, the other half to be disposed of by either party according to his own free choice, with effect that

Ninthly, should one of the above-mentioned marriage partners depart this world leaving one or more children, the survivor shall not only inherit the half share referred to in the preceding paragraph, but also have the full and entire use of the assets for the exclusive benefit of the children ['usus fructus'], to provide them with a decent Christian upbringing; not until they come of age shall each receive his portion, moreover

[5] The 'Morgengabe' was a traditional gift to the bride from her husband, paid after the wedding-night.

Tenthly and lastly, each partner may make additional bequests by will, codicil or other gift.

All the above made honestly and in good faith. Two identical copies of this true record of the marriage contract, have been drawn up and signed in their own hands by both marriage partners and by the witnesses—without risk or prejudice to the latter. Made in Vienna, 3 September 1750.

Signed: Maria Anna Bergin, bride

Theres Bergin, widow, bride's mother	Christoph Gluck, bridegroom
Franz Xav. v. Concin JUDr., witness	Giov. Pietro Sorosina, witness for the bridegroom[6]
Joseph Salliet, legally appointed guardian	

The contract was ratified four days later on 7 September 1750, on which occasion Gluck was identified as a 'famous composer', 'a reputed virtuoso of good standing'.[7] The marriage took place on 15 September 1750 at St Ulrich's church. A nineteenth-century transcript of the parish record confirms the biographical details:

The nobly born Herr Christophorus Gluckh, bachelor, born in Neumarkt in the Upper Palatinate, son and legitimate issue of the nobly born Herr Alexandri Gluckh, former head forester to His Serene Highness the Grand Duke of Tuscany, and Frau Anna Walburga, his wife, both deceased, take to wife the nobly born spinster Maria Anna Pergin, resident in the Laurant's house in Oberneustift,[8] a daughter born locally to the noble Herr Josephi Pergin, former merchant, deceased, and Frau Maria Theresia, his surviving spouse. They were married in accordance with the rites of the holy Catholic Church, on 15 September 1750, through the dispensation of the Honourable Herr P. Aemilian, curate of the parish, in the presence of Herr Joh. Peter Sorosina, agent in the Italian Office, and Franz Xav. von Consin, retired lawyer, and Josef Salliet, in the imperial Commercial Office, as witnesses.[9]

Gluck's marriage marked a significant turning-point. He gained a loyal partner, who supported and protected him for the remainder of his life; the Bergin wealth brought him immediately a considerable degree of financial

[6] Vienna, Archiv der Stadt Wien, AZJ.-Akt Fasz. 132–3. Transcribed in Kratochwill, 'Heiratskontrakt', 237–8. For details of the witnesses, see the marriage certificate.

[7] Kratochwill, 'Hieratskontrakt', 239.

[8] It is generally presumed that the young married couple lived with Maria Theresia Bergin in the Laurant's house (no longer standing). See Brauneis, 'Gluck in Wien', 43–5.

[9] Transcribed by the parish priest of St Ulrich's, Heinrich Münzer, in 1844, and reproduced in Tenschert, *Gluck . . . Reformator der Oper*, 172.

independence, which was gradually transformed into creative independence; and membership of the Bergin family brought him closer to the
court, where Marianne's sister Maria Petronella Josepha had been a lady-
in-waiting to the empress and was now married to Mauro Ignazio
Valmagini, inspector of buildings to the court, later privy counsellor.
Although he did not at once obtain a court appointment, and he continued
to travel wherever commissions were to be had, Gluck's home was now in
Vienna.

6

THE COMPLETE METASTASIAN
(1751–1756)

THERE is no trace of Gluck's activities in the year following his marriage. He is presumed to have remained in Vienna, and he can hardly have disappeared from notice, in view of a passing comment by Metastasio: in a letter to Farinelli, dated 6 November 1751, Metastasio mentions 'two masters of German music; one is Gluck, the other Wagenseil. The former displays a marvellous but wayward passion; the latter is a prodigious harpsichord player.'[1] But it was outside Vienna that his reputation was made in these years.

Gluck continued as a member of Locatelli's troupe, becoming its director for the carnival season of 1751–2. During this season—the exact date of the first performance is not recorded—his setting of yet another Metastasian libretto, *Issipile*, was given at the Teatro nuovo in Prague. The libretto confirms Gluck's standing in the company, revealing that 'the music is in the graceful and newest manner of Sig. *Maestro di Cappella* Gluck'.[2]

In March 1752, he was commissioned to write a festival opera for the name-day of King Charles III of Naples. It was Gluck's first invitation from the impresario Diego Tufarelli to write for the Teatro San Carlo, the moist prestigious opera-house in Italy. With his wife, Gluck arrived in Naples on 30 August:

As soon as he learned that the drama allotted to him to compose for 4 November was *Arsace*, [Gluck], with eloquent reasons and pressing eagerness, sought instead to be allowed to compose, for the said occasion, Metastasio's *La clemenza di Tito* (which I had promised to Sig. Abos for 18 December), on account of the latter [libretto] being enriched strong

---

[1] Metastasio, *Tutte le opere*, iii. 681–2.   [2] Wotquenne, *Thematisches Verzeichnis*, 196.

situations, and provided with more attractive and varied scenery. To satisfy his demand, which was an entirely reasonable one, and to do him justice with all the means at my disposal (the opera on 4 November being the more important one, because during its run the patrons attended the theatre more frequently) I granted his request.[3]

This occasion afforded Gluck his first opportunity to write for the great castrato Caffarelli. Another anecdote from Reichardt's French manuscript dramatizes their meeting:

When [Gluck] was invited to Naples, to compose two [*sic*] operas there, he found the great Caffarelli, idolized by the whole nation and inundated with superlative tributes from all and sundry. All musicians showed great respect and deference towards him. Gluck was informed of this, and invited to pay his respects. He, however, visited no one, even though he knew that Caffarelli was to sing in his opera. The latter, astonished by this outrageous behaviour, had no alternative but to visit Gluck. Afterwards they became the best of friends.[4]

Perhaps because of the short composition period (though surprising in view of the importance Gluck apparently attached to this opera) there are many borrowings from previous works: the overture, a march, and two arias were taken from *Ezio*, with further arias from *Issipile*, *Sofonisba*, and *Le nozze*. More discussed at the time, however, was a newly composed aria which Gluck was to reuse at the end of his creative life, 'Se mai senti spirarti sul volto', written for Caffarelli in the role of Sextus. Reichardt's manuscript is the earliest source of a widely cited tale:

While in Naples, Gluck wrote for this singer the celebrated aria 'Se mai senti spirarti sul volto', against which all the composers who were there at that time united; they asserted that the rules were violated in one passage, where, during a long sustained note from the ringing tones of Caffarelli, the instruments were too active. They hastened, with the score of this aria, to [Francesco] Durante, the oracle of composition, to hear his judgement. The great master examined the passage and told them: 'I do not wish to pronounce on whether this is completely in accordance with the rules of composition; I only wish to

---

[3] Diego Tufarelli, in Archivio di Stato Napoli, fasci teatrali no. 9, quoted in Ulisse Prota-Giurleo, 'Notizie biografiche intorno ad alcuni musicisti d'oltralpe a Napoli nel settecento', *Analecta musicologica*, 2 (1965), 118. Girolamo Abos was a Maltese composer who spent all his working life in Naples, pupil of Durante, and teacher of Paisiello. He appears to have composed neither an *Arsace* nor a *Clemenza*.

[4] Reichardt, 'Fortsetzung', 72.

say to you all that every one of us, myself before anyone, should be very proud to have conceived and written such a passage.'[5]

In Naples, Gluck revived his glass-harmonica recitals. An anonymous eyewitness gives more exact information on Gluck's method of playing this instrument than any other source; the reference arises in connection with a German musician, Anton Bebber, who claimed in 1775 to have invented the instrument:

There were fifty-five numbered glasses of various sizes, arranged on a table, tuned by means of water to create the different pitches. Bebber then dipped his fingers in the water and rubbed the rim of the glasses with the same fingers, which produced a sound like a delicate little organ. . . . It would not be wrong to credit him with the invention of this method of playing the glasses, because although *Maestro di Cappella* Gluck once gave this same entertainment with glasses in Naples, he, for his part, struck them with little rods, which did not produce so pleasant a sound as that achieved by Bebber.[6]

The reputation of the aria 'Se mai senti spirarti sul volto' preceded Gluck's return to Vienna, and helped to secure him his next position. An informative source for the next few years exists in the autobiography of Carl Ditters von Dittersdorf. Ditters, who dictated his memoirs to his son half a century later (and who cannot therefore be relied upon for every detail) was just 13 at the time, and himself a new member of the lavish musical establishment of Prince Joseph Friedrich von Sachsen-Hildburghausen:

Gluck came to Vienna in December [1752]. The prince already knew from his correspondent how great a success this worthy man had had in Italy. The same correspondent had sent the prince, a few weeks earlier, the score of the celebrated air 'Se mai senti spirarti sul volto', with which Gluck had made such a sensation throughout Italy. The prince had it performed by Mlle Heinisch, a very famous Viennese chamber singer, and it was widely admired. A natural

---

[5] Ibid. 72–3; quoted in Schmid, *Gluck*, 48–9. Francesco Durante (1684–1755), venerable Neapolitan composer and teacher, was widely regarded as an arbiter of composition. Burney (*General History*, ii. 426) notes that 'his masses and motets are still in use, [as] models of correct writing, with the students of the several conservatories of Naples.' The first section of the controversial aria appears as 'O malheureuse Iphigénie' in *Iphigénie en Tauride*, Act II; the middle section of the aria is used for the chorus 'Que d'attraits' in *Iphigénie en Aulide*, Act I, and is later reused for the Act II finale in *Tauride*.

[6] Naples, Archivio di Stato Napoli, fasci teatrali no. 19, quoted in Prota-Giurleo, 'Notizie', 119–20.

consequence of this was that the prince wanted to know Gluck in person. This was brought about by Bonno, who effected the introduction.[7]

Gluck was engaged by the prince immediately, and early in 1753 he became concert-master of the famous Hildburghausen orchestra:

Gluck was always jovial in carrying out his duties; besides his professional skills, he was well-read and had a knowledge of the wider world, and consequently soon became an intimate friend of the prince's. Gluck always led the orchestra for the concerts, for which a rehearsal was invariably held on the previous evening, so that everything, especially new items, should be brought off in an orderly and accurate manner. On the rehearsal and concert days, the prince's orchestra was reinforced with a considerable number of select orchestral players. No wonder our concerts were acknowledged as the best in all Vienna![8]

Ditters identifies some of the household musicians, and names the singers brought in for the concerts: Vittoria Tesi-Tramontini, who had sung the title role in *Semiramide*, and Theresia Heinisch, who, according to Ditters, refused theatrical engagements and chose only to sing in chamber concerts, appeared regularly. In addition, Bonno negotiated the engagement of visiting celebrities, including the singers Caterina Gabrielli and Tommaso Guarducci (both soon to star in *L'innocenza giustificata*). Ditters continues, 'Gluck had many of his compositions, such as sinfonias and arias, copied for the prince, and each piece from the pen of that talented composer was a newer and more delicate feast for our ears.'[9]

Gluck appears to have written no opera in 1753. The following year, however, an opportunity arose which was to consolidate his Viennese reputation and set his career in a new direction. In September 1754, the summer residence of Prince Joseph Friedrich at Schlosshof an der March was to receive a four-day imperial visit of more than ceremonial significance, for the empress was contemplating buying the estate as a gift for her husband. Gluck was invited to contribute a festival piece, a setting of Metastasio's libretto *Le cinesi*. The choice of this work was no doubt designed to gain in appeal from the fact that it was originally written in

[7] *Lebensbeschreibung* (Leipzig, 1801, repr. Munich, 1967), 59. Giuseppe Bonno, friend of Metastasio, was a composer of operas, oratorios, and church music and the teacher of many young musicians including Ditters; he was Kapellmeister to Prince Joseph Friedrich in 1749 and directed the prince's concerts at the Palais Rofrano every Friday during the winter season.

[8] Ibid. 59. Ditters implies that the prince and Gluck conversed in Italian, though the evidence is not conclusive, and the point of the anecdote may have been to demonstrate Ditters's own language skills.

[9] Ibid. 60.

1735 for a royal domestic performance, with two of the three Chinese women played by Maria Theresia and her sister Maria Anna. Metastasio had revised the text in 1751, adding a male role; it was this expanded text that Gluck set.

Hildburghausen took on new forces for the occasion. Besides an 'engineer, a painter, and a sculptor', Ditters mentions 'a double-bass player, a cellist, and three violinists, of which my younger brother, Alexander, was one. . . . By the time we arrived at Schlosshof, it was swarming with artists and artisans, carpenters, joiners, painters, varnishers, gilders, etc., so that wherever one went, one bumped into busy people, running hither and thither, heartily disenchanted with the forthcoming visit of the court.'[10] One of the workforce was the designer Giovanni Maria Quaglio, principal designer for the court theatres, whom Ditters complimented with the epithet 'Bibiena restored to life', comparing him with the celebrated and widely influential family of stage designers and architects.[11]

For Gluck, the preparations were longer than usual. He arrived at Schlosshof in mid-May. *Le cinesi* was given on 24 September, the second day of the royal visit. (Two pieces by Bonno, *Il vero omaggio* and *L'isola disabitata*, had opened the festivities.) The singers in *Le cinesi* were Joseph Friebert as Silango, Vittoria Tesi-Tramontini in the empress's role of Lisinga, Theresia Heinisch (tempted onto the stage for the occasion) in Maria Anna's role of Sivene, and Caterina Starzer, sister of the ballet composer Joseph Starzer, as Tangia.[12]

I see before me still the exquisite performance of the little comic opera . . . adapted by Metastasio from his work *Il ballo cinese*, and set to music by Gluck. Quaglio's diaphanous decorations were completely in the Chinese taste. Sculptors, varnishers, and gilders had rendered them richly with all the resources of their art. But what gave the design the greatest brilliance were glass prisms, which had been polished in Bohemian glassworks, and arranged closely together in the empty spaces which would normally be filled with brightly painted scenery. The splendid, most amazing sight produced by these prisms, already very effective in broad daylight, and here illuminated by innumerable lights, is indescribable. Even if one could imagine the reflected glitter of the azure-lacquered panels, the shimmer of the gilded foliage, and, as final

---

[10] Ibid. 66–7.

[11] Ibid. 76. Among the illustrious Bibiena family, Francesco (1659–1737) built the theatre in what was later to become the Redoutensaal of the imperial palace, where court opera during the reign of Charles VI was given. His elder brother Ferdinando (1656–1743) also worked on this theatre. Ferdinando's sons, Giuseppe and Antonio, had been employed by the imperial court as theatrical engineers in the 1740s.

[12] Joseph Starzer, violinist and composer, collaborated with Franz Hilverding in a series of ballets which paved the way for the even more innovative partnership of Gluck and Angiolini.

touch, the rainbow colours sparkling multifariously from the hundreds of prisms, as from the finest diamonds, the most vivid imagination must fall short of this magic. And then the heavenly music of one such as Gluck! It was not only the enchanting flow of the brilliant sinfonia, accompanied here and there by little chimes, triangles, small hand-drums and bells, now singly, now all together, which immediately delighted the audience, even before the curtain was raised, but the whole of the music, from first to last, was magical.

After the work concluded, the emperor and the prince went to the pit and asked for the curtain to be raised again. This was done. The monarch took his opera-glasses and was conducted onto the stage, where Quaglio explained everything to him. He asked for a piece of prism, at which Quaglio brought him a whole hatful, and he put three or four pieces in his pocket. He then requested the prince to have someone sent out from Vienna to make a drawing of the decorations. Quaglio, however, undertook the task himself, and finished it the following evening, for which he was rewarded with a fine gold watch with a gold chain.[13]

The rewards were high. The emperor was given the estate; the prince received the price of 400,000 gulden, and a present of four fine horses; Tesi was presented with two diamond bracelets, Heinisch and Starzer, expensive dresses; Gluck and Bonno each received a gold snuffbox containing a hundred ducats; the servants and military escort were also rewarded. Even the young Ditters received double pay. But for Gluck, the value of *Le cinesi* was not to be measured in coin or gift. Firstly it effected his entry into the imperial circle, and was to guarantee him a degree of royal favour for years to come. But no less importantly, the work had also caught the subject of the moment: it illustrated rival operatic styles, and demonstrated the composer's versatility in both the tragic and comic manners. Consequently it attracted the attention of the new theatrical management in Vienna, where, in 1754, Count Giacomo Durazzo became sole director of the court theatres.[14]

The commission for Gluck's next opera, *La danza*, arose directly from the success of *Le cinesi*. Metastasio's slight occasional work, a one-act pastoral drama, was performed for the celebration of Archduke Leopold's birthday at the summer palace of Laxenburg. Khevenhüller, always more

---

[13] Ditters, *Lebensbeschreibung*, 80–2. Ditters incorrectly identifies the 'little comic opera' as *La danza*. The description of Quaglio's prismatic decorations is ambiguous, and other translators have suggested that they took the form of hollow cylinders which fitted into each other, ignoring the fact that round edges do not refract light.

[14] Durazzo came to Vienna in 1749 as Genoan ambassador; in 1752 he was made assistant intendant under Count Franz Esterházy; in spring 1754 he became director of the Burg and Kärntnertor theatres.

concerned with the social status of the audience than with the quality of the entertainment, mentions the work briefly: 'On 5 [May] an informal celebration for Archduke Leopold was held, from which the ambassadors excused themselves. Nevertheless, the nobility was present at the summer theatre, where a new pastoral drama called *La danza* was produced, with a cast of only two singers, [Caterina] Gabrielli and the tenor Sig. [Friebert], and serving as introduction to a new ballet.'[15] The work consists of an overture, four arias, and a duet finale. It introduced Gluck to the dancer and choreographer Gasparo Angiolini, the leading male dancer in the *Ballet des bergers* (music by Joseph Starzer, choreography by Franz Hilverding), which followed *La danza*.[16]

Later in the same year Gluck forged closer links with the new imperial intendant, Durazzo. The occasion was *L'innocenza giustificata*, given on 8 December in the Burgtheater to celebrate the emperor's birthday, as Khevenhüller records: 'In the evening, the emperor and the younger nobility attended the court theatre where a little opera in two acts, called *L'Innocenza giustificata* was given for the first time, together with two new ballets.'[17] The empress did not see the opera until 14 December.[18] The soloists included Caterina Gabrielli and Tommaso Guarducci. A much longer account, which gives some hint of the unusual manufacture of the libretto, appears in the *Journal encyclopédique*, an influential periodical published at this period in Liège, aiming to explain Viennese life and culture to those in other European cities, principally Paris. *Innocenza* is described as an 'Italian pastoral'. In common with most French notices of plays and operas, it begins with a lengthy narration of the plot. The anonymous correspondent continues:

The author had no difficulty in incorporating Metastasio's excellent aria [texts], which find their place naturally in his subject. He drew the attention of the public to this fact in good faith, although he did not want to reveal his identity, which fact is all the more praiseworthy and all the more unusual, in that his drama had the most outstanding success.

The music to this poem is by M. Christoph Gluch, already known for other works in this genre, all of which have done infinite credit to this skilful composer. The two [scenes] each conclude with very striking ballets, contrived so that neither taste nor expense were spared. This birthday celebration was

---

[15] *Tagebuch*, 1752–5, 237.

[16] Franz Hilverding, dancer and choreographer, who held various posts at the imperial court between 1737 and 1758, is associated with the creation of ballet-pantomime. His pupil Gasparo Angiolini developed his work, succeeding him at the court, and defended his reputation in the face of rival claims from Noverre. Angiolini was to choreograph Gluck's most important ballets.

[17] *Tagebuch*, 1752–5, 271.   [18] Ibid. 272.

carried out by order of M. le Comte Durazzo, Superintendent of Theatres at the imperial court.[19]

The notice, possibly contributed by Durazzo himself,[20] hints at the unusual construction of the *Innocenza* libretto, in which Durazzo made a selection of aria texts by Metastasio, taken out of their original contexts, and wrote a drama around them, adding recitatives and incorporating a dramatically active chorus.

At the end of 1755 Gluck travelled to Rome to set an authentic Metastasian text, *Antigono*, at the Teatro di Torre Argentina on 9 February 1756. On the libretto, he is identified as Kapellmeister to the Prince of Sachsen-Hilburghausen. Little is known of the production or reception of this work, but it drew a revealing comment from Metastasio himself: 'I am most curious to learn how the music of our own Gluck has fared in Rome. His writing has a particular energy, and according to the current taste which I'm told prevails in Rome, I do not discount the possibility that it might please that public.'[21]

Rome honoured Gluck. His portrait was painted, probably at the request of Cardinal Albani, a notable patron of the arts. Durazzo later possessed a copy of this portrait, which he had 'updated' to represent a more mature Gluck; the composer had a copy of the altered version sent to Padre Martini in 1773.[22] He was also dignified with the papal title of Knight of the Golden Spur (Cavaliere dello Sperone d'Oro). The exact date of the award is not known, but Ditters associated it with Gluck's visit to Rome in 1756:

At this time Gluck was invited to Rome, where he had a great success and became Knight of the Golden Spur.

This order was conferred in Rome, and the members bear the title *Comites palatii romani*. They receive a diploma, written on parchment and authenticated by a great seal. In Rome, as in all the papal states, they enjoy all the privileges of nobility, and may freely enter the papal palace; moreover they hold the same rank as chamberlains at other royal courts. Their insignia is a gold Maltese cross in a yellow enamel setting. It is worn round the neck on a poppy-red ribbon; there is also a smaller cross, sometimes made entirely of gold, which hangs on the chest from a red ribbon through the buttonhole. The order is a very old one, and used to be held in more regard than it currently is.

[19] 15 Jan. 1756, 67–8.

[20] But see the discussion in Brown, 'Gluck and Opéra-Comique', 196–7.

[21] Letter to Francesco d'Argenvillières, 19 Feb. 1756, in Metastasio, *Tutte le opere*, iii. 1099. Metastasio's words are 'una vivacità particolare'.

[22] See Gluck's letter to Martini, 26 Oct. 1773, in Ch. 12 below. The portrait is reproduced and discussed in Gerhard Croll, 'Il mio ritratto fatto in Roma', *Österreichische Musikzeitung*, 42 (1987), 505–17.

To encourage the fine arts and the sciences to flourish more abundantly, the popes have recently bestowed this order on men of great and outstanding genius, such as Metastasio, Bibiena, Guarini, etc. This is how Gluck came to receive the order, and thereafter always signed himself *Cavaliere, Chevalier*, or *Ritter* Gluck.[23]

Ditters does not refrain from adding that he himself received the same honour in 1770, in which year Mozart was similarly honoured.[24]

Back in Vienna, Gluck composed for the emperor's birthday the Metastasian pastoral *Il rè pastore*, premièred at the Burgtheater on 8 December 1756. Khevenhüller mentions the newly honoured Gluck by name—a reliable indication of the composer's growing reputation at court: 'The opera they performed was the *Rè pastore* by Abate Metastasio, previously produced at Schönbrunn by a company of ladies and gentlemen [of the court], but to which Sig. Gluck, recently made a Knight of the Golden Spur by the Pope, composed the music; of the new cast, the Bavarian chamber virtuoso, Sig. Mazzanti, made an impression.'[25] A report published almost a year later in the *Journal encyclopédique* shows that Gluck's name was also being made known to French readers as guarantee of quality:

To praise [the work] in a few words, it is sufficient to say that the words are by M. l'Abbé Metastasio, the music by M. le chevalier Pluch [*sic*], the dances by M. Hilverding, that the famous singer, the Sieur Mazzanti, undertook the leading male role, and Mlle [Caterina] Gabrielli that of Elisa. This fine singer surpassed herself in this work, and above all in the ariette in Act III ['Io rimaner divisa'], a moment of such beauty that the admiring public could not decide whether she deserved more applause for the beauty of her voice, or for her skill, or for the varied expression of her singing.[26]

Most valuably, a third account comes from the librettist himself. After describing festivities earlier in the day, to celebrate the successful delivery of a prince, Maximilian, to Maria Theresia, Metastasio continues:

The opera which was performed this evening in the public theatre was certainly applauded: but what could displease on such a day? The libretto is my

---

[23] *Lebensbeschreibung*, 92–3.

[24] Leopold Mozart to his wife, 7 July 1770, in Wolfgang Amadeus Mozart, *Briefe und Aufzeichnungen*, ed. Wilhelm Bauer, Otto Erich Deutsch, and Joseph Heinz Eibl (Kassel, 1962–75), i. 368.

[25] *Tagebuch*, 1756–7, 55. The earlier Viennese setting (1751) was by Bonno. Lásló Somfai notes some close correspondences between Bonno's setting and Gluck's in Gluck's *Sämtliche Werke*, ed. R. Gerber, G. Croll, *et al.* (Kassel and Basle, 1951–), III/21, p. viii.

[26] 15 Sept. 1757, 127–8.

Rè pastore, the music is by the Bohemian *maestro di cappella* Gluck, whose vivacity, reputation, and invention have served him well in more than one theatre in Europe; I can well understand this, and those who think similarly are not in the minority, for here there is no scarcity of those who praise extravagantly. The prima donna is the Roman Signora Caterina Gabrielli; the young woman certainly has no equal in the excellence of her voice, her taste, and her acting. (Incidentally, I assure you that I'm not in love with her.) The first time our M. L'Augier heard her, he broke out into unheard-of expressions of delight and wonder, not unreasonably, and with total justification. The first [male] soprano is Sig. Mazzanti ... he does not lack admirers, because we have a taste for all that is piquant. I, for my part, whenever I listen to singing, am not content merely to admire, but desire that my heart enter into that which my ears experience. But the skill to move the heart is bestowed on few, and nature does not often take the trouble to make a Farinelli.[27]

The following comment from Reichardt's manuscript is attached to no specific occasion, but, if it has any basis in fact, probably stems from the 1750s:

Wherever possible, Gluck contrived his music to suit those who were to sing it, and to the place and circumstances [of performance]. This once caused a rift between himself and Metastasio, for Gluck wanted to alter the ordering and distribution of roles, the better to suit the particular singers present. The result vindicated Gluck's judgement, which always stemmed from his proper feelings.[28]

[27] Letter to Farinelli, Vienna, 8 Dec. 1756, in Metastasio, *Tutte le opere*, iii. 1152–4.
[28] 'Fortsetzung', 73.

7

THE COURT COMPOSER
(1756–1762)

AFTER the success of *Le cinesi* and *La danza*, Gluck began his official court career. In 1755 he was appointed court composer, and in the following year director of music academies; from 1759 he was named composer of ballets, and in 1760 'director of theatre music' appears in his official title.[1] The variety of his activities is made clear in a document in which Durazzo retrospectively catalogues Gluck's outstanding contribution to Viennese musical life over a decade:

The acknowledged talent of the Sieur Gluck for theatrical composition, and the readiness he has shown to apply himself to all the kinds of music that I have asked of him, whether for ballets, for opéras-comiques, or for opera seria, in which he has always distinguished himself, from *L'innocenza giustificata* of ten years ago up to the present, and moreover the fact that he is sought after by every Italian town and many German courts, prompts me to beseech your majesty to allow me to make sure of retaining him, by promising him a pension for himself of 600 florins, which he will enjoy when he is no longer able to serve, which, in view of his age, must be very distant. I am sure that thereby he can be bound to Your Majesty's service at no cost to Your Majesty, both for that which pertains to the direction of theatrical entertainments, and for the provision of vocal music for the chamber or the table, in which [latter] he has been employed till now without recompense. He will continue to work in these two areas, without asking anything in addition to the regular salary which the theatre management has assigned him in respect of his compositions.[2]

---

[1] Gluck's official positions and salaries in 1755–64 are listed in Bruce Alan Brown, *Gluck and the French Theatre in Vienna* (Oxford, 1991), 486. Much of the content of this chapter is derived, with grateful acknowledgement, from Brown's researches into Vienna in the 1750s.

[2] Letter to Maria Theresia, Vienna, 21 Jan. 1763: Vienna, Hofkammerarchiv, Camerale 2186, Fasz. 67, fos. 8–9; reproduced in Brown, 'Gluck and Opéra-Comique', 867.

A personal perspective on the busy life of a court musician in this period is given by Ditters, who left the Prince of Hildburghausen's orchestra when it was disbanded in 1761. The prince arranged with Durazzo for his musicians to be taken on by the court, but Ditters found the move disadvantageous:

No one was more badly affected [by the change] than I, for I had not only to play almost every day for the opera and ballet rehearsals from ten in the morning till two in the afternoon, and at the performances in the theatre in the evenings from half past six to ten o'clock, but also to play at the theatre concerts every Friday, and perform a concerto every fortnight. I was also contracted to appear before the imperial court on high days and holidays.

It is obvious that with this heavy burden of work, I had no time to take on pupils, or appear at private concerts, so that I was debarred from all supplementary [paid] work. . . . My monthly salary of 37 florins 30 kreutzer was all spent on breakfast, lunch, and dinner. . . .

Gluck had been Kapellmeister to the court and theatre at a salary of 2,000 gulden for the last two years. He already held me in affection when we were with the prince. . . . I therefore looked to him for help and explained my circumstances, at which he promised to interest himself on my behalf.

One day I went with him to Count Durazzo. Gluck explained everything to him, and I asked for either an increase in pay or release from my contract. Gluck did everything he could to support me. At last the count said to me, 'Dear child, it is not in my power either to increase your pay or to release you, for I can do nothing beyond your contract. But I can give you leave for four days each week, so that on these days you can earn something for yourself as you wish, and in this way you will be somewhat more comfortable.[3]

The official titles of his positions suggest that Gluck was initially concerned with the academies (concerts) given in the Burgtheater during Lent. These were put on a regular footing by Durazzo in 1755, the year of Gluck's appointment. Like so much cultural life in Vienna, they were devised in imitation of a Parisian phenomenon, the Concerts spirituels, and Metastasio refers to them as *concerti spirituali* in this ironic account of Durazzo's first Lenten season:

To increase our devotion, we have here *concerti spirituali* three times a week in the public theatre next to the court. There can be heard the judicious alternation of sacred or moral arias and cantatas, oratorios, psalms in the vernacular,

---

[3] *Lebensbeschreibung*, 106–8.

choruses, madrigals, caprices, and every elegant thing that the holy fathers of harmony have conceived. . . . The battlefield boasts all the splendour of majesty and all the refinement of good taste. The large orchestra and many singers who serve in the chorus are positioned on the stage which rises in well-proportioned steps, and are surrounded by scenery of the finest design.[4]

(Burney called such staged concerts in London 'oratorios in still life'.[5]) Gluck's concert-direction scarcely impinged upon his creative life; it led neither to an outburst of symphonic writing, nor to a flood of sacred oratorios, the repertory of both genres being dominated in the 1750s by Wagenseil. Although an anonymous tribute described him as 'a man truly created for the orchestra',[6] there is no account of him in this role. His creative energies were soon to be directed elsewhere.

In 1752, the year in which Pergolesi's intermezzo *La serva padrona* was rapturously received in Paris, a troupe of French actors was established in Vienna.[7] Both events were to impact on Gluck's career, the latter more immediately and more constructively than the former. The performance of opéras-comiques, initially imported from Paris, but increasingly revised and refurbished with new music in Vienna, became regular events in the mid-1750s; they filled a gap in the social calendar left by the suspension of opera seria in 1756 (an economy due to the outbreak of the Seven Years War). Writing to the Parisian librettist Charles-Simon Favart, who was to supply him with opéras-comiques over a number of years, Durazzo describes the relationship between the Viennese audience and the French repertory:

That which pleases in Paris is sometimes unsuitable for Vienna. French comedy given in foreign courts is more an entertainment for the nobility than a national tradition. It is not a question of using the French plays to provide moral instruction for the Germans, but only of avoiding everything in the presentation of these works that could damage or corrupt standards which are simple and naturally sound. . . . The theatre at the Viennese court is

[4] Letter to Antonio Tolomeo Trivulzio, Vienna, 17 Feb. 1755, in Metastasio, *Tutte le opere*, iii. 989.

[5] Reporting a performance of Handel's masque *Acis and Galatea* in 1732, Burney quotes from an advertisement which promised 'There will be *no action* on the stage, but the scene will represent, in a picturesque manner, a rural prospect with rocks, groves, fountains, and grottos, among which will be disposed a chorus of nymphs and shepherds, the habits and every other decoration suited to the subject', and comments, 'And this seems to have been the origin of Handel's performance of oratorios in still life, and of serenatas and other secular musical dramas, during Lent, *in the manner* of oratorios' (Burney's italics). *General History*, ii. 776.

[6] *Wienerisches Diarium*, 84, suppl., 18 Oct. 1766. The document is discussed in Ch. 9 below.

[7] The French troupe was installed and protected by the Imperial Chancellor, Count Wenzel Anton Kaunitz.

comparable to that at Paris, except that the auditorium here is finer and larger, and although it is almost always less crowded, the presence of the imperial family compensates for the [smaller] number of the spectators.[8]

Gluck's involvement in the early opéras-comiques was slight, though the case for his contribution to at least one, *Tircis et Doristée* (1756), has been convincingly argued.[9] The first opéra-comique for which he provided all the music was *La Fausse Esclave*, given in the Burgtheater on 8 January 1758. The text, by Louis Anseaume and Pierre Augustin Lefèvre de Marcouville, had been performed in Paris a year earlier. Gluck's setting was reviewed in the *Journal encyclopédique*, in an account shaped by the typical compulsion to compare Viennese theatrical practice with that in Paris. It is worth noting that Gluck is referred to as an established and successful composer, making his 'first attempt' at writing an opéra-comique, and that his setting of the French language was seen to be a crucial issue, despite the fact that the words were said to be without merit. With hindsight, the wish to have Gluck's music performed in Paris appears significant:

On the eighth of January, in the presence of their royal and imperial majesties, *La Fausse Esclave*, an opéra-comique in one act, was performed.

Although in modern opéras-comiques it is the custom to distort the French text to accommodate it to the Italianate music which is being parodied, M. le Chevalier Pluch, renowned for his talents in the composition of several serious Italian operas which have been admired in the most prestigious theatres in Europe, has himself written wholly new music for the words of the ariettes in this opéra-comique, which has been widely applauded, and which has continued to be heard with equal pleasure right up to the closure of the French Theatre on Tuesday 7 February last.

The text provided for the composer has no merit. All that has been done is to reduce to one act the two-act opéra-comique *La Fausse Aventurière*, which had already been performed in Paris in the Théâtre de la Foire. . . .

After the success of this work, it is to be hoped that the music of this talented composer might be performed in Paris, so that it can be determined whether, at the first attempt, he has managed to retain all the expressive truth of the French words, while adding, as he has undoubtedly done, all the brilliance of accompaniments in the Italian style.[10]

---

[8] Vienna, 20 Dec. 1759, in Charles-Simon Favart, *Mémoires et correspondances littéraires, dramatiques et anecdotiques* (Paris, 1808), i. 2–3.

[9] See Brown, *Gluck and the French Theatre*, 202–5.

[10] *Journal encyclopédique*, 1 Mar. 1758, 131–2.

The brilliance of Gluck's accompaniments is muted for us by the fact that the work survives only in the form of a vocal score; and the ballet which concluded it is missing. The soloists were Louise Joffroy-Bodin, Jean-Baptiste Rousselois, Pierre-Auguste Clavereau, and Mimi Favier, members of the versatile French troupe, who were in general as well able to act and dance as to sing. In particular, Joffroy-Bodin and Favier were regarded primarily as dancers.

Louise Joffroy-Bodin delayed the performance of Gluck's second opéra-comique, *L'Isle de Merlin, ou Le Monde renversé*, as Khevenhüller explains: 'The new opéra-comique called *Le Monde renversé* was performed on 3 [October] in the theatre at Schönbrunn. It should already have been given at Laxenburg, but had to be deferred till now because of the recent confinement of Mme Bodin or Geoffroi [Joffroy]. The admission was organized on the old footing, and the small boxes on the left were made available to the ambassadors and their wives. The opera was followed by a new ballet, devised for the work.'[11] The ballet, which survives,[12] may have been written by the official ballet composer Starzer, or by Gluck. The work opens with a descriptive overture representing a storm, which Gluck later adapted for the overture to *Iphigénie en Tauride*. The *Journal encyclopédique* warmly welcomed the work in a delayed review. Without naming Gluck, it gives somewhat fulsome credit to Durazzo for his role in promoting the French genre:

The music, ballets, and decoration in both Viennese theatres are redolent of the taste of their director. A passionate enthusiast and refined connoisseur, in a country where the arts are not sufficiently widely esteemed, Count Durazzo takes pride in welcoming the talented, and in seeking out all who are gifted with genius. When I speak of music, I do not only refer to that which accompanies dancing, but also that which enhances the little stage works called opéras-comiques. This genre has too often been impaired by trivial vaudevilles; here they try to improve it by the power of harmony. Since you ceased to mention the Viennese theatres, performances have been given here, a description of which deserves a distinguished place in your journal. One of these, *Le Monde renversé*, under the title *L'Isle de Merlin*, made an enjoyable impression which still remains. Cuts and additions have made this entertainment from the fairground [the Théâtre de la Foire] truly worthy of the court and the town. The sung airs are almost all new, and the decorations capture the magic which lies at the heart of this work.[13]

---

[11] *Tagebuch*, 1758–9, 66.

[12] In the MS collection at Český Krumlov, in the former Czechoslovakia.

[13] 15 Dec. 1759, 130–1. Reports from the Viennese theatres had been absent from the *Journal* for over a year.

The growing taste for opéra-comique is signalled by the fact that Gluck produced three such works in 1759. For the first, *Le Diable à quatre*, he provided ariettes, accompaniments, and a ballet to a French version of Charles Coffey's ballad opera *The Devil to Pay*, which had already enjoyed an eventful life in Germany as the Singspiel *Der Teufel ist los*.[14] The libretto of Gluck's opera, by Jean-Michel Sedaine, derives from Coffey's original. Khevenhüller notes the première on 28 May 1759: 'Then we had a new opéra-comique, called *Le Diable à quatre*, which had been adapted by Count Durazzo to the requirements of our theatre, fitted up with various new airs by the present gifted composer and Kapellmeister of the theatre, cavalier Kluck. It was followed by a new ballet of servants, devised for the work.'[15] There is no other account of the reception, but its success is indicated by revivals in 1761 and 1762. The air 'Je n'aimois pas le tabac beaucoup' (adapted, not composed, by Gluck), was used by Haydn in 1761 in his Symphony No. 8, 'Le Soir'.[16]

Another opera from 1759, *Cythère assiégée*, marks Gluck's first direct professional contact with Favart, the librettist of this work, who was to play a significant role in introducing Gluck's music to Paris. The date of the first performance is not known. A description of it follows the review of *L'Isle de Merlin* in the *Journal encyclopédique*:

Le Siège de Cythère is another entertainment no less bewitching. The costumes, all the decorations, and the music formed a unity which aptly recreated all the illusions which poetry had imagined on this fictitious island. There were outstanding choruses composed of young lovers and children of both sexes, numbering sixty in all. The walls of Cythera fell only to reveal the interior of this marvellous city, and the Temple of Love. Voluptuous music invited one thither, and extended the sweet influence of the divinity over all present.[17]

The libretto describes the temple as being 'transparent'—another of Quaglio's experiments with glass. *Cythère assiégée* was performed the same year before the Elector Carl Theodor at his summer palace of Schwetzingen. Burney mentions the occasion:

[14] See Walter Marshall, ' "The Devil to Pay" and its Influence on the Eighteenth-Century German Singspiel', Ph.D thesis (Open Univ., 1985).

[15] *Tagebuch*, 1758–9, 105.

[16] Daniel Heartz, 'Haydn und Gluck im Burgtheater um 1760: *Der neue krumme Teufel, Le Diable à quatre*, und die Sinfonie "Le Soir" ', *Bericht über den Internationalen Musikwissenschaftlichen Kongress, Bayreuth 1981*, ed. Christoph-Helmut Mahling and Sigrid Wiesmann (Kassel, 1983), 120–35.

[17] 15 Dec. 1759, 131–2.

A few years since, a comic opera of Gluck's was performed at the Elector Palatine's theatre, at Schwetzingen: his Electoral highness was much struck with the music, and enquired who had composed it; and, upon being informed that it was the production of an honest German, who loved old hock; 'I think, says the Elector, he deserves to be made drink for his trouble;' and ordered him a tun, not indeed quite so big as that at Heidelberg, but a very large one, and full of excellent wine.[18]

A new eyewitness was shortly to enter the picture. Count Carl Zinzendorf, member of a celebrated Protestant family, came to Vienna in 1761 and filled many volumes of his diary, written in French, with a social, political, and cultural commentary on Viennese life. His references to music are all too brief (often confined to relating to plot), but sometimes provide vivid one-line descriptions of events unrecorded elsewhere. Zinzendorf attended the revival of *Cythère assiégée* in 1762, and confirms the outstanding impression made by the set: 'The decorations in *Cythère assiégée* were very beautiful. At the end, [we saw] a dome, supported by columns, with balustrades to each side, with urns piled with fruit, the whole illuminated.'[19] The music was turned into a ballet, *Citera assediata*, given at the Burgtheater on 15 September 1762; Gluck also reworked it as an opera-ballet for Paris, performed on 1 August 1775.

The last opéra-comique of 1759 was *L'Arbre enchanté*, libretto by Jean-Joseph Vadé, given at Schönbrunn on 3 October. It seems to have been no less successful than the others. On the occasion of the 1761 revival, Zinzendorf found 'the airs pretty and the music enchanting'; he was sufficiently impressed with the composer to find it worth recording that 'the Chevalier Gluck [was] near me as he directed the music'.[20] Gluck adapted this opera for performance at Versailles in 1775 as a compliment to the visiting Archduke Maximilian. The following year Gluck wrote only one opéra-comique. *L'Ivrogne corrigé*, to a libretto by Anseaume, was given some time in 1760.[21] There are no sources relating to the 1760 performance. Zinzendorf saw a revival on 30 May 1761 and found the mock fury scene 'so bad that I regretted having gone to see it.'[22]

Gluck's next opéra-comique was more to the count's taste. *Le Cadi*

---

[18] *Present State . . . Germany*, i. 291–2.

[19] Diary, 17 Feb. 1762. His diaries cover the years 1752–1813 in more than 50 vols. of cramped handwriting. They are unpublished, and housed in the Haus-, Hof- und Staatsarchiv in Vienna.

[20] Diary, 12 May 1761.

[21] Croll suggests April (see pref. to Gluck's *Sämtliche Werke*, III/22, p. vi). Brown (*Gluck and the French Theatre*, 253) argues persuasively for the end of the year, after the ballet-pantomime *Les Aventures champêtres* (19 Nov.), which included music from every one of Gluck's opéras-comiques except *L'Ivrogne*.

[22] Diary, 30 May 1761.

dupé, given on 9 December 1761, caught the fashion for Turkish opera, which was to become a characteristic sub-genre in German-speaking Europe for some decades. Durazzo reported to Favart that it 'enjoyed all imaginable success',[23] and Zinzendorf particularly delighted in the grotesque travesty role of the ugly daughter, sung by the tenor Gabriel Soullé in a casting tradition dating back to the seventeenth century: 'Gluck's music was very good, and the airs pretty. Soullé did extremely well in the role of the dyer's daughter'.[24]

In his plea for a pension for Gluck, cited at the beginning of this chapter, Durazzo placed ballet at the head of the list of Gluck's manifold contributions to Viennese musical life. Durazzo's own efforts in facilitating these entertainments were untiring, as he claimed in his own words:

Ballets are in general done better in Vienna than in Paris, at least as far as the decorations and the music are concerned. Costume is given great attention here. The designs for the ballet are by a fine master. As for the subject, it is usually Count Durazzo who names it, or who suggests it, and he has made it his study to maintain the attraction of the theatre by the variety of the entertainments. . . . The ease with which the theatre director can assemble the dancers, the musicians, and the decorations of the two theatres on a single stage, and the magnificence which he takes pride in lavishing on the court entertainments, gives scope to the imagination of a poet who is to create the subject-matter of fêtes or ballets.[25]

The extent of Gluck's contribution to the ballet has only recently begun to be understood, and many recently discovered scores are in the process of being attributed to him.[26] He acquired the title 'Composer of Music for the Ballets' in 1759, and it is presumed that the majority of the ballets performed in both the Burg and Kärntnertor theatres in 1759–61 were composed by him. The following review contains a sentence which is possibly the earliest brief description of his ballet music. The presence of so detailed a report in the *Journal étranger*, published in Paris and edited by François Arnaud, is further evidence of the enthusiastic cultural interchange between the two capitals. *Les Amours de Flore et Zéphire* was first performed at Schönbrunn on 13 August 1759 and revived at the Burgtheater in the spring of 1760:

[23] Favart, *Mémoires*, i. 213.   [24] Diary, 13 Dec. 1761.

[25] Letter to Favart, Vienna, 20 Dec. 1759, in Favart, *Mémoires*, i. 3–4.

[26] See Rudolf Gerber, 'Unbekannte Instrumentalwerke von Christoph Willibald Gluck', *Die Musikforschung*, 4 (1951), 305–18; Gerhard Croll, 'Neue Quellen zu Musik und Theater in Wien 1758–1763', *Festschrift Walter Senn*, ed. Erich Egg and Ewald Fässler (Munich, 1975), 8–12; Brown, *Gluck and the French Theatre*, 282–357.

I come to the subject of those entertainments which I believe to be superior in Vienna, that is, the ballets. I have seen some here that were quite magnificent. Those which impressed me the most were *Le Port de Marseille* and *La Boutique du perruquier*, given at the German Theatre [Kärntnertor], and *Flore et Zéphir* and *Le Berger magicien* at the French Comedy [Burgtheater]. . . .

The *Ballet de Flore* was as elegant as one could imagine. There was an *entrée* of North Winds in attendance upon Boreas, who, in a jealous rage, had devastated the flowers opening beneath the feet of his beloved. The decoration of this scene was magical. The winds emerged from the depths of clouds which darkened the sky. A wild dance was accompanied by music that was both menacing and thrilling. Zephyr flew away in fear; Flora, distraught, sank onto a grassy bank. It was necessary to have seen Mme Angiolini, to imagine just how moving the attitude of her head made the languor of her expression. Her steps might have been more delicate, her movements more accurate, her arms more controlled in their motion, or her carriage lighter; but Nature and Art have created no more harmonious whole than Mme Angiolini.[27]

Through his collaboration with Angiolini, Gluck found himself caught up in innovations at least as far-reaching as those which were shaping opéra-comique—nothing less than the creation of a new genre which attempted to raise ballet to the status of spoken tragedy. Angiolini himself identified three of the ballets he created with Gluck as significant 'novelties'. With their substantial and coherent dramatic content, and articulate use of gesture, *Don Juan*, *Citera assediata*, and *Sémiramis* break new ground (though their primacy was challenged by Jean-Georges Noverre, with whom Gluck was to collaborate in *Alceste* and *Paride ed Elena*):

It was not until the year 1761 that my ideas began a little to clarify themselves, to come together, and to germinate. And so after many difficulties of various kinds, I discovered, without help or example, a fruitful and interesting way of introducing into [ballet]-pantomime a comedy, a drama, and, a little while later, an entire tragedy. In 1761, then, I gave the ballet *Don Juan*, accompanying its programme with a Dissertation in which theory predominated over practice, because at that time I had learnt more from reading than from experience.

In 1762 I gave another novelty suggested to me by the ancients; this was to turn *Citera assediata*, the witty opéra-comique by Sig. Favart, set to music by the famous Sig. Cavaliere Gluck, into ballet-pantomime. . . . My feeble productions no longer fell into those crude errors which ignorant youth thoughtlessly commits through not having analysed the meaning of gestures, nor

---

[27] May 1760, 106–10. The dancer Maria Teresa Fogliazzi married Angiolini in 1754.

understood how they connect and how they represent, nor recognized their significance and unity, whereas with proper use, these might be employed in a way appropriate to human customs, characters, and passions. By these means, I sought as best I could to bring colour to historical and mythical ballets, which to me had seemed the coldest of all; and not content with these genres, I progressed to the terrible and sublime pathos of true tragedy. . . .

In 1765 I devised and produced the ballet *Sémiramis*, the most terrible subject that antiquity has handed down to us.[28]

Don Juan was given on 17 October 1761. Zinzendorf gave a detailed description of the action, concluding:

Suddenly hell is represented, furies dance with lighted torches and torment Don Juan. At the back of the stage can be seen a fine firework display, representing the fires of hell; demons are seen aloft. The ballet lasts a very long time; finally the demons bear Don Juan away and leap with him into the fiery abyss. All this was very well performed, and the music extremely beautiful.[29]

The stage effects of the last scene are a reminder that fire was a constant hazard in eighteenth-century theatres. Fire did break out in the Kärntnertortheater, on 3 November 1761, following a performance of a German comedy on the subject of Don Juan, given for All Souls' Day (2 November), though there is no evidence that the stage effects caused the disaster: 'On the very day after the comedy—by the grace of God there was no one left, apart from a few gentlemen who continued to amuse themselves—the theatre unfortunately caught fire, so that it was entirely burnt down, with damage to two neighbouring houses'.[30]

Describing a less disastrous occasion, Reichardt's French manuscript contains the following scene, which if not true, is at least plausible. (The date of the event and the work concerned are not specified):

One day in Vienna, as Gluck was directing his opera at the keyboard, at the end of the first ballet, fire broke out in the wings. There was uproar in the theatre; the male dancers fled and the audience sought to save themselves. Meanwhile the fire was extinguished, and orders were given that the second act of the opera should start. Gluck tried to resume the rehearsal, but as the

---

[28] Gasparo Angiolini, *Lettere di Gasparo Angiolini a Monsieur Noverre sopra i balli pantomimi* (Milan, 1773), 16–19.

[29] Diary, 17 Oct. 1761.

[30] Philipp Gumpenhuber, *Répertoire*, quoted in Brown, *Gluck and the French Theatre*, 101–2. See also Croll, 'Glucks *Don Juan* freigesprochen: Bemerkungen zum Brand des Kärntnertortheaters von 1761', *Österreichische Musikzeitschrift*, 31 (1976), 12–15.

tumult had not yet completely subsided, he sat down again to wait for the
noise to die down. A great argument arose. The women dancers were still
shivering with fear, and the male dancers had already changed out of their costumes. At last Gluck rose from his chair and, in the presence of the court,
shouted loudly across the stage, 'Either the ballet is danced again, or the opera
will be cancelled for today.' They were compelled to begin the ballet again.
When the opera was performed, it was given with the most tremendous success. This admirable courage stood him in good stead on many occasions,
especially in France.[31]

Another aspect of Gluck's duties as court composer was to supply occasional dramas for royal festivities. One such took place in October 1760,
with the marriage of Archduke Joseph to Isabella of Bourbon-Parma, a
dynastic alliance devised to forge closer links with France. The occasion
was celebrated in Parma with an opera-ballet, *Le feste d'Imeneo* by Traetta,
and in Vienna with two Italian operas, which genre was only gradually
reappearing in Vienna after the austerities of the mid-1750s. The principal
work was an opera seria by Hasse, *Alcide al bivio*, given the day after the
wedding, on 8 October; additionally, the serenata *Tetide*, by Gluck, was
performed on 10 October. A complete account of the festivities appears in
a thirty-one-page essay in the *Journal étranger*, in which Gluck is briefly
mentioned:

This entertainment, with words by M. [Gianambrosio] Migliavacca,
Counsellor to the legation of His Majesty the King of Poland and Elector of
Saxony, was performed for the first time on the tenth of last October in the
Redoutensaal, and has been repeated several times. . . . The music . . . which
was considered original, harmonious, and full of touches worthy of the great-
est masters, is by M. le Chevalier Gluk, who is not unknown in France.[32]

The cast included Caterina Gabrielli (Thetis) and Giovanni Manzuoli
(Apollo). The first performance of the serenata is commemorated in a
painting which, despite the great impact made by Servandoni's stage
design, is almost entirely devoted to the brilliant auditorium of the
Redoutensaal and the even more illustrious audience.[33]

Gluck worked on another text by Migliavacca during this period. For
the *festa teatrale Arianna*, given on 27 May 1762, he arranged pre-existing
music to a new text. The libretto shows that the cast included Gluck's

---

[31] 'Fortsetzung', 73.   [32] Nov. 1760, 198–9, 205.
[33] Attributed to Dophonias Dederich; discussed and reproduced in Otto Erich Deutsch, 'Gluck
im Redoutensaal', *Österreichische Musikzeitschrift*, 21 (1966), 521–5.

Orpheus and Eurydice (Guadagni and Bianchi) as Ariadne and Bacchus, with the tenor Giuseppe Tibaldi as Theseus. The score is lost, and it is not known how much of his own music was included in this pasticcio.[34]

A final comment on Gluck's assured position in Viennese theatrical life, from both an artistic and a financial point of view, appears in a letter to Favart from Louis Hurtaut Dancourt, newly arrived in the imperial capital and alert to waxing and waning reputations. It is unlikely that the worldly Gluck in fact gave up his post of official composer of ballets in favour of his protegé Giuseppe Scarlatti because he was 'rich enough'; more probably he was now totally immersed in a fresh project (*Orfeo*) which was to take him in new directions:

Gluck . . . is a musician well thought of by our people, and particularly by our singers. Their opinion, however, seems suspect to me: I have the greatest difficulty in conceiving that a German could sing well in French; allow me to say no more on this subject until I have heard him. . . . Another virtuoso, called Scarlatti, has been appointed here in place of Gluck, who has been reproached with no other fault than that of being rich enough to be able to give way to an Italian who is not.[35]

---

[34] See Klaus Hortschansky, '*Arianna*: Ein Pasticcio von Gluck', *Die Musikforschung*, 24 (1971), 407–11. Tibaldi was shortly to take the leading roles of Porsena in *Il trionfo di Clelia* and Admetus in *Alceste*.

[35] Vienna, 25 Apr. 1762, in Favart, *Mémoires*, 263–6.

8

ORFEO
(1762)

GLUCK's next opera transformed his standing both among his contemporaries and for all time. There are, however, few sources to tell how it came to be written, and the most explicit is not necessarily the most reliable. More than twenty years later, aware of the epoch-making nature of the little *azione teatrale* called *Orfeo*, and knowing that he had achieved nothing comparable since his collaboration with Gluck ended, the librettist Ranieri de' Calzabigi gave the following account:

I am no musician, but I have made a great study of declamation. . . . It is twenty-five years since I became persuaded that the only music suitable for dramatic poetry, and especially for dialogue and for those airs that we call 'action numbers' [*d'azione*], was the lively and energetic music that conformed most closely to natural declamation. I held, moreover, that declamation itself was no more than imperfect music, and could be notated as such if only we had invented enough signs to indicate the pitches, the increases and diminutions in volume, and, so to speak, the infinitely varied nuances with which the voice is used in declaiming. I held that music, on whatever verses, was no more than skilful, studied, declamation, further enriched by the harmony of its accompaniments, and that therein lay the whole secret of composing excellent music for a drama; and that the more taut, energetic, impassioned, and touching the poetry, the more the music which sought to express it well, according to its proper declamation, would be the right music for this poetry, the best music. . . .

I arrived in Vienna in 1761, full of these ideas. A year later, his excellency Count Durazzo, then the director of entertainments at the imperial court and now its ambassador in Venice, to whom I had recited my *Orfeo*, encouraged me to have it performed in the theatre. I agreed to it, on condition that the music should be written according to my wishes. He sent me M. Gluck, who, he assured me, would fall in with all of them.

M. Gluck was not at that time considered among our greatest masters (no doubt erroneously). Hasse, Buranello [Galuppi], Jommelli, Peres, and others occupied the highest ranks. No one understood what I call declamatory music, and as for M. Gluck, who did not speak our language well, it was impossible for him to declaim even a few lines coherently.

I read him my *Orfeo*, showing him, by repeating several passages, the nuances that I put into my declamation and that I wanted him to make use of in his composition: the pauses, the slowing down, the speeding up, the sound of the voice now strong, now weaker and in an aside. At the same time, I begged him to forgo passage-work, cadenzas, ritornellos, and all that is gothic, barbaric, and extravagant in our music. M. Gluck went along with my ideas.

But declamation evaporates into the air and often cannot be recalled . . . only the poet himself can recite his verses, for better or worse.

I therefore tried to find signs which would at least indicate the most salient points. I invented some; I wrote them between the lines throughout *Orfeo*. It is on such a manuscript, accompanied by notes written in those places where the signs would give insufficient information, that M. Gluck composed his music. (Later, I did the same thing for *Alceste*.) This is so true an account that when, at the first performances, the success of *Orfeo* was undecided, M. Gluck blamed me for it. . . .

I hope that after this explanation, you will acknowledge, monsieur, that if M. Gluck has been the creator of dramatic music, he has not created it from nothing. I provided him with the matter, or if you will, the chaos; the honour of this creation is thus shared between us.[1]

Calzabigi, born in Livorno (Leghorn) in the same year as Gluck, was the dynamic of the partnership. Quick to spot a new artistic trend, on arriving in Vienna he interested himself in Angiolini's preparations for *Don Juan* (perhaps writing the preface to the ballet).[2] His critical attitude to Metastasio's librettos was already hinted at in his famous *Dissertazione su le poesie drammatiche del Sig. Abate Metastasio*, published in 1755,[3] and continued exposure to French aesthetics prepared him to attempt a closer union of words and music than had been undertaken in Italian opera. A thoroughgoing eighteenth-century adventurer, he came to Vienna with a trail of scandals behind him, including a poisoning in Naples and a dubious lottery in Paris. His partner in the latter enterprise was Casanova, who describes the poet in 1757: 'I saw a man in bed, covered with sores, but that did not prevent him from eating with an excellent appetite, writing, conversing, and carrying out all the functions of a man in good health. . . . [He

---

[1] Letter to *Mercure de France*, Naples, 15 June 1784, pub. 21 Aug. 1784, 133–6.
[2] Gerhard Croll, 'Calzabigi', *New Grove*, iii. 635.
[3] In *Poesie del Sig. Abate Pietro Metastasio* (Paris, 1755), vol. i., pp. xix–cciv.

was] very calculating, well-versed in theoretical and practical finance, familiar with commerce in all countries, learned in history, witty, worshipper of the fair sex, and poet.'[4] When, ten years later, Casanova visited Calzabigi in Vienna, he found him (still afflicted with his skin condition) now unequivocal in his opinion of Metastasio: 'I often dined with Calzabigi, who boasted of his atheism, and always impudently slandered Metastasio; the latter despised him, but Calzabigi ridiculed him for it.'[5]

Orfeo must have been well advanced by the summer. Zinzendorf was present at two private previews: '[On 8 July] we dined at Calzabigi's in the Kohlmarkt, with the Duke of Braganza, M. de Durazzo, Count Philipp, who sat between us, the Chevalier Gluck, and Guadagni. Everything was carried off well, the wine excellent. After dinner, Guadagni sang some airs from an opera which Calzabigi has written, called *Orfeo ed Euridice*. Gluck acted the Furies.' In his entry for 6 August, he added: 'Then to the Duke of Braganza where we dined with Calzabigi, L'Augier, Guadagni, Lion, and M. le Chevalier Gluck, who played airs from the opera *Orfeo*, and Guadagni sang.'

The castrato Gaetano Guadagni played a crucial role in the creation of *Orfeo*. Calzabigi himself admitted that '*Orfeo* went well, because we discovered Guadagni'.[6] He had made his reputation initially in England, where he worked with Handel and Garrick. Burney knew him well, and his description of the singer's technique suggests how certain passages in the role of Orpheus might have been performed; his account of Guadagni's appearance in a performance in London on 7 April 1770 indicates how far Gluck's insistence on dramatic integrity was out of step with the custom of his age:

[Guadagni's] figure was uncommonly elegant and noble; his countenance replete with beauty, intelligence, and dignity; and his attitudes and gestures were so full of grace and propriety, that they would have been excellent studies for a statuary. . . . The Music he sung was the most simple imaginable; a few notes with frequent pauses, and opportunities of being liberated from the composer and the band, were all he wanted. And in these seemingly extemporaneous effusions, he proved the inherent power of melody totally divorced from harmony and unassisted even by unisonous accompaniment. Surprised at such great effects from causes apparently so small, I frequently tried to analize [*sic*] the pleasure he communicated to the audience, and found it chiefly arose from his artful manner of diminishing the tones of his voice, like the dying notes of the Aeolian harp. Most other singers captivate by a swell or

---

[4] Jacques Casanova de Seingalt, *Histoire de ma vie*, ed. Fritz Brockhaus (Paris, 1960–2), v. 28.
[5] Ibid. x. 238–9.   [6] Letter of 6 Mar. 1767; see Ch. 10 below.

messa di voce; but Guadagni, after beginning a note or passage with all the force he could safely exert, fined it off to a thread, and gave it all the effect of extreme distance. . . .

His attitudes, action, and impassioned and exquisite manner of singing the simple and ballad-like air: *Che farò*, acquired him very great and just applause . . . [but through] his determined spirit of supporting the dignity and propriety of his dramatic character, by now bowing acknowledgement, when applauded, or destroying all theatrical illusion by returning to repeat an air, if encored at the termination of an interesting scene, he so much offended individuals, and the opera audience in general that, at length he never appeared without being hissed.[7]

No such detail exists on the other soloists. Marianna Bianchi won few plaudits in the role of Eurydice. The even smaller role of Cupid was taken by Lucile Clavereau, a singer from the opéra-comique troupe, whose voice Zinzendorf had described a year earlier as 'piercing'.[8]

The rehearsals were unusually lengthy,[9] and Gluck's own account of them to Burney tells the time-honoured tale of the exacting master imposing unprecedentedly high standards on his forces:

M. Gluck and I had a long conversation concerning musical and dramatic effects; concerning *those* which had been produced in his *Orfeo* at Vienna ten years ago, when it was first performed. . . . He is a great disciplinarian, and as formidable as Handel used to be, when at the head of a band; but he assured me, that he never found his troops mutinous, though he, on no account, suffered them to leave any part of their business, till it was well done, and frequently obliged them to repeat some of his manœuvres twenty or thirty times. This was the best proof he could give of the wholesomeness of his discipline; for there is a strong presumption, that when it is endured without murmur, by men not absolute slaves to their commander, they are convinced of its expediency.[10]

Calzabigi had suggested that the reception of *Orfeo* was initially 'undecided'. But other sources written closer to the event suggest that the work was immediately perceived as something new and remarkable. Debates arose over aspects of the action and particularly the scenery, for which Quaglio's designs were perceived as puzzlingly original. The first performances are recorded in Zinzendorf's diary, in which he communicates both his own appreciation of the opera and the criticisms of his circle:

[7] *General History*, ii. 876–7; see also Patricia Howard, 'Guadagni', *International Dictionary of Opera*, ed. Steven LaRue (Detroit, 1993), i. 561–2.

[8] Diary, 12 May 1761, quoted in Brown, *Gluck and the French Theatre*, 367.

[9] Ibid. 373.   [10] Burney, *Present State . . . Germany*, i. 344–5.

To the theatre, which was filled to capacity. *Orfeo ed Euridice* was performed, an opera by Calzabigi, the music by Gluck. It was sublime, very pathetic, wholly apt for the subject; the decorations were very beautiful. There was criticism that the work lacked unity of place, that the passions were not sufficiently strongly expressed, that [the music] passed too quickly from one to another, and that at the end of the second act, Orpheus went off with Eurydice without one knowing what they did off-stage. The decorations were criticized in that when the Shades brought on Eurydice, she was not dressed like them, as a Shade, as she should have been because she was no longer on the earth, and that in the Elysian fields, the flowers, trees, and plants are not the colour of budding greenery, but the colour of autumn leaves. To the latter objection, it was answered that Virgil mentions that the Elysian fields have a kind of brilliance which dazzles the eyes, which was intended to be represented by this colour.[11]

At Princess Esterházy's where the colour of the Elysian fields was much discussed; some said it was reddish, others a flaxen-grey, yet others the colour of autumn leaves, or of dawn. The ambassador's wife found the music of the air 'Che farò senza Euridice' too gay for a man on the point of suicide, but she said, however, that the whole made a very beautiful entertainment. Mme de Sternberg [Countess Stahremberg] found the music of the last ballet frightful, full of tedious repetition. Mme de E[sterházy] of Poland said that the overture was poor. All disapproved greatly of Eurydice.[12]

An extended review appeared in the *Wienerisches Diarium*, the official Viennese newspaper of the time, which was published twice weekly and which had recently begun to include arts news in a supplement. In common with most journal reviews of this period, it concentrates on the story with minimal coverage of the music. It may well have been contributed by Calzabigi:

On the fifth of this month the new Italian Singspiel *Orfeo ed Euridice* was performed for the first time in the theatre near the Hofburg in the presence of the imperial court. Describing this Singspiel with the expression that first comes to mind when making a sympathetic judgement of one of our dramas, we could say that this was a successful work, and that it was received with extraordinary acclaim. Assessment of its inner value depends, however, not on the often hasty opinions of amateurs, but on the stringent pronouncements of the connoisseurs of musico-dramatic art. The latter have also found it beautiful, and judged both the invention and the execution superb. They already knew

[11] 5 Oct. 1762.

[12] 7 Oct. 1762. Zinzendorf's words for the colours in the controversial Elysian fields are 'feuille-morte', 'moyen rouge', 'gris de lin', and 'aurore'.

the merit of its author, Herr Ranieri de Calzabigi of Livorno, titular counsellor for the court at the Netherlands Finance Office, who has published in
France a new edition of the works of Herr Abate Metastasio, and is known to
scholars through his fine introduction to that work; he has also elsewhere
demonstrated his philosophical insight into poetry.

The myth of Orpheus and Eurydice remains recognizable throughout,
however poetically it has been dressed; it has lost nothing of its beauty at the
hands of the poet. He has indeed made some changes, but all are reasonable
ones! They are in the nature of embellishments, and are to be regarded as clear
traits that indicate the hand of a master. The outline is new and the unity natural. Tenderness and the miraculous are the general rule; the expression is
condensed into the language of tender passion, without superfluous ornament.
We shall now follow the author back to his original outline.

Orpheus mourns the loss of his beloved Eurydice. The gods hear his weeping, and the god of love tells him he has their permission to bring Eurydice
back from the underworld. The prohibition not to look at her before their
arrival in the upper world is familiar from the myth, but the enjoined secrecy
over this command is a fruitful invention of the author's. The tender Orpheus
believes himself to be strong enough to fulfil both demands. He overcomes all
obstacles. He finds the reawakened shade of his wife; with face averted, he
leads her towards the upper earth. That he withholds a glance must seem
strange to her; her question is answered with the request for her to follow him
with faster steps. The most tender husband must in these circumstances arouse
suspicion. Eurydice weeps; she reproaches him; death seems preferable to her;
sorrow overwhelms her heart; she sinks. . . . To keep a secret is not the most
difficult task for a reasonable man; but it is asking too much for an already
soft-hearted husband not to help a suffering wife. Orpheus turns back, sees his
wife, and she dies. . . .

We are grateful to the author for not representing Orpheus as a despicable
man who, through recklessness or impiety, has forever lost a beloved wife. He
has rather portrayed the tender husband, and has shown us a crime caused
only by love and tenderness. Orpheus turns back, sees his wife, and she
dies. . . . No one can better put right a failing in love than the god of love himself. The poet brings him back to restore Eurydice to life. Here again the
author's prudent judgement should not be overlooked, which he has exercised
out of a pleasing concern for our theatre here, and which he has himself mentioned in his preface. The tragic outcome of the myth is thus turned into a joy-
ful one. All the audience, who would otherwise have returned home burdened
with compassion, are most grateful to him for this happy alteration. And has
not Orpheus, shown throughout as virtuous, deserved a happier fate?

We have joyfully accompanied the poet through a series of changing emo-
tional states, and shared the pleasant feelings he has prepared for us in his
poetic treatment of the myth.

We welcome the reintroduction of the choruses, and the active role Herr Calzabigi has contrived for them, as sufficient evidence of his familiarity with the usages and customs of the ancients. The value of the opera as a whole is in proportion to the success of the two leading roles. They progress from one passion to another without the slightest distraction. The airs, which tend to carry the burden of expression, are here located correctly, where they do not interrupt the emotion but rather intensify it.

The music is by our celebrated Herr Cavalier Christoph Gluck, who has surpassed himself in it. Perfect harmony rules throughout; both characters and passions are clearly and feelingly expressed; the emotions of the listener are constantly engaged, through judicious changes of speed and a good choice and variety of instruments. Herr Gasparo Angiolini has again proved his particular skill in the composition of the dances by integrating them with the choruses and with the myth in such a way as to render them as striking as they are articulate.

Herr Quaglio, who undertook the decoration of the stage, has once again shown himself to be an inventive artist, especially in his particular way of representing the Elysian fields. With a stage arranged thus, even a spectator who was ignorant of the content of the production could expect nothing other than the appearance of the blessed shades of dead heroes. The design of the cavern through which Orpheus leads his Eurydice to the upper earth is indeed beautiful; but we cannot persuade ourselves that the painter's brush has realized the true intentions of the designer.

The text of the Singspiel has been translated into German by Herr Jac. Ant. Edler von Ghelen, whose pen is already known through similar work.[13]

Other accounts are similarly biased in favour of the libretto. A six-page review in the *Journal étranger* mentions Gluck only in its closing paragraphs, where, despite his growing reputation in France, the writer still ranks Gluck below the 'greatest masters': 'The music, which is by the Chevalier Gluck, was widely relished; it is throughout perfectly adapted to the subject, and doubtless the greatest masters would have congratulated themselves on having written it.'[14] A valuable light on the opera's reception is shed by a comment at the end of a long review of a French translation of the libretto in the *Journal encyclopédique*: 'Although the music of this opera is entirely in the French taste, M. Gluck has had the greatest success. The Viennese court could not leave off acclaiming the music and words of this drama, which has had some thirty performances at which their majesties have regularly been present.'[15]

The next stage in the history of *Orfeo* is much more fully documented: the protracted and ultimately frustrating process of the engraving of the

---

[13] 82, suppl., 13 Oct. 1762.   [14] Aug. [*sic*] 1762, 235.   [15] 15 Feb. 1763, 134.

score. The initiative was Favart's, though not in connection with *Orfeo* and not exclusively in relation to Gluck: 'There is a desire here for Mm. Hasse and Gluck to have their scores published. The status and reputation that they have acquired should sell many copies. Why do Italian and German musicians confine their works to copyists? We lose by their modesty; their role is to enlighten us.'[16] Durazzo must have decided to send the score of *Orfeo* to Paris within weeks of its first performance. It was nearly lost in transit, and Favart supplies evidence of its wide pre-publication circulation, evidence, that is, of a lively interest in the work among those who had not had the opportunity of seeing it, and a sufficiently wide circulation among potential buyers partially to explain the eventual lack of sales of the engraved score:

Your excellency advises me in two of his letters of [the arrival] of the opera *Orfeo ed Euridice*. I do not believe I have received this work, though it could be that it has been delivered to me . . . I have made enquiries but without success. I sent M. Duni to investigate; he has told me that M. Blondel had been charged with delivering the score of *Orfeo* to me, but that he had first of all given it to Baron d'Holbach and then to Baron van Swieten who, after having had several airs copied from it, gave it back to M. Blondel.[17]

The score turned up within days, and was subject to further scrutiny.[18] Favart was told that the score was full of errors and needed Gluck's presence to make the corrections. Besides Egidio Duni, Favart showed the score to other potential rivals including Jean-Joseph Mondonville, who 'was enraptured by Gluck's talent'[19] and François-André-Danican Philidor, who cannot be acquitted of duplicity in the matter:

Duni has made a bugbear out of the *Orfeo* score. He said that he did not want to undertake to correct the copyist's mistakes even for 500 *livres*. I showed the score to Philidor, who was not nearly so obstructive. He offered to correct the wrong notes for nothing, and to undertake personal supervision of the engraving of the work. He asks no more of your excellency than a single copy. He has examined the opera carefully and he finds that the copyist's errors amount to a small number. He was enchanted with the beauty of the work, and in several places he shed tears of pleasure. He has always greatly esteemed Gluck's talents, but since getting to know *Orfeo*, his esteem has turned to veneration. We can therefore begin the engraving straight away, without having to wait for Gluck's arrival.[20]

---

[16] Favart to Durazzo, Paris, 10 Nov. 1760, in Favart, *Mémoires*, i. 113–14.

[17] Letter to Durazzo, Paris, 28 Jan. 1763; ibid. ii. 58–9.

[18] It is now in Paris, Bibliothèque de l'Opéra, Mus. Ms. 3971.

[19] Favart, *Mémoires*, ii. 67.   [20] Letter to Durazzo, Paris, 19 Apr. 1763, ibid. ii. 102–3.

Philidor appears to have monopolized the score for several months, declaring his intention of being its 'patron' and 'godfather',[21] the result of which was that he plagiarized 'Chiamo il mio ben così' in his opéra-comique *Le Sorcier* (1764). The corrections, such as they were, were later undertaken by Carlo Sodi.[22]

Meanwhile, Durazzo warned Favart to expect Gluck's arrival in Paris. The composer had left Vienna for Bologna on 24 March for the production of *Il trionfo di Clelia* (see Chapter 9), which was produced there on 14 May:

Our Chevalier Gluck will soon be leaving Bologna, where I hope he will cover himself with honour on the occasion of the opening of the new theatre, to come to Paris. I recommend him to your friendship. . . . You must get Gluck to correct the score of *Orfeo* as soon as he arrives, and I beg you to insist he does this, because he is indolent by nature and very indifferent towards his own works.[23]

Favart hastened to offer Gluck hospitality:

My lord the Count Durazzo informs me that you are to come to Paris in the course of this month. No lover of genius can be ignorant of your reputation. I do not have the honour of knowing you personally, but I have always wished to do so. May I hope that you will answer my entreaty? Yes, I dare hope as much, in view of the opinion I have always held of your goodness. For this reason, I hope that you will take no accommodation other than with me. I have in my house a furnished apartment to offer you. You will find there a good harpsichord and other instruments, a little garden, and complete freedom—that is to say, you will be as if in your own home, and you need see no one whom you do not wish to see. Although situated in one of the noisiest districts of Paris, our house, with its courtyard and garden, has a kind of solitude where one can work as peacefully as in the country. If I am so fortunate, monsieur, that you accept my offer, I beg you to let me know the day of your arrival. My address is rue Monconseil, near the Italian theatre, opposite the great gate of the cloister of St Jacques de l'Hôpital.[24]

Gluck's journey to Paris was delayed for nine months:

You will see nothing of the Chevalier Gluck. He has returned here. He was just stepping into his post-chaise at Bologna to set off for Paris, when he received a letter from the Count [Durazzo] summoning him to Vienna,

[21] Ibid. ii. 108.   [22] See Brown, *Gluck and the French Theatre*, 377.

[23] Vienna, 6 May 1763, in Favart, *Mémoires*, ii. 111–12.

[24] Paris, June 1763, ibid. ii. 113–14.

because having learned that the Opéra had burnt down, it seemed to him that the Chevalier's journey was useless.[25]

In view of the fact that the postponement was caused by a major outbreak of fire at the Paris Opéra, we can infer a hidden agenda for the visit: in his letter of 6 May, Durazzo had not only advised Favart to 'insist' on Gluck supervising the correction of his score, but made it clear that the main purpose of Gluck's visit was for the composer to inform Favart in detail on Viennese taste and the requirements for the forthcoming season, so that Favart could continue to send appropriate librettos and recruit needed singers. Neither activity would have been prevented by the fire; only if Durazzo had planned that Gluck should take steps to have *Orfeo* performed in Paris would the burning of the Opéra render the journey 'useless'.

Durazzo continued his negotiations at a distance, taking an active role in the design of the score, and in particular in the devising of a fitting frontispiece for a work that was already assuming the importance of an 'epoch-making' masterpiece which would be 'handed down to posterity'.[26] He also foresaw the dangers of the long production period, warning Favart that he would not be able to buy the entire stock, 'because, while awaiting it, almost all the work's admirers have had time to make themselves copies of it.'[27] In January 1764, Gluck's visit was again talked of as imminent, and in March, he arrived, in company with Durazzo and Marco Coltellini, who was shortly to write the libretto for *Telemaco* (30 January 1765). We know nothing of what passed between Favart and Gluck, but another clue to Gluck's growing reputation is recorded on the occasion of his visit to the expatriate Viennese engraver, Jean-Georges Wille: 'M. le Chevalier Gluck, the celebrated composer, so renowned throughout Europe wherever good music is valued, came to see me [on 9 March 1764]. He is besides a most excellent fellow. He stayed with me several hours . . . he was accompanied by M. Coltellini.'[28]

Not until 1766 did Favart reveal to Durazzo that no more than nine copies of the score had been sold,[29] presumably because of its wide circu-

[25] Dancourt to Favart, Vienna, 5 July 1763, ibid. ii. 279–80.

[26] Favart twice claims that *Orfeo* 'doit passer à la posterité', in letters of 29 Dec. 1763 (ibid. ii. 180) and 2 Jan. 1764 (ibid. ii. 184). The story of the frontispiece is told in detail in Brown, 'Durazzo, Duni, and the Frontispiece to *Orfeo ed Euridice*', *Studies in Eighteenth-Century Culture*, 19 (1989), 71–97.

[27] Durazzo to Favart, 17 Dec. 1763: Bibliothèque de l'Opéra, Fonds Favart Carton I A II; reproduced in Jacques-Gabriel Prod'homme, *Christoph-Willibald Gluck*, 2nd edn., rev. Joël-Marie Fauquet (Paris, 1985), 131–2.

[28] Jean-Georges Wille, *Mémoires et journal de J.-G. Wille, Graveur du Roi*, ed. Georges Duplessis (Paris, 1857), i. 249.

[29] Letter of 13 Apr. 1766, in Favart, *Mémoires*, ii. 225–6.

lation in manuscript in an age when copying was the more usual method of acquiring music. One copy fell into the hands of Baron Friedrich Melchior von Grimm, editor of a widely circulated cultural journal, the *Correspondance littéraire*, subscribed to by a select readership of noble and royal enthusiasts for the arts. Like the reviewer in the *Journal encyclopédique*,[30] Grimm considered *Orfeo* as an opera 'entirely in the French taste'. His comments resonate with pro-Italian polemic, typical of the *philosophes*, which Gluck was not to encounter personally for a decade. Grimm attaches his opinions to a report of the death of Francesco Algarotti, mentioning the latter's projected reform of Italian opera by introducing into it aspects of *tragédie lyrique*:[31]

Count Durazzo, intendant of the theatres at the Viennese court, has had a similar experiment tried, with the opera *Orfeo ed Euridice*, with music by the Chevalier Gluck. This work, of which I have had the opportunity to see the score, seemed to me almost barbaric. Music will be ruined if this genre is ever to get established. But I have too great an opinion of the Italians, our only masters in the art, to fear that this false genre might ever please them. I believe I have demonstrated, in the *Encyclopédie*, in the article 'Poëme lyrique', that the design and constitution of French opera are as wrong-headed as its music is cold and tedious.[32]

The 'epoch-making' quality of Gluck's best-known opera can be shown no more convincingly than by comparing Grimm's initial reaction with his response to *Orphée et Euridice*, the version adapted by Gluck for Paris ten years later (though in order to praise this, Grimm in his obstinacy had now to find the music 'wholly Italian'):

The *Académie royale de Musique* . . . gave us at last, on Tuesday 2 [August], the première of *Orphée et Euridice*, an opera in three acts. M. [Pierre-Louis Moline], the author of the words, has certainly abused the licence to be mediocre allowed to those who attempt to make a liberal translation of a libretto, and who put French verses to wholly Italian music. But it would be ungrateful not to credit him with some taste in his work, such as it is, because we owe to him the pleasure of hearing the most sublime music that has perhaps ever been performed in France.[33]

[30] See above and n. 15.

[31] Francesco Algarotti, *Saggio sopra l'opera in musica*, 2nd edn. (Livorno, 1763). Algarotti worked for many years in Parma, admired Traetta's operas there, and advocated many of the reforms later carried out by Gluck and Galzabigi, especially the merging of recitative with aria, the cultivation of a realistic acting style, and the pursuit of simplicity.

[32] Melchior Grimm (ed.), *Correspondance littéraire, philosophique et critique* (1813), 3rd edn., ed. Maurice Tourneux (Paris, 1877–82), vi. 35.

[33] Ibid. x. 472.

9

BETWEEN *ORFEO* AND *ALCESTE*
(1762–1766)

DURAZZO'S claim, in his position for a pension for Gluck,[1] that the composer 'is sought after by every Italian town' receives some support from the commission, in the summer of 1762, for Gluck's next opera, *Il trionfo di Clelia*. Documents of a very different kind from Khevenhüller's and Zinzendorf's diaries and the Viennese and Parisian journal articles illuminate the genesis of this work. An exchange of letters between Count Luigi Bevilacqua, in charge of the theatre in Bologna, and his agent in Vienna, Abate Lodovico Preti, show Gluck's negotiating skills. Bevilacqua's intention was to invite Gluck to compose a new opera for the opening of the Teatro comunale, rebuilt after (again) a fire. The work chosen was the Metastasian text which had, in Hasse's setting, been highly successful in Vienna earlier in the year.

Two almost identical contracts were drawn up in July 1762, differing only in their financial details. Preti was asked to try to get Gluck to agree to the lower sum, and to produce the second contract only if Gluck remained obdurate. Aware that the expenses of the journey, which the contract specifically excludes, might prove a stumbling-block, Bevilacqua instructs Preti: 'if Sig. Gluck does not raise the subject of board and lodging, say nothing about it yourself, and let the contract remain as it is.'[2] The two contracts put the fee for the opera at 180 and 200 *ungari* respectively, but Gluck stood out for 240 *ungari*, which seems to have been agreed. (When Maria Theresia rewarded Gluck for writing *Orfeo* with 'a rich purse, lined with a hundred ducats' she knew her man.[3])

---

[1] See Ch. 7 above.

[2] 10 Sept. 1762. Part of the correspondence is reproduced in the original Italian, together with the whole sequence of letters translated into German, in Max Unger, 'Zur Entstehungsgeschichte des *Trionfo di Clelia* von Gluck', *Neue Zeitschrift für Musik*, 82 (1915), 269–75. The originals of the letters are in private possession.

[3] Burney, *Present State . . . Germany*, i. 291.

Most Reverend Sig. Abate,

From your most kind letter dated the 23rd of last month which I received a few days ago in Ferrara, I saw how much longer my letter took to reach you than it should have done, so that I have only now received from you the contract from Sig. Gluck; this gave me cause for disquiet, for I did not know the reason for the delay, but I am still more disturbed on account of the uncertainty in which the said Sig. Gluck has left me as to whether he will be in Bologna by the date already determined in the contract; he must, as he maintains, arrange to be granted permission for the journey. It is not important that he himself stay in Bologna for the entire run of performances,[4] but I would find it regrettable if he were to delay his arrival in Bologna later than 1 April [1763]. I beg you to make him aware of this so that no mistakes or inconveniences arise. As to the choice of libretto that we have made, of which he appears not to approve, we no longer have time to change our plans, since we have already half-finished the decorations and ordered the costumes.[5] All we can do to accommodate in part his worries and desires is to grant him the freedom to approach Sig. Abate Metastasio himself, so that the latter can advise how the libretto might be altered, provided that he does not find it unfitting [to do so], and also to change a number of arias at his discretion. We would have no difficulty in allowing him about 20 *ungari* [for this work], always provided that the changes of scenery stay as they are, so that we do not have to rebuild any of them nor break up some which are already constructed. . . .

To the proposal that he should write an *Olimpiade* for us, I gather that he considered that he was at liberty to please no one but himself, without thinking that when an opera is written it should attempt to please everybody. I know that nowadays it is difficult for an opera to succeed, especially on the occasion of the opening of a theatre, if it lacks beautiful decorations; *Olimpiade* would be just such a work, as it admits almost nothing of that sort. These days decorations are commonly valued more highly than the substance of the libretto and the charm of the music, and I think the reason for this is that all have eyes to see with, but few have sharp ears to savour the music, and only a very few besides have the gift to understand the development of the plot, the skill of the author, and the quality of the writing. These reasons have determined our choice of libretto, although we are aware that it lacks the beauty and charm of many other compositions by the same Sig. Metastasio. To turn to the people who are to present the opera, the first man will be the castrato [Giovani] Manzuoli and Sig.ra Antonia Girelli[-Aguilar] the first woman; both singers are known to Gluck, as is also the tenor Sig. [Giuseppe] Tibaldi. For second man we have a certain Sig. Giovanni Toschi, a young man in his

---

[4] Bevilacqua later stipulates that Gluck should play continuo harpsichord in '10 or 12 performances' (14 Dec. 1762, in Unger, 'Zur Entstehungsgeschichte', 273).

[5] Gluck's preferred choice of text was *Olimpiade*.

first season, but who sings with much grace and good taste, whose singing, in short, touches the heart. The second woman is a certain [Cecilia] Grassi, who, they say, sang very gracefully at the feast of the Ascension in Venice. The last role is not yet settled; it needs a middle-range contralto. As Girelli has a husband who is a very fine oboist, she has written to ask that she might have an aria with obbligato oboe, but it rests with Gluck whether or not to grant her wish. I believe that with this answer, I have dealt with all the questions that Sig. Gluck has raised with me.[6]

Gluck sought the help of an 'anonymous poet' (Migliavacca?) in altering Metastasio's text.[7] While awaiting Gluck's arrival, Bevilacqua learned of the success of *Orfeo*: 'It has given us great pleasure to hear of the reception his last opera has enjoyed, and of the gift that he has received from the empress. Here he will receive no gifts, but we can promise him applause and loud acclaim.'[8]

Another source informs us of the journey, and adds to the evidence of Gluck's cautious attitude to money at this time. The irrepressible Ditters was Gluck's chosen travelling companion for the journey:

One day Gluck told me that he was bound for Bologna, to write an opera there, and asked me at the same time whether I would like to go with him to Italy. He stipulated, however, that I would have to pay from my own resources half the travelling expenses and my own food. He would obtain permission from Count Durazzo. 'Oh I would like it tremendously,' I replied with a high degree of enthusiasm, which a man like Gluck, who knew both my love of art and my whole circumstances, should have understood; 'But,' I added sadly, 'I cannot afford it.' 'Well then,' Gluck replied coldly, turning away, 'nothing can come of it.'[9]

It is the only instance, in all the words attributed to Gluck, on which he is said to have spoken coldly ['kalt']. Ditters, however, had friends who supplied him with the necessary gifts and loans, and Gluck, apparently delighted to hear that Ditters could after all accompany him, secured leave from Durazzo. They travelled via Venice, in the company of the singer Chiara Marini and her mother:

---

[6] Bevilacqua to Preti, Bologna, 16 Oct. 1762, in Unger, 'Zur Entstehungsgeschichte', 271–2 (trans. direct from the original Italian text). Manzuoli had sung Apollo in *Tetide*; Tibaldi was back in Vienna at the end of the year to sing Massimo in Gluck's revised *Ezio*; four years later he created the role of Admetus in *Alceste*. The last singer to be engaged for *Clelia* was Gaetano Ravanni. Girelli did not get her obbligato aria.

[7] Ibid. 273.

[8] Ibid.

[9] Ditters, *Lebensbeschreibung*, 108–9.

We travelled [from Venice to Bologna] through the night between Holy Saturday and Easter Day. The old theatre which had burnt to the ground a year ago, had been replaced by a splendid, new, stone-built opera-house, paid for by the subscriptions of the most prominent and wealthiest of the nobility, and due to be opened at Whitsuntide. The director, Count Bevilacqua, a member of the [rebuilding] committee, had chosen the Metastasian libretto *Il trionfo di Clelia* for the inauguration, and Gluck was commissioned to compose the music for it.[10]

Bevilacqua later praised the acoustics of the new building, in which the singers 'could be heard from the most obscure corners'.[11] Ditters names the singers and mentions some of the orchestra, which was led by Lucchini, who had been brought from Milan for the occasion, with Spagnoletti, recruited from Cremona, leading the second violins. According to Ditters, the orchestra numbered about seventy players, necessitating two harpsichordists; Gluck played first harpsichord, the Bolognese *maestro di cappella* Mazzoni the other:

Gluck told the count of his wish to hear the opera singers, so he immediately arranged a concert of thirty of the best performers at his house on the following afternoon, for no other audience but the three of us. I was particularly delighted with Girelli, Manzuoli, and Tibaldi, but most of all with an aria in which [Sig.] Aguilar accompanied his wife on the oboe. Lucchini and Spagnoletti each played a violin concerto. Gluck said quietly to me, 'You need not fear these two magicians.' I thought the same. . . .

Now Gluck began to compose. But because he had already done much preparatory work in Vienna, he was able to deliver the first act to the copyist ten days later.

Gluck never worked in the afternoon, only in the evening and in the morning. After lunch we would go visiting, and then to the coffee-house, where we generally remained until supper.

One of our first visits was to the great Farinelli. . . . He was then a veteran of nearly 80 years. He invited us several times, and treated us royally. But that was not surprising since he was almost a millionaire. . . .[12]

We also visited that universally celebrated dictator of classical music, Padre Martini. He was almost as old as Farinelli, and they were intimate bosom friends. Gluck had known him for many years, and never travelled through Bologna without paying his respects to the 'father of all the masters' ['padre di tutte i maestri'] (as all Kapellmeisters call him to this very day).[13]

---

[10] Ibid. 113.   [11] Letter to Preti, 23 May 1763, in Unger, 'Zur Entstehungsgeschichte', 274.
[12] 'gegen eine Million reich'.   [13] Ditters, *Lebensbeschreibung*, 114–15.

Ditters is uncharacteristically brief on the eventual performance of *Clelia* on 14 May 1763:

At last came the moment for the performance of Gluck's opera. It pleased to an uncommon degree, despite the fact that the execution fell far short of the composer's intentions. Gluck was the more disappointed because the fame of Italian orchestras had been made so much of. There had been seventeen full rehearsals, yet the production lacked the ensemble and precision we were accustomed to hearing in Vienna.[14]

The truth seems to be that *Clelia* failed to please the Bolognese, and the underwriters were called upon to make good the theatre's losses. Bevilacqua told Preti of his disappointment: 'The music of Sig. Cav. Gluck has not had the success that we expected. There are very beautiful passages in it, but as a whole it failed to please.'[15] Gluck and Ditters left Bologna after the third performance, travelling back through Parma, where they heard J. C. Bach's *Catone in Utica*.

Gluck spent the remainder of 1763 preparing a revival of *Orfeo*, writing a new opéra-comique, *La Rencontre imprévue*, and revising *Ezio*, first performed in Prague in the winter of 1749–50. His work on *Ezio* constituted the first of those thoroughgoing revisions he was subsequently to make to a number of his works (including the transformation of *Orfeo* into *Orphée*). The nature and extent of this revision suggest that Gluck was conscious of the new path he had taken in 1762.[16] The première was on 26 December 1763; the *Wienerisches Diarium* reviewed it warmly:

Gluck has recently newly composed the music of *Ezio*, one of the finest works of the immortal Metastasio. His genius, known throughout Europe, does not need our praise. No other composer is so faithful to Nature. He has sacrificed almost everything to art. [Formerly], arias, trills, and other artifices were often used absurdly to interrupt the flow of feelings and passions, instead of themselves reinforcing or intensifying the expression, so that the poet was the slave of the composer, who would tickle the ear without the poet being able to stir the heart. Herr Cavaliere Gluck does completely the opposite. With him, the poet does not pursue his objective alone, but his work gains new advantages, and new stimulus from being combined with a well-matched art. All this he seems to have achieved in the newly composed *Ezio*, and the public were justifiably outraged by [Guadagni in the title role] when he did badly in the first

---

[14] Ditters, *Lebensbeschreibung*, 124.   [15] Unger, 'Zur Entstehungsgeschichte', 274.

[16] The revs. are detailed in Hortschansky, *Parodie und Entlehnung*, 79–83; also in Gabriele Buschmeier, '*Ezio* in Prag und Wien: Bemerkungen zu den beiden Fassungen', in *Gluck in Wien*, ed. Croll and Woitas, 85–8.

performance, and seemed likely to prevent the universal success which the music enjoyed. He however has been instructed in his task, and we can now watch the work with unalloyed pleasure, in which Mme Tibaldi especially distinguishes herself.[17]

No more is known of the exact nature of Guadagni's shortcomings. Both Giuseppe Tibaldi and his wife Rosa Tartaglini-Tibaldi sang in *Ezio*. The work was given with two ballets, composed by Florian Gassmann, who had taken over the responsibility for providing ballets for the operas during Gluck's journey to Bologna.

The following year saw Gluck's last opéra-comique. Durazzo had selected a popular French text by Le Sage and D'Orneval, which he had assigned to Dancourt to adapt to the Viennese taste:

All the works of this sort succeed greatly here,[18] which is why I would like to find more of the same quality to entertain our rulers. For example I have just had arranged *Les Pèlerins de la Mecque* by the late M. Le Sage. I have had all that was licentious in it suppressed, and have retained only the noble element, and the humour which could be linked to it. I do not doubt that this text, adapted in this way to the current taste of the nation, will make an impact, especially as it is supported by music composed by the Sieur Gluck, who is incontrovertibly unique in his field.[19]

The opera was already in rehearsal on 31 October, but its planned première was cancelled due to the illness and subsequent death of Archduchess Isabella, whose wedding to Joseph had been celebrated so lavishly in 1760.[20] Under the new name *La Rencontre imprévue*, the work was performed for the first time on 7 January 1764 and noted in the *Wienerisches Diarium*:

That which we reported in the previous issue,[21] on the occasion of *Ezio*, concerning the merit of Herr Cavaliere Gluck, has been recently confirmed in a new trial. He has again surpassed himself in the music for the French opéra-comique *La Rencontre imprévue*. It can truly be said that the acclamation with which connoisseurs received this work was both exceptional and universal.[22]

[17] 2, suppl., 7 Jan. 1764.
[18] Durazzo was reporting the success of *Le Roi et le fermier* by Monsigny and Sedaine, a comparatively refined example of the popular genre, strewn with edifying maxims.
[19] Durazzo to Favart, Vienna, 19 Nov. 1763, in Favart, *Mémoires*, ii. 169.
[20] See the description of *Tetide* in Ch. 7 above. A detailed account of the need to revise the opera and the effect on the content is given in Bruce Alan Brown, 'Gluck's *Rencontre imprévue* and its Revisions', *Journal of the American Musicological Society*, 36 (1983), 498–518.
[21] See n. 17 above.   [22] 3, suppl., 11 Jan. 1764.

Zinzendorf was more discriminating:

A new and very long opéra-comique was given, which had been called *Les Pèlerins de la Mecque*, and which now, after the changes made to it following the death of the Archduchess, is called *La Rencontre imprévue* . . . The subject-matter is very thin, badly unified, badly integrated, and disfigured by the representation of a mad painter. The music is very fine and in the Italian style . . . [but] I preferred the airs in *Le Roi et son fermier* and many people were of my opinion.[23]

Barely three weeks later, however, he mentioned that he 'listened with pleasure from start to finish'.[24]

After the widespread success of *La Rencontre*, Gluck, together with Durazzo and his future librettist Coltellini, travelled to Paris in connection with the publication of the score of *Orfeo*.[25] From Paris, he went to Frankfurt for Joseph's coronation, on 3 April, for which occasion he is thought to have composed the cantata *Enea e Ascanio*, the music of which is now lost. Ditters could have told us much of this event, but his account is characteristically focused on his own status and rewards:

The time drew near for the coronation of Archduke Joseph. Count Durazzo, went himself to Frankfurt, and summoned Gluck, the castrato Guadagni, myself, and twenty other members of the imperial Hofkapelle to this great ceremony. The first two received 600 gulden travelling expenses and six gulden a day for subsistence, but I and the other twenty had only half this in total. . . . On our return to Vienna, Gluck and Guadagni received, in addition to their subsistence allowance, another 300, while I, poor devil, got no more than fifty ducats![26]

The coronation marked Gluck's last engagement with Durazzo, who resigned while on the Frankfurt expedition, on 1 April 1764.[27] After this event (but not necessarily because of it) Gluck wrote no more opéras-comiques, though he revised *L'Arbre enchanté* and *Cythère assiégée* for Paris in 1775. During the summer, Gluck was occupied with a new ballet, *Les Amours d'Alexandre et de Roxane*, performed in the Burgtheater on 4 October 1764, the last name-day festivity he was to offer to the Emperor Francis, who died the following year.

Joseph remarried on 23 January 1765; his new consort was Maria

[23] Diary, 7 Jan. 1764.   [24] Diary, 26 Jan. 1764.
[25] See Ch. 8.   [26] *Lebensbeschreibung*, 129–30.
[27] For a discussion of the complex reasons behind Durazzo's downfall, see Brown, *Gluck and the French Theatre*, 425–45.

Josepha of Bavaria. Gluck contributed three very different works to the festivities. The first, *Il Parnaso confuso*, was 'commissioned, conceived, written, set to music, rehearsed, designed, and produced in five weeks'.[28] The words are Metastasio's, and the occasion is the only one in which Gluck appears to have worked in direct collaboration with the poet. The work, given at Schönbrunn in a specially erected theatre, on 24 January 1765, was exceptional in other respects:

In the evening the first entertainment was performed, in the guise of a little operetta called *Il Parnaso confuso*, for which Abate Metastasio wrote the words and Cavaliere Gluck the music. The stage was erected for the occasion in the big antechamber, the so-called *Salon des batailles*, and as the area for the spectators was very small, the empress was very sparing with the invitations . . . It was indeed a sight well worth seeing, such as has perhaps never been seen at a court before, not only because of the presence of the four archduchesses, Elisabeth, Amalia, Josepha, and Charlotte, and the two youngest [royal children] dancing in it, and Archduke Leopold playing the [harpsichord] or directing the orchestra, but also because all these noble persons distinguished themselves above all expectations and to universal wonder, both in singing (on account of the natural beauty of their voices), and in deportment, whether in acting or dancing (in the latter the Archduke Ferdinand performed quite admirably, as to the manner born).[29]

Since the one-scene *azione teatrale* contains no dances, Bernd Baselt suggests that Khevenhüller's remarks on the dancing refer to Gassmann's ballet *Il trionfo d'amore*, given the following day.[30] The *Wienerisches Diarium* described the action of the 'Italian Singspiel' at length, concluding: 'The music of this piece is by Cavaliere Gluck, and again received the universal acclaim that is always accorded to this talented composer.'[31] The occasion is recorded in two paintings by Johann Franz Greipel, one depicting the interior of the theatre, with stage, orchestra, and audience represented, and the other a scene from the opera.[32]

On 30 January the court moved back to town for more public celebrations, and Gluck's second contribution to the festivities, an opera seria called *Telemaco, ossia L'isola di Circe*, was given in the Burgtheater. The librettist was Coltellini, and the work may have been planned during the

[28] Metastasio to Farinelli, 28 Jan. 1765, in Metastasio, *Tutte le opere*, iv. 380.
[29] Khevenhüller-Metsch, *Tagebuch*, 1764–7, 77–8.
[30] In his edn. of *Il Parnaso confuso* in Gluck's *Sämtliche Werke*, iii/25, p. ix.
[31] 9, suppl., 30 Jan. 1765.
[32] Both images are reproduced in Otto Erich Deutsch, 'Höfische Theaterbilder aus Schönbrunn', *Österreichische Musikzeitschrift*, 22 (1967), 577–84.

journey to Paris undertaken by the two in 1764. Khevenhüller broke into Italian to record the occasion: 'In the evening one attended a semi-public ['in mezzo publico'] performance of the new opera *Telemaco*, written by Sig. Coltellini with music by Cavaliere Gluck—it was given without a new ballet, which shocked the spectators not a little.'[33] The score of *Telemaco* ends with Circe's recitative describing universal devastation; it is followed by a programme for a substantial ballet, in which Apollo and Venus restore order, ending with 'a festive dance'. Khevenhüller's comment suggests that rather than new music, an old ballet was borrowed to conclude the work.[34]

The third work Gluck wrote for the festivities, the ballet-pantomime *Sémiramis*, was given in the Burgtheater on 31 January, following a performance of Racine's tragedy *Bajazeth*. Angiolini described the ballet as his most tragic—'the most terrible subject that antiquity has handed down to us'[35]—and the choice of a subject (based on Voltaire's tragedy), featuring not only death and vengeance but incest and an interrupted wedding, seems curiously misjudged. Khevenhüller recorded that it found 'absolutely no approval, and was indeed far too pathetic and melancholy for a wedding feast'.[36] The action was structured by Calzabigi, as Van Swieten's lively account makes clear:

I must say a word to Your Excellency concerning the wedding festivities which have been boring everyone; I speak only of the public events, because the archduchesses' opera [*Il Parnaso confuso*] was an event unique of its kind, and could not be sufficiently admired, independently of the rank of the performers. But the opera seria [*Telemaco*] is of the saddest sort, and, a degree worse, on the second day of public rejoicing, the dark tragedy of *Bajazeth* was performed, followed by an even darker ballet-pantomime, which brought together in a quarter of an hour all the horrors of the tragedy of Semiramis, and enacted them before the eyes of the audience; both the court and town were revolted by it. There is an association of hypochondriacs here, headed by M. Calzabigi, who are dedicated to introduce among us all the severity of English theatre, and for the last three years all the operas given here contain nothing but the apparitions of ghosts, demons, murders, and assassins. The result, however, is not wholly bad, in that it has bought about the creation of partisans, who give a kind of liveliness to the entertainments which was not to

[33] *Tagebuch*, 1764–7, 80.

[34] See, however, Karl Geiringer, 'Zu Glucks Oper *Il Telemaco*', *Bericht über den Internationalen Musikwissenschaftlichen Kongress Bonn 1970*, ed. Carl Dahlhaus (Kassel, 1972), 400–2, and Josef-Horst Lederer, ' "e con una danza festosa finisce lo spettacolo": Bermerkungen zum Schluss von Glucks *Telemaco*', *Gluck in Wien*, ed. Croll and Woitas, 116–23.

[35] See Ch. 7 n. 28.   [36] *Tagebuch*, 1764–7, 81.

be found before. M. Calzabigi has taken the trouble to write a long dissertation[37] to prove to all those who do not admire the ballet of *Sémiramis* that they
are fools. The ballet was designed to display the talents of Mlle de Nancy
[Levier], former mistress of the Duke of Württemberg, who pulls some fine
faces but who cannot dance. Calzabigi says that true dancing is done not with
the feet but with the face; the young lady likewise does not concern herself
with her feet, for she turns her feet in like a parrot; but we are told that good
dancing does not require to have the feet turned out, and that that is a modern
invention—all this is debated in the liveliest manner, and is treated as seriously as the French would treat it. The two sides can be distinguished by their
physiognomy: all the supporters of Semiramis pull faces, and the others
laugh.[38]

Whatever the immediate reception of *Telemaco* and *Sémiramis*, for Gluck
these works proved to be treasure stores, which he plundered extensively
in his French operas, extracting no fewer than eleven numbers from
Sémiramis for *Iphigénie en Tauride*.[39]

Gluck composed two more ballets in 1765. *Ifigenia in Aulide* was performed at Laxenburg on 19 May. Naming Angiolini but not Gluck,
Khevenhüller records the première of 'a serious ballet, taken from the
tragedy of *Iphigénie*, and much better than *Sémiramis*'.[40] More interest-
ingly, Archduke Leopold (the harpsichordist in *Parnaso*) mentions the
work warmly:

At last the weather has turned fine again. You will be thinking that in consequence we are enjoying ourselves, but on the contrary; I don't know why, but
I always have the capacity to be bored here, because one spends all day doing
nothing. We go out once or twice a day from time to time, and then we have
some enjoyable plays; yesterday we had among other things a tragic ballet on
the story of Iphigenia, which pleased me greatly, the music of it being very
beautiful, composed by Gluck.[41]

---

[37] The *Dissertation sur les ballets pantomimes des anciens pour servir de programme au ballet pantomime tragique de Sémiramis* (Vienna, 1765), pub. in Angiolini's name.
[38] Letter to Count Johann Karl Philipp Cobenzl, Vienna, 16 Feb. 1765: MS in Brussels, Archives
générales, Secrétairerie d'État et de Guerre, No. 1238, fos. 108–9; pub. in part in Klaus
Hortschansky, 'Unbekannte Aufführungsberichte zu Glucks Opern der Jahre 1748 bis 1765',
Jahrbuch des Staatlichen Institutes für Musikforschung Preussischer Kulturbesitz 1969 (Berlin, 1970), 31.
I am grateful to Edward Olleson for drawing the MS source to my attention.
[39] See Hortschansky, *Parodie und Entlehnung*, 303–6.
[40] *Tagebuch*, 1764–7, 97.
[41] Letter (in French) to Franz Thurn-Valsassina, Laxenburg, 20 May 1765, quoted in Gerhard
Croll, 'Ein unbekanntes tragisches Ballett von Gluck', *Mitteilungen der Gesellschaft für Salzburger
Landeskunde*, 109 (1969), 275.

His last ballet, *Achille in Sciro*, was probably designed to be Gluck's contribution to Archduke Leopold's wedding with Maria Luisa of Spain, which took place in Innsbruck on 5 August. The ballet was, however, never performed. The death of Emperor Francis on 18 August cut short the festivities and closed the theatres for a prolonged period of mourning.[42] Gluck's last composition of 1765 suffered a similar fate. *La corona* was planned to repeat the success of *Il Parnaso confuso*, and to be performed in the same Schönbrunn salon by the four archduchesses on the emperor's name-day in October. It was to be the last Metastasian text Gluck set: the end of an era.

The closure of the theatres silenced Gluck for over a year, during which time he is likely to have been preparing his next contribution to opera reform. The prevailing mood of mourning, presided over by the widowed empress, was wholly conducive to his subject, *Alceste*. His next operatic activity, however, took him to Florence, at the invitation of Archduke Leopold, now Grand Duke of Tuscany, where he conducted a performance of Traetta's *Ifigenia in Aulide* (written on a libretto by Coltellini) and his own work *Il prologo* (libretto by Lorenzo Ottavio del Rosso), a staged cantata for solo and chorus; the solo role of Jove was sung by the castrato Giacomo Veroli. The performance took place in the Teatro della Pergola on 22 February 1767; archival records dwell more on the brilliant illumination of the theatre by means of 564 lamps than on the reception of the music.[43]

A summary of Gluck's position in Vienna at this time is provided in a much-discussed article in the *Wienerisches Diarium*, 'On the Viennese Taste in Music'.[44] Heartz plausibly attributes the article to Ditters. Heaping lavish and flowery praise on Kapellmeister Reutter, Leopold Hoffmann, Wagenseil and his pupil Joseph Steffan, Haydn, Ditters himself, and Gluck, with brief references to Zechner, Ordonez, Starzer, and Gassmann, the article has an immediacy which a more balanced assessment might lack:

Gluck is a man truly created for the orchestra. Even if he were to write nothing more besides, he is a man who would already be immortal through his

---

[42] *Achille* is discussed in Brown, *Gluck and the French Theatre*, 341–51.

[43] Quoted in Andrea Della Corte, *Gluck e i suoi tempi* (Florence, 1948), 115–16.

[44] 84, suppl., 18 Oct. 1766; the article is reproduced in Robert Haas, 'Von dem Wienerischen Geschmack in der Musik', *Festschrift Johannes Biehle zum 60. Geburtstage*, ed. Erich Hermann Müller von Asow (Leipzig, 1930), 61–5, and further discussed in Norbert Tschulik, 'Musikartikel aus dem Wienerischen Diarium von 1766', *Studien zur Musikwissenschaft*, 30 (1979), 91–106, and in Daniel Heartz, 'Ditters, Gluck und der Artikel "Von dem Wienerischen Geschmack in der Musik" (1766)', *Gluck in Wien*, ed. Croll and Woitas, 78–80.

Orfeo, *Rencontre imprévue*, and *Alessandro* [*Alexandre et Roxane*]. He is a man who has breathed life into the works of a Metastasio, pleased the English, entertained the French, and as for us, his very notes give voice to our thoughts. He writes passages in the presence of which the little talent that one has disappears: one is full of self-doubt. (Only musicians will understand us here.) Our courage does not return until the impression he has made on us is gradually dispersed. When he represents the passions with strong pen-strokes, he tears the heart as he pleases. Ever successful, ever the ruler of our hearts! Each turn of phrase, each rise and fall, gives the soul its true expression. It is impossible to feel it completely if one is not at the same time both poet and composer. It can furthermore be said that he brought opéra-comique to perfection because his genius was the rich source which refreshed the arid French areas hereabout and made them fruitful.

10

ALCESTE
(1767–1769)

WHEN Gluck visited Florence in February 1767, *Alceste* was already finished. He may well have played portions of it to Archduke Leopold, whose interest from an early stage is implied in the celebrated dedication of the score. A letter from Calzabigi written in March of that year shows that the new opera was complete and its performance expected soon. Calzabigi addresses the imperial chancellor Prince Wenzel Anton Kaunitz, his employer and patron, who, after Durazzo's resignation on 1 April 1764, had taken a leading role in protecting both the interests of the French company at the Burgtheater and Gluck's and Calzabigi's operatic innovations.[1] Calzabigi's letter is an uncharacteristically disorganized confusion of manifesto and plea for resources:

Your Highness,

While communicating to Your Highness the enclosed letter from Sig. Gluck, to which I must draw your attention, I find it necessary to add some important thoughts of my own to what he says about my *Alceste*.

When it may please Her Imperial Majesty and Your Highness to decree that *Alceste* be staged, it will be essential to choose suitable singers for *Alceste*, since it is impossible to have the roles of Alcestis and Admetus played by the usual run of singers, partly because of the nature of this new sort of drama, which approaches everything through the eye of the spectator and thus through the acting, and also because of the music associated with this genre, which is aimed more towards expression than to that which the Italians presently call song.

The dramas of Sig. Abate Metastasio, the scheme of which seems designed

[1] See e.g. his 'Réflexions sur les spectacles de la ville de Vienne, 1765', quoted in Oscar Teuber, *Das k. k. Hofburgtheater seit seiner Begründung* (Vienna, 1896), 105.

to deter the attention of the spectator (because of their length, resulting from the quantity of verses and the elaboration of the music), have the sole virtue of being *saddles for all horses* ['Selles à tous chevaux'], so that it has always been a matter of indifference whether a character in these dramas was sung by Farinelli, Caffarelli, Guadagni, or Toschi, or by Tesi, Gabrielli, or Bianchi, since from these singers the public anticipated and demanded no more than a pair of arias and a duet, without expecting to be moved by the words. Even before the performance they would abandon all thought of becoming involved with the action, because it is impossible to pay attention for five hours to six actors, four of whom are usually so inept that they scarcely know how to pronounce, in order to secure at such a cost the pleasure of thrilling to an insipid Clelia, a cold Ersilia, an unreal Aristea, an impertinent Emira, an indecent Honoria, and a shameless Mandana, all of whom are really no more than little Roman or Neapolitan courtesans who speak in polished phrases and gossip about love on the stage. I say nothing of the heroes—they are completely unnatural, for characters so full of philosophy as Metastasio's Horace, Temistocles, Cato, and Romulus are not to be met with in this world.

Since the performance of these dramas could not please the mind, they needed all the more to entertain the senses: the eye, by real horses in painted forests, real battles on stage battlefields, and conflagrations made from coloured paper; the ear, by treating the voice as a violin and performing concertos with the mouth—hence the musical gargling which in Naples is called 'trocciolette' (because it closely resembles the noise made by wheels passing over the ropes of a pulley)—and many other musical caprices which could be compared to those stone offcuts with which Gothic architecture decorated, or rather, disfigured, its monuments, once so much admired, now objects of disgust and ridicule to anyone who stops to look at them. To make room for these strange embellishments, the poet was ready to fill his dramas with similes of storms, tempests, lions, warhorses, and nightingales, which sit just as well in the mouths of passionate, desperate or angry heroes as patches and make-up, hair powder, and diamonds on the face, head, and neck of an ape.

Things are quite different in the new scheme of drama, which has been if not invented by me, then at least carried out for the first time in *Orfeo*, then in *Alceste*, and then continued by Sig. Coltellini. Here nature and feeling prevail. There are no maxims, no philosophy, no politics, no similes, no descriptions, and no bombast: these are only a means to avoid difficulties, and as such are met with in all [conventional] librettos. The duration is limited to what will not tire or weaken concentration. The subjects are simple, with no overelaborate plots, so that a few lines are enough to allow the spectators to understand the action, which is always unified, not complicated or duplicated through unnecessary, servile obedience to the crazy rule about the 'second man' and 'second woman'. Reduced to the form of Greek tragedy, the drama has the power to arouse pity and terror, and to act upon the soul to the same degree as spoken tragedy does. In this scheme Your Highness will easily see that the music expresses nothing but that which arises from the words. Consequently the words are not buried in notes, and are not used to prolong the performance inappropriately. I consider that a note should never have the value of more than one syllable: it is ridiculous to extend the pronunciation of 'amore' (for example) to a hundred notes when nature has limited it to just three.

If this scheme, with the addition of pantomime in the choruses and ballets in imitation of the Greeks, satisfies both the public taste and the refined taste of Her Majesty (who actually attended fourteen performances of *Orfeo* and who, as a sign of her great pleasure, rewarded both the *maestro di cappella* and the *musico* [Guadagni]), it is necessary to adhere to that taste, and not to confuse it with that of Sig. Metástasio, since a beautiful brunette requires different ornaments from those which suit a blonde. In the Abate's dramas, it is of no importance if the Gabriellis and Bastardellas and similar warblers trill and get out of breath in an aria about a murmuring stream, so that not a word can be heard. But in *Orfeo*, in [Traetta's] *Ifigenia*, in *Telemaco*, and in *Alceste*, we need actresses who will sing that which the composer has written, and not presume to write a trunkful of notes by repeating a 'Parto' or an 'Addio' thirty or forty times in musical hieroglyphics of which one could say politely, 'Pulchrum est, sed non erat hic locus'.[2]

To put *Alceste* in the mouth of these warblers, and singers like them, would both ruin the music and the poetry and frustrate the appointed aim, which is to give pleasure by bringing them together. Where the spirit of the Gabriellis and the Apirles still holds sway, let them be satisfied by assigning to them an opera by our Arcadian shepherd, Artino Corasio [Metastasio], and turn to Mingotti or Francesina, and to Manzuoli or Tibaldi for *Alceste*. Furthermore another two basses are needed to strengthen the choruses (I have already advised Sig. Gluck of this), and for the roles of priest and oracle, and as characters for the pantomimes besides. In this way, *Alceste* will be able to succeed as a novel, majestic, and appealing work, worthy of this court, of this capital city, and of the taste of Your Highness, who has happily taken an interest in it. Otherwise it would have been better to leave buried this product of my poor talents and the sublime gifts of Sig. Gluck, and to await circumstances more suitable for it, rather than have it crippled at birth. *Orfeo* went well because we discovered Guadagni, for whom it seemed tailor-made, and it would have fared disastrously in other hands. But *Telemaco*, with the finest poetry and exceptionally sublime music, went very badly indeed because [Rosa Tartaglini-]Tibaldi was no actress, Guadagni was a rogue, and the famous [Elisabeth] Teyber was unsuited to play the part of Circe, with too small a

---

[2] 'It is beautiful, but this was not the place for it.'

voice for a sorceress, or to do justice to music worthy of an enchantress and an enchantment.

I conclude with the expression of my most profound respect, Your Highness's most humble, most devoted and most obedient servant,

De Calzabigi.[3]

Gluck's and Calzabigi's intention to find singers who could act was widely misunderstood. Leopold Mozart connected the lack of interest in opera seria in Vienna with the dearth of suitable singers: 'No operas of that sort are being given at present, and what is more, people do not like them . . . There are no singers here for opera seria. Even Gluck's tragic opera *Alceste* was performed by a cast of opera buffa singers.'[4] Leopold Mozart does, however, praise Antonia Bernasconi, who created the title role in *Alceste*.

The looked-for performance of *Alceste* was delayed for nine months. Scarcely had the long period of court mourning for the emperor concluded than the early death of Archduchess Maria Josepha in October again closed the theatres. *Alceste* opened the season on 26 December 1767:

Today the theatres were open to the usual crowds, and at the Burgtheater a new opera, called *Alceste*, was produced, composed by Cavaliere Gluck, for which Sig. Calzabigi wrote the libretto. It was once again found by the public to be pathetic and lugubrious. Fortunately at the end there was a ballet by M. de Noverre in the grotesque style, which was greeted with tremendous applause.[5]

Jean-Georges Noverre now enters the scene as Gluck's new choreographer. In the period of inactivity following the emperor's death, Angiolini seized the opportunity of succeeding his teacher, Hilverding, at the court of Catherine the Great in St Petersburg. In 1767 his place was taken by Noverre, who had first crossed Gluck's path in Dresden in 1747.[6] In the intervening years, Noverre had worked in France, England, and latterly Stuttgart, and pursued choreographic experiments on similar lines to Angiolini's pantomime-ballets (though each contested the other's claims to have invented the genre, and pursued the dispute in polemical tracts, which

---

[3] Vienna, 6 Mar. 1767, first pub. in Vladimir Helfert, 'Dosud Neznámý dopis Ran. Calsabigiho z r. 1767', *Musikologie*, 1 (1938), 115–18. See also Hans Hammelmann and Michael Rose, 'New Light on Calzabigi and Gluck', *Musical Times*, 110 (1969), 609–11. The actual signature is 'De Calsabigi l'ainé': the French spelling was adopted by the poet while living in Paris; he first used it in 1755 in his edn. of Metastasio's works (his younger brother had been a party to his financial schemes in Paris in the 1750s). The enclosed letter from Gluck, mentioned in Calzabigi's letter, is missing.

[4] Letter to Lorenz Hagenaur, 30 Jan. 1768, in Mozart, *Briefe und Aufzeichnungen*, i. 258.

[5] Khevenhüller-Metsch, *Tagebuch*, 1764–7, 280.

[6] See the details of *La spartana generosa* in Ch. 4 above.

have proved invaluable in tracing the development of their fugitive art).[7] The disjunction between the concentrated tragedy of Gluck's opera and the popular 'grotesque' concluding ballet suggests that Gluck's collaboration with Noverre was neither as close nor as productive as his work with Angiolini. For a subsequent performance in Bologna, Calzabigi relayed Gluck's instructions that

In the dance introduced in the temple scene (Act I, Scene 4), and in the scene in the royal chambers where Admetus unexpectedly recovers (Act II, Scene 3), the composer recommends that there should not be long additions to the pantomime . . . the dancers called 'grotesque' must not intervene in these places. At the end of the tragedy, any kind of dance may be performed; there they will have the chance to dance to their hearts' content.[8]

In the same document, Calzabigi also wrote of Tibaldi's interpretation of Admetus in terms which reveal how far this poignant role has been misunderstood: 'When Tibaldi played the part of Admetus for the first time, he proved to be a most excellent actor, because he has a soul, and means what he says . . . he will have the same effect on the audience of Bologna as he did on the Viennese: attention, involvement, tears.'[9]

A highly enthusiastic account of the early performances appears in a series of five articles by the writer Joseph von Sonnenfels:

I find myself in the land of miracles. A serious Singspiel without castrati, music without solmization—or, as I would prefer to call it, gargling—an Italian libretto without bombast and trumpery. With this threefold miracle, the Burgtheater has reopened. Indeed I would like to add a fourth, and it is perhaps not the least: the principal woman singer is a native German. . . .[10]

Gluck's powers of imagination are prodigious: consequently, the limits of all national styles are too narrow for him. From the music of all nations, he has made a music for himself—or rather, he has plundered Nature for all the sounds of true expression and made them his own. . . . *Alceste* provided this gifted man with a spacious canvas on which to show the fertility of his thought. It is difficult with such material, in which the tragic and the melan-

---

[7] Noverre, *Lettres sur la danse, et sur les ballets* (Stuttgart and Lyons, 1760), replied to by Angiolini in *Lettere* and followed by Noverre's *Petite réponse aux grandes lettres du Sr. Angiolini* (Vienna, 1774).

[8] Calzabigi, 'Documenti sull' esecuzione dell'*Alceste* . . . Bologna, 1778', in Corrado Ricci, *I teatri di Bologna nei secoli XVII e XVIII* (Bologna, 1888), 630.

[9] Ibid. 628–9.

[10] 27 Dec. 1767. 'Briefe über die Wienerische Schaubühne', *Gesammelte Schriften* (Vienna, 1784), v. 150.

choly are equally and unrelievedly spread, to escape from monotony and repetition. Gluck has overcome this difficulty with many glories. His choruses are always fundamentally differentiated, his recitative is eloquent, and its accompaniment is not a simple, dry harmony, or a futile filling-up of spaces, but an essential part of the expression, and often so integrally expressive, that it makes the whole content comprehensible, rendering the words almost superfluous. His arias are new, with simple but heartfelt melodies, of which the cadences in particular transported me. . . .

Universal approval has crowned his endeavours, and this approval is all the more flattering since it increases with every repeated performance of *Alceste*. We await the publication of this Singspiel, without which I would find it diffi-cult to enter into a discussion of the beauty of individual parts.[11]

Tibaldi . . . surpassed himself, and played with true feeling, especially in the scene where he tears from Alcestis the confession of her great vow. . . . Bernasconi played Alcestis with a truth, feeling, and sympathy which exceeded all expectations.[12]

Calzabigi later claimed that '*Alceste* ran very successfully for two runs of sixty performances in Vienna.'[13]

Notwithstanding the commercial failure of the published score of *Orfeo*, publication of *Alceste* was seen as essential to clarify the new dramatic aims. And not just the score, but an explanatory preface: Calzabigi became increasingly eager to articulate his dramatic theories, which he scattered throughout a wide range of correspondence dating from the turn of the decade.[14] In the following letter, offering the score to Antonio Greppi, Milanese financier and member of the board of the Teatro Regio Ducal, he claims authorship of the famous preface (not too much reliance should be placed on this statement: Gluck made a similar claim in 1770).[15] The letter also contains evidence of the early date of composition of *Paride ed Elena*, which had to wait even longer than *Alceste* for performance:

Sig. Gluk called on me yesterday with a draft copy of the words and music of *Alceste*. . . . The agreement between Gluk and myself is that he will not pub-lish his music without my knowledge, since I must preface the printed score with an introduction which explains the motive, or rather the motives, for the extensive changes we have made to dramatic compositions such as this.

[11] 5 Jan. 1768. Ibid. v. 165–7.   [12] 15 Jan. 1768. Ibid. v. 176.

[13] Letter to Antonio Montefani, 1 May 1778, in Ricci, *I teatri di Bologna*, 635.

[14] See e.g. letters pub. ibid. 631–44; Carlo Antonio Vianello, *Teatri, spettacoli musiche a Milano nei secoli scorsi* (Milan, 1941), 237–53; Mariangela Donà, 'Dagli archivi milanesi: Lettere de Calzabigi e di Antonia Bernasconi', *Analecta musicologica*, 14 (1974), 268–300.

[15] In his letter to Martini, 14 July 1770; see Ch. 11.

Currently I have not yet written this preface, and the score still lacks a title-page, a dedication, and this very essential preface. . . . I beg you to obtain from your colleagues a justly ample and generous fee for the said composer, and to be so kind as to relieve him of the costs of publication, which you can do discreetly by subscribing for a certain number of copies that you can distribute there or elsewhere in Italy, either as gifts or even by selling them on behalf of the theatre in a bookshop. For example: 'Sig. Greppi, for 10 copies'. It would be no bad thing, and you would be repaid by being the first to get other productions from our partnership, one of which, entitled *Paride ed Elena*, has been written by me and set by Sig. Gluk. . . . I leave matters with you, knowing that you will act wisely, especially after reflecting that in giving you a copy of his composition before anyone else, Sig. Gluk will not be able to offer it as something 'brand new' to any other person, as he had intended.[16]

The score was eventually published by Trattnern in Vienna in the spring of 1769 (the advertisement in the *Wienerisches Diarium* appeared in the issue of 29 March). It was accompanied by one of the most celebrated statements in operatic history:

Your Royal Highness

When I undertook to write the music for *Alceste*, I decided to strip it completely of all those abuses, introduced either by the ignorant vanity of singers or by composers over-eager to oblige, abuses which have for so long disfigured Italian opera, and turned the most sumptuous and beautiful of all spectacles into the most ridiculous and the most tedious. I thought to restrict music to its true function of helping poetry to be expressive and to represent the situations of the plot, without interrupting the action or cooling its impetus with useless and unwanted ornaments. I thought it should act in the same way as an accurate and well-executed drawing is brought to life by colour and by the well-chosen contrast of light and shade, which serve to animate the figures, without changing their shapes. I did not therefore want to hold up an actor in the white heat of dialogue to wait for a tedious ritornello, nor let him remain on a favourite vowel in the middle of a word, or display the agility of his fine voice in lengthy passage-work, nor let him wait while the orchestra gives him time to recover his breath for a cadenza. I did not feel it my duty to skim quickly over the second part of an aria, which may well contain the most passionate and significant words, in order to have space to repeat exactly, four times over, the words of the first part, nor to accommodate a singer who wants to show in how many ways he can capriciously vary a passage, rather than ending the aria where its meaning ends. In short, I have sought to abolish all

---

[16] Vienna, 12 Dec. 1768: autograph in Milan, Archivio di Stato di Milano, Archivio Greppi, cartella 56; pub. in Donà, 'Dagli archivi', 280–1.

those abuses against which reason and good sense have for long cried out in vain.

I considered that the sinfonia should inform the spectators of the subject that is to be enacted, and constitute, as it were, the argument; that the ensemble of instruments should be formed with reference to the interest and feeling, without leaving that sharp division in the dialogue between aria and recitative; that [the orchestra] should not break up a sentence nonsensically, nor interrupt the force and heat of the action inappropriately.

I also considered that my greatest efforts should be concentrated on seeking a beautiful simplicity. I have avoided making a show of complexities at the expense of clarity; and I did not think it useful to invent novelties which were not genuinely required to express the situation and the emotions. There is no convention that I have not willingly renounced in favour of the total effect.

These are my principles. By good fortune, the libretto lent itself miraculously to my plan. The celebrated author, conceiving a new scheme for dramatic art, had throughout substituted florid descriptions, unnecessary similes, and affected, cold moralizing, with the language of the heart, strong passions, interesting situations, and a constantly varied spectacle. Success justified my precepts, and the universal approbation of so enlightened a city has clearly shown that simplicity, truth, and nature are the great principles of beauty in all artistic endeavours. Although highly respected people have repeatedly urged me to issue this opera of mine in print, I have been fully aware of the risk which would be run in combating widely held and deeply rooted prejudices, and I have thought it necessary to arm myself with the most powerful patronage of Your Royal Highness, entreating the favour to preface my opera with your August Name, which so justly unites the support of an enlightened Europe. Great protector of the fine arts, you reign over a nation which has the glory of seeing them rise again from universal oppression, a nation itself producing one of the greatest models, in the form of a city which was always the first to shake off the yoke of popular prejudice by blazing a trail to perfection, and which alone can undertake the reform of this noble spectacle in which all the fine arts have so great a share. When this should come about, I shall retain the glory of having moved the first stone, and this public testimonial of Your Highness's protection for which favour I have the honour of declaring myself, with most humble deference, Your Royal Highness's most humble, devoted, and obedient servant,

Cristoforo Gluck.[17]

---

[17] Gluck to Archduke Leopold of Tuscany, Vienna, 1769, in *Alceste* (Vienna, 1769), pp. xi–xii; also in Nohl, *Musiker-Briefe. Eine Sammlung Briefe von C. W. von Gluck, Ph. E. Bach, J. Haydn, C. M. von Weber und F. Mendelssohn-Bartholdy* (Leipzig, 1867), 1–5. The fine trans. by Blom in Alfred Einstein, *Gluck*, 2nd edn. (London, 1964), 98–100, has become the standard one; my version is made not through presumption but in the interests of consistency. Blom's language is, however, becoming dated to the point of obscurity, e.g. his use of 'paragon' for 'simile'.

A lengthy review of the score in the *Allgemeine deutsche Bibliothek* by Johann Nicolaus Forkel answers Gluck's preface point by point, and treats the music in similar detail. It illustrates how hard Gluck found it to be judged on his own terms and in the light of his declared intentions:

There are several arias, constructed especially in accordance with the composer's declared aims, where the expression is natural and good, for example . . . 'Io non chiedo'. The accompaniment is also well thought out, especially at the beginning. The oboe leads with the main melody, against which the violins play pizzicato, two solo violas have weaving quavers, and the bassoon and horns sustain long notes, to be joined by the oboe after the voice enters. Metre, speed, and accompaniment are subsequently varied several times, following closely the meaning of the words, which are sung once and never repeated. But scarcely has one passage been enjoyed, than it is superseded by another, so that at the end little or no overall impression remains. This criticism can be applied to many other arias.[18]

Metastasio also remained unimpressed by the new path opera was taking. In a letter to Count Bolognini, dated 7 February 1776, he asserts, 'The author of *Alceste* must believe my unfavourable opinion of his drama, and be sorry for it. He very much displeases me, so much so that I do not think it proper to have victory attributed to me in a presumed contest, since the author has obviously taken . . . a course of action diametrically opposed to mine, which precludes all comparison.'[19]

---

[18] 14 (1771), 19. See also Forkel's earlier attack in issue 10 (1769), 28–32. The same aria was criticized in similar terms by Rousseau in 'Fragments d'observations sur l'*Alceste* italien de M. le chevalier Gluck', *Traités sur la musique* (Geneva, 1781), 392–427. Forkel quotes Rousseau's definitions of 'air' and 'roulade' from the latter's recently published *Dictionnaire de musique* (Paris, 1768).

[19] Pub. in Joseph Guerin Fucilla, 'Nuove lettere inedite del Metastasio', *Convivium*, 26 (1958), 588.

11

TRANSITIONAL YEARS
(1769–1773)

IF Calzabigi's claim, that *Paride ed Elena* was already written by the end of 1768 is true, then Gluck's years between then and his first French opera were singularly barren. He revised *L'innocenza giustificata*, under the title *La Vestale*, for a performance at the Burgtheater in the summer of 1768; only the libretto survives, providing the information that Gluck had been elected as a member of the Arcadian Academy under the name of 'Armonide Terpsicoreo'.[1]

A family letter from 1769 shows Gluck in moralistic mood. It is addressed to his brother-in-law, Johann Friedrich Crommer, of whom little is known except that he married Gluck's second-youngest sister, and that the couple had three children.[2] Gluck's excessively formal tone distances him from someone who was clearly a troublesome relative:

Most honoured brother-in-law,

I have not received a letter from you informing us of the change in your circumstances, but nevertheless, I cannot but rejoice with you, because you have found a wife who honours you by [bearing] your children, and whom you have won at little cost to yourself, for to tell the truth, I did not reply to your former letter to me because I did not have the means to help you. I hope that by good conduct and by abstaining from drink, you may make your position a permanent one. Please be so good as to tell me whether you received the clothes I sent you over two years ago through [Herr] Alexander. My wife sends her compliments to you on the change in your condition and fortune, and we both wish you and all your family well.

---

[1] See Alfred Einstein, 'Gluck's *La Vestale*', *Monthly Musical Record*, 66 (1936), 151–2.
[2] Schmid, *Gluck*, 12.

If you should discover a pretty little estate for me, capable of yielding a certain income, please be so good as to tell me of it.

I remain the obedient servant of my most honoured brother-in-law,

Chevalier Gluck.[3]

In 1769 Gluck fulfilled his duties as a court composer by providing music for the wedding celebrations of Archduchess Maria Amalia and Prince Ferdinand of Parma. But the occasion yielded little new music: the festival work, *Le feste d'Apollo*, was devised as a composite of three independent acts with a prologue, the libretto to be composed by four different authors. Nothing could have seemed more remote from the new dramatic principles expounded in the *Alceste* preface. Gluck expended little energy on the music. Twenty of the numbers of the prologue and first two acts were taken from earlier works;[4] the last act was an adaptation of *Orfeo*, arranged for the soprano castrato Giuseppe Millico. An unsigned letter, in French, from an unnamed Viennese doctor to an unknown recipient, describes a far from enthusiastic Gluck:

The court of Parma summoned Clouc, director of music at the Viennese court, to compose the opera which is to be given on the occasion of the wedding festivities. When these were deferred (for the reason you know,)[5] he asked permission to return home to manage his affairs. He obtained leave on condition that he would return to Parma when he was needed. He returned here a few days ago.

Yesterday evening, someone who is very familiar with the court at Parma, who admires its administration, and has some affection for the country, told me that Clouc was saying that at Parma everything exuded poverty, repression, and fear, and that he did not want to stay there because everything was in disorder, and that the administration was violent and despotic. I made some show of not believing this, telling him that all foreigners spoke of Parma as if delighted with the court and the administration, and other matters besides. This person replied that he had not heard anything himself, but that those who repeated it had no motive other than to tell him what was said. In addition, they said that [Gluck] is a coarse German, a [work]horse who sees no further than his music, and for that reason he had found nothing to praise at Parma

---

[3] Vienna, 16 Jan. 1769: autograph in New York, Pierpont Morgan Library, Mary Flagler Cary Collection; the letter has never been published. It is hard to know how to interpret Gluck's plea of poverty in the first sentence. He had, however, purchased a sizeable country estate in 1768 (see Burney's comment of 2 Sept. 1770, below) which might have limited any possible generosity towards his family.

[4] Discussed in detail in Hortschansky, *Parodie und Entlehnung*, 115–46.

[5] The delay was due to the interregnum between two popes. Clement XIV was elected in the summer of 1769.

except the music at court. This in truth agrees to some extent with what I have heard elsewhere. I have been told that Clouc praised the music at the court of Parma, and no one has told me that he spoke well of anything else. The other day, Calzabigi, Clouc's friend, said, while speaking of the election of the Pope, that it was as well that the wedding had been deferred, because his friend had told him that nothing was ready at Parma, that everything was in confusion, and that no one had known where the married couple were to live. I replied to that by saying that Clouc must have seen only the ruined palace, and saw nothing of the [summer palace], or the palace at Colorno, or the residence opposite St Paul's. Incidentally, this same Calzabigi told me that Clouc had come back to Vienna for three months, which would indicate that the wedding will not take place any earlier. If all these things are true, and they seem likely, I would be very sorry if anyone sang as bad a song about Vienna. We have here an excellent opinion of Parma, but people are quick to form adverse impressions. Calzabigi has invited me to dine with him on several occasions; I shall go there with a purpose, and I shall endeavour to choose a day when his friend will be there.[6]

Le feste was eventually performed on 24 August. For Gluck, the most positive outcome from the Parma visit was the close and lasting friendship he developed with Millico. Their meeting is given typically dramatic treatment in Reichardt's French manuscript:

The great singer Millico lamented when he was given the role of Orpheus to sing at the court theatre in Parma, for it seemed to him that it was in no way a proper role for a 'first man' in the Italian style. After he had studied the role under Gluck's direction, however, he was ashamed of his short-sightedness. He enjoyed the greatest success in the role, and became so completely attached to Gluck that he resolved on living with him in Vienna for several years.[7]

Back in Vienna, Gluck gathered more friends around him. He may have sought pupils for the same reason that Calzabigi wrote polemics, in an attempt to reinforce his 'reform' by attaching adherents. One such pupil was Salieri, who, as a youth of 19, benefited from Gluck's encouragement. He described one instance in these words:

Without saying anything to me, [Giovanni Gastone] Boccherini[8] had whispered to Calzabigi that I had made good progress with my opera. The latter,

---

[6] Vienna, 15 May 1769: F-Pn, Gluck lettres autographes, no. 2; partially reproduced in Julien Tiersot, *Lettres de musiciens* (Paris, 1924), 55–6. The writer's profession emerges later in the letter, where he describes his friendship with Van Swieten.

[7] 'Fortsetzung', 73.   [8] Brother of the composer Luigi.

a friend of the impresario's,[9] wanted to arrange for a little rehearsal in his own home to hear all that had been completed. He invited me there, and I, without knowing the reason for the invitation, went there together with my librettist [Boccherini], taking the completed vocal numbers. I was a little taken aback on finding the impresario, Kapellmeister Gluck, and [Giuseppe] Scarlatti there, but thought that they had come merely out of curiosity, and was delighted that they were there. I sang and played all that was completed. Gluck and Scarlatti sang with me in the ensembles. Gluck, who had already befriended and encouraged me, showed himself pleased with my work from the outset. Scarlatti, who from time to time rebuked little grammatical errors in the music, by and large praised each piece. At the end both masters said to the impresario that if I were to finish the missing numbers, the opera could be put into rehearsal without delay, and performed, 'Because the work contains enough to please the public,' were Gluck's very words.[10]

The impresario, a background figure in the above tale, played a much larger role in Gluck's life at this time. From 1767, the theatre direction had been in the hands of the so-called Count Afflisio, a man of many aliases. Afflisio, an adventurer in the same mould as his friends Calzabigi and Casanova, obtained his appointment in the teeth of well-founded opposition from Maria Theresia.[11] From May 1767 he managed not only the Burg and Kärntnertor theatres, but a popular theatre, or Hetztheater, which included a menagerie among its entertainments.[12] On 11 October 1769, Gluck entered into a partnership with Afflisio and Francesco Lopresti, in which he invested 30,000 florins on the understanding that he would receive a quarter of the profits from the theatres.[13] A month later, Afflisio was declared bankrupt. On 13 November, Gluck wrote to Kaunitz, asking him to extricate him from his legal obligations; on Kaunitz's refusal, Gluck appealed to Emperor Joseph, who urged him to recoup his losses by putting on German comedies three times a week (both of Gluck's letters are lost). At the end of December, Gluck made a second appeal to Kaunitz:

[9] Giuseppe d'Afflisio, or Affligio; see below.

[10] Quoted in Ignaz Franz Edlen von Mosel, *Über das Leben und die Werke des Anton Salieri* (Vienna, 1827), 34. Mosel's biography was written at Salieri's request, and based on 'a bundle of papers' in the composer's own hand. Salieri's opera was *Le donne letterate*, first performed at the Burgtheater in Jan. 1770.

[11] Prod'homme, *Gluck*, 157.

[12] Id., 'Giuseppe d'Affligio', *Rivista musicale italiana*, 23 (1916), 209.

[13] Gustav Zechmeister, *Die Wiener Theater nächst der Burg und nächst dem Kärntnertor von 1747 bis 1767* (Vienna, 1971), 83.

Most Serene Prince,

Most Gracious Lord,

The high protection and especial favour with which Your Serene Highness has always distinguished me encourage me to have recourse to Your Highness for help to escape from my present unfortunate situation. I am, according to the most gracious word of His Majesty the Emperor, committed for the next year to the board of theatre management, together with Lieutenant Colonel Afflisio, on the understanding that he, by virtue of your decree, could dismiss the French troupe, and to this end, I advanced 30,000 florins as my share and entered into a bond with Baron [Johann von] Fries and [Johann Blasius von] Bender to pay the former at 3,000 florins a year, the latter at 8,000 florins, including interest, to meet their demands over a period of six years. Since by the latest decree of His Majesty the Emperor this arrangement is utterly invalid, I am not only unable to make the payments I am committed to, but, thanks to this chicanery, must also be at risk of a lawsuit and see the money I have advanced be gradually spent and disappear into the bargain, for I cannot seek any redress in the courts ['per viam juris'] from Afflisio, as his debts far exceed his assets. He owes 50,000 florins to Herr Bender, 25,000 florins to Baron Fries, and 30,000 florins to me, exclusive of what he owes to the imperial court, to which his whole liability, with the deposit, and the stock of the Hetz and other theatres, and not including those debts which have not yet come to light, may run to some 90,000 florins. Now I freely admit that the said Afflisio may have earned Your Highness's disfavour, but the philanthropy which Your Highness always manifests to the world emboldens me to hope that Your Highness will not allow my family to be ruined. Everyone knows that no living man has suffered any harm through Your Serene Highness, but that Your Serene Highness has set before the eyes of the world sufficient proof of your good-hearted disposition.

This allows me to entertain the most confident hope that Your Serene Highness will either most graciously intervene in Afflisio's fate, or, through your great goodness, find a means whereby I may soon be able to settle my family's affairs, especially as, although part of this money has been advanced by me, the other is the property of my wife, a circumstance which has already so distressed her that her health has suffered on account of it.

I ask most humbly that my plea be heard, and remain, with the deepest respect, Most Serene Prince, Your Serene Highness's most humble and obedient servant,

Christoph Gluck.[14]

---

[14] Vienna, 31 Dec. 1769: the autograph is in private ownership, and the German text has never been published. I am most grateful to Dr Gabriele Buschmeier for providing me with a facsimile.

Kaunitz's response is not extant. Afflisio remained nominally in charge of the theatres until 31 May 1770, when the Hungarian Count Kohary took over the direction. Gluck lost a major part of his fortune in the enterprise, an event which seems to have increased his natural caution in subsequent years.

Afflisio did not escape retribution. By the middle of 1770 he had fled to Italy. He was arrested in Bologna at the end of 1778 and a year later convicted of forgery on a massive scale.[15] A vivid account of his last days in Pisa is recorded by the tenor Michael Kelly:

a man was pointed out to me, whose head was shaved, and who wore the dress of a galley-slave, sweeping the baths. He did the most laborious work by day, and at night was chained on board a Tuscan galley, which lay in the Arno. This man was the well-known Giuseppe Afrissa [*sic*], who had visited and been received at all the courts of Europe; and at Vienna, had been in such favour with the Emperor Francis I, and his Empress, Maria Theresa, that he sat at their table, and was appointed Master of the Revels at Schönbrunn and all the royal palaces! He was banished from Vienna for some disgraceful act, but not before he had contrived to lose at the gaming-table every shilling of a large fortune, which he had originally acquired there.[16]

Early in 1770, Gluck engaged in correspondence with Gaspare Caroli, a double-bass player he had met in Parma. The letters refer in the main to the Bolognese singer Gabriella Tagliaferri, who was employed at Parma in the season following Gluck's visit, and who sought a position in Vienna; but the correspondence opens with reference to one of Gluck's purchases made during his visit to Parma the previous year:

Monsieur,

You could not have managed better to avoid embarrassment in letting me have the cloak than by giving it to Sig. Napolioni, and since there is a remittance of 100 *ungari* to be paid in your town, which will follow in the near future, I shall take advantage of that occasion to repay you the amount agreed according to the account, twelve and a quarter florins, which I would ask you to pay to Sig. Giambattista Piloti on my behalf. My obligation towards you, after causing so much inconvenience, and after all your favours and kindness, will never be forgotten, and I continually hope that I shall have the opportunity to show you my sincere appreciation—I trust that I shall be fortunate enough to have this chance. Since I rely totally on your frankness and good judgement, I should like you to give me hour honest opinion regarding the talent of this Sig.ra

---

[15] Prod'homme, 'Affligio', 218.   [16] *Reminiscences* (London, 1826), i. 102–3.

Tagliaferri: whether she presents herself well, whether she has a good voice, and whether she has as much talent for acting as she has for singing. I assure you that whatever you are kind enough to write to me shall be kept in the utmost confidence. On behalf of myself and my wife, I send many best wishes and much affection to your dear wife, to the most amiable Sig. Pio Piazza, and to all your friends, in the hope that I may succeed in having the pleasure of seeing you again, and embracing you.

It is with great honour that I sign myself sincerely your most devoted and obedient servant,

Chevalier Gluck.[17]

Monsieur,

By now you will already have received from Sig. Pulcherio reimbursement of your expenses on my behalf. I remain, however, indebted to you for the many numerous inconveniences I have caused, which I fervently hope to be able to repay at the earliest opportunity.

I must thank you for the information which you gave me regarding Sig.ra Tagliaferri, which has convinced the director to make her an offer, if her terms, which she has already communicated through Sig. Pulcherio, are reasonable.

In the hope that she will still be there [in Parma] when you receive this, I inform you that next Monday you should receive a letter from Sig. Pulcherio, stating Sig.ra Tagliaferri's demands, and we shall probably respond by sending her the contract, so that, to avoid any delay, she may return to Vienna accompanied by this gentleman, who could both conclude the contract and arrange the visit for her.

I ask your pardon once more for this further inconvenience I lay upon you. Always remember me with affection, and be assured of my great respect. I remain your most devoted and obedient servant,

Chevalier Gluck.[18]

'The director' at this time still meant Afflisio, and a contract signed by him was despatched to Caroli on 26 February. A duplicate was sent to Bologna, as the next surviving letter makes clear:

My dear Signor Caroli,

A communication arrived this week from Sig. Pulcherio and from Sig.ra Tagliaferri herself, with the lady's application to this theatre; we have sent the

---

[17] Gluck to Caroli, Vienna, 26 Jan. 1770. The autographs of this and the next three letters are in Parma, Archivio di Stato di Parma, Cartella no. 88; pub. in Cesare Alcari, 'La cartella no. 88', *Musica d'oggi*, 14 (1932), 257–60. All are in Italian, despite the greeting 'Monsieur' and signature 'Chevalier'.

[18] Gluck to Caroli, Vienna, 22 Feb. 1770.

contract to her in Bologna, where you say she will go immediately after the last of her present performances. I am passing on this information in case our letters cross, because I had asked that she remain [in Parma] until she received my reply.

The difference in fee between her request and our offer is almost negligible, and it will be so easy to reach an agreement that we can call the transaction concluded. It remains only for me to thank you for the inconvenience which I have caused you in this matter, and to offer you my eternal gratitude and heartfelt respect, with which I remain your most devoted and affectionate servant and friend,

Chevalier Gluck.[19]

Postal delays nearly cost Gluck his singer. Tagliaferri left for Bologna on 1 March, and never received the offer from Vienna, owing to the machinations of the Bolognese negotiator, who suppressed letters forwarded by Caroli to secure the singer for his own company:

Monsieur,

I acknowledge receipt of your letters dated the 6th and 9th of this month, and thank you for the information contained in them. I only hope that I can also be of service to you as far as it is in my capacity to do so. It was with great surprise that I heard of the unhelpful action taken by Sig.ra Tagliaferri. Be so kind as to inform her of how her conduct seems to the management, stressing that hers is not very professional behaviour—but from such people one cannot hope for anything better. It distresses me that on my account the management finds itself without any women singers, and I therefore ask you to do all that is in your power, in the event of not being able to secure this lady, to write to Mme Suardi, asking if she would like to start immediately as second woman in the opera seria, and alternate with the other first woman in the opera buffa. The lady told me herself that she would not be averse to singing in the opera buffa. My dear friend, I beg you not to lose one moment of time, and to arrange everything as you think best.

I send my best wishes to everyone, and also those of my wife. Whenever I can be of service, you have only to ask. I remain your most devoted and obedient servant,

Chevalier Gluck.[20]

Tagliaferri was eventually engaged for the Viennese theatres, and played the second woman's role of Pallas in Gluck's next opera, *Paride ed Elena*.

The next letter from Gluck's pen shows him again trying to gather

---

[19] Gluck to Caroli, Vienna, 1 Mar. 1770.   [20] Gluck to Caroli, Vienna, 19 Mar. 1770.

support for his new path in opera. It is addressed to Padre Martini, whom he had met in Bologna on the occasion of *Il trionfo di Clelia*. Gluck now sends him a score of *Alceste* and a carefully worded declaration of his dramatic aims:

If I were not confident of the friendship with which you honour me, I would not have ventured to expose my music of *Alceste* to your all-seeing eyes, despite the extraordinary impact it has had in our local theatres, for I am well aware that the numerous faults in it, which have arisen partly from the carelessness of the publisher, and partly as the result of my own inexperience, do not fit it to undergo so scrupulous a judgement. The favourable view you entertain of me has brought about praise rather than excuses for my music, and this, coming from so great a man, is both flattering and precious to me. In the music of this opera, my sole aim was to enter into the [whole] content and situation of the drama, and to seek to give expression to these, not to express the meaning of single isolated words or a fragment of dialogue, as some have imagined. I have always believed that if the fundamental rules of music cannot add to the effect, cannot, that is, clothe the passions and reinforce their strength, then it is useless to immerse oneself at great cost in such arduous study.

Your opinion could do more than anything that I have said in the dedication to *Alceste* to impress these basic truths on the masters of this noble art, and produce that rational reform of opera, so long awaited and hoped for in vain by the most enlightened people, and by those most supportive of this truthful and sublime spectacle.

I shall always feel gratified that I took the first step in the attempt, and thereby earned the approval both of the public and also of the leading lights of the century. I thank you with all my heart, and long for a further opportunity to express my perfect respect and the complete esteem with which I have the honour to sign myself, Most Reverend Father, your most humble, devoted and obedient servant,

Chevalier Gluck.[21]

In the autumn of 1770, Gluck put on *Alceste* with Millico in the role of Admetus. He also sang in *Paride ed Elena*, which was given on 3 November 1770. Khevenhüller records a cool reception: 'In the evening in the Burgtheater a new opera called *Paride ed Elena* was performed . . . which because of its unusual and somewhat strange taste did not find great approval.'[22] The *Wienerisches Diarium* gives a different impression:

[21] Vienna, 14 July 1770; reproduced in Klaus Hortschansky, 'Glucks Sendungsbewusstsein: Dargestellt an einem unbekannten Gluck-Brief', *Die Musikforschung*, 21 (1968), 30–1.
[22] *Tagebuch*, 1770–3, 48.

The new Singspiel from the talented pen of Herr Calzabigi received well-earned general approbation both from the imperial court and from the assembled public, not only on account of the skilful and pleasing music by the well-known Cavaliere Gluck, the brilliant decoration of the theatre, and the great number of supernumeraries, but because of the very famous Italian singer Millico, and a young German singer, Mlle [Catarina] Schindler, who performed the leading roles with artistry and spontaneity.[23]

As has been noted, Tagliaferri appeared as Pallas, the second-woman role Gluck had promised her; he wrote her a formidably dramatic *scena* in the last act. The ballets, which play a major role in the drama, were by Noverre. Zinzendorf found 'the music agreeable, the decorations very beautiful, and the ballets charming'.[24]

This time, Gluck and Calzabigi realized that publication was a crucial step in ensuring understanding of their work, and the score was published at around the time of the première. The preface is again signed by Gluck, but the elegant language suggests Calzabigi at his most polished:

Your Highness,

In dedicating to Your Highness this my newest work, I seek less a protector than a judge. A mind fortified against the prejudices of convention, with sufficient knowledge of the great principles of art, and taste formed not so much on great models as on the unvarying fundamentals of beauty and truth—these are the qualities I seek in my Maecenas, and which I find united in Your Highness. The only reason that induced me to issue my music for *Alceste* in print was the hope of finding successors, who would take the path already opened, and, urged on by the full support of an enlightened public, would be encouraged to eliminate the abuses introduced into Italian opera and bring it as close to perfection as possible. I regret that I have so far attempted this in vain. Countless arbiters of taste and pedants, who form the greatest barrier to progress in the fine arts, have pronounced against a method which, were it to gain a footing, would destroy at a stroke all their pretensions in the direction of criticism and all their capacity to achieve anything themselves. These people believed they could make an assessment of *Alceste* on the basis of informal rehearsals, badly directed and worse executed; they calculated what the effect might be in a theatre on the basis of what took place in a room—with the same cunning means as those employed in olden days in a town in Greece, where statues which were designed to stand on very high columns were judged from a distance of a few feet. Perhaps one sensitive ear found a vocal line too harsh, or a transition too violent, or badly prepared, without realizing that in its

---

[23] 89, suppl., 7 Nov. 1770.   [24] Diary, 3 Nov. 1770.

proper place it might perhaps sound greatly expressive or make the most beautiful juxtaposition. A single pedant seized upon an intentional licence, or perhaps condemned a printing error, as an unforgivable sin against the mysteries
of harmony, and then voices were raised in unison against this barbaric and
eccentric music. It is true that other scores are assessed by the same criterion,
and that they are judged with the same confidence which admits no possibility
of error, but Your Highness can at once see the reason for this. The more that
truth and perfection are sought, the more necessary are precision and exact-
ness. The differences which distinguish Raphael from a host of ordinary
painters are imperceptible, and any change of contour which would not damage the likeness of a caricature would completely disfigure the portrait of a fine
lady. Nothing but a change in the mode of expression is needed to turn my aria
from *Orfeo*, 'Che farò senza Euridice', into a dance for marionettes. One note
held or shortened, a neglected increase in speed, a misplaced appoggiatura in
the voice, or a trill, passage-work, or roulade can ruin a whole scene in such
an opera, though it does nothing to, or does nothing but improve, an opera of
the common sort. The presence of the composer is therefore as important to
the performance of this kind of music as, so to say, the presence of the sun to
the works of nature. [The sun] is absolutely the spirit and the life, and without
it everything remains in chaos and darkness.

But we have to be prepared to meet such obstacles as long as we live in the
world of people who believe themselves empowered to judge the fine arts
because they have the advantage of possessing a pair of eyes and a pair of ears,
no matter of what sort. A passion for wanting to talk of that of which they
understand least is a defect unhappily all too common among men, and I have
recently seen one of the greatest philosophers of the century struggle to write
about music, and pronounce, like oracles, 'Dreams of the blind and follies of
romance'.[25] Your Highness will have already read the text of *Paride*, and will
have noticed that it did not provide the composer's imagination with those
strong passions, those noble portraits, and those tragic situations which
moved the spectators in *Alceste*, and which give so much opportunity for
grand musical effects; you will therefore surely not expect the same force and
energy in the music; just as one does not demand in a painting in full light the
same degree of chiaroscuro and the same strong contrasts that the painter can
employ in a subject which allows the choice of subdued light. Here we are not
dealing with a wife on the point of losing her husband who, to save him, has
the courage to summon the infernal gods from the black shadows of the night
in a fearful forest, and who in the final agony of death fears for the fate of her
sons, and tears herself from a husband she adores. We are dealing with a
young lover confronted with the waywardness of a proud and virtuous

---

[25] The philosopher referred to is presumably Rousseau, whose dictionary articles were cited by
Forkel in his attack on *Alceste*; see Ch. 10 above.

woman, who finally triumphs by using all the ingenuity of a cunning passion. I was obliged to strive to find some variety of colour, seeking it in the different characters of the two nations of Phrygia and Sparta, by contrasting the roughness and savagery of one with the delicacy and tenderness of the other. I believed that since singing in opera is nothing but a substitute for declamation, I must make Helen's music imitate the native ruggedness of that nation, and I thought that it would not be reprehensible if in order to capture this characteristic in the music, I descended now and then to create a coarse effect. I believed that I must vary my style in the pursuit of truth, according to the subject in hand. The greatest beauties of melody and harmony become defects and imperfections when they are misplaced. I do not expect any more success with my *Paride* than with *Alceste* in achieving the aim of producing among composers of music the desired change, on the contrary, I foresee ever greater obstacles in the way; but I myself shall not desist from making new attempts on the worthy aim, and should I win Your Highness's confidence, I shall be happy to repeat, *Tolle Syparium sufficit mihi unus Plato pro cuncto populo.*[26]

I have the honour to be, with the deepest respect, Your Highness's most humble, devoted, and obedient servant,

Chevalier Christof Gluck.[27]

Gluck's reputation grew steadily in these years. When Burney travelled to Vienna in 1772, he found Gluck a celebrity and a 'character'. He visited him on 2 September at his recently acquired country house in St Marx. Burney gives the useful information that Gluck's next opera, *Iphigénie en Aulide*, was already complete:

Countess Thun . . . has been so kind as to write a note to Gluck on my account and he had returned, for *him*, a very civil answer; for he is as formidable a character as Handel used to be: a very dragon, of whom all are in fear. However, he had agreed to be visited in the afternoon. . . . At five o'clock, lord Stormont's coach carried madame Thun, his lordship, and myself, to the house of the chevalier Gluck, in the Fauxbourg St. Mark. He is very well housed there; has a pretty garden, and a great number of neat, and elegantly furnished rooms. He has no children; madame Gluck, and his niece, who lives with him,[28] came to receive us at the door, as well as the veteran composer

---

[26] A misspelt quotation from Cicero's *Brutus*: 'Up with the curtain! One Plato rather than all the people is enough for me.'

[27] Letter to Duke Giovanni of Braganza, Vienna, 30 Oct. 1770, in *Paride ed Elena* (Vienna, 1700), pp. ix–xii. Reproduced in Nohl, *Musiker-Briefe*, 8–11. The Duke of Braganza had been a warm admirer of Gluck's music for some years; he was present at the previews of *Orfeo* described in Zinzendorf (see Ch. 8 above), and at Lord Stormont's dinner for Burney (see n. 30 below).

[28] Marianne, known as Nanette, was the daughter of Gluck's youngest sister, Maria Anna Rosina, who had died in the early 1760s.

himself. He is very much pitted with the small-pox, and very coarse in figure and look, but was soon got into good humour; and he talked, sung, and played, madame Thun observed, more than ever she knew him at any one time.

He began, upon a very bad harpsichord,[29] by accompanying his niece, who is but thirteen years old, in two of the capital scenes of his own famous opera of *Alceste*. She has a powerful and well-toned voice, and sung with infinite taste, feeling, expression, and even execution. After these two scenes from *Alceste*, she sung several others, by different composers, and in different styles, particularly by Traetta.

I was assured that mademoiselle Gluck had learned to sing but two years, which, considering the perfection of her performance, really astonished me. She began singing under her uncle, but he, in a precipitate fit of despair, had given her up; when Signor Millico, arriving at Vienna about the same time, and discovering that she had an improvable voice, and a docile disposition, begged he might be allowed to teach her for a few months only, in order to try whether it would not be worth her while still to persevere in her musical studies, notwithstanding the late decision against her; which he suspected had its rise from the impatience and impetuosity of the uncle, more than the want of genius in the niece. . . .

When she had done, her uncle was prevailed upon to sing himself; and, with as little voice as possible, he contrived to entertain, and even delight the company, in a very high degree; for, with the richness of accompaniment, the energy and vehemence of his manner in the *Allegros*, and his judicious expression in the slow movements, he so well compensated for the want of voice that it was a defect which was soon entirely forgotten.

He was so good-humoured as to perform almost his whole operas of *Alceste*; many admirable things in a still later opera of his, called *Paride ed Elena*; and in a French opera, from Racine's *Iphigénie*, which he has just composed. This last, though he had not as yet committed a note of it to paper, was so well digested in his head, and his retention is so wonderful, that he sang it nearly from the beginning to the end, with as much readiness as if he had had a fair score before him.[30]

Burney met Gluck two days later at a dinner at Lord Stormont's, where his niece sang again: 'She executed, admirably, several entire scenes in her uncle's operas, of which the music was so truly dramatic, picturesque, and well expressed, that, if my conjecture be admissible, of the first vocal music being the voice of passion and cry of nature, the chevalier Gluck's

---

[29] It is thought that Burney took advantage of this visit to sell Gluck a piano; I am grateful to Dr David Rowland for this information.

[30] 2 Sept. 1772. *Present State . . . Germany*, i. 259–65 *passim*.

compositions, and his niece's performance, entirely fulfil that idea.'[31] Burney's leave-taking, on 11 September, affords another vivid, human impression of the composer:

This morning I went to take leave of the chevalier Gluck; and though it was near eleven o'clock, when I arrived, yet, like a true great genius, he was still in bed; *Madame* told me, that he usually wrote all night, and lay in bed late to recruit. Gluck, when he appeared, did not make so good a defence, but frankly confessed his sluggishness, *je suis un peu poltron ce matin*.[32]

Gluck was developing other interests in these years. He discussed with Burney his ambition to make a new setting of Dryden's *Ode on St Cecilia's Day*, which he had heard in Vienna in Handel's setting.[33] He had evidently given much thought to the problems of setting a long narrative poem as a dramatic cantata, and had already attempted something similar with Friedrich Gottlieb Klopstock's epic tragedy *Hermannsschlacht*, setting some of the bardic choruses in 1769. Writing to his intimate friend Johann Gleim, Klopstock revealed that 'Gluck, a composer from Vienna, who according to the word of one who knows is uniquely a poet among composers, has set some strophes from the bardic choruses, with the full ring of truth. I have actually not yet seen his composition, but all those who have heard it are very taken with it.'[34] Gluck continued to play extracts from his setting for many years, but nothing was ever written down. He did, however, complete and publish the much smaller-scale declamatory settings of some of Klopstock's odes:

Most nobly born,

Most honourable Counsellor to the Legation,

Father Denis[35] has told me that you desire to have those strophes I have composed from your *Hermannsschlacht*. I would long ago have done you this service, had I not been categorically assured that many would not find them to their taste, because they must be sung in a certain style which is not yet much in fashion. It seems to me that although you have excellent musicians, music which calls for a passionate delivery is still completely unknown in your country, a fact which I have clearly inferred from the review of my *Alceste* published in Berlin.[36] I have so great an admiration for you, that I promise you

---

[31] 2 Sept. 1772. *Present State ... Germany*, i. 293.
[32] 'I'm a bit of a coward this morning'; ibid. i. 343.   [33] Ibid. i. 241–4.
[34] 2 Sept. 1769, in Klamer Schmidt (ed.), *Klopstock und seine Freunde: Briefwechsel der Familie Klopstock* (Halberstadt, 1810), ii. 227–8.
[35] Father Johann Denis was a Jesuit poet, author of some bardic songs in his own right.
[36] The criticism of *Alceste* referred to is almost certainly Forkel's trenchant art. quoted in Ch. 10 above.

that, if you do not think of coming to Vienna, I shall visit Hamburg next year to make your personal acquaintance. Moreover I promise to sing you not only much from *Hermannsschlacht*, but also from your sublime odes, in order to show you to what extent I have aspired towards your greatness, or how far I have obscured it by my music.

Meanwhile I am sending you several songs, which are utterly simple in style and easy to perform. Three of them have a German character, and three of them are in a more modern Italian taste, to which I have added, as an experiment, two songs in the old bardic style, which can, however, always be discarded. It will be necessary to choose a good pianist for these, so that they may appear less intolerable to you. I remain honoured to call myself, with deepest respect, Your Honour's most obedient servant,

Chevalier Gluck.[37]

[37] Gluck to Klopstock, Vienna, 14 Aug. 1773. Gluck's relationship with Klopstock is discussed in Josef Müller-Blattau, 'Gluck und die deutsche Dichtung', *Jahrbuch der Musikbibliothek Peters*, 45 (1938), 30–52, which includes the text of the letter (p. 32). Also pub. in Klopstock, *Briefe von und an Klopstock*, ed. Johann Martin Lappenberg (Brunswick, 1867), 252–3; *Christoph Willibald Gluck: Briefe*, ed. Wilhelm M. Treichlinger (Zurich, 1951), 77–8.

12

IPHIGÉNIE EN AULIDE

(1772–1774)

ON Burney's evidence, the composition of *Iphigénie en Aulide* was completed, though the score still unwritten, by September 1772. A month earlier, Gluck's new librettist, François Louis Gand Leblanc du Roullet, a minor diplomat at the French embassy in Vienna, had taken the first steps to arrange its performance in Paris through a letter to Antoine d'Auvergne, one of the directors of the Opéra, which was published in the *Mercure de France*:

The honour which is due to you, monsieur, on account of your very distinguished abilities, and your reputation for integrity, with which I am familiar, have persuaded me to undertake to write to you to inform you that the celebrated M. Glouch, famous throughout Europe, has composed a French opera which he would like to have performed on the Parisian stage. After having written more than forty Italian operas, which have enjoyed the greatest success in all the theatres where that language is in usage, this great man has become convinced, by a close reading of authors ancient and modern, and by profound reflection on his art, that in their theatrical compositions, the Italians have strayed from the true path, that the French genre is the true genre of music drama, and that if it has not yet been perfected, it is not the acknowledged talents of French musicians which are to blame, but rather the authors of the poems, who, ignorant of the scope of musical style, have in their librettos preferred wit to feeling, gallantry to the passions, and restraint and the refinements of versification to pathos in style and situation. As a result of these thoughts, he communicated his ideas to a man of considerable shrewdness, ability, and taste, and got from him two Italian poems which he set to music. He himself has directed these two operas in the theatres of Parma, Milan, Naples, etc. They were incredibly successful there, and have brought about a revolution in the genre in Italy. Last winter, the town of Bologna put on one of these operas in M. Glouch's absence. Its success in this town drew more than 20,000 visitors, eager to see the performances, and when the takings were reckoned, Bologna gained, by this one production, more than 80,000 ducats, about 900,000 French *livres*. On his return here, M. Glouch, enlightened by his own experiences, became convinced that the Italian language, well suited because of its frequent repetition of vowels to what the Italians call 'passages', had neither the clarity nor the energy of French, and that the advantage which we used to concede to the Italian language was in fact destroying the true style of music-drama, in which all 'passages' are unsuitable, or at least weaken the expression. After making these observations, M. Glouch was filled with indignation against the brazen assertions of those of our famous writers who have dared to denigrate the French language by insisting that it does not lend itself to great musical composition. No one can be more competent to judge this matter than M. Glouch: he has a sound knowledge of both languages, and although he speaks French haltingly, he understands it thoroughly; he has made a special study of it; he knows all its niceties, particularly its rules of versification, which he observes most diligently. For a long time he has exercised his talents in both languages in a variety of genres, and has met with success in a court where both are equally familiar (although French is there the preferred usage), a court all the better qualified to judge ability in this area because there ears and taste are constantly exercised. After arriving at these opinions, M. Glouch wanted to be able to support his argument in favour of the French language with a practical demonstration. By chance the tragic opera of *Iphigénie en Aulide* fell into his hands. He believed that in this work he had found what he was seeking.

The author or, more correctly, the editor of this poem seems to me to have followed Racine with the most scrupulous accuracy. It is his very own *Iphigénie* made into an opera. To attain this end, it was necessary to shorten the text and to cut the episode of Eriphyle. In the first act, Calchas has been introduced in place of the confidant Arcas; by this means, the plot is set in motion, the subject-matter simplified, and the tauter action progresses more quickly towards its end. These alterations have in no way diminished the interest: it seems to me to be as complete as in Racine's tragedy. The omission of the episode with Eriphyle makes the denouement of that great man's play inappropriate for the opera, so it has been replaced by a dramatic denouement which should have an excellent effect; the author gleaned the idea for this as much from Greek tragedy as from Racine's own preface to his *Iphigénie*. The whole work is divided into three acts, a division which seems to me to be the best for a genre requiring a fast-moving plot. A brilliant divertissement has been introduced into each act, related convincingly to the subject-matter of which it forms a part, and emerging from the plot in such a way that it either enhances the action or completes it. Great pains have been taken to create contrasts between situations and between characters, producing that piquant variety necessary to hold the spectator's attention and sustain the interest throughout the duration of the performance. Without recourse to machines or very expensive effects, a way has been found to provide the spectator with a noble and magnificent spectacle. I think there has never been a new opera requiring less expense but at the same time producing a more sumptuous effect. The author of this poem, the complete performance of which should take no more than two-and-a-half hours including the divertissements, has made it his task to use Racine's thoughts and even his verses, when the circumstances of the differing genres permitted. These verses have been inserted so skilfully that it is impossible to detect any inconsistency in the total style of the work. The subject of *Iphigénie en Aulide* seemed to me to be especially well chosen in that by following Racine as closely as possible, the author is assured of the effect of his work, and this certainty of success will fully compensate him for what he might lose in self-esteem.

The name of M. Glouch alone, monsieur, would exempt me from speaking of the music of this opera, if the pleasure which several hearings have given me allowed me to remain silent. It seems to me that this great man has expended all the resources of his art in this composition. A simple, natural vocal line, always shaped by the most accurate and sensitive expression, and by the most seductive melody, an inexhaustible variety of theme and treatment, the grandest harmonic effects equally at the service of terror, pathos, and charm, recitative which is rapid but also noble and expressive in its style, in effect, our very own French recitative perfectly declaimed, the most varied airs for dancing, written in the latest fashion and with a most pleasing freshness, choruses, duets, trios, quartets, all equally scrupulously observed— everything in this composition seems to me to be in our tradition, nothing struck me as being foreign to French ears. It is the work of ability; M. Glouch is at once both poet and musician, and everywhere gives evidence of his genius and his taste; nothing is weak or careless.

You know well, monsieur, that I am no partisan, and that in the disputes which have arisen over the advocacy of musical styles, I have maintained an absolute neutrality. I am therefore persuaded that you will not be prejudiced against the praise which I have here heaped upon the opera *Iphigénie*. I am convinced that you will be eager to applaud it. I know that no one wishes more than you to see advances in your art. You have already contributed much by your productions and by the recognition which I have seen you give to those who distinguish themselves in them. You will, therefore, both as a man of talent and as a good citizen, be pleased to see a foreigner as famous as M. Glouch working in our language, and defending it in the eyes of all Europe from the calumnious imputations of our native authors.

M. Glouch would like to know whether the management of the Académie de musique would have sufficient confidence in his abilities to decide to put on his opera. He is prepared to make the journey to France, but he wishes to be assured in advance both that his opera will be given, and approximately when this might be. If you have nothing arranged for the winter, for Lent, or for the reopening after Easter, I think you could not do better than to assign him one of these periods. M. Glouch has received a pressing invitation to Naples for next May; he does not want to accept any offer from that quarter, and is determined to sacrifice the rewards offered him if he can be assured that his opera will be accepted by your Académie, to whom I beg you to communicate this letter, and inform me of their decision, which will decide that of M. Glouch. I would be greatly flattered to share with you, monsieur, the honour of demonstrating to our nation her language's true potential, enhanced by the art which you profess. With this expression of my sincerest regard, I am, monsieur,

Your most humble and obedient servant,

[Du Roullet]

PS   If the management has not sufficient confidence in the judgement which I have formed of the text of this opera, I will send it to you at the earliest opportunity.

I forgot to tell you, monsieur, that M. Glouch, very disinterested by nature, asks no more for his work than the sum fixed by the management for the authors of new operas.[1]

The letter gave new life to a long-running controversy. Du Roullet's blatant flattery was satirized by Forkel in an article 'in which a composer may learn how to arouse the enthusiasm of the director of the Académie royale de Musique in Paris for a new opera'.[2] The poet and scholar Michel-Paul Guy de Chabanon was prompted to contribute to the old debate on the suitability of the French language for opera, initiated by Rousseau in 1753 through his *Lettre sur la musique française*.[3] Then Gluck entered the campaign with another of the formal declarations with which he was becoming accustomed to signal the stages of his reform:

---

[1] Vienna, 1 Aug. 1772, pub. as 'Lettre à M. D., un des directeurs de l'Opéra de Paris', *Mercure de France*, Oct. 1772, 169–74. Reproduced in François Lesure (ed.), *Querelle des Gluckistes et des Piccinnistes* (Geneva, 1984), i. 1–7; Jean-Georges Prod'homme, *Écrits des musiciens* (Paris, 1912), 387–93. The opera performed in Bologna in 1771 was *Orfeo*. The chief representative of the French writers who 'have dared to denigrate the French language' is Rousseau.

[2] 'Schreiben, woraus ein Componist lernen kann, auf welche Weise man den Direktoren der Académie royale de Musique in Paris Lust zu einer neuen Oper machen müsse', in *Musikalischer Almanach für Deutschland*, 4 (1789) 151–63.

[3] 'Lettre de M de Chabanon sur les propriétés musicales de la langue française', *Mercure de France*, Jan. 1773, 171–91.

I might be justly reproached, and I would seriously reproach myself, if, after having read the letter written from here to one of the directors of the Académie royale de musique, which you published in the *Mercure* last October, on the subject of the opera *Iphigénie*, if, I say, after having expressed my gratitude to the author of this letter for the praises he was pleased to heap upon me, I did not hasten to declare that he was undoubtedly influenced by friendship and too warm a partiality, and that I am very far from deceiving myself that I deserve the praise he lavishes on me. I would be even more seriously to blame if I were to take the credit for the invention of a new genre of Italian opera, the attempt at which has been vindicated by success: the principal merit belongs to M. de Calzabigi. And if my music has had some acclaim, I must acknowledge my debt to him, because it is he who set me on the path to develop the resources of my art. This writer of invention and ability has, in his poems *Orfeo*, *Alceste*, and *Paride*, followed a path unfamiliar to the Italians. These works are full of those choice situations, and moments of terror and pathos, which provide the composer with the opportunity to represent great emotions and to create powerful, moving music. Whatever ability the composer has, he will never write music which rises above mediocrity if the poet does not arouse in him that enthusiasm without which all artistic creation is flat and feeble. The imitation of nature is the acknowledged end at which all must aim. It is the one I endeavour to attain. Always as simple and natural as possible, my music aspires only to achieve the fullest expression and to follow the declamation of the poetry. This is why I never use trills, passage-work, or cadenzas, which the Italians employ in profusion. Their language, which lends itself particularly well to this kind of writing, has therefore no advantages for me in this respect, though it has, without doubt, many others. But since I was born in Germany, such study as I have been able to make of the Italian and French languages is insufficient to enable me to appreciate the precise distinctions which could enable me to prefer one to the other, and I think that all foreigners should abstain from judging between them. I do, however, feel able to say that the language which suits me best will always be that in which the poet provides me with the most varied means to express the passions. It is this quality which I believed I found in the words of the opera *Iphigénie*, a poem which seemed to me to have all the power necessary to inspire me to write good music. Although I have never had occasion to offer my works to any theatre, I cannot blame the author of the latter to one of the directors for having suggested my *Iphigénie* to your Académie de musique. I confess that I would be delighted to produce it in Paris, because by the effect of this work, and with the help of the famous M. Rousseau of Geneva, whom I propose to consult, we might perhaps together, through seeking a type of melody which is noble, expressive, and natural, and declaimed exactly according to the prosody of each language and the character of each nation, manage to determine the means to achieve my plan—which is to produce a music fit for all nations and to do away with the ridiculous differentiation between national musical styles. I have studied this great man's writings on music, including the letter in which he analyses the monologue from Lully's *Armide*; they prove the extent of his knowledge and the accuracy of his taste, and have filled me with admiration. I am strongly persuaded that if he had chosen to apply himself to the practice of this art he might have realized the marvellous effects which the ancients attributed to music. I am delighted to have here the opportunity to make public my tribute of the praise I believe he deserves.

I beg you, monsieur, to be kind enough to publish this letter in your next *Mercure*.

I have the honour to be, etc.

Chevalier Gluck[4]

D'Auvergne responded by requesting to see the first act of *Iphigénie*. His cautious offer of a production depended on Gluck agreeing to supply six more works of the same kind.[5] Gluck took the precaution of enlisting the patronage of the *dauphine* Marie Antoinette. Finally, in the autumn of 1773, he was ready to set off for Paris. The following letter to Martini indicates his awareness of the difficulty of the undertaking:

Most Reverend Father and friend!

I have learned, reverend sir, through Sig. Teyber of your wish to have a portrait of me. Sensible as I am of the honour the wish does me, I am all the more sorry that I cannot come in person in the hope of finding a skilled artist on the spot, for I am certain that the pleasure of seeing you would render me more handsome.

His Excellency Count Durazzo, Imperial Ambassador to Venice and my good patron for many years, obtained a copy of the portrait of me made in Rome on the occasion of my last journey there, and he has had it altered by one of his young protégés to represent my present appearance and situation.

Of the compositions mentioned to you, I think only *Orfeo* is known over there. The others have obtained some approval at this court, and I am just on the point of going to Paris with the intention of producing the most recent of them, that is, *Iphigénie en Aulide*, in the great opera-house. The enterprise is certainly a bold one, and there will be considerable opposition, because it will run counter to national prejudices, against which reason is no defence. If I can be of service to you there, I am at your disposal.

---

[4] Letter to the editor of the *Mercure de France*, Vienna, 1 Feb. 1773, pub. Feb. 1773, 182–4. Reproduced in Lesure, *Querelle*, i. 8–10; Nohl, *Musiker-Briefe*, 15–17; Prod'homme, *Écrits*, 394–7.

[5] D'Auvergne's reply is not extant, but its content is reported in Reichardt, *Studien für Tonkünstler* (Berlin, 1739), iv. 67.

I am indebted to His Excellency the Ambassador for the favour of sending you the aforementioned portrait as soon as he returns from Venice. He values and promotes the fine arts, and has a special regard for you, although he has never made your personal acquaintance.

I am, reverend sir, with the greatest respect and friendship,

Your most devoted and obedient servant,

Cavaliere Cristoforo Gluck[6]

Gluck arrived in Paris in mid-November 1773. The painter Mannlich is an attractive source for this period. His descriptions of Gluck's appearance, behaviour in rehearsals, and manner in society are consistent with other sources, the closeness of the verbal parallels suggesting that Mannlich, writing in the early nineteenth century, may have relied on the contemporary *Mémoires secrets* to prompt his memory. The few discrepancies point to one significant difference between Mannlich's account and the journals of the period: writing with hindsight and in the light of preconceptions typical of the Romantic movement, Mannlich aimed to paint a picture of genius at work; he saw the composer as a larger-than-life figure, and emphasized his defiance of conventions. The journals provide more accurate insight into how Gluck's reputation was constructed on a day-to-day basis. Gluck's critical attitude to the Parisian musicians, for example, was at first smoothed over by diarists, until they found that the stormy rehearsal scenes carried their own news value. On 24 March 1774, the *Mémoires secrets* had reported that 'this foreigner is delighted with our actors and especially with our orchestra, who perform his composition with the greatest precision.'[7] Mannlich tells a different tale of the composer he came to know when Gluck took up residence in the *hôtel* of Duke Christian IV, in whose household Mannlich was court painter. Since Mannlich did not come to Paris till February 1774, Gluck had presumably already spent more than two months in furnished lodgings before his move to more congenial accommodation:

My Lord the Duke, who loved the French while hating their music, invited Gluck (who had just arrived in Paris to produce one of his operas) to come and stay in his residence, an invitation which Gluck accepted with genuine gratitude. Several people were moved up a floor to make an apartment for the Chevalier Gluck, who had with him his wife, his [adopted] daughter, a chambermaid and a manservant. He became my nearest neighbour: my studio had

---

[6] Vienna, 26 Oct. 1773, reproduced in Nohl, *Musiker-Briefe*, 19–20; Schmid, *Gluck*, 475. The portrait is discussed in Croll, 'Il mio ritratto'.

[7] vii. 167.

a door opening onto his lodgings. His opera *Iphigénie* was well advanced; already the first two acts were in rehearsal, and the rehearsals were always stormy, because the Chevalier was openly at war with his poet, M. du Roullet, Knight of Malta, who would refuse to sacrifice lines by Racine to have them substituted by words the composer thought more 'musical'. He was also at war with the orchestra and the singers, who, in his opinion, knew neither how to sing, nor to declaim, nor how to get the best out of their instruments. Their French vanity was sorely wounded to be taught all these things by a Teutonic master; they would have more easily bent to the yoke of an Italian. Mme Gluck trembled every time she attended those opera rehearsals, which might be described as lessons in taste, singing, and declamation, that he tried to impose on the accomplished singers and instrumentalists. (These, adulated by the Parisians and accustomed to the applause of their compatriots, genuinely thought they were the finest virtuosi in the world.) She accompanied him every day throughout the course of these tumultuous lessons, called rehearsals, in order to calm his ardent, Germanic plain speaking.

The whole public joined in the dispute; they were naturally on the side of Lully and Rameau, and seemed pledged not to admit any other taste, or any other style than that which had for so long delighted them. This was the state of things when Gluck, with his family, moved into his apartment in the residence.[8]

Du Roullet made sure that his attempt to resist Gluck's interference in the libretto was well known. His preface, quoted in both the *Mercure de France* and the *Mémoires secrets*, attempted to anticipate and deflect criticism:

It will doubtless seem surprising that in adapting one of Racine's immortal masterpieces for our lyric theatre, more of its beauties have not been retained, and particularly that in preserving several of the great poet's thoughts and images, these have been expressed in other words than his. But we were working under orders; it was necessary either to submit or to abstain from making known in France a new type of music never before heard there.[9]

Mannlich's descriptions of the Gluck family are the more valuable in that he observed Gluck with a painter's eye:

It was the first time I had seen this famous man, whom all Paris was discussing so extensively and so variously. I am here going to attempt to sketch his portrait from memory. Although it is almost thirty-nine years since I lost sight of

---

[8] Mannlich, 'Mémoires', 161–2.   [9] *Iphigénie en Aulide*, libretto (Paris, 1774).

him, the impression which he made on me, and the true, sincere friendship I felt for him, have so impressed his traits and mannerisms in my memory and in my heart that I seem to see and hear him.

Those who met Gluck without recognizing him, in his greatcoat and round wig, would certainly not have realized at first glance that here was a great man, a creative genius. His figure was above average height; without being stout, he was stocky, strong, and very muscular; his head was round, his face broad, ruddy, and pock-marked; his eyes were small and rather deep-set, but sparkling, fiery, and expressive.

His nature was blunt, animated, and quick-tempered. He was incapable of conforming to the rules and conventions of polite behaviour in the fashionable world. Bluntly spoken, he called a spade a spade, and for this reason he would shock the delicate ears of the Parisians twenty times a day, accustomed as they were to the flattery and exchange of white lies which go by the name of polite behaviour. Untouched by praise when it issued from those whom he did not esteem, he only wanted to please true connoisseurs. He loved his wife, his daughter, and his friends, while never petting them or pandering to them.

He was given to copious eating and drinking, without ever becoming intoxicated or dyspeptic. He was self-seeking, unashamedly fond of money, and did not conceal a strong tendency to egotism, especially at table, where the choicest morsels belonged to him by right. This is a true portrait of the famous Chevalier Gluck and it does not flatter him.

His wife's conduct was as simple as it was dignified; she loved her husband with devotion, watched over his smallest acts, knew how to master him without appearing for a moment to cease to be subject to his wishes. He had no children; he had adopted and taken to live with him the daughter of his brother[-in-law], a lieutenant-colonel in the service of the emperor. She was 16 years old, shorter than average height for a woman; very handsome, very pale, with blue eyes in a face more long than round, a generous mouth, and very white teeth. She was very well brought up, light-hearted, gentle, pleasant, full of spirit, and above all gifted.[10]

Gluck's conduct of the rehearsals soon became the talking-point of Paris:

Every day, from nine till noon, M. Gluck attended the rehearsals of his opera. When he returned from them, accompanied as always by Mme Gluck, he was bathed in sweat from the exertion. Then, without saying a word to him, Mme Gluck would remove his wig, rub his head with a hot towel, and change his clothing. He was prostrated and did not speak again till meal-time . . .

[10] Mannlich, 'Mémoires', 163.

Mme Gluck did not hesitate to share with me the fears and worries she felt daily at the rehearsals in the Opéra, where on the one hand her husband's unyielding resolution, and on the other the singers' and musicians' ill will, made her dread disagreeable scenes and consequences. 'I would be greatly obliged to you, my dear neighbour, if out of kindness to us, you could attend these rehearsals, help me restrain my husband within the limits required by French manners, and diminish the hostility that the orchestra and above all the women singers have for him.' I gladly promised to do my best, and from that day onwards I did not fail to go with them to the rehearsals. Mme Gluck stayed in a box, but I would go sometimes to the orchestra but most often onto the stage, among the actors.

The overture and two-thirds of the opera had already gone reasonably well, although the composer still found a thousand things to repeat, making them start again twenty times 'from the top'. But when it came to work on performing the third part, Gluck ran about like one possessed, from one end of the orchestra to the other; sometimes it was the violins who offended, sometimes the basses, or the horns, or the violas, etc. He stopped them short and sang them the passage, with the expression he required, but soon stopped them again, crying at the top of his voice, 'That's damnable rubbish!' On several occasions I could envisage the moment when all the violins and other instruments besides would be sent flying at his head. Being acquainted with the leader of the orchestra, and M. Canavas, whom I had often seen at the house of Mme Vanloo, I begged them to calm the hotheads, and to persuade them that M. Gluck, as a foreigner, did not always know the strength of the expressions he let slip when carried away, that he was far from wanting to give offence, but that he held dear the success of his opera, and wanted them all to share the credit with him, etc., consequently they must ignore his brusqueness at this critical moment, on which all the success of the work depended. These gentlemen, who in any case knew very well that Gluck was in the right, took the hint and calmed the others.

In one of these scenes, M. Gluck was down stage, in the thick of things, listening to each instrument, when the basses made a mistake. He turned his head so rapidly in their direction that his old round wig could not follow the swift movement; it froze and fell to the ground. In his enthusiasm for the music, he was unaware of the incident, and saw no more than that Mlle Arnould, with mock-seriousness, having picked up the wig from the floor with two fingers, the other fingers extended, replaced it on his head. When it came to the turn of the singers, Mlle Arnould complained that in her role as Iphigenia there was only recitative and that she wanted to sing great arias. 'To sing great arias,' replied Gluck, 'you have to know how to sing.' 'Oh well,' said the famous actress, as much astonished as nettled by this truth, 'since you have so little confidence in me, you won't be surprised if I tell you that I no longer have any confidence in the success of your opera. I care very little about singing in it and sharing in its glory.' 'If you mean what you have just said, mademoiselle, have the goodness to repeat it! I've already found someone who can replace you right away.' The witty Sophie did not long withstand the German Orpheus. Her jokes could not extricate her from the situation and she did not try them. She had to yield, follow his advice, take lessons from him like a schoolgirl, and put a brave face on it.[11]

Sophie Arnould was not the only singer to fall foul of Gluck during the *Iphigénie* rehearsals. The baritone Henri Larrivée, who sang Agamemnon, features in a widely told anecdote, which paints a more benign portrait of Gluck in rehearsal. This is how Salieri relates it:

There was at the great Paris Opéra, during the time when Gluck's immortal masterpieces were spreading astonishment and delight there, a popular singer and actor by the name of Larrivée, who boasted that he could bring such variety to his representation of characters on the stage, through appropriate alteration of his voice, his singing style, his bearing, his acting, etc. that, as he used to declare, 'his best friend would not be able to recognize him'. . . . At the first rehearsal Gluck well pleased with everything that befell; only a single place seemed to him to lack the spirit of the role, and he amicably pointed this out to the singer. But the latter replied, 'Only let me get into costume, and you won't recognize me.' The master waited patiently for the complete run-through, which in that theatre was always done with costumes and scenery just like a first night. Gluck, who sat in one of the boxes near the stage, in order to judge his music from the position of a member of the audience, noticed that the place in question was no better than in earlier rehearsals, and called out to Larrivée, 'I spy you, my friend!'[12]

Gluck's reputation in these months rested not only on his notoriety as disciplinarian, but on his position as the representative of new French music against the supporters of both the old French music (of Lully and Rameau) and the new Italian music (Piccinni). The latter rivalry, which was not seriously to trouble Gluck for another two years, was attributed to competition between the adherents of the Countess Du Barry, mistress of Louis XV, and those of Marie Antoinette, who had supported Gluck from the moment of his arrival in Paris. The *Mémoires secrets* had reported on 14 January: 'As Gluck has the honour of being known to the *dauphine*, it is hoped he will have sufficient support to put on his opera. The princess has

---

[11] Mannlich, 'Mémoires', 164–6.   [12] Mosel, *Anton Salieri*, 76.

PLATES

PLATE I. Gluck, oil painting, anonymous, 1773; copy of portrait made in Rome in 1756. Reproduced by permission of Giovanni Battista Martini Conservatorio di Musica, Bologna. (*Discussed in Chapter 12*)

PLATE II. Gluck, oil painting by Jean-Silfrède Duplessis, 1775. Reproduced by permission of the Kunsthistorisches Museum, Vienna. (*Discussed in Chapter 15*)

PLATE III. Gluck, copy of bust by Jean-Antoine Houdon, 1775.
Reproduced by permission of the Herzogin Anna Amalia Bibliothek,
Weimar. (*Discussed in Chapter 15*)

IV(a)

Meiner frau macht ihm ihr Compliment wegen
der Veränderung ihres stand und glück, und
wir wünschen ihm alles gutes mit sambt Ihrer
gantzen familie.

Wan sie fein mahl ein hübsch gütl hörung
vor mich auß fündig machen, welches die gewisse
interessen tragt, so bericht sie fl mir. Womit
Verbleibe

Meiner hochgschätzter
Hr. Schwagers

Wien den 16 Jenner
1769

ergebener rur Diener
Chevalier Gluck

IV(b)

Madame

On m'a si traccassè sur la Musique, et j'en suis si degoutè, qu'à present
je n'écrirois pas seulement une notte pour un louis; conçevez par là
Madame, le degrè de mon devouement pour vous, puisque j'ai pu me
resoudre à vous arranger pour la Harpe les deux chansons, que j'ai
l'honneur de vous envoyer. jamais on a livrè une battaglie plus
terrible, et plus disputée de celle que j'ai donnè avec mon opera Armide,
les cabales contre Iphigenie, Orfée, et Alceste n'etoint que des petites
rencontres entre les trouppes legeres en comparaison. l'Ambassadeur
de Naples pour assurer un grand succes à l'opera de Piccini, est infati=
=cable pour cabaler contre moi tant à la cour, que parmi la Noblesse,
il a gagnè Marmontel, la Harpe, et quelques accademiciens pour ecrire
contre mon sisteme de Musique, et ma maniere de composer, M.r l'Abbè
Arnaud, M.r Suard et quelques autres ont pris ma defence, et la querelle
s'est échauffè au point, qu'après des injures ils seroint venu aux faites
si les amis comunes n'auroint pas mis l'ordre entre eux; le journal
de Paris qu'on debite tous les jours en est plein, cette dispute fait la
fortune du redacteur, qui a deja au dela de 2500 abbonnes dans Paris.
Voilà donc la revolution de le Musique en France, avec la pompe la
plus éclatante, les entousiastes me disent: Monsieur, vous etes heureux de
jouir des honneurs de la persecution, tous les grands genies ont passè par
là, je les envoyerai volontier au Diable avec leur beaux discours.

V(a)

PLATES V(a) AND V(b). Autograph letter from Gluck to Anna von
Fries, dated Paris, 16 November 1777. The Mary Flagler Cary Music
Collection in the Pierpont Morgan Library, MFC G 5675. F 912.
Reproduced by permission of the Pierpont Morgan Library, New
York. (*Discussed in Chapter 19*)

la fait est, que l'opera qu'on disoit d'être tombé, a produit en 7 represen=
=tations 37200 livres, sans compter les loges louez par l'Année, et sans
les abonnées. hier 8me representation on a fait 5767 livres, jamais
on a vu une plaine si terrible, et un silence si soutenu, le parterre
etoit si serré, qu'un homme qu'avoit le chapeau sur la tête, et à que la
sentinelle disoit de l'oter, lui a repondu, venez donc vous même à me
l'oter, car je ne puis pas faire usage des mes bras, cela a fait rire,
j'ai vu des gens en sortant les cheveux delabré, et les abits ßraignés,
comme s'ils étoint tombez dans une riviere; il faut être Francois, pour
accheter un plaisir à ce prix la; il y a 6 endroits dans l'opera qui
forcent le public à perdre la contenance, et desenporter. Venez y Madame
à voir tout ce tumulte, il vous amusera autant que l'opera même,
je suis au desespoir de ne pouvoir pas encore partir à cause du mauvais
chemin, ma femme a trop de frayeur. je vous prie de faire mes com=
=plimens à Monsieur le Baron, et à Monsieur Gontard, je suis
avec la consideration la plus parfait

Madame

P:S: ma femme vous fait mille
tendres complimens.

Paris 16 Novembre
1777.

votre treshumble et tres obeissant
serviteur le Chevalier Gluck

V(b)

admitted him to her presence at all times.'[13] A later entry (3 April) reveals the formation of a counterplot:

The supporters of the Countess Du Barry have advised her that she could not enhance her fame more effectively than by undertaking a conspicuous sponsorship of the arts; they have urged her to take up a rival position to the *dauphine* in this respect, and as the princess strongly protects the Sr Gluck and has fostered his coming to France, they have persuaded her to set up a competitor to Gluck in the person of the Sr Piccinni, whom she is to summon from Italy.[14]

The first complete dress rehearsal (*répétition générale*) was given on Saturday 9 April, and attracted a great crowd. Rumour had it that the Countess Du Barry watched the triumph of her rival's favourite from behind a specially erected grille. The first performance, planned for Tuesday 12 April, was deferred for a week because of Larrivée's indisposition:[15]

The day is awaited with the greatest of impatience. No one doubts that it will mark a milestone in our music. This work, to the delight of the connoisseurs, is remarkable for is expressive power; the composer has contrived a vocabulary and a style for every emotion. He himself is so absorbed in his work that when he is on stage he hears and sees nothing but the characters he is concerned with; he expends himself in convulsive outbursts, surely symptomatic of the demon which possesses him. Moreover, the execution was first-rate, and the singers, carried away by the composer's genius, acted incredibly well, even the S[r] Le Gros, who till now could never be called an actor.[16]

The première took place on 19 April 1774. The *Mémoires secrets* emphasized the role of the *dauphine* in securing a degree of success:

The Chevalier Gluck did not have as complete a success as his supporters had predicted. The greater part of the applause lavished on him could well be attributed to the audience's desire to please the *dauphine*. This princess seemed to have manipulated the acclaim, and would not stop clapping, which

[13] *Mémoires secrets*, vii. 125–6.

[14] Ibid. vii. 174. Piccinni's invitation was urged by Domenico Carraccioli, Neapolitan ambassador to Paris.

[15] For the Du Barry rumour, see ibid. xxvii. 238–9 (13 Apr. 1774). For Larrivée's illness and the postponement, see ibid. xxvii. 239–40 (13 Apr. 1774), also Reichardt, 'Fortsetzung', 73.

[16] *Mémoires secrets*, vii. 178–9 (10 Apr. 1774).

obliged the Countess de Provence, the princes, and all those in the boxes to do the same.[17]

Evidence of keenly partisan support in court circles emerges from a variety of documents. Count Mercy-Argenteau, Austrian ambassador to Paris, hastened to send an enthusiastic report back to Vienna concerning 'our celebrated Gluck': 'This music is expected to mark a milestone in the reformation of French music, which is, as you know, very vapid and monotonous.'[18] The *dauphine* sent news of the première to her sister:

What a triumph we had at last, my dear Christine, on the 19th, at the first performance of Gluck's *Iphigénie*; I was quite carried away by it, and could talk of nothing else. Everyone is in a greater ferment over this event than you could imagine; it is incredible. People are divided and antagonistic, as if it were a religious matter. At court, there are factions and remarkably sharp discussions, although I have spoken publicly in favour of this work of genius, and it seems things are even worse in town. I had desired to see M. Gluck in advance of the trial of the performance, and he himself expounded to me his strategy to establish what he calls the true character of music for the stage, and to bring it back to nature: if I may judge this by the effect it had on me, he has succeeded better than he could have wished. M. le Dauphin was roused from his composure, and found something to applaud throughout. But at the performance, as I expected, whenever there were affecting passages, there was a general air of holding back; this new approach needs getting used to after being so accustomed to the old one. Today everyone wants to hear the piece, which is a good sign, and Gluck seems very satisfied; I am sure you will be as happy as me at this event . . . Gluck has written me out several passages of his music which I sing at the keyboard. Farewell.

Marie Antoinette[19]

Daily fluctuations in public opinion are registered in the *Mémoires secrets*. Successive entries show how Gluck's opera gradually won adherents:

The crowds were no less on Friday [22 April] for *Iphigénie*, and the tickets for the stalls and other seats became objects of speculation, with individuals secur-

---

[17] *Mémoires secrets*, vii. 185–6; this entry is dated 21 Apr. 1774 and refers incorrectly to the première occurring 'yesterday'.

[18] Maria Theresia, *Correspondance secrète entre Marie Thérèse et le Comte de Mercy-Argenteau*, ed. Alfred von Arneth and Mathieu Auguste Geoffroy (Paris, 1874), ii. 131 n. 1.

[19] Marie Antoinette to Marie Christine, Versailles, 26 Apr. 1774, in *Correspondance inédite de Marie Antoinette*, ed. Paul Vogt de Hunolstein (Paris, 1864), 48–50.

ing them and reselling them at six, twelve, or fifteen francs, etc. The entrance to the stalls had to be guarded to control the crowd and ensure that no one was crushed. For the rest, the opera seemed to have been much better received. The ear, still unused to this type of sung declamation, begins to be accustomed to it and to distinguish its qualities. It is incontestably to the credit of the composer that although the scenes are sometimes very long, the recitative is not tedious, because one is constantly moved by the passions which stir the actors; and in contrast to other operas in the same vein, it is the dances and the divertissements which have become the wearisome part, because they are quite insignificant, they do not relate to the plot, and they express nothing. Another innovation is the silence of the orchestra between the acts. Such a thing has never happened till now, and it allows the listener to calm down if he has been strongly roused by what has gone before.[20]

Gluck was given a lengthy ovation ('lasting half of a quarter of an hour') but, suffering the physical reaction habitual to him, was unable to acknowledge it in person, being ill in bed.

It was not long before the opera received professional scrutiny. Although most reactions to the work were governed by strict partisanship, one notable conversion showed that it was possible to change sides. Mannlich attaches this vivid anecdote to the occasion of the final rehearsal:

On our return to the residence [on 17 April], Gluck asked me to stay to dine with him (a frequent occurrence for me). We were taking dessert when a little Savoyard brought a letter addressed to him; he opened it and, as was his custom, he began by looking at the signature. I was surprised to see that he was moved by it and was reading it with unmistakable pleasure. 'Ah!' he cried, after reading it through twice, 'here at last is praise in which I can delight; I have not been wasting my time, then. Come, read it,' he said, giving it to me, 'read it aloud!' As far as my memory serves me, it was couched more or less in these terms: 'M. le Chevalier, I have just come from the rehearsal of your opera *Iphigénie*: I am delighted with it. You have brought about that which up till this moment I thought impossible. Be so good as to receive my most sincere compliments and humble greetings. J.-J. Rousseau. Paris 17 April 1774.'[21]

From this moment Rousseau won won over to Gluck's cause. Grimm notes the conversion, which was thought remarkable by his friends:

---

[20] vii. 186–7 (23 Apr. 1774).
[21] 'Mémoires', 166–7. Rousseau's letter has never been traced.

Jean-Jacques has become the most zealous advocate of [Gluck's] new system. He has declared, with a readiness to self-abnegation little known among our wise men, that he has been mistaken till now, that M. Gluck's opera throws all his theories into reverse, and that he was now totally convinced that the French language could be as apt as any other for strong, passionate, and expressive music.[22]

Gluck's own theories had already been laid before the Parisian public in a translation of the *Alceste* preface published in the *Gazette de politique et de littérature*.[23] One of his most articulate—and most prejudiced—supporters was the Abbé François Arnaud.[24] His detailed, at times technical, analysis of *Iphigénie* shows, however, that his partisanship was informed and rational:

Listen to the overture; observe how, having bound the opening of it to the subject, not by vague connections but by the very structure, the composer suddenly brings in all the instruments on the same note; how, after having climbed in unison to the octave above this note, the instruments separate and converge, each one independent of the rest, in order to prepare the mind for a great event . . .

What is sublime, what can only emanate from a profound sensitivity, roused and stirred into action by genius, is the manner in which the composer signals and articulates the cries which Nature provokes in the depths of Agamemnon's heart. This mournful voice in the oboes with its sombre answer from the basses, the chromatic progression in the vocal line and in the distant accompaniment—this soft consonant infilling which, bridging the plaintive monosyllables of the oboes and basses, harmonizes and unites the orchestral strands, without detracting from the effect of the dialogue—these are beauties which would cover a multitude of failings.[25]

The May 1774 issue of the *Mercure de France* devoted an extended section to *Iphigénie*, recapitulating Du Roullet's preface, his letter of August 1772, and Gluck's statement of February 1773; it also briefly acknowledged Arnaud's analysis.[26] Arnaud's letter was translated into German and pub-

---

[22] *Correspondance littéraire*, x. 416. A third ref. in the *Mémoires secrets* (vii. 187–8, 24 Apr. 1774) places the change of heart after the première, recording that Rousseau 'has attended two performances of *Iphigénie*, and admits that he is obliged to recant, and that good foreign music can be made on French texts'.

[23] Feb. 1774, reproduced in Lesure, *Querelle*, i. 15–17.

[24] 'Abbé Arnaud and several other learned persons became Gluck's zealous supporters.' Mannlich, 'Mémoires', 166.

[25] 'Lettre de M. l'A[bbé] A[rnaud] à Madame D['Augny], *Gazette de littérature*, Apr. 1774, reproduced in Lesure, *Querelle*, i. 29–39.

[26] pp. 157–80.

lished the following year in a small collection of documents gathered by Gluck's admirer, Riedel, to mark Gluck's growing international status.[27] A review of Riedel's pamphlet by Gluck's old adversary, Forkel, shows the rigour of the opposition. Forkel takes Arnaud's eulogy point by point, and supports his attack with extensive quotation from the score:

We find nothing praiseworthy in bringing in the instruments suddenly on one note and then having them rise to the octave above this note. A passage in which all the instruments sound in unison must have a certain degree of importance; its content must be so constructed that it merits performance by all instruments in unison, and to be given significance by the intrinsic splendour and power. If it has no particularly important and interesting content, if its content is not so focused and concentrated that it communicates to us a wholly significant musical thought in a short space, then it is as inappropriate to give it to all instruments in unison, thereby endowing it with an unearned splendour, as when an orator contrives to give powerful weight and expression to the most insignificant thing in the world. It needs to be a passage which is outstanding on account of its magnificence or because of some other form of beauty, in order to earn especially prominent and powerful performance.

In Herr Gluck's *all'unisono* passage, however, we find neither magnificence nor any other possible form of beauty to justify it and merit it being given the marked prominence of performance by all voices in unison.

. . . Who can find the plaintive voice of the horns [*sic*] when none are to be found? The sombre answer of the basses, the chromatic progression in the vocal line and in the instruments which ever accompany it in the distance . . . they are pure fantasies which only someone in a particular state of mind could impute to this passage, and which no disinterested music-lover would take to be true. Where are the horns with their broken and plaintive notes? Where is the chromatic progression in the vocal and instrumental parts? Is it chromatic if it moves through part of the circle of fifths? And finally, who can find such beauties in this passage, a single glance at which were sufficient to discover a thousand faults?[28]

Duke Christian was active in promoting his distinguished guest's interests. Mannlich reports that the day after the première, the duke congratulated Gluck on the success of his opera: 'Have a fair copy made of the score, and get it nicely bound so that it can be offered to the king. I myself will present you to the monarch as soon as it is ready.'[29] The presentation of the

---

[27] *Ueber die Musik des Ritters Christoph von Gluck*, ed. Friedrich Justus Riedel (Vienna, 1775). This was the basis for the earliest biographical entries on Gluck, in dictionaries by Gerber and Dlabač.

[28] *Musikalisch-kritische Bibliothek* (Gotha, 1778–9), i. 131–2, 148.   [29] 'Mémoires', 167.

score gave Mannlich the opportunity for further insights into Gluck's character:

The score of *Iphigénie* was bound in fine sky-blue satin, and my Lord the Duke took Gluck with him to Versailles. He was prepared for the occasion, and had donned a coat richly embroidered in gold.

At about two o'clock the duke brought Gluck back to the residence and sat down with us . . . at table. Our composer, who was that day dining later than was usual for him, and therefore devoting himself the more readily to satisfying his large appetite, said not a word of his reception at Versailles, and scarcely responded to the compliments the ladies made him on his great talent. My Lord the Duke seemed to me to be a little nettled by this silence. The custom was that when strangers, even those of high rank, were presented to the king, he would pause for barely a moment in crossing the gallery on his way to mass, and, without saying a word to them, would acknowledge them with no more than a nod of the head; but on this occasion he had stopped, surrounded by all the court, in order to speak to M. Gluck. He accepted the score with pleasure, thanked Gluck, and complimented him on the spectacular success his opera had met with. All the courtiers and the many observers were astonished by this, and asked themselves who this extraordinary man was. Soon all Paris knew of this mark of high favour, and M. Gluck's real reputation rose a hundred per cent in the estimation of the Parisians. He alone did not feel the full value of this. Eventually, the duke, amazed at his protégé's silence, asked him, 'Well, M. Gluck, are you pleased with the manner in which you were received and welcomed by the king?' 'Yes, my Lord,' he replied, 'I was told that His Majesty very rarely spoke to those who were presented to him: I ought therefore to be very flattered to see him stop and talk to me, and receive my gift. However, if I write another opera for Paris, I would rather dedicate it to a tax farmer, because he would give me [ducats] rather than compliments.' This reply froze the assembled friends, who were all good courtiers, and visibly displeased the duke, who changed the subject.

Without approving of M. Gluck, but knowing him more intimately, I regarded the affair in a different light from these gentlemen. He was uninhibited, and wiser than he seemed; he took no vanity in pleasing either great men or the masses; acclaim never went to his head. All questionable praise, that is to say praise coming from someone he thought unfit to judge, all distinction of rank based on chance, on the caprice of the nobility, or on wealth, had little value in his eyes. He distrusted reputations, and did not render them homage until he had investigated their foundation. I never heard him speak ill even of his antagonists, but he was at the same time very sparing of praise. He flattered no one, and wanted to please only through his abilities. If he did not get his own way, it was difficult, even armed with authority, to make him do what he did not want. Such a man needs must hold independence dear, and seek the means to ensure it in private life. That was the only reason why, without avarice, he loved money: he regarded it as the means to break the chains of slavery, of subjection to social convention, of the tedium of ministers' antechambers, of patronage and humiliation—inseparable companions of poverty. Without being ruthless in the pursuit of the money he needed to earn, he cherished that which he possessed as the guarantee of liberty, and the source of that independence which, for a man of his character, was beyond price.[30]

The final stage in the campaign for *Iphigénie* was marked by the publication of the score. After his unhappy experiences with the lengthy preparation and poor sales of *Orfeo*, Gluck took early steps to ensure that this time the score would be ready soon after the première. He entrusted the publication to Le Marchand, a decision which was to cause him great trouble in the following year. (His choice of Le Marchand may have been the result of a relationship established when the publisher had issued *Six ariettes nouvelles avec simphonie* from *La Rencontre imprévue*, undated, but before 1774.) The engraving was under way by February, and its progress is tracked in a surviving 'Mémoire des planches d'étain', which records the accounts for the period 14 February to 8 August 1774.[31] Licence to publish was granted on 4 August. The score was dedicated to the new king, Louis XVI, who had succeeded to the throne on 10 May, though the wording of the first sentence suggests that it had been prepared as an address to Louis XV:

Sire,

In accordance with the example of the Greeks, when Augustus, the Medicis, and Louis XIV welcomed and supported the arts, they had a more important object than to increase the number of amusements and entertainments; they saw this field of human knowledge as one of the most precious links in the political chain; they knew that only the arts have the power to soften men without corrupting them, and to make them governable without degrading them.

Since your accession to the throne, Sire, you have shown yourself to be moved by the same principles and the same outlook. While Your Majesty works ceaselessly at the sustenance and the happiness of your subjects, you do not disdain the homage I make so bold as to offer you, and in granting me the first proofs of your protection of the arts, you guarantee the happiness and the

[30] 'Mémoires', 168–9.
[31] F-Pn, Gluck lettres autographes, no. 21. Gluck evidently signed a contract with Le Marchand on 6 Mar., authorizing him to print not only the score, but any number of airs extracted from the opera: see Ch. 15 below.

pride of a foreigner who yields to no Frenchman in zeal, in gratitude, and in devotion to your sacred person.

It is with these sentiments together with the deepest respect that I am, Sire, Your Majesty's most humble and obedient servant,

Chevalier Gluck[32]

---

[32] Paris, 4 Aug. 1774, in *Iphigénie en Aulide*, score (Paris, 1774), fo. 2ʳ. Reproduced in Nohl, *Musiker-Briefe*, 22–3; Prod'homme, *Écrits*, 400–1.

13

SUMMER IN PARIS

(1774)

AFTER only five performances of *Iphigénie en Aulide*, the death of Louis XV on 10 May 1774 caused the theatres to be closed. During the period of mourning, Gluck prepared his next opera, the transformation of *Orfeo* into *Orphée et Euridice*. Calzabigi's libretto was translated by Pierre Moline, the opera was considerably amplified, and the castrato role rewritten for a tenor.[1] The première was on 2 August.

Meanwhile Gluck dined out, clearly in his element while giving previews of his opera and defending his dramatic theories. Numerous diaries record private gatherings, where 'after a good dinner and interesting conversation, some delightful music would be studied'.[2] As in Vienna, it was Gluck's single-handed representation of the furies that made the greatest impression:

It was at the dinners given by Abbé Morellet . . . that for the first time in Paris was heard Gluck's *Orphée*, which Jean-Jacques [Rousseau] had desired either never to hear or to hear constantly. At the first sounds of Millico singing the romance, all hearts were touched, and all eyes shed tears. . . . At the supplications to the spirits and the furies, hell itself seemed moved. And when Gluck alone, representing all the furies, made the terrible cries of 'No!' ring out . . . one seemed to see Millico surrounded by demons and flares, like Orpheus in hell.[3]

---

[1] For a detailed account of the changes between the two versions, see Patricia Howard, *C. W. von Gluck: Orfeo* (Cambridge, 1981).

[2] Amélie Suard, *Essais de mémoires sur M. Suard* (Paris, 1820), 97.

[3] Dominique-Joseph Garat, *Mémoires historiques sur la vie de M. Suard, sur ses écrits, et sur le XVIIIᵉ siècle* (Paris, 1820), i. 360–1. By 'romance' is meant the first aria, 'Chiamo il mio ben'/'Objet de mon amour'. See the discussion in Brown, *Gluck and the French Theatre*, 365.

Mme de Genlis, who had been a regular attender at the rehearsals and performances of *Iphigénie*, entertained Gluck twice a week: 'With no voice and no keyboard ability [*sans voix, sans doigts*], Gluck is captivating when he sings his beautiful airs, accompanying himself on the piano. . . . He made me sing all his lovely airs and play his overtures on the harp.'[4] Besides Millico, Gluck was invariably accompanied by his wife and niece. Nanette often sang, and her small voice was warmly praised, the Abbé Arnaud christening her 'the little muse'.[5] Count d'Escherny supplies a vivid detail on Gluck's conversation:

Gluck was a gifted man. He defended his system of opera very ably. He was Bohemian. He spoke three or four languages without knowing any of them properly; he mangled them all equally, which gave his conversation a hint of the unconventional and the unpolished which charmed and attracted more than studied speech. I always thought that he owed much to the warmth and energy he put into his conversation and opinions—these qualities sustained his operas.[6]

'We are all for Gluck at Ferney'.[7] Having notoriously converted Rousseau to his cause, Gluck soon found an equally illustrious adherent in Voltaire, who defended his taste in a series of letters to the Marquise du Deffant.[8] The marquise was a traditionalist, a supporter of Lully and Rameau; she found Gluck's music 'hateful . . . and neither French nor Italian'.[9] Voltaire responded by drawing parallels between the new music and the new king: 'It seems to me that you Parisians are about to witness a great and peaceful revolution both in your government and in your music. Louis XVI and Gluck will found a new French nation.'[10]

---

[4] Stéphanie Félicité Ducrest de Saint Aubin Brulart de Genlis, *Mémoires inédits de Mme la Comtesse de Genlis pour servir à l'histoire des dix-huitième et dix-neuvième siècles* (Paris, 1825–6), ii. 216–17 *passim*.

[5] In the memoirs of both Garat and Suard; see nn. 2 and 3 above.

[6] François-Louis d'Escherny, *Mélanges de littérature, d'histoire, de morale, et de philosophie* (Paris, 1811), ii. 366–7. D'Escherny was the brother-in-law of Gluck's banker, Baron von Fries. Gluck's articulate defence of his system is vividly reconstructed in Corancez's obituary; see Ch. 25 below. We need not take too literally Garat's assertion (*Mémoires historiques*, i. 356) that Gluck had Montaigne's essays by heart, but Corancez's claim that he had read 'all of Corneille, Racine, Molière, and La Fontaine' is probably true ('Lettre sur le Chevalier Gluck', *Journal de Paris*, 24 Aug. 1788, 1023).

[7] François-Marie Arouet de Voltaire to the Chevalier Delisle, 27 May 1774, in Voltaire, *Œuvres complètes* (Kehl, 1785–9), lxii. 330.

[8] Ibid. lxii. 335, lxiii. 16.

[9] Letter of 3 Aug. 1774, in Joseph Trabucco (ed.), *Lettres à Voltaire* (Paris, 1922), 231.

[10] Letter of 28 July, Voltaire, *Œuvres complètes*, lxii. 352–3. Voltaire uses almost identical language in a letter of 16 Aug. to Marin (ibid. lxii. 361): 'It seems to me that Louis XVI and M. Gluck will create a new era.'

Well before the première of *Orphée*, Gluck arranged for the publication of the score, which was issued in August simultaneously with that of *Iphigénie en Aulide*.[11] A letter records an act of unusual generosity, or carelessness, on Gluck's part, and marks the beginning of a troublesome relationship with the enterprising publisher Le Marchand:

I the undersigned acknowledge having given of my own free will, as of now, the manuscript score of my opera *Orphée et Euridice* to M. Marchand, giving him permission to have it engraved for his own profit, complete or in parts, as he thinks fit, on the understanding that no one shall interfere with the gift I have made him, and ceding to him all the rights in this work accorded to me through the *privilège* which I have obtained from the king, which, to prevent forgery by others, I give him so that he can act in my name; he will be responsible for such expenses as he will incur.

Chevalier Gluck.[12]

The score was dedicated to Queen Marie Antoinette:

Madame,

Overwhelmed with your acts of kindness, I consider the most precious to be that which keeps me in the midst of a nation, which is the more worthy to possess you in that it is aware of the extent of your virtue. Honoured by your protection, I undoubtedly owe to it the applause I have received. I have never aspired, as many have wished to accuse me of doing, to lecture the French on their own language, nor have I tried to prove that they have had no single author worthy of their admiration and recognition up to the present time. There exist here some works to which I have given the praises they merit; several of their living authors deserve their reputation. My intention was to try to adapt the new style of music, that I adopted in my last three Italian operas, to French words. I have noted with satisfaction that the accent of nature is a universal language. M. Rousseau has used it with the greatest success in the field of comic opera. His *Devin du village* is a model which no author has yet imitated. I do not know how far I have succeeded in my aim, but I know I have the approbation of Your Majesty, because you allow me to dedicate this work to you; that is the most flattering success I could have. The style I am trying to introduce seems to me to return art to its original dignity. Music will no longer be limited to the cold, conventional forms of beauty which authors used to be obliged to choose.

[11] Cecil Hopkinson, *A Bibliography of the Printed Works of C. W. Gluck 1714–1787*, 2nd edn. (New York, 1967), 38, 43.
[12] Paris, 10 July 1774: F-Pn, Fonds français 21966, 288. Pub. in Maurice Cauchie, 'Gluck et ses éditeurs parisiens', *Le Ménestrel*, 89 (1927), 309.

With this expression of the most profound respect, I am, Madame, Your Majesty's most humble and obedient servant,

Chevalier Gluck.[13]

In a telling phrase, Sara Goudar attributes the whole success of *Orphée* to the queen's support: 'Orpheus was likely to have remained entombed for ever in the underworld till at one of the performances a pair of beautiful hands clapped and applauded his strains. No more was needed to make him emerge from thence, glorious and triumphant. All Paris was delighted at it.'[14]

Long reviews in the *Mercure de France*[15] and the *Journal des beaux-arts*[16] analysed the opera scene by scene, the former concluding that 'The music . . . confirms the impression already given by the opera *Iphigénie* of the genius and great talent of the Chevalier Gluck for scene-painting and for expressing the heart's affections.'[17] Moline's libretto was more harshly judged. The *Journal des beaux-arts* noted a current criticism which compared Gluck unfavourably with Rameau, and *Orphée* with *Castor et Pollux*:

M. Gluck appears to have sustained in *Orphée* the reputation which *Iphigénie* won for him in France, and perhaps *Orphée* only seems inferior because of the enormous difference between the two librettos. Some ill-humoured wits have called *Orphée* a 'demi-*Castor*', either because Orpheus, like Pollux, descends to the underworld, passes through the Elysian fields, resists their blandishments, and brings back the object of his desires, or because *Orphée* seems inferior to *Castor*—but in this latter case the epigram is unjust. If one compares libretto with libretto, it is too kind, and does too much honour to the libretto of *Orphée*; if one compares music with music, the epigram is so severe as to be untrue. The means which Rameau and M. Gluck have used to achieve equal success are so different that it would be almost impossible to make even a limited comparison.[18]

The tenor Joseph Le Gros in the title role received universal praise, and Gluck was complimented on his skilful training of a singer who 'sang the principal role with such warmth, taste, and even soul, that it is difficult to recognize him, and his metamorphosis is to be regarded as one of the major miracles wrought by Gluck's magic art.'[19] Perhaps Rousseau's was the

---

[13] *Orphée et Euridice* (Paris, 1774), fo. 3. Reproduced in Nohl, *Musiker-Briefe*, 23–4; Prod'homme, *Écrits*, 401–2.

[14] *Le Brigandage de la musique italienne* (Paris, 1780), 15.

[15] Sept. 1774, 190–8.

[16] Sept. 1774, 520–47.

[17] *Mercure de France*, Sept. 1774, 195.

[18] Sept. 1774, 546.

[19] Grimm (ed.), *Correspondance littéraire*, x. 473.

finest tribute to the opera; it was recorded by Jean-François de La Harpe, himself no Gluckist: 'If one can experience two hours of such great pleasure, I can understand that life may be worth living.'[20]

Gratified with this reception, Gluck considered making his permanent home in Paris. He used the Austrian ambassador to Paris, Count Florimond Mercy-Argenteau, to negotiate terms:

Your Excellency,

I can find no words to express to Your Excellency the gratitude I owe you for the zeal with which you have had the goodness to pursue my interests. But I do not think I could subsist in Paris on less than ten or twelve thousand *livres*, because I would need a carriage for my wife and a decent house. Moreover if I were to settle in Paris and give up my position in Vienna, I would need to be assured of this sum on a permanent basis, guaranteed and independent of any circumstance, even in the event of a change in the administration at the Opéra. Every year, unless I were to fall ill, I would give an opera without fee; I would also undertake to give advice and direct the studies of young composers who wished to consult me about their works, so that a standard of good taste might be established for all time. I would try to make the orchestra as excellent as possible; I would also coach the singers; and I would take all possible pains so that we might have the finest theatre in Europe. As for titles, I aspire to none unless it were the intention of the king or the queen to bestow one; I wish only to have the authority necessary to change certain abuses which hamper the perfection of our theatre. For the rest I leave everything to the percipience of Your Excellency, and I am sure that you will take my interests as much to heart as I do. I have the honour to be, with deepest respect, Your Excellency's most humble and most obedient servant,

Chevalier Gluck[21]

The count appears to have responded favourably, for Gluck's next letter to him gives the impression that his move to Paris had been informally agreed:

Your Excellency,

I do not know how to find words to express the gratitude I feel. Your Excellency has arranged everything admirably. The singers will improve at the pace at which I put on operas (to form a singing-school other

---

[20] *Correspondance littéraire*, 2nd edn. (Paris, 1804–7), i. 25.
[21] Gluck to Mercy-Argenteau, Paris, 11 Aug. 1774: F-Pn, Fac-Sim 147, no. 14. Pub. in L.R., 'Correspondance inédite de Gluck', *La Revue musicale*, 10 (1914), 1; Tiersot, 'Pour le centenaire de Gluck: Lettres et documents inédits', *Le Ménestrel*, 80 (1914), 215.

arrangements would have to be made); I shall however give all my attention to Mlle Rosalie [Levasseur], and I am hopeful that she will develop admirably.

If the court does not return until the beginning of next month, I would prefer to come to Compiègne, because I shall have more time to arrange my affairs in Vienna; but if Your Excellency thinks it better that I await the return of the court, I shall be pleased to stay till then; I await your orders on the matter. I make so bold as to ask Your Excellency again if I may tell my friends of the favour I have been granted, or if I must wait until the deed has been done with all the requisite formality. I have difficulty in keeping silent because the arrangements give me so much pleasure, in that I hope to be always near enough to pay my respects to Your Excellency in Paris, so that we can sometimes make fine music together. I have the honour to be, with deepest respect, Your Excellency's most humble and most obedient servant,

Chevalier Gluck[22]

Exactly what happened to these plans is not clear. No permanent position with the Opéra was forthcoming, and when Gluck left Paris for Vienna in mid-October, he was trying to negotiate his future contract on a more limited basis:

PRO MEMORIA

1. The Chevalier Gluck has received 3,000 *livres* from the Académie royale de musique for his opera *Iphigénie*, and 3,000 which he has received on behalf of the poet; he was promised an honorarium which he hopes to receive, particularly as his journeys to and from Paris, together with the expenses of his stay, come to at least 6,000 *livres*.

2. It has been agreed that he would receive the sum of 6,000 *livres* for each of the operas he might compose; he himself is not required to pay the poet, and if the poet were to give his poem without fee, he would still be paid 6,000 *livres* for his work, and [the poet] would ask nothing for the libretto. Thus when *Cythère assiégée* is put on, the Académie royale will itself undertake to recompense the poet, as it did on the occasion of *Orphée*.

3. As he has now fulfilled his engagements according to the contract granted him for 6,000 *livres*, he wants to know whether, if his contract is not renewed, he may from 8 October 1774 draw pro rata upon a sum equivalent to that which has previously been paid him.

4. If the Académie renews his contract, he undertakes to compose three more operas, namely *Alceste*, *Electre*, and *Iphigénie en Tauride*, or instead of one of the latter two, an opera in the vein of *Cythère assiégée*; he restricts his

---

[22] Paris, 16 Aug. 1774: F-Pn, Fac-Sim 147, no. 15. Pub. in L.R., 'Correspondance inédite', 1–2; Tiersot, 'Pour le centenaire', 215. Levasseur took the part of Cupid in *Orphée* and was to sing the roles of Alcestis, Armida, and Iphigenia (*Iphigénie en Tauride*); she was the count's mistress.

promise to this number, as his age and health do not permit him to promise more; in this event, he would return in the spring of 1776 to give two operas together, one for the summer, with the second [weaker] cast, and the other, which would be *Alceste*, for the season proper.[23] In this way he would be in a position to train the singers for the roles in which they would be employed. Furthermore, he believes that with the six operas he will have given, the groundwork of the revolution in music will have been achieved.

5. As he is on the point of leaving for Vienna, he begs to be informed at once what is intended on the subject of these articles.[24]

The Académie's reply is not extant. Although no permanent position was offered him in Paris, on his return to Vienna Gluck at last received the coveted promotion to the position of court composer, with a salary of 2,000 florins. Maria Theresia's interest in her employee had been stimulated by his success in Paris, and she acted to keep him in her service, 'on account of both his thorough knowledge of music and his proven ability in various compositions . . . and so that he may broaden his own exceptional artistic experience with all possible diligence.'[25] Gluck was to follow this directive to the letter.

[23] 'l'un pendant l'été pour les doubles': Gluck refers on several occasions to operas designed for the weaker singers; see his letter to Du Roullet, 1 July 1775 (Ch. 16 below), and Mercy-Argenteau's suggestion in a letter of 19 Jan. 1775 of 'a new piece, devised so that it could be sung by those weaker singers who are intended, in case of need, to understudy the first singers' (Ch. 14 below).

[24] Gluck to the Directors of the Académie royale, Oct. 1774: Fac-Sim 147, no. 16. Pub. in L.R., 'Correspondance inédite', 16.

[25] Tenschert, *Gluck . . . Reformator der Oper*, 194.

14

THE TRAVELLING COMPOSER
(1774–1775)

ON his return to Vienna in early November, Gluck received the following letter from Herder, offering the libretto of *Brutus*, which had already been set by J. C. Bach. The letter confirms Gluck's growing reputation as an innovator:

You will find enclosed, honoured Sir, a musical drama, a first reading of which will doubtless displease you. Please be so good as to allow me, therefore, to explain something of its purpose.

The great dispute between poetry and music, which has so deeply divided these two arts, concerns the question, which of them should serve, and which rule. The musician wants his art to rule, the poet likewise, and so they impede each other. Each aspires to create a beautiful entity, and often ignores the fact that he must supply only a part, for the entity arises only from the conjunction of the work of both.

Could it ever come about that the musician might yield, and be content to serve—and that in your musical compositions you have so noble an aim?

Or could it be the poet who is to yield, by only sketching in an outline, and inserting words only to give precision to the otherwise unspecific emotions in the music?—that is what is attempted here. He should be only what the inscription is to a painting or a sculpture, *explaining* and *directing* the stream of music, by inserting words into it here and there.

That is why, esteemed Sir, the reading will seem disjointed and broken up. It is to be heard, not read. The words should merely bring life to the stirring sounds of the music, and the music should speak, act, rouse, transport, following only the poet's spirit and outline.

But to which composer should the muse now turn? Not to one who conforms to the old rules of music, which make everything as comfortable as the armchair or couch, in which he periodically nods. Rather he should turn to one who fills each scene with action, emotion, and articulate thoughts, as when Portia and Brutus are *compelled* to pour out their hearts in speech. In short, he turns to Gluck.

It would be useless for me to attempt to say what the effect has been on me of the few pieces, in which I have heard *your* folk-like simplicity. Unfortunately I know only a few of them. But if, noble Sir, reading this moves you to be so kind as to look at this poem, and to set it, even if only in certain scenes and passages—I know what I am asking, and what I desire! But I will not ask! The outcome must be decided by a fortunate or an unfortunate spirit, aroused by the reading of this piece.

Plutarch's 'Life of Brutus' and Shakespeare's *Julius Caesar* tell it all, and this drama can only be a commentary on them in *musical hieroglyphics*.

Perhaps I have written in such a way that Brutus might be a noble German! And perhaps Gluck, if he does not hear him in vain, may feel himself to be a *noble German*.

With deepest respect,

Herder.[1]

Gluck's reply is lost. A few days later he set off for Paris again, with Maria Theresia's encouragement for him to build his reputation abroad: 'Gluck, having been admitted into our service with 2,000 florins' worth of appointments, asked me for permission to return to Paris for a period, which I willingly granted him.'[2] He broke his journey at the court of the Margrave of Baden in Karlsruhe, where he was warmly received. Here he met Klopstock for the first time. The visit is recorded in the following letter to a diplomat at the margrave's court; the writer is Gluck's friend and house guest, Johann Friedrich Riedel:

God knows, my dear friend, how your letter delighted my heart. . . . It was particularly interesting to me because it dealt with my friends. I had already predicted to them that they would be well received by you, and now Gluck's wife has told me that my prediction has been fulfilled. But it was precious to me to hear it also from you. It also pleased me that the 'deutsches Mädchen' [Nanette][3] won your approval. I have often debated with her whether there is anything superior to Paris, and I hope fervently I shall continue to debate it. You say nothing about Mme Gluck; perhaps you did not have much opportunity of talking to her. For wisdom and intelligence, she is truly a Solomon

---

[1] Bückeburg, 5 Nov. 1774: autograph in Graz, Steiermärkisches Landesarchiv Autographen-sammlung, HS 1506/2.

[2] Letter to Mercy-Argenteau, 11 Nov. 1774, in Maria Theresia, *Correspondance secrète*, ii. 251.

[3] The German maiden; the ref. is to one of Klopstock's odes, 'Ich bin ein deutsches Mädchen', set by Gluck, and often sung by his niece. The phrase became Nanette's soubriquet.

among women. . . . I would so much like to have seen Klopstock and Gluck together. Perhaps I shall see them on another occasion, for if Gluck goes again to Paris a few years hence, and I am still hale and hearty, I have not ruled out the possibility of accompanying him.[4]

Gluck had taken Riedel into his household in Vienna towards the end of 1774, to enable him to write an account of his operatic reform. The result was the short biography, together with documents indicating the warmth of the reception of *Iphigénie*, which Riedel published in 1775.[5] Gluck is alleged to have exploited his friendship ruthlessly, at least while the family were in residence in their country house in St Marx: 'Herr Riedel led an almost animal existence in Gluck's house, spending more time toiling in the garden with his shovel than in studying and writing.'[6] More details on the 'debate' about Paris are supplied by another source, which also provides a unique description of Mme Gluck at the keyboard:

For two evenings in succession [Gluck, his wife, and his niece] regaled the court with their heavenly music, though no one besides a few gentlemen, Klopstock, and I were admitted. The old man sang and played, truly *con amore*, many passages that he had set from the *Messiade*; in a couple of other pieces his wife accompanied him, and the delightful niece sang several times the song, by Klopstock, 'Ich bin ein deutsches Mädchen' quite enchantingly. . . . [On another occasion] I arrived late and took my place beside Mlle Gluck. 'You have come just in time,' said the charming girl, 'You shall judge between Herr Klopstock and me.' 'What is it all about?' I asked. 'Whether or not the French are a likeable nation. Klopstock insists that they are not, and will not give way, although Herr von P. here' (her neighbour on the right) 'and Herr von M. contradict him.' 'And you, mademoiselle,' I asked. 'Ah, I cannot say enough of how all Paris, from the highest to the lowest, has fêted me with favours and thoughtful acts and presents.' 'Then the question is decided,' said I.[7]

---

[4] Letter to Counsellor Ring, Vienna, 10 Dec. 1774, quoted in Heinrich Funck, 'Glucks Zusammentreffen mit Klopstock am Hofe Karl Friedrichs von Baden, 1774 und 1775', *Euphorion*, 1 (1894), 790–2.

[5] *Ueber die Musik*; see Ch. 12 n. 27.

[6] Tobias Philipp von Gebler, letter of 7 Nov. 1775, in Richard Maria Werner (ed.), *Aus dem Josephinischen Wien: Geblers und Nicolais Briefwechsel während der Jahre 1771–1786* (Berlin, 1888), 72.

[7] Georg Wilhelm Petersen to Johann Heinrich Merck, Karlsruhe, Nov. 1774, in David Friedrich Strauss, *Kleine Schriften* (Leipzig, 1862), 42–4. Strauss attributes the Paris debate to Gluck's return visit in Mar. 1775, but Riedel's letter (above) suggests otherwise, unless his 'often' implies that this was a constant topic of Nanette's conversation. The ref. to Klopstock's *Messiade* is presumed to be an error for *Hermannsschlacht*.

A further account of the visit is related by Carl Friedrich Cramer, whose *Magazin der Musik*, published between 1783 and 1786, contains a number of anecdotes on Gluck. Cramer's source was Klopstock himself:

Klopstock made Gluck's acquaintance at the court of the Margrave of Baden, where in the summer [*sic*] of 1774, Gluck spent a few days, together with his wife and niece. . . . Klopstock tells of how Gluck, sitting at the keyboard, would often interrupt his niece suddenly in the middle of a most delightful performance of a song, in the very presence of the court, breaking in quite sharply with, 'Stop! That was wrong! Do it again!' And if it so happened that someone in the company, even a connoisseur, thought they had noticed not the slightest error in intonation or in expression, and said to Gluck, 'But what was the error?', such a question put him in a complete 'musical indignation': 'What? You don't hear it? Woe betide you if you do not hear it! You lie!' For there was indeed some shade of refinement, which in the course of the piece no one but Gluck detected or could have detected.

He had his own hierarchy among his compositions, and there were some favourite pieces in which even his niece's singing did not satisfy him. In vain Klopstock wished to hear her sing his 'Sommernacht' ('Willkommen, O silbener Mond').[8] 'She cannot sing that yet!' he said, and sang the same work of Klopstock's in his own expressive voice. The piece appeared to be very easy—but the emotion! It was only in this way that its demands were made evident.[9]

Gluck arrived in Paris no later than 27 November: a bill for repairs to his coach records details of its maintenance between 28 November 1774 and 10 March 1775.[10] A revised version of *Iphigénie en Aulide* was given on 10 January 1775.[11]

Meanwhile in Vienna, Maria Theresia entered into a plan with Mercy-Argenteau to have members of the Opéra brought to Vienna to perform *Iphigénie en Aulide* on the occasion of the projected visit of her son, Archduke Ferdinand of Milan. Among an exchange of letters dealing mostly with the expense of the undertaking, the odd phrase throws light on the empress's view of Gluck's character: 'As I want to make the

---

[8] An apparent confusion: 'Die Sommernacht' is the fifth of Gluck's settings of Klopstock's odes; the song beginning 'Willkommen, O silbener Mond' is the sixth, entitled 'Die frühen Gräber'.

[9] *Magazin der Musik*, I (1783), 561–4. The material appears as an editorial footnote to Kämpfer's description of Gluck in Vienna; see Ch. 23 below.

[10] 'Mémoire des réparations faites à la voiture de Monsieur Clouc', 18 Feb. 1775, and 'Quittance faite à Paris', 10 Mar. 1775: F-Pn, Gluck lettres autographes, no. 22.

[11] For a discussion of the differences between the two versions, see Julian Rushton, ' "Royal Agamemnon": The Two Versions of Gluck's *Iphigénie en Aulide*', in *Music and the French Revolution*, ed. Malcolm Boyd (Cambridge, 1992), 15–36.

performance of this opera a surprise for the emperor [Joseph II], for my daughter, and for the public, I need to have the negotiations kept secret, and although I am of the opinion that you may speak of it to Gluck, you must be somewhat reticent, because I do not trust too much in his taciturnity.'[12] The count had to inform the empress that the forces of the Opéra were directly in the service of the king, and were not to be hired like any other troupe:

I consulted Gluck at once, enjoining him to secrecy in such a way that I am confident that he will not violate it. As it is impossible that the Paris Opéra should be suspended at any time, I suggested to Gluck that he might immediately compose a new piece, devised so that it could be sung by those weaker singers who are intended, in case of need, to understudy the first singers, the latter being indispensably necessary to perform the opera *Iphigénie*. The new work, on which Gluck is already working, will perhaps involve him in staying here a few weeks longer than his permission allows, but I dare to believe that Your Majesty will condescend to consent to this, in view of the fact that it will come about only as a necessary expedient in the execution of her wishes.

In seeking to diminish the obstacles as far as possible, Gluck has decided that five of the first singers and twelve voices for the choruses would suffice to put on his opera *Iphigénie*; it is, then, a matter of sending seventeen people to Vienna. The only way to transfer these singers would be by express order of the king, and there is not the slightest doubt that the monarch would have pleasure in accommodating Your Majesty in the matter; in this way, everything can be arranged so that the performances in Paris are not interrupted. . . . I conclude by mentioning that the people here would be certainly very flattered that Your Majesty wanted to see an entertainment on whose value the French nation has always prided itself, perhaps more than it should.[13]

The empress, clearly wary of incurring expense, was nevertheless reluctant to abandon her idea:

As a result of the information you send me about the footing on which the singers for the opera *Iphigénie* are employed in Paris, I find the idea of bringing them here as awkward as it is expensive. It is, therefore, no longer an issue—unless Gluck could bring a couple of them to give an idea of the performance, for the month of June until October; but I do not want to be involved in any expenditure, nor to burden myself with too many people.[14]

[12] Letter to Mercy-Argenteau, 15 Nov. 1774, in Maria Theresia, *Correspondance secrète*, ii. 253.
[13] Mercy-Argenteau to Maria Theresia, Paris, 19 Jan. 1775, ibid. ii. 285–7.
[14] Maria Theresia to Mercy-Argenteau, Vienna, 4 Feb. 1775, ibid. ii. 293–4.

Mercy-Argenteau responded with the suggestion of a further economy:

I made known to Gluck Your Majesty's wishes concerning the plan to have a trial of the French opera in Vienna, but I think they could be carried out without bringing singers from here; they could be easily substituted by French singers from touring companies. Gluck's skill will suffice to get the best from them, and thereby much certain expenditure will be saved.[15]

The empress found even this proposal too inconvenient, and dropped the entire project.[16] Whether Gluck's revision of the undemanding opéra-comique, *L'Arbre enchanté*, was made as a result of Mercy-Argenteau's suggestion of a work which could be performed by understudies is not proved. In January he was already working on a more extensive revision of *Cythère assiégée*. *L'Arbre enchanté* had, in any case, another function, since it was given on 27 February at Versailles, in honour of a visit by Archduke Maximilian. It may, however, be significant that it was performed not by members of the Opéra, but by the Opéra-Comique, with the original sung vaudevilles replaced by new spoken verses by Moline.[17]

Gluck set off to return to Vienna in mid-March 1775. On this short visit, he evidently had time to sit for his portrait to Duplessis, painter to the French court; he asked after the progress of this work later in the year.[18] Before leaving Paris, he appointed Franz Kruthoffer, secretary to Count Mercy-Argenteau, as agent to oversee the publication of his scores. Kruthoffer was to become Gluck's intimate friend, and the correspondence between the two contains the fullest sequence of Gluck's letters that has been handed down. He makes his first appearance in a formal document, granting him power of attorney to act on Gluck's behalf:

In the presence of the undersigned Privy Counsellors and notaries at the Châtelet, Mre Christophe de Gluck, Chevalier of the Holy Empire, residing in Paris at rue Villedot in the parish of St Roch, has made and appointed as his general attorney Sr François Kruthoffer, Secretary to the Ambassador of their Imperial and Royal Majesties, to whom he accords the power to negotiate, on his behalf and in his name, with such persons as he shall think fit, to sell them, and to transfer to them at such prices and charges, clauses, and conditions as he will find the most advantageous: 1° the complete score of *Le Siège de Cithere* [*Cythère assiégée*], of which the aforementioned party is the author, with all its

---

[15] Letter to Maria Theresia, Paris, 20 Feb. 1775, ibid. ii. 301.   [16] Ibid. ii. 305.

[17] The score identifies the performers as 'les comédiens italiens ordinaires du roi', a troupe which had merged with the Opéra-Comique in 1762, but whose title was often retained in notices and on scores and librettos well after this time.

[18] See his letter to Arnaud, 12 May 1775, in Ch. 15 below.

accessories and appendages; 2° the plates of the score of the opera called *Iphigénie*, of which the aforementioned party is also the author, together with the plates of the airs taken from the same opera, in sum, everything that may belong to it. Also to process and sign all documents concerning the aforesaid sales and dealings, agree the price of the aforesaid objects, receive all or part of that price, negotiate on all time clauses, give consents, hand over all the objects included in the aforesaid sales, issue receipts for all payments and valid expenses, and in general, through the above means, do all the appointed attorney shall think fit, even if not specified in this document, providing that the aforesaid S[r] appointee is in full agreement and furnishes deeds of ratification as required.

Signed: Chevalier Gluck, Fourcaut, Deherain.[19]

A receipt dated the following day records the fact that the *Iphigénie* plates were transported from Le Marchand to Gluck.[20] The break with Le Marchand, revoking the agreement freely entered into on 10 July 1774, is puzzling. In 1774, Le Marchand had brought out the scores of *Iphigénie* and *Orphée*; he had also had engraved some extracts from *Iphigénie*, Achilles' Act III ariette, 'J'obtiens Iphigénie', and some airs arranged for two violins; in addition, he was preparing to publish vocal extracts from both the operas, together with a short score of *L'Arbre enchanté*.[21] There is no evidence of any dishonesty on Le Marchand's part, and some suggestion in the correspondence of Kruthoffer and Peters of a conspiracy between the two Germans to wrest the profitable publication of Gluck's scores away from the Frenchman.

On his return journey to Vienna, Gluck again passed through Karlsruhe. Klopstock travelled on with him to Rastatt. An enchanting letter from Nanette suggests that on this occasion she sang 'Che farò' and 'Io non chiedo' (or perhaps 'Ah! per questo già'), studied during her stay in Paris:

I the undersigned, sorceress of the Holy Roman Empire, as also of the Unholy Gallic Empire, herewith testify and declare that which I have promised Klopstock: I promise that as soon as I, arch-enchantress, have returned to the arch-house in the arch-city called Vienna, and have spent three days and three nights consecutively, recovering my breath after my journey, I shall forthwith, straightway, and without any delay, send him: 1. the aria in which Orpheus calls after Eurydice, 2. the aria in which Alcestis calls after her

[19] Gluck to Kruthoffer, Paris, 9 Mar. 1775, in Cauchie, 'Gluck et ses éditeurs', 310.
[20] 'Compte avec M. le Chevalier Gluck'; F-Pn, Gluck lettres autographes, no. 35.
[21] Details in Hopkinson, *Bibliography*, items 40A, 40B, 40D, 40E; 41A, 41BB; 42A.

children; and that under each of these arias I will put a few words, in which shall be contained, so far as words can contain such things, the nature, method, constituents, and essence, and as it were the nuances of my magical musical performance, so that the aforesaid Klopstock can, on his part, send these my words, together with the arias, to his niece in Hamburg, who according to his assertion is also given up to sorcery.[22]

[22] Letter to Klopstock, Rastatt, 17 Mar. 1775, in Adolf Bernard Marx, *Gluck und die Oper* (Berlin, 1863), 143-4; Nohl, *Musiker-Briefe*, 29-30; Tenschert, *Gluck . . . reformator der Oper*, 195. Gluck's letter to Klopstock of 24 June 1775 (see Ch. 15 below) suggests that Gluck himself intended to annotate the arias.

15

PROBLEMS WITH PUBLISHERS
(1775)

KRUTHOFFER lost little time in finding a publisher to replace Le Marchand. In a document drawn up on 28 March 1775, he signed an agreement with his compatriot Anton de Peters:

... To transfer to him with the promise to guarantee him against any troubles and difficulties ...

1° The complete score of the opera called *Le Siège de Cythère*, of which the aforementioned Sr Gluck is the author, with all its accessories and appendages,

2° The complete score of the opera called *Iphigénie*, of which the aforementioned Sr Gluck is also the author,

3° The engraved plates, both of the said opera *Iphigénie*, and in addition the ariette and the separate airs, in sum, everything that could form part of the said two operas, without exception, retention, or reserve,

4° Finally, the rights belonging to the aforementioned Sr Gluck to have engraved and printed the said operas and associated material ... and all his musical compositions of whatever nature, past or future ['faits ou à faire'].[1]

The last clause clearly exceeds the authority entrusted to Kruthoffer by Gluck in the deed of 9 March. In the same document, Peters acknowledged receipt of the plates for *Iphigénie* and for the separate airs taken from it, and agreed that Kruthoffer should deliver him the score of *Cythère assiégée* within a month.[2] For this he was to pay Kruthoffer 5,000 *livres*. A private agreement between Kruthoffer and Peters, signed on the same day but

---

[1] F-Pn, Gluck lettres autographes, no. 23. Pub. in Tiersot, 'Pour le centenaire', 243–4; Cauchie, 'Gluck et ses éditeurs', 310–11.

[2] Peters peremptorily requested the return of the plates in an undated memo to Le Marchand headed 'Il faut que M. Le Marchand rende les comptes à M. Gluck' (F-Pn, Gluck lettres autographes, no. 29). The first act of *Cythère* was already in Berton's hands; see Cauchie, 'Gluck et ses éditeurs', 311.

without witnesses, contains two clauses, one dividing the payment into two instalments, the other stipulating that Peters 'shall not interfere with the S^r Le Marchand on the subject of the volume of airs taken from the opera *Iphigénie* arranged for two violins or flutes, on condition that no words are added to the airs.'[3] Kruthoffer promptly reported these negotiations to Gluck. The repercussions of the following letter dominated Gluck's correspondence for many months:

A few days after your departure, I decided, monsieur, to conclude the arrangements with M. de Peters relating to your operas *Iphigénie* and the *Siège de Cythère*, using the authority you have given me in this respect. Before proceeding in the matter, I urged M. de Peters to make all the necessary arrangements with the Sr Marchand, concerning both his contract and the publication of the little airs for two violins which he has taken from *Iphigénie*. M. de Peters undertook this with great goodwill, but M. le Marchand did not think fit to reply. Being for my part confident of M. de Peters's way of thinking, and being equally confident of your assurance to me that you had given nothing in writing to the Sr Marchand which might allow him to publish any airs from the opera *Iphigénie* other than those engraved last year for two violins, and not wanting to lose any time in settling this affair, I hastened to sign a contract with M. de Peters, in the presence of a lawyer, in which I transferred to him, in your name, the full and complete ownership of the said operas on the conditions agreed between you and him, further pledging, in a document under private seal, that M. de Peters should not interfere with the Sr Marchand in the publication of his volume of airs for violin solo. After concluding this business, all that remained to do was to transfer the *privilège* [permission] to publish the opera *Iphigénie*, which you have purported to grant to the Sr Marchand. . . . I was surprised to learn that he held a licence, signed by you, authorizing him to extract from *Iphigénie* such airs as he thinks fit, besides those mentioned above. I cannot conceal from you, monsieur, that this assertion, which contradicts your word, shocked me greatly. I did not want to believe it, but I was forced to concede, on seeing the paper in question. It was dated 6 March last [i.e. 1774], signed by you and witnessed.[4]

I must not conceal from you that your inclination to issue such documents can damage your interests in general, and in this particular case it is a source of embarrassment to me. On your assurance that no such permission existed, I had drawn up the contract with M. de Peters . . . and after all this trouble, the Sr Marchand produces an authorization whose existence had not been

---

[3] See n. 1 above.

[4] The contract dated 6 Mar. 1774 is missing; it must have been similar to that issued in relation to *Orphée* on 10 July 1774 (see Ch. 13 above). Georg Kinsky quotes from the *privilège* of 4 Aug. 1774 in confirmation of Le Marchand's rights: see *Glucks Briefe an Franz Kruthoffer* (Vienna, 1927), 14.

suspected, and announces in the press a new volume of airs taken from *Iphigénie* and arranged for the harpsichord. You must realize, monsieur, that such an incident is bound to displease those who deal openly and honestly in their affairs. The publication of this new volume must harm the present owner, the more so as he had planned to make a similar collection of ariettes, and strictly speaking he would be justified in seeking damages from you. But judge now between the probity of M. de Peters and the conduct of the Sʳ Le Marchand: M. de Peters, out of regard for you, monsieur, was willing to let this publication stand . . . on condition that, 1° he rather than you should grant the permission to allow the new volume to be published . . . and 2° that M. de Peters might, in his turn, publish airs taken from the opera *Orphée* if he should wish. These conditions, whose justice will not escape you, were rejected by M. Marchand. . . .

There remains one last matter of which I must inform you: under the contract, the *privilège* for *Iphigénie* has to be given up to M. de Peters. As you have in your possession a receipt for the document purporting to give up this *privilège* to the Sʳ Le Marchand, it is absolutely necessary for me to have this receipt, either to return to the Sʳ Le Marchand, when he gives up the *privilège* to M. de Peters, or as insurance for the latter, in case Le Marchand, through his habitual lack of good faith, were not to agree to this act. I therefore beg you to send me this receipt without delay.[5]

Gluck's response was placatory:

My dear friend,

At the time when I asked you to complete my business with M. Peters, I never dreamt that you would have so much trouble on my account. This distresses me so much that I would rather that the whole sum should be lost, than see you further harassed. M. Marchand has written to me, complaining as usual about the great injustice done him. I am sending you my answer, which, when you have read it, please send on to him. If he remains obstinate, then reimburse him at your discretion, provided that M. Peters will permit a deduction from the 5,000 *livres*, for I am quite resolved that in future you shall have no more annoyance on my account. I only wish that I could recompense you for the past. M. Marchand's receipt, which you ask from me, does not exist because I never asked him for one, as I could not believe he would ever be capable of becoming a rogue. You teach me, however, to be more careful in future with such people. Anyway, the matter is common knowledge, and he can be referred to enough witnesses, if it should be necessary. I ask you to present my

⁵ Kruthoffer to Gluck, Paris, 31 Mar. 1775: F-Pn, Gluck lettres autographes, no. 28; this source includes a summary of the letter, headed 'Idée de la lettre à écrire à M. Gluck'. Pub. in Tiersot, 'Pour le centenaire', 244.

compliments to M. Peters, and to warn him that the last Allegro of the overture may be changed, so he should not have it engraved until it is decided
whether it should remain.[6] My wife and Nanette send their best wishes to you
and also to M. de Blumendorff. Write us something cheerful, for here in
Vienna the weather is very wild and melancholy, we have a hard frost and
snow, and envy you the fine weather in Paris. Adieu. Do not tire of my friendship, for you will not wear it out. I shall always remember the troubles I have
caused you, and through my gratitude, I shall endeavour to convince you that
I am, dear friend, your most devoted servant,

Chevalier Gluck.

PS   Be sure to let me know whether you have found a good outcome for those
[quartets] by M. Aspelmayer, which I got for you.[7]

The letter enclosed to Le Marchand does not suggest that Gluck was plan-
ning to make a decisive break with the publisher:

I was sorry to hear of the troubles you have had in connection with your
action, as I am convinced that M. Kruthoffer and M. Peters have always been
the most honest and reasonable of men. Perhaps you have not co-operated
with good grace in the arrangements they wanted to make with you. I have no
wish to take sides, as I have received a letter which complains even more of
you. In view of the friendship you have for me, I cannot believe that you
would cause the contract I have with M. Peters to be annulled; I therefore beg
you not to put any obstacle in the way of the execution of my arrangement
with M. Peters. I have been told that I gave you written permission to publish
from the opera *Iphigénie* other airs besides those for two violins, engraved last
year. Having sold my *Iphigénie*, I cannot honestly give this permission; so if
you have such a document from me (which I do not remember writing), either
I did not understand the contents, or I wrote it in a moment when I was thinking of something else. Therefore I ask you to give up this paper to M. Peters,
if you do not want me to be regarded in Paris as a dishonest man. I am not yet
dead, thank Heaven! I shall still have any opportunities to be useful to you,
and to compensate you, if you value my friendship. See to it, then, that I hear
no more of quarrels, and that everything is settled. I need all my energies for
work, because I tell you in confidence that I shall arrive next year with three
operas instead of the two I had promised. You will readily understand that I

---

[6] See Max Arend, 'Die Ouvertüren zu Glucks *Cythère assiégée*', *Zeitschrift für Musikwissenschaft*,
4 (1921–2), 94–5.
[7] Letter to Kruthoffer, Vienna, 15 Apr. 1775, pub. in Kinsky, *Glucks Briefe*, 13. Franz von
Blumendorff was a diplomat in the Austrian embassy in Paris. Franz Aspelmayer [Asplmayr] had
been composer for the ballet at the German theatre in Vienna, and wrote several symphonies and
quartets.

do not have time for arguments, and that I have to work like a dog. Be sensible, because I have the means in hand to make you a reasonable profit when I arrive. My wife and my daughter embrace you and Mme Marchand likewise. Write to me with news of the operas. I am always you very devoted friend and servant,

Chevalier Gluck.

PS   I hope to hear without delay that your affairs with M. de Peters have been amicably arranged. Do your utmost to settle the business once and for all.[8]

Kruthoffer forwarded this letter to Le Marchand on 30 April, enclosing it in one which reiterated Gluck's requests.[9] Before then, however, another aggravation had arisen. In a letter dated 21 April, Peters told Kruthoffer that he had requested the score of *Cythère assiégée* from Pierre Berton, director of the Opéra, and had been refused it, on the grounds that Gluck had given or sold the work to the Académie; Peters threatened to withhold part of the 3,000 *livres*, and to sue for damages if he were not able to bring out the score at the time of the first performance.[10] Kruthoffer again stepped in to negotiate,[11] and Peters's firm, the Bureau d'abonnement musical, was able to bring out *Cythère* to coincide with the première, on 1 August 1775. A communication to Du Roullet, in which Kruthoffer reiterates his complaints against Le Marchand, adds information about the rehearsals of *Cythère*, for which Berton had provided a long closing ballet. The source is a memorandum of a letter, undated and headed 'Note':

M. Kruthoffer feels bound to inform M. le Bailli du Roullet that it seemed to him, when he was present at a rehearsal of the opera of the *Siège de Cythère*, that the orchestra fell far short of performing the music in the spirit and in accordance with the principles of M. Gluck. He noticed that M. Berton had actually allowed badly rendered passages to pass uncorrected. Moreover, there is a widespread rumour that M. Berton appears to be more concerned with the success of his ballet than with the rest of the opera, and that he is giving his whole attention to securing a good performance for his own work, to such an extent that he has left that of M. Gluck to the discretion of the orchestra. Although this rumour may have its basis in mischief-making, it could, however, have arisen in part through the

---

[8] Vienna, 15 Apr. 1775: F-Pn, Gluck lettres autographes, no. 25. Pub. in Tiersot, 'Pour le centenaire', 244.

[9] F-Pn, Gluck lettres autographes, no. 26. Pub. ibid. 244.

[10] F-Pn, Gluck lettres autographes, no. 31. Pub. ibid. 252. The word concerning Gluck's transmission of the score to the Académie appears to be 'rendu' (given), and Tiersot prints this; but in his own copy of the letter (see n. 11 below), Kruthoffer writes clearly 'vendu' (sold).

[11] F-Pn, Gluck lettres autographes, no. 32 (copy).

indifference with which M. Berton seems to perform the music of M. Gluck.[12]

Gluck was now suffering from the first of the serious illnesses which were to dog him for the remainder of his life. A letter from Nanette to Abbé Arnaud explains that Gluck was to ill to write.[13] Arnaud did not reply to this letter, and drew the following rebuke from Gluck when he was well enough to write for himself:

My very dear friend,

We are all astonished that you have not replied to my daughter's letter. Has Grétry taken my place in your heart? Is it necessary to forget one, in loving another? You give so much of yourself to your friends and acquaintances, that everyone makes demands on you. Do likewise with your affections, so that you always keep a small place in your heart for me, and I can expect to have a few kind words from you from time to time, for such words come easily to you, and give so much pleasure. If you do not write to me soon, I promise to take my vengeance on you when I arrive in Paris, for I shall not let you hear a single bar of my *Alceste*, which I am working on at present. On this subject, I would ask you to urge this count or marquis who wants to translate *Olimpiade* to send me the poem as soon as possible, for if it is well done, I shall start to set it to music at once; tell me, I beg you, whether or not I can rely on him. My wife and daughter send you a thousand tender wishes, and I remain always,

Your most humble and obedient friend and servant,

Chevalier Gluck.

PS   I beg you to tell me whether or not M. Duplessis will finish my portrait for the Salon.[14]

Gluck's enquiry referred to the portrait which Jean-Silfrède Duplessis had begun in 1774. During its long gestation, the artist made numerous sketches and painted at least one alternative pose (some of these studies have survived). He also drew attention to his work by issuing engravings of the portrait in advance of its exhibition at the Salon du Louvre in the autumn of 1775. The portrait was widely acclaimed, though a handful of

[12] c.30 Apr. 1775: F-Pn, Gluck lettres autographes, no. 27. Pub. in Tiersot, 'Pour le centenaire', 244–5.

[13] I have not been able to trace this letter. A translation appears in Hedwig and Erich Müller von Asow, *The Collected Correspondence and Papers of Christoph Willibald Gluck* (London, 1962), 209. Nanette apparently refers to herself as 'your little Chinese girl', which suggests that she had included arias from *Le cinesi* in her private performances in Paris.

[14] Vienna, 12 May 1775: F-Pn, Gluck lettres autographes, no. 4. Pub. in L.R., 'Correspondance inédite', 2. Metastasio's *Olimpiade*, which Gluck had hoped to set for Bologna (see Ch. 9 above), had been trans. by Framery, and was set by Sacchini in 1777.

critics, Diderot among them, criticized the painting of the hands—a reservation which made a deep impression on Gluck.[15] At the same salon, the sculptor Jean-Antoine Houdon exhibited a bronze bust of Gluck. It was regarded as a more 'realistic' portrayal than the Duplessis, and was criticized for representing all too accurately the composer's skin blemishes.[16] There was considerable demand for copies of both images, and several copies of the bust survive today.

The dispute with Le Marchand and the shortcomings of Berton continued to distract Gluck:

My dear friend,

I have received no reply from Herr Marchand to my letter; if I do receive one, I shall follow your advice fully. If you think fit, speak to Herr Bailli du Roullet about the matter; perhaps he can get Herr Marchand to see reason. This time I shall warn him that I really want this matter settled once and for all. If you or M. Peters, to whom I send my compliments, should want a ticket [for the Opéra] at any time, please ask Herr Bailli du Roullet for one; I shall write to him about it. I have written to ask M. Berton to tell M. Peters about the change in the overture when it is ready. As far as the final divertissement is concerned, I deliberately did not intend to write one, because it is an appendage to the plot ['ein hors d'œuvre']: my work finishes with the last chorus. If, however, M. Peters wants there to be such a piece, I will ask M. Berton to try to work out something of the sort, although I believe that the opera will be sufficiently strong, and long enough, without it, and without incurring extra expense in this way. I send my compliments to Herr von Blumendorff; tell M. Kohaut that I shall write to him as soon as possible; if you encounter M. Lamotte, tell him to write to his mother, if he does not wish her to die! I remain, my dear friend, you most obedient servant,

Chevalier Gluck.

PS   Please let me have news of the theatre.[17]

Gluck's next letter refers to Nanette's promise to provide Klopstock with copies of the arias she had sung, annotated to show her interpretation, in order that Klopstock might instruct his own niece in the refinements of her performance:

---

[15] See *Mercure de France*, Oct. 1775, 194; *Mémoires secrets*, xiii. 176. Gluck refers metaphorically to 'disfigured hands' in his letter to Arnaud of 31 Jan. 1776; see Ch. 16 below.

[16] Anon., *Observations sur les ouvrages exposés au Salon du Louvre* (Paris, 1775), 55.

[17] Letter to Kruthoffer, Vienna, 30 May 1775: F-Pn, Gluck lettres autographes, no. 5. Pub. in L.R., 'Correspondance inédite', 3; Marie Louise Pereyra, 'Vier Gluck-Briefe', *Die Musik*, 13 (1913–14), 10–11; Kinsky, *Glucks Briefe*, 15. Kohaut was a fellow Bohemian composer, working in Paris. Franz Lamotte was a Viennese violinist.

I hope you have safely received the arias you wanted from Herr Graf von Cobenzl. I took advantage of this opportunity to send them to you in order to save the cost of postage. I had to omit the annotations because I did not know how to express myself as I wished. I think it would be equally difficult for you if you wanted to tell someone by letter how, and with what expression, he should declaim your *Messiade*. Everything depends on the feeling, and cannot be properly explained, as you know better than I. I certainly do not lack the desire to implant [my ideas], but I have not yet been able to act, for hardly had I arrived in Vienna, than the emperor left, and has not yet returned; in these circumstances, one must wait the 'academic quarter of an hour' before anything can be done.[18] At large court gatherings there is rarely the opportunity to achieve anything; I hear, however, that an Academy of Science is to be established here, and that the earnings from its publications and periodicals are to form part of the funds, in order to meet the expenses. When I am better informed on the matter, I will be sure to tell you about it. Meanwhile, remember me affectionately until I have the pleasure of seeing you again. My wife and daughter send you their compliments, and are delighted to hear from you.

I remain, your most devoted

Gluck.[19]

---

[18] 'die gutte Virtelstunde beobachten': probably referring to 'das akademische Viertel', the quarter of an hour traditionally allowed between the published time of a lecture and its actual commencement.

[19] Letter to Klopstock, Vienna, 24 June, 1775, pub. in Forkel, *Musikalisch-kritische Bibliothek*, ii. 368; Schmid, *Gluck*, 239–40; Marx, *Gluck*, ii. 144–5; Nohl, *Musiker-Briefe*, 28–9; Klopstock, *Briefe*, 263; Treichlinger (ed.), *Briefe*, 34. Klopstock continued to press Gluck to devise a system to represent the nuances of his declamation; see Gluck's letter to Klopstock, 10 May 1780, in Ch. 22 below.

16

FROM *CYTHÈRE* TO *ALCESTE*
(1775–1776)

GLUCK responded to the rumours of Berton's inadequate preparation of *Cythère* in a long letter to Du Roullet, who was working on the translation and adaptation of *Alceste*, and also preparing a libretto on the subject of *Iphigénie en Tauride*, later finished by Guillard.[1] Gluck's letter, besides affording a window onto his working relationship with his librettist, also conveys the stress of composition, mentioned increasingly frequently from this point onwards. The illness that kept Gluck in Vienna in the summer of 1775 has not been identified, but the symptoms he describes are typical of the hypertension that led to his subsequent strokes: 'a hive of bees in my head, that buzz continually':

Here is a letter in three acts. You will find it a little blunt, but I abandon my polite manners in addressing the friend to whom I am at least as devoted as to my wife.

Act I *Siège de Cythère*

In the first place, I believe M. Berton to be something of a rogue, because he has not replied to two letters I have sent him. And since he has been unwise enough to put on *Orphée* again [in my absence], I suspect he cares very little whether my works are performed well or badly. I have similarly very little hope that *Siège de Cythère* will please, especially if the end of the second act is not performed with great precision, and if the soloists and choruses are not made to act with passion. If you see that the work is being ruined, I beg you to persuade the ambassador [Mercy-Argenteau] to join with you in having it removed from the stage; I shall rehearse it myself when I come to Paris, and then it will be apparent how it should be performed.

---

[1] See Ch. 20.

Act II *The Opera Buffa, or La Fidelité recompensée*[2]

You tell me that the author is a poor devil who must be paid, but you must negotiate the fee with him, because according to my contract, I am given 6,000 *livres* for the opera on the understanding that I do not have to pay [the poet] for the libretto. You might clarify this clause with M. Berton. This is, moreover, an opera which should be given only by the second cast, and only on Thursdays; although the work will be weaker than the other operas, it will be good enough for the days on which it will be given, and for the singers who are to perform it.[3] But do tell the author not to forget to introduce choruses wherever the situation permits it.

Act III *Alceste*

In Act I, Scene 5, I had removed the second line of Alcestis's monologue, 'Voilà donc le secours que j'attendais de vous': it must be restored as in the original. I think the divertissement in the second act must not be too long, otherwise it will be out of proportion with the rest of the opera. It should comprise a very lively dance for the whole ensemble, while the chorus sings, with no *pas de deux* or solo, because I feel that the mood of rejoicing must prevail, and any dance not for the full ensemble would weaken this effect. *I want your opinion on this matter.* I am delighted that you think my arrangement [of the libretto] to your taste, but I do not find your denouement at the end of the third act a happy one. It would be good enough for an opera by Chabanon, or Marmontel, or the Chevalier Saint-Mard,[4] but it is useless for a masterpiece like *Alceste*. What the deuce do you think Apollo is doing here in the company of the Arts? They are only appropriate to accompany him on Mount Parnassus—here, they will detract too much from the interest of the catastrophe. A [new] denouement has come to me like a thunderbolt; I think it infinitely better, and it will set the seal on the beauty of your work. Here it is:

Apollo: Vos malheurs ont touché les Dieux, et le destin, à leur prière, consent de revoguer ses ordres rigoureux. Allez, consoler vos sujets que la perte d'Alceste a mis dans une situation déplorable, etc. etc., Et vivez désormais heureux. *Apollo goes away and Admetus and Alcestis sing a couple of lines together, thanking Apollo, while the machine rises; they leave at the same moment that the machine reaches its full height. Last scene: a large room or a well-lit space, with the choruses and the dancers grouped in attitudes of great sadness. The people still believe that Alcestis is dead, and know nothing of what*

---

[2] An abortive project. Gluck wrote no opera with this as title or subtitle.

[3] It was the custom at the Académie to devote Thursdays to the performance of occasional works, usually of a lighter nature, sung by the second cast.

[4] Three writers whose views on opera were inimical to Gluck's. On Chabanon, see Ch. 12 and n. 3, Jean François Marmontel was a future Piccinnist; Rémond de Saint-Mard was a conservative: see his *Réflexions sur l'Opéra* (The Hague, 1741).

has happened in the wood. The dancers surround the children, and look on them with compassion.

Evander, in dialogue with a coryphée: Qu'est-ce que deviendrons-nous! Alceste n'existe plus, le sort d'Admète est affreux, je tremble!

Coryphée: Je suis de glace; la terreur, l'épouvante me saisis!

Both: O nous miserables! Qui nous donnera du secours? Qui nous donnera de la consolation?

Chorus, in a long phrase: Pleure, ô Patrie, ô Thessalie, Alceste est morte! *Several verses of outcry between the coryphée and Evander, then the chorus repeats*: Pleure, ô Patrie, *etc. etc.,* following the original Italian. After this whole scene, Admetus and Alcestis [enter]. All this must be delivered with wonder and urgency—

Admetus: O mes amis!

Alcestis, to her children, who run downstage immediately: O mes enfants!

Chorus: Ciel!

Alcestis, to her children: Enfin je vous revois.

Chorus: O bonheur inattendu! O puissance éternelle!

Admetus: Dissipez les nuages de la tristesse, livrez vous à l'allégresse, benis-sons les Dieux de leur bonté suprême.

Alcestis and Admetus sing several lines together, then the full chorus sings the lines I have already indicated to you.

After this, there will be just a chaconne for the ballet, and that will be the end, because, after hearing the opera, it is impossible that the public should have a taste for anything more. [Even] after the end of *Iphigénie*, no one wanted to hear or see any more, and this is something altogether different. I myself become almost distracted when I run through it. The nerves are strained for too long, and the attention is held from the first word to the last, without respite. This opera is like a cask of late-season wine,[5] the flavour of which is concentrated in the heart of it; it is truly superb, but too full-bodied to be drunk freely. Woe betide the poet and the musician who would under-take to create a second work of the same kind! The first act lasts only forty minutes, the third, up to the entry of Apollo, twenty minutes, so *Alceste* will never be an opera for the winter season, and I am well pleased at that. We shall produce it immediately on my arrival, otherwise, if I had to wait longer, I would become mad. For the last month it has kept me awake at nights, and my wife is in despair. I seem to have a hive of bees in my head, that buzz continu-ally. Operas of this sort are very pernicious, believe me. I now begin to under-stand the shrewdness of Quinault and Calzabigi, who fill their works with subsidiary characters to give the spectator some respite, enabling him to enjoy

---

[5] 'vin gelé': Gluck translates 'Eiswein' literally—wine made from grapes which are not har-vested until after the first frosts.

a peaceful episode.[6] An opera such as [*Alceste*] is no entertainment, but a very serious occupation for whoever listens to it. Be sure to tell me yourself if you hear any [theatre] news. In writing *Iphigénie en Tauride*, be guided by my thoughts. Do not encourage anyone else to write [librettos] for me, because I have already decided on my third, which I shall bring with me when I come to Paris. I am not going to tell you the subject yet, because you might dissuade me; I feel that you have too much influence over my mind, and I think I shall only tell you of it when I am so far on that there will be no time left to draw back.[7]

Meanwhile, Peters was preparing to publish the score of *Cythère*. Less than a month before the première, Peters complained to Kruthoffer that changes and corrections threatened to delay publication and eat into his slender profit, and 'in his obstinacy, M. Berton has capped it all by giving the divertissements to M. Le Marchand. Imagine what effect that will have on the public, and how many complaints I shall have to deal with from all sides, claiming that the work is incomplete, and that it is too dear at 24 *livres*!'[8] Kruthoffer forwarded Peters's letter to Gluck, eliciting the following response:

My dear friend,

I gathered from his letter that M. Peters considers my *Siège de Cythère* to be incomplete, even though I have already explained to him that my work ends with the last chorus. The ballet which M. Berton wants to add to it, whatever it may be called, is from my point of view an hors d'œuvre. As I see it, if my work were too short and someone wanted to extend the duration by adding an act by another composer, this would not mean that my opera had been incomplete. M. Peters may well be right to complain about *Iphigénie* in connection with Le Marchand, but over the *Siège de Cythère* he is wrong, because [he has been given] the complete work for which the Académie paid me. I will go further and say that in future I shall write no more ballet airs for my operas, apart from those that arise during the course of the action, and if people do not like that, then I shall write no more operas, for I will not let myself be reproached in all the journals that my [final] ballets are weak and mediocre, etc. The rogues shall hear no more from me, and my operas will always end where the text ends.

Concerning Le Marchand, I beg you to be so good as to explain the whole

---

[6] Philippe Quinault was Lully's librettist. One of the many changes Du Roullet made to Calzabigi's *Alceste* was to remove the confidants.

[7] Gluck to Du Roullet, Vienna, 1 July 1775: F-Pn, Gluck lettres autographes, no. 8. Pub. in L.R., 'Correspondance inédite', 3–5.

[8] Peters to Kruthoffer, Vienna, 15 July 1775: F-Pn, Gluck lettres autographes, no. 33. Pub. in Tiersot, 'Pour le centenaire', 253. Le Marchand did not in fact publish the divertissements.

affair to M. Bailli du Roullet. He will surely make him see reason. I have already warned him that you will speak to him about it.

I ask you also to give M. Kohaut a message from us, and tell him that his brother came to see me, and that I found him very well disposed towards him, and that I do not doubt that his affairs will very soon be concluded. I expect another visit from him, which he has promised me.

One more commission: my Nanette's roll of Indian cotton has been lost, and I would like to get her another. The package is small; could it not, with your help and that of Herr von Blumendorff, be brought to the local customs point by courier? Or must I bother His Excellency the Count [Mercy-Argenteau] with it? Advise me what needs to be done. Now my womenfolk send a thousand compliments to you and to Herr von Blumendorff, in which I join, and remain ever, dear friend, you most devoted servant,

Chevalier Gluck.[9]

Cythère was performed in Gluck's absence on 1 August. The *Mémoires secrets* evidently expected the work to repeat the success of *Iphigénie:*

Cythère assiégée—for that is the true title of the opera—is nothing more at bottom than the opéra-comique of the same name by the Sr Favart, given for the first time in 1754. The Chevalier Gluck has thought this subject to be worthy of his music, and according to the well-attended rehearsal held the day before yesterday, he has fulfilled his task very agreeably. This lyrical drama has the rare merit of being very lively and avoiding tedium.[10]

The initial cool reception was attributed to a cabal.[11] But after a week of tepid interest, the journal was forced to acknowledge the failure of the opera, despite the queen's efforts to support it; Favart, the singers, and Berton's closing ballet bore the blame.[12] Grimm's *Correspondance littéraire* repeated the same criticisms, in particular the mismatch between the light and graceful words of the libretto and Gluck's music, which was found 'too strong for the genre . . . heavy and unrefined, with monotonous and undistinguished airs.'[13] Gluck's friends conspired to keep the poor reception of *Cythère* from him. He was seriously ill throughout the summer, and there are no letters from him until the autumn, when he wrote at length to Du Roullet:

[9] Gluck to Kruthoffer, Vienna, 31 July 1775: F-Pn, Gluck lettres autographes, no. 7. Pub. in Pereyra, 'Vier Gluck-Briefe', 11–13; Kinsky, *Glucks Briefe*, 16–17; fragment in L.R., 'Correspondance inédite', 13–14.
[10] *Mémoires secrets*, viii. 152 (2 Aug. 1775).
[11] Ibid. viii. 154 (4 Aug. 1775).   [12] Ibid. viii. 162 (10 Aug. 1775).
[13] xi. 107–8.

I am most grateful to Mme de la Ménardière and to you for the concern you have both shown during my illness and recovery. I shall never in my life forget how indebted I am to you for the friendship you have shown me, and for the interest you take in all that concerns me. My wife also sends her thanks to you both, and presents her compliments; she is in tolerably good health, although she did not have a moment's respite during my illness, and felt the effects of it almost as if it were her own. She kept back all the letters you wrote to me, and gave me them all together when I recovered. Consequently I have many things to tell you, but I do not know how to answer you, as I am still very weak. I shall therefore deal only with the most essential points.

I shall not be able to leave here before the end of March or the beginning of April, because if I leave during the winter, I shall be sure to catch cold once again. This will not prevent us from giving *Alceste* after Easter, because as I work through the piece, I shall send it to be copied and distribute the roles, so that when I arrive, I shall be able to start rehearsals at once, and in two weeks I shall be able to instruct everyone in their parts. The *Siège de Cythère* could be given again in the summer! The opéra-comique is, in my opinion, too mediocre,[14] and I think it could be given only on Thursdays in the winter season. I acknowledge that the libretto is very weak, but the music is amusing and original, and should make more of an effect than the wretched scraps which it is always the custom to give. The act by M. Ghibert, which you recommend me to compose, reads well, but I find it the most wretched thing in the world for setting to music. For a start, the choruses and ballet are supposed to consist of young pupils, which we do not have, and adults do not have the same effect; then Alexander is always on stage, and he is the most foolish person in the world. In Noverre's ballet, he was absent, and he made his appearance only to surprise the two lovers—that was effective.[15] Here, Alexander and his officers are superfluous, and Campaspe has only one romance to sing at the end, so you can see the insufficiency of the piece as a whole. It could never produce a big effect. I am thinking of trying a new approach with *Armide*; I do not intend to remove a line from Quinault's libretto, but in many of the scenes the music must be made to trot, or rather gallop, in order to disguise the coldness and the tedium of the work, which hinder involvement. When I study the fifth act, I cannot prevent myself from weeping at the situation, which is so lifelike and so tender. If my plan succeeds, your old music will be crushed for ever. All the same, I am resolved to write no more; [if I did] I would either burst or go mad! My nerves are too sensitive not to give way in the end.

Next I shall reply to the proposal made by you and our dear friend M. l'Abbé Arnaud that I should settle in France. Firstly, although I have no

---

[14] 'l'opéra Buffon est selon moi trop mediocre': probably a ref. to *La Fidelitée recompensée* (see n. 2 above).

[15] Noverre's ballet *Apelles et Campaspe ou Le Triomphe d'Alexandre* (music by Aspelmayr) was performed in the Burgtheater in 1773.

duties here, I could not leave my post unless the queen obtained permission for me, otherwise everyone would think me crazy. Secondly, I would not like to be in France when the change of administration [at the Opéra] takes place, because I would not want to be suspected of having intrigued for a post, and to be the cause of those presently in employment losing their work so that I might obtain it. Thirdly, as I feel my health will not permit me to write any more operas, I could only contribute to the improvement of music in France, and help the new administration, by working with Gossec, and others who have a talent for collaboration, like M. Laborde and M. Berton—that would allow many musicians to develop their ideas and their gifts, and would produce good opera composers more rapidly than if I were to write my operas by myself.[16] I beg you to communicate my thoughts to M. l'Abbé Arnaud, because he is so great a friend, and always takes so warm an interest in me that it would be wrong of me to hide my ideas from him, besides which his advice is never anything but very sound. Tell him that his friendship is always very precious to me, that my wife and daughter send him a thousand compliments, and that I ask him to arrange for M. Duplessis to send me my portrait, which we are curious to see here. I have nothing to say in answer to his letter, except that I thank him for all his expressions of friendship, that I love him with all my heart, and that I very much look forward to the time when I shall be able to talk with him once more. I also ask you to send my thanks to all those who were concerned at my illness, principally Mlle Durancy.[17] I am still too weak to reply myself to all my friends. As for you yourself, I say nothing, because I feel that all my expressions are too feeble to tell you of the feelings I have for you.

PS   Do not forget Alcestis's air at the end of the second act.[18]

The next letters concern Mme Gluck's interception of one from Kruthoffer, who had written bluntly that

the public anticipate the end of the run of performances of the *Siège de Cythère* with great indifference; if the number of spectators and the sales of the score are true measures, the conclusion that the *Siège de Cythère* has not been a success is inescapable. Moreover the Sr Peters is most unhappy and could well sue M. Gluck unless he compensates him in some way.

Kruthoffer's letter is missing, but Mme Gluck had a French translation made, and sent it to Du Roullet, who then wrote to Kruthoffer, quoting the

---

[16] The advantages of collaboration with Berton are perhaps intended ironically.

[17] Magdeline-Célice de Frossac Durancy was to sing Hate (La Haine) in *Armide*.

[18] Gluck to Du Roullet, Vienna, 14 Oct. 1775: F-Pn, Gluck lettres autographes, no. 9. Pub. (with errors) in L.R., 'Correspondance inédite', 6, and Tiersot, 'Pour le centenaire', 261. I have been unable to identify Mme de la Ménardière, whom Gluck greets in many letters to Du Roullet.

above passage and rebuking Kruthoffer for his insensitivity towards the convalescent Gluck.[19] In Kruthoffer's apology to Du Roullet the translation ('more literal than faithful') is blamed; Kruthoffer repeated his damning assessment of *Cythère*, but added the comment that 'the enlightened section of the public rendered [Gluck's] work full justice, despite the poor performance which spoiled it.' He blamed Peters's discontent on continued aggravation from Le Marchand.[20] After warning Kruthoffer of Gluck's poor health, Du Roullet wrote confidently of the composer's plans for his return: 'There will be a revival of the *Siège de Cythère*, with some changes to the words. . . . Then M. Peters will see sales as abundant as he could wish for. Each new work M. Gluck gives will create renewed demand for the score of *Iphigénie*; *Alceste*, which is to be given at Easter, is completely ready'.[21] The latter claim proved to be exaggerated as the following letter from Gluck to Du Roullet reveals:

My very dear friend,

It gives me infinite pleasure to hear from you that you sympathize with me, but if that is prejudicial to your health, I wish you would love me a little less; nothing is more precious to me than your health, and I am glad to have known nothing of your illness, because it would have affected me too strongly. I hope that with your cordial we shall in future make light of all the illnesses which threaten us. I am also glad that you have not abandoned work on your *Iphigénie* [*en Tauride*]—it would be too great a loss to be deprived of a libretto by an author with so much knowledge of the stage, so much talent, and so much taste. Concerning your *Alceste*, I cannot say which of the two denouements I shall choose until I finish the accompaniments of all three acts, when I shall be able to judge how everything is combined and integrated; meanwhile I can tell you that the poetry you have written following my suggestions seems very good to me. I hope to be able to send you by the January courier both the music and the poem together, so that you can have the orchestral and vocal parts extracted and copied while awaiting my return. As for *Armide*, I shall not decide about the music until I come to Paris, because I want to consult you first about whether we should leave the poem as it is, or make cuts. I hope soon to receive the end of the second act of *Alceste*, incorporating the other changes. As for the rest, I think it will be difficult unless I am able to stay in Paris, because there are many problems to be overcome if the project is to succeed.

---

[19] 20 Oct. 1775: F-Pn, Du Roullet lettres autographes, no. 6. Pub. in Tiersot, 'Pour le centenaire', 261–2.

[20] Letter to Du Roullet, 21 Oct. 1775: F-Pn, Gluck lettres autographes, no. 34. Pub. in Tiersot, 'Pour le centenaire', 262.

[21] Letter to Kruthoffer, 21 Oct. 1775: F-Pn, Du Roullet lettres autographes, no. 7. Pub. in Tiersot, 'Pour le centenaire', 262.

Since I have been in Vienna, I have tried to sell my garden, but till now I have found no one who wants to snap it up—things never go as one would wish. Le Marchand has written to me, and asked me to grant him a deferment of his debt; I agreed to his request, so please demand nothing from him at present. For my journey, I shall consult Madam Moon, and I believe she will not prevent me from arriving in Paris towards the middle of March, which will give sufficient time to put on *Alceste* after Easter. Please present our most affectionate compliments to Mme de la Ménardière, and tell her that we heartily rejoice that she is restored to health. My wife and daughter always have tears in their eyes when I read them your letters; they send you a thousand compliments, and sing your praises as if you were their dearest lover. Do not forget to present our compliments to M. l'Abbé Arnaud, and to Mlle Rosalie, and to all the company at table. I think it will be necessary to notify M. Berton that we expect to give *Alceste* after Easter. Since you do not want compliments, I send you none; nevertheless I am ever yours,

Chevalier Gluck.[22]

The next time Kruthoffer sent Gluck criticism of *Cythère*, it was apparently selected for its light touch, and designed not to disturb the convalescent. Gluck responded:

My dear friend,

I am deeply indebted to you for sending the brochures and the criticism of the *Siège de Cythère*, which I find witty, and which has my approval. I also safely received the bill of exchange, and am indebted to you for this, too. I shall send you something from *Alceste* with the next courier, as I plan to put on this opera after Easter. You could therefore sound out M. Peters (to whom I send my compliments) as to whether he would like to undertake it, as I would give him preference over all others, on account of his honesty. I hope to be able to embrace you, and also Herr von Blumendorff, by the middle of next March at the latest. Meanwhile my wife, my niece, and I all send our compliments. I remain, ever, dear friend, your most devoted servant,

Chevalier Gluck.[23]

---

[22] Vienna, 22 Nov. 1774: F-Pn, Gluck lettres autographes, no. 10. Pub. in L.R., 'Correspondance inédite', 7. The garden Gluck was trying to sell was presumably that in which Riedel wielded his shovel (see Ch. 14).

[23] Letter to Kruthoffer, Vienna, 29 Nov. 1775: F-Pn, Gluck lettres autographes, no. 6. Pub. in L.R., 'Correspondance inédite', 10; Pereyra, 'Vier Gluck-Briefe', 13–14; Kinsky, *Glucks Briefe*, 18. Kinsky suggests that the witty criticism was Arnaud's *bon mot*, 'Hercules is better with the club than the distaff'.

Two letters to Du Roullet within the space of a fortnight afford further insights into Gluck's thoughts on opera:

I am much obliged to you for the news you send me; it greatly entertains me, especially [the suggestion] that you will prevent the performance of *Iphigénie* if M. Larrivée does not play in it. For the rest, when will you abandon your scruples over *Alceste?* Do you want to become as pale and thin as you were when we produced *Iphigénie?* I shall certainly not allow it, and I am resolved to cure you once and for all in this matter. Firstly, you are writing for the lyric theatre, not a tragedy for actors, and that totally changes the way you have to set about it. Although they are superb masters at writing tragedies, neither Racine nor Voltaire has ever known how to write an opera, and indeed no one has judged the requirements of the genre as well as you. It is, therefore, sometimes necessary to ignore the old rules, and to make new ones for oneself, in order to create grand effects. These old Greeks were men with one nose and a pair of eyes, just like us. We do not have to submit to their rules like servile peasants. On the contrary, we must throw off their clothes, break free of the chains they would bind us with, and seek to become original. Those people who wept when you read them your work, but then found the denouement poor, are, I concede, perceptive, have a sound instinct, and judge from the heart. But are they infallible? My wife and I also wept when you read us your work, but nevertheless, when I grasped the totality of the thing, I found many passages inappropriate for a musical setting. You mock me when you say that the third act is my work; you must think me either foolish or vain. Do you think that if someone gives a man fifty pictures, arranged according to his taste, and he arranges them a little differently, anyone could think the man had painted them? The injustice you do yourself infuriates me, and I am going to make you angry in your turn, by praising my denouement and criticizing yours. Firstly, with your denouement, the opera becomes an inverted pyramid, because you begin with the chorus, who, *nota bene,* are actors, and have an acute interest in the actions of the other characters in the work. So it starts with pomp and ceremony, the chorus always participates, and in the first two acts the work unfolds to a great extent through them, for they do not wish to lose so perfect a king and queen. When we turn to the third act, this chorus, which has taken such an interest in the preservation of its rulers, is forgotten and seen no more. I declare that the work cannot finish until these poor people have been consoled. It is no use your telling me that Apollo will bring them back. That seems to me an hors d'œuvre, dragged in by the skin of its teeth.[24] Besides, Apollo would have to play the part of a magician, because if he transforms the scene in the wood into a magnificent interior, he must make another

---

[24] 'hors d'œuvre' was a strong term of disapprobation for Gluck, who used the expression to condemn Berton's unwanted ballet in *Cythère.*

pass with his wand to transport the people there, who sing their chorus abruptly, without being gradually prepared for their happiness. In my denouement, everything follows naturally, without the need to have recourse to magic. The work finishes without the help of any spirit or supernatural arts, with the same pomp and ceremony that began it. It is not because of the music that I advocate this, for there is very little music here, and what there is is very short. But on reading and rereading the opera, I have never been persuaded that the progression is natural or that it would be effective. If all this still does not reassure you, I will persuade you, or you will persuade me otherwise, when I come to Paris. Please keep writing to me with all your news, even if I do not reply, as I must work now so that I can send you the first and second act by the courier who leaves on the first of January next. You tell me that Mlle Rosalie wants to leave, and, in another letter, Mlle Laguerre too. Who shall we have for the operas? I foresee that *Alceste* will be the last opera I shall be able to put on, as battles cannot be fought without troops. My wife, the little one, and I send our compliments to Mme la Ménardière, to you, and to M. l'Abbé [Arnaud]. Adieu, my dear friend. I embrace you with all my heart.

Chevalier Gluck.[25]

I have given some thought to what M. Berton has to say, and on looking closely into things, I conclude that I shall not be able to give any opera other that *Alceste* next year; having been ill for four months, I lost a good deal of working time, and until I leave I shall have to devote myself to *Alceste*, which requires infinite care. Furthermore, *Armide* has such a large cast that I do not know where we shall find the singers: for the role of Armida we need either Rosalie or Laguerre, for the role of Renault, M. Le Gros, for Hate [La Haine], Mlle Duplant or Durancy, and for Armida's old father [Hidraot] we need M. Gélin. The other roles are so weighty, and the public so critical, that I don't know who to give them to. *Nor could I risk the opéra-comique,*[26] *because it needs at least ten singers, among whom I must have M. Le Gros and Larrivée, otherwise I would hand the critics a delightful opportunity to attack me, as they did with the* Siège de Cythère, *where they treated me like a little schoolboy without conceiving that anything could be said in my defence. I made a point of escaping as far as I could from their clutches. Because I do not live in Paris, all these criticisms prejudice my reputation in Germany and Italy, because here they are taken literally, whether for or against an author. So whilst I kill myself with my efforts to entertain the French, they are trying to deprive me of the little reputation I had acquired*

---

[25] Vienna, 2 Dec. 1775: F-Pn, Gluck lettres autographes, no. 11. Pub. in L.R., 'Correspondance inédite', 8–9. Marie Josephine de Laguerre remained at the Opéra, as did Rosalie Levasseur.

[26] 'je ne pourrois non plus hazarder l'Opéra Bouffon': an ambiguous statement. Either Gluck contemplated using members of the Opéra-Comique for *Armide*, or (his habitual lack of paragraph-breaks concealing a change of topic) he planned a revival of an old opéra-comique (*La Recontre imprévue* has a cast of ten), or he referred to *La Fidelité recompensée* (see nn. 2 and 14 above).

before I came to Paris. I hope to send you, without fail, the first act by next month's courier. You might suggest to M. Berton that if M. Larrivée would like to undertake the part of High Priest, he would be sure to please the public as much as or more than in the role of Agamemnon, as his recitative is the most striking number in the whole opera, and cannot fail once I have communicated my intentions to him; otherwise, the part must be given to M. Gélin. The role of Evander is for the singer who took the role of Olgar in the *Siège de Cythère*, the coryphées for Mlle Châteauneuf and a young girl who understudied Rosalie in *Iphigénie*; she had a pretty voice but I do not remember her name. Please tell Mlle Rosalie to be sure to learn her role in outline only, because she cannot possibly understand the nuances, and the delivery, without me; otherwise the correction of bad habits acquired in my absence would be infinitely troublesome to both of us. The chorus should be given their roles, because as they are always in action, they must know their music by heart, as if it were the *Pater noster*. We send our respects to Mme de la Ménardière and to you.

Chevalier Gluck.[27]

Gluck was able to finish the first two acts of *Alceste* in time for the courier who left on 1 January. Kruthoffer continued as his agent:

My dear friend,

I am most grateful to you for the very kind wishes you sent me, and for the packages, all of which I received safely. I must trouble you again with this package, which contains the two acts of *Alceste*, and the enclosed letters for forwarding to their addresses. With regard to M. Peters, to whom I send my compliments, I can do no better than to leave matters in your hands, as I am convinced that you are a true friend to both of us. I place my complete confidence in you to manage this business. Please embrace Herr von Blumendorff on my behalf. My old lady and my little lady both send you many kind greetings, and ask to be remembered to you. I remain, dear friend, ever your most devoted servant,

Chevalier Gluck.[28]

One of the enclosed letters was to Arnaud, reiterating Gluck's concern for the ending of *Alceste*:

---

[27] Letter to Du Roullet, Vienna, 13 Dec. 1775: F-Pn, Gluck lettres autographes, no. 13. Pub. in L.R., 'Correspondance inédite', 9; Tiersot, 'Pour le centenaire', 266. Gluck secured most of the singers mentioned, with the exception of Larrivée, who did not sing in the first French production of *Alceste*. The first sentence may refer to Berton's proposal that Gluck should set *Roland*; see Ch. 18 below.

[28] Letter to Kruthoffer, Vienna, 31 Dec. 1775, in Kinsky, *Glucks Briefe*, 19.

Monsieur,

I am most grateful to you, my dear friend, for the perseverance you show in all that concerns me, and for your friendship, which appears never to diminish. You can at least be sure that my esteem for you, and for your knowledge of the fine arts, could not be greater. I must tell you in a few words that I had devised several scenes from the opera *Armide* when I fell ill; afterwards, having heard of the cabals against the *Siège de Cythère*, I stopped working on it, because I could not understand the animosity of the public towards a foreigner who was prepared to kill himself to entertain them, and to enlighten them in many matters. Now, it could be set exactly as it is, but I confess that it is very weak in many places, and that it would make a better effect if it were reduced to three acts. As for *Alceste*, I can tell you that the whole is more consistent than in the Italian version, and if I can obtain from the chorus and soloists the expression and the action I have in mind, you will have a tremendous work, which will be difficult to follow. I admit, however, that I am not satisfied with the denouement. The opera resembles a fine portrait, the hands of which are disfigured. M. le Bailli [du Roullet] rightly says that the action ends with the death of Alcestis. But Euripides, who, I believe, also knew the rules of the theatre, brings on Hercules after her death, to give her back to Admetus, and in this way avoids strangling the work with its own rules. In order to give full expression to the grief of the people at her death, it needs a different location from the scene where the catastrophe occurred. The music will be fully effective only in the proper situation—which is why military music with drums is not suitable in a church, and church music is not appropriate in the theatre. We shall decide this matter when I get to Paris, which I shall hasten to do as soon as the season permits. Meanwhile accept my respects, and those of my wife and my niece, who are, like me, devoted to you.

Chevalier Gluck.[29]

Gluck left Vienna in mid-February as he had planned, and, travelling more slowly than usual, arrived in Paris in mid-March. The première of *Alceste* was on 23 April, with Rosalie Levasseur in the title role and Le Gros as Admetus. Some of the advance publicity stressed the Italian origins of the work, in an attempt to deflect a possible attack from the adherents of Sacchini and Piccinni:

The tragic opera *Alceste*, which is to be given today on the stage of the Opéra, is a kind of translation. M. le Bailli du Roullet states in his announcement that he has not only followed in part the Italian design of M. Calzabigi, but that he

---

[29] Gluck to Arnaud, Vienna, 31 Jan. 1775: F-Pn, Gluck lettres autographes, no. 12. Pub. in L.R., 'Correspondance inédite', 11–12, and excerpted in Tiersot, 'Pour le centenaire', 266.

has also borrowed several details from it, in order to retain a good many passages of the most passionate, vigorous, and dramatic music ever heard in any theatre in Europe since the renaissance of this fine art. He confirms this by quoting the Chevalier Planelli, one of the greatest connoisseurs in Italy today[30] ... We shall see whether the French connoisseurs are of the same opinion. The verdict arrived at in the course of the rehearsals, attendance at which has not been limited to fifty people of taste, as the regulation intends, but which were almost as well attended as usual,[31] was that the first two acts were very fine, but that the last was worthless.[32]

Yesterday in the theatre was the most brilliant affair. The Queen, Madame, Monsieur, and the Count and Countess d'Artois all honoured it with their presence. Her Majesty did her best to support the Chevalier Gluck's alleged masterpiece, but all the efforts of this German's partisans could not defend the poor effect of the third act, which received no applause at all. The music of the first two was found to be vigorous, colourful, and very spirited; but the other, being no more than a continuation of the same, seemed only monotonous and tedious.[33]

On 3 May, the *Mémoires* revealed that Gluck and Du Roullet were working to create more variety in the third act by introducing the character of Hercules. A few days later they recorded an outburst from Gluck on a theme which was to become increasingly characteristic of his attitude to his music:

The changes to *Alceste* are expected tomorrow. The Chevalier Gluck is perfectly confident. He asserts that if his music is not successful at the first performance, it will succeed at the last, if not this year, then next year, or in ten years' time, because his music is very close to Nature, and he knows nothing that is truer to it. This confidence, which would be absurd and senseless in an average man, must be seen in this great man as an innate belief in his own ability, like the noble audacity of genius, which is aware of its strengths and its worth, and which judges itself with the same impartiality as if it were a stranger to itself.[34]

---

[30] Antonio Planelli, *Dell'opera in musica* (Naples, 1772): Planelli upheld the Viennese *Alceste* as a model opera, and quoted (pp. 148–51) from the preface.

[31] A series of rules concerning the Académie royale were brought in during 1776; one aimed to control attendance at the open rehearsals, made popular by *Iphigénie*. See Maurice Barthélemy, 'Les Règlements de 1776 et l'Académie royale de musique', *Recherches sur la musique française classique*, 4 (1964), 239–48.

[32] *Mémoires secrets*, ix. 90 (23 Apr. 1776).

[33] Ibid. ix. 91 (24 Apr. 1776).   [34] Ibid. ix. 105 (6 May 1776).

Gluck defended his opera in similar terms to the journalist Olivier de Corancez: 'I declare that it will please two hundred years hence . . . because I have grounded it in Nature, which is not subject to fashion.'[35]

Alceste became the focus of controversy. Arnaud made a vigorous defence of it in a celebrated essay describing an evening at the opera, in which he pretended to be distracted from enjoying the performance by having to answer the objections of Gluck's detractors. It is necessary to quote a short extract from this because of subsequent events:

A fourth [detractor] said: 'Here is a pleasing chorus, but it has been stolen from the opera *Golconde*.' 'Have patience, monsieur; there is at the end of the second act one of the most beautiful airs ever heard in any opera-house, and in this air, the most moving and faithful inflexions that Art has yet borrowed from Nature. To be sure, you will find the same accent and the same expression in an air from M. Sacchini's *Olimpiade*, but you must learn that long before both M. Sacchini's *Olimpiade* and the opera *Golconde*, *Alceste* saw the light, and the full light at that—that is to say, it was performed, engraved, and made public.'[36]

Neither polemic, nor the new ending, nor a change of cast, with Laguerre taking over the title role from Levasseur, could make any impact on the opposition, which was not a unified attack, but came from conservatives who cherished the Lullist tradition, modernists who supported Italian opera, and a few members of the troupe who had suffered at Gluck's hands, notably Sophie Arnould, who had been displaced by Rosalie Levasseur. Even Gluck's faithful supporters claimed to prefer the opera 'in its old dress'.[37] Not till the last weeks of its run was the opera widely acclaimed, by which time Gluck was following the controversy at a distance:

My dear friend,

I am very much obliged to you and also to Herr von Blumendorff for the pamphlets you sent, which entertain me greatly. Please forward me absolutely everything by way of anecdotes relating to the opera [*Alceste*]. I am enclosing the letter for M. Berton. You can let the opera be engraved in the form in which it is performed. The little that Herr Gossec may have added to it can be of no consequence; it will make the opera neither better nor worse, because it comes at the end of it. Concerning Le Marchand, I have written to M. le Bailli du Roullet, who is going to attempt to make peace with the scheming fellow.

[35] *Journal de Paris*, 24 Aug. 1788, 1022; see Ch. 25 below.
[36] 'La Soirée perdue à l'Opéra', in Lesure, *Querelle*, i. 47–8.
[37] *Mémoires secrets*, ix. 107 (12 May 1776).

My wife sends you both her best wishes, and hopes to have the pleasure of your company in Paris next spring or next summer. I remain, with my best compliments to Herr von Blumendorff, your most devoted friend and servant,

Chevalier Gluck.

PS   As the courier escaped me this time, I am sending this by post.[38]

Gluck had left Paris in the third week of May, not because of his opera's turbulent reception, but because he had news from Vienna of the death of Nanette.[39]

---

[38] Letter to Kruthoffer, Vienna, 30 June 1776, in Kinsky, *Glucks Briefe*, 20. Kruthoffer had probably sent Arnaud's pamphlet 'La Soirée perdue'; see n. 36 above. Gossec composed additional ballet movements for the end of *Alceste*.

[39] *Mémoires secrets*, ix. 114 (19 May 1776).

17

NANETTE
(1776)

NANETTE died of smallpox on 21 April. Gerber records a few details of her last illness, including the fact that she was a favourite with the imperial family, and that Emperor Joseph sent for news of her several times each day.[1] Writing to Klopstock, Gluck declared that his was a grief to be assuaged only through music:

Honoured Sir and dear friend,

There is no greater comfort for those who are unhappy than the sympathy of friends. I look to receive this comfort from you, dear friend. I have lost my Nanette. Your 'deutsches Mädchen', with her good and noble heart, who was so proud of your approval and of your friendship, is no more. In the spring-time of her life, she faded like a rose, and losing her I lose the joy of my old age. How poignantly I feel the loss! Just at the moment when I might enjoy the fruits of a happy upbringing, she was snatched from me, snatched during my absence, and without my receiving the last impressions of her pure soul before her passing. How desolate and lonely everything about me now is. She was my only hope, my comfort, and the inspiration of my work. Music, usually my dearest occupation, has lost all attraction for me; if it is ever to lighten my grief, it must be hallowed by the memory of this beloved creature. Is it asking too much of your friendship if I desire to move your sensitive heart to feel my loss, and if I hope your illustrious muse might stoop to strew a few flowers on the ashes of my beloved niece? With what delight would I avail myself of this powerful consolation! Fired by your genius, I would seek to express my grief in the most moving of music. Nature, friendship, and, what is more, a father's love would be the sources of my inspiration.

---

[1] Gerber, *Lexicon*, i. 518. It is on Nanette's death certificate that we learn for the first time that the Gluck family had recently taken up new lodgings in Vienna, in a house belonging to Lopresti in Kärntnerstrasse.

Noble friend, do not let me sigh in vain for a gift worthy of this beautiful soul. I am on the point of returning to Vienna, where I shall eagerly await your answer. Then each time I think of you, together with the emotions of sincerest friendship, will be those of heartfelt gratitude, and both will seal for all time the perfect respect with which I have the honour to be, dearest friend, your most devoted servant,

Chevalier Gluck.[2]

Gluck applied unsuccessfully to several of his literary friends for a memorial text. The following, from Wieland, acknowledges such a request:

I am quite ashamed, most worthy Sir, to have kept silent for so long after your kind and intimate letter from Paris, and now to appear before you with empty hands. When I received your letter, I was in a state to weep with you, to feel your loss deeply, and to mourn; but to put something into words which would be worthy of the departed angel, and of your grief, and your genius, I could not, and will not be able to do. Other than Klopstock, only Goethe could do it. I sought him out and showed him your letter, and the very next day I found him full of a grand idea which had taken possession of his mind. I saw it begin to form, and hope to rejoice greatly at its completion, whatever the difficulties, for what is impossible to Goethe? I saw him brood over it lovingly, and only some quiet days of solitude were needed for him to put on paper that which he had let me see was in his heart. But fate did not allow him or you this consolation. Just at this moment, his position here became increasingly unsettled, and his energies attracted elsewhere. For several weeks now, with our duke's unbounded confidence and particular affection, he has taken a position in the Privy Council from which he cannot withdraw. Now there is almost no hope that he may soon be able to complete the work he has begun. . . .

I have moments when I keenly wish that I could write a lyrical work worthy to be given life and immortality by Gluck. . . . But I lack a subject which might suit lyrical drama and also be capable of making a great effect. Perhaps, my dear Gluck, you know of one which you would like to have written so that you could work on it? . . . At one time *Antonius und Cleopatra* was strongly in my head and in my heart—but even if I could work on it, this is no subject for Vienna, where the excess of love would doubtless be found too indecent. You have already set the three greatest subjects, Orpheus, Alcestis, and Iphigenia—and what is left that is worthy of you?

---

[2] Paris, 10 May 1776, pub. in Klopstock, *Auswahl aus Klopstocks nachgelassenen Briefwechsel*, ed. Christian August Heinrich Clodius (Leipzig, 1821), i. 266–8; Treichlinger (ed.), *Briefe*, 39–40. The phrase 'deutsches Mädchen' refers to Gluck's setting of Klopstock's ode; see Ch. 14 above.

... The enclosed letter from [Duke] Carl August has been in my hands for some time.[3]

Dear Chevalier Gluck,

Just how closely the death of your dearest niece has touched me, must be felt not said. It is well for the good soul, that she feels no more the suffering and oppression of this wretched earth—no, not the earth, which is good, but the world [of men]. She was one of the dearest creatures on earth. Let us mourn her loss inconsolably, as long as the Creator allows us feelings. Suffering is not to be shunned, for it breaks through the coldness of this world. Her spirit is near us in every lovely moonbeam and every lovely sunset. The spirits of good souls envelop us worthy people, and protect us from the pestilential air of cold, insincere, superficial beings, interposing between us, so that although these may oppress the body they cannot touch the soul. Farewell, and allow us to feel the nearness of the dear blessed one in each warm summer night! Think of me often!

Carl August, Duke of Sachsen-Weimar.[4]

Gluck's reply to Carl August is lost, but his letter to Wieland survives:

Honoured Sir and dear friend,

Your letter of 13 July was all the more pleasant a gift because I had awaited it with such impatience. Although time has diminished my grief, as it tends to subdue all human suffering, even joy, your letter did not arrive too late to fill the void created by the loss of my child. The friendship of a Wieland, a Klopstock, and other such men suffices to comfort a suffering man for all the sorrows of this world. You bring me the hope that in Herr Goethe I may win a new friend of this kind, and my joy is now complete. Although I may not expect a poem on the good, snow-white departed soul of my little one, either from you or from Herr Goethe, however much I might wish it, your muse, my dear Wieland, will never desert you without your bidding. And Goethe— whose writings, like yours, I have read thoroughly, Goethe—of whom Klopstock said to me: 'This is the great man'—cannot shut out inspiration just because of his official duties, and cannot refrain from laying one of his roses on a grave worthy of roses. Is anything impossible for you and Goethe? Present my compliments to this excellent man, and tell him that I would have composed the songs for his *Erwin und Elmire* for this theatre, if there had been people available to perform them.

[3] Letter to Gluck, Weimar, 13 July 1776, pub. in Christoph Martin Wieland, *Auswahl denkwürdiger Briefe*, ed. Ludwig Wieland (Vienna, 1815), i. 315–18; Tenschert, *Gluck . . . Reformator der Oper*, 195–7.

[4] Weimar, July 1776, pub. in *Litterarische Monate*, ed. Friedrich Justus Riedel, 1 (1776–7), 145. Mentions of moonbeams, summer nights, etc. refer to the text of Klopstock's odes.

Instead of forgetting your *Antonius und Cleopatra*, forget instead your thought that the 'excess of love' would shock the people in Vienna, where there is now no German opera, only the opera buffa. If you would like to send me your poem, I would gladly work with you and for you. In Weimar, under such a duke, in the excellent company of Goethe and others, it is impossible that you lack encouragement. My request is only that instead of the usual confidants, you should include choruses, of Romans on Antony's side, and of Egyptian women on Cleopatra's. Confidants and other secondary roles make the work tedious, because they are too uninteresting; furthermore, it is rarely easy to find more than one good soprano. But choruses create interest, and when they fill the stage, especially at the end, they are tremendously acclaimed.

Perhaps my arrangements with Vienna and Paris will allow me to undertake an excursion through Germany. Weimar will then be the first place I shall visit, in order to meet the finest assembly of people, and to draw inspiration at their source.

I ask you to deliver the enclosed [letter] to the duke, and to say on my behalf as much about it as you think fit, to keep me in the favour of this worthy nobleman.

Farewell, and enjoy all the blessings you deserve!

Gluck.[5]

---

[5] Vienna, 7 Aug. 1776: autograph in Weimar, Goethe- und Schiller-Archiv, 93/III, 1, 27a.

18

THE PICCINNI WAR: FIRST SHOTS
(1776–1777)

IN July 1776, Gluck's Parisian friends planned to honour him by commissioning a marble copy of Houdon's bust, to be placed in the Opéra beside those of Lully and Rameau. The tribute was intended to mark Gluck's acceptance as a French composer of classic status. A subscription was set up by the cellist Jean-Baptiste Janson (or Jannson) and underwritten by six of Gluck's colleagues and friends: (in order of signing) Gossec, Du Roullet, Larrivée, Le Duc (director of the Concert spirituel), Berton, and Le Gros. The marble bust was completed in 1777 and exhibited in the Salon du Louvre that autumn. In March 1778 it was installed at the Opéra. The full effect of the tribute was marred, however, by an insufficient number of subscribers coming forward to raise the 4,000 *livres* required by Houdon. Despite a contribution of 600 *livres* from the queen, only the sum of 2,500 *livres* was raised, and the underwriters had to make good the shortfall.[1]

Meanwhile the anti-Gluckists, headed by Marmontel in collusion with the Neapolitan ambassador Domenico Carraccioli, selected Piccinni as their champion, and prepared a trial of strength by offering both composers the same subject, *Roland*. The following letter from Gluck to Du Roullet exposes the plot. It was published in the *Année littéraire* with this editorial note: 'This letter, written in the confidence of friendship, was, as is obvious, not intended for publication. It has been printed with the consent neither of M. Gluck nor of the person addressed.' But several clues, including the timing, suggest that the letter was written solely with publi-

---

[1] The bust was destroyed by fire in 1873. Documents relating to the subscription are reproduced in Prod'homme, 'Les Portraites français de Gluck', *Rivista musicale italiana*, 25 (1918), 47–51. Several (perhaps all) of the guarantors, including Janson, were freemasons and members of the lodge 'Des neuf soeurs', which Gluck is also thought to have attended. Janson became a member of Gluck's household in Vienna, where he gave a benefit concert which included music by Gluck; see Ch. 22 below.

cation in mind; the unusually coherent content sends a clear message to the directors of the Opéra, and the repeated endearments ('mon cher ami') scarcely serve to camouflage the public statement.

I have just received your letter of 15 January, my dear friend, in which you exhort me to continue working on the libretto of the opera *Roland*. This is no longer feasible, for when I learned that the administration at the Opéra, aware that I was working on *Roland*, had given the same piece to M. Piccinni, I burnt everything I had already done—which was perhaps not worth much, in which case the public must be grateful to M. Marmontel for having prevented them from hearing bad music. Besides, I am not the man to enter into competition. M. Piccinni would have too great an advantage over me, for, apart from his personal merit, which is certainly very great, he would have the advantage of novelty, in that I have already given four works in Paris, whether good or bad it matters not, and that taxes one's invention. I have paved the way for him, and he has only to follow in my path. I say nothing to you of his supporters. I am sure that a certain politician of my acquaintance [Carraccioli] will invite three-quarters of Paris to dinner or supper to win him proselytes, and that Marmontel, who is so good at inventing stories, will tell the whole kingdom about the exclusive merit of the Sr Piccinni. I am sincerely sorry for M. Hébert for having fallen into the clutches of such people, one of whom admires nothing but Italian music, the other a librettist of would-be opéras-comiques. They will make a fool of him! ['Ils lui feront voir la lune à midi.'] I am really sorry about it, because M. Hébert is a gentleman, and that is why I shall not withhold my *Armide* from him, but only on the conditions I set out in my previous letter to you, of which I repeat to you the essential ones: that when I come to Paris, I must be allowed at least two months to train the actors and actresses, that I must have the authority to hold as many rehearsals as I think necessary, that there will be no understudies, and that another opera is held in readiness in case some actor or actress be indisposed. These are my conditions, without which I shall keep *Armide* for my own pleasure. I have written the music in such a manner that it will not quickly age.

You tell me, my dear friend, in your letter that nothing will ever equal *Alceste*, but I do not endorse your prophecy. *Alceste* is a pure tragedy, and I confess to you that I think it very little short of perfection. But you can have no idea of how many nuances and variations music is capable. The totality of *Armide* is so different from that of *Alceste* that you will not believe they are by the same composer. I have used all the little power that remains to me to complete *Armide*, and in doing so I have tried to be more painter and poet than musician—you will be able to judge this, if they decide to put it on. I confess I should like to end my career with this opera. It is true that the public will require as much time to understand it as they did to understand *Alceste*. There is a kind of refinement in *Armide* which is not present in *Alceste*, because I have found the way to make the characters speak so that you will know at once, from their manner of speaking, when it is Armida who speaks, or a confidant, etc. etc. I shall say no more, or you will think I have become a madman or a charlatan. Nothing makes a worse impression than singing one's own praises; that was only proper for the great Corneille. When Marmontel or I praise ourselves, people mock us and laugh in our faces. As for the rest, you are quite right to say that French composers have been too much neglected; unless I am much mistaken, Gossec and Philidor, who understand the style of French opera, would be of infinitely more service to the public than the best Italian composers, if only people did not enthuse so much over everything that has an air of novelty. Then again you tell me, my friend, that *Orphée* loses in comparison with *Alceste*. But good heavens! How can these two works be compared, when nothing about them is comparable? One might please more than the other, but if you perform *Alceste* with poor actors, and with any actress except Levasseur, and give *Orphée* with the best you have, you will see that *Orphée* will turn the scales. The best-written things, if performed badly, become utterly intolerable. There can be no comparison between two works of a different nature. Now if, for example, Piccinni and I each wrote our own setting of [Quinault's] *Roland*, it would be possible to judge which of the two was better composed. But different librettos must necessarily produce different music to express the words in the most faithful manner, according to the nature of each poem. Comparisons are odious.[2] I almost fear lest anyone should compare *Armide* with *Alceste*. The poems are so different; one must evoke tears, the other arouse a voluptuous sensation. If such a comparison is made, I shall have no other course than to pray to God that the good city of Paris may come to its senses.

Farewell, my dear friend, I embrace you, etc. etc.[3]

At about the same time, Gluck took further steps to promote his name at the Opéra. By the end of the season, *Alceste* was an acknowledged success, and Gluck recorded his gratitude to the company, though he could not refrain from adding a barbed comment on the probity of Parisian musicians:

They write to tell me that you perform *Alceste* with a remarkable perfection, tackling it with extraordinary zeal. I cannot tell you how much pleasure this token of your friendship in this connection has given me. I beg you to believe

---

[2] 'toute comparaison claudicat': literally, every comparison distorts.

[3] Vienna, summer, 1776, in *Année littéraire*, 7 (1776), 322–3. Reproduced in Nohl, *Musiker-Briefe*, 32–4; Prod'homme, *Écrits*, 405–9; Einstein, *Gluck*, 227–8; Lesure, *Querelle*, i. 42–5; a copy, not in Gluck's hand, exists in F-Pn, Gluck lettres autographes, no. 43. Hébert was a member of the administration at the Opéra. Carraccioli was the admirer of Italian music, Marmontel the librettist, who adapted Quinault's *Roland* for Piccinni.

that I shall lose no opportunity to show you my gratitude. Meanwhile, my dear friends and companions, accept my heartiest thanks, and if I may ask for another token of your friendship, do take all the pains you can to make M. Cambini's opera succeed, as I have been told that quite apart from his talents, he is a very worthy man—a very rare thing in our profession in this age. I am always, gentlemen and dear friends, your very humble [servant], etc.[4]

A series of letters to more intimate friends record Gluck's daily concern with the Paris scene. Kruthoffer was the recipient of the majority of these bulletins:

My dear friend,

I am much obliged to you for sending the parcel. We have not yet received the atlas from the architect, because the courier does not know where he lives; we hope soon to find this out. My wife, who joins with me in sending kindest regards to you and Herr von Blumendorff, asks you to send the two rolls of muslin at the earliest opportunity, provided they are of the same colour. Concerning Le Marchand, I have sent him *Le Poirier* [*L'Arbre enchantée*], in the hope that his manners will one day mend, though I observe that neither good fortune nor bad helps to improve him, as I never hear from him at all.[5] Write and tell me when the score of *Alceste* will be ready; I am pestered about it from Paris even here. I hear that M. Noverre is engaged by the Opéra; if this is true, then next year, if God spares me, I shall produce *Siège de Cythère* again, because this opera, with appropriate dances created for it, will win an altogether different reputation, and I have no doubt as to its success.[6] Your story about Mlle Arnould made us laugh heartily. You will remember that I have always said that when the public had once understood *Alceste*, the work would make a deep and lasting impression, and now it seems that I guessed right. *Armide* will have difficulty in standing comparison with it, because the libretto has less tension than *Alceste*, and contains many episodes. But if M. Janson's

[4] Letter to the musicians in the orchestra at the Opéra, Vienna, 14 Aug. 1776, in François Métra, *Correspondance secrète* (London, 1787), iii. 280–1; Prod'homme, *Écrits*, 411–12; id., 'Lettres de Gluck et à propos de Gluck', *Zeitschrift der Internationalen Musikgesellschaft*, 13 (1912), 257. Giovanni Giuseppe Cambini had worked in Paris since 1770; his ballet *Les romans* had been given on 2 Aug. and failed immediately. It is possible that the whole letter was intended ironically; Gluck had chafed at the low performance standards under Berton, and was aware that Cambini's failure enhanced his own success. See, however, his generosity over Laurenti (n. 9 below).

[5] Le Marchand published a short score of *L'Arbre enchantée*, together with some extracts and the orchestral parts; see Hopkinson, *Bibliography*, item 42A and 42B.

[6] Noverre took up a position at the Opéra in Aug. 1776; see *Mémoires secrets*, ix. 189 (18 Aug. 1776). Although he created the ballets for a revival of *Iphigénie en Aulide* and for *Armide* in 1777, and for *Iphigénie en Tauride* and *Écho et Narcisse* (1779), besides those for Piccinni's *Roland* (1778), there is no trace of work on *Cythère*.

subscription [for the bust] comes about, then out of gratitude to the public, I shall scarcely be in a position to withdraw the work. If I have deserved this honour, it is not so much on account of my good music, for in my opinion much good music has been written by many before me, and will be written in the future, but because I have shown them how to produce their operas, and I have trained an actress and an actor whom they thought nothing of—for which I may deserve some reward. In any case, it is M. Janson who receives the greatest honour from it. I remain, dear friend, your most devoted servant,

Gluck.[7]

My dear friend,

I have received everything in good order. My wife thanks you particularly for the fine cloth, and sends many good wishes to you and to Herr von Blumendorff. You forgot to send me the twelve volumes of *Le Nouveau Spectateur*, and [you sent] absolutely no news. Another time, prepare your letter in advance, so that you do not leave it till the last minute to write to me. If M. Peters does not consider it profitable to have *Alceste* engraved, then give it to Le Marchand, so that it will soon be ready, for the emperor keeps asking me when he will receive a copy, and I no longer know what I should reply.[8] It has now been known for almost a year that I intend to give *Armide*, and Mme Laurenti has taken no steps to find underwriters who could be of help to her in producing her *Armide*.[9] The administration is scarcely likely to accept her opera without guarantee, as it is expensive, and her husband did not previously work for the Académie. This is essential: she must do as M. Floquet has done; he sought underwriters, and [as] the Parisian public is compassionate, his poverty contributed as much to his success as the music itself.[10] She must act. Now is the right time, because the administration does not know what to produce next. I have written to ask M. Bailli [du Roullet] to speak for me to M. Berton, so that everything possible is done to make this affair succeed. This is all I can do in the matter; I cannot force her [to act]; that would be construed as impertinence and arrogance on my part. But I would like nothing better than for the opera to be given, so that I could be released from the perpetual harassments with which I am bombarded by every post, to bring *Armide* with me (I [still] find it very superficial in several places). I have suggested to the

---

[7] Letter to Kruthoffer, Vienna, 29 Aug. 1776, in Kinsky, *Glucks Briefe*, 20. The actress and actor in whose training Gluck took most pride were Levasseur and Le Gros.

[8] Le Marchand advertised *Alceste* in the *Mercure de France* in Dec. 1776, but the only surviving copies were issued by Peters; see Hopkinson, *Bibliography*, 53–4.

[9] Mme Laurenti was the widow of an amateur composer who had also written a setting of *Armide*. Gluck appears to have supported diligently and with disinterest her attempts to get the work performed. No such composer or work is mentioned in the records at the Opéra.

[10] When at first the success of *Alceste* had seemed doubtful, the ballet *L'Union de l'amour et des arts* by Étienne Joseph Floquet had been revived and performed alternately with the opera; see *Mercure de France*, June 1776, 184.

administration that I postpone my *Armide* until next carnival season in 1778, so that no obstacle is raised on my account. This is what I have done in response to your request. I remain forever, dear friend, your most devoted servant,

Gluck.

PS   Please present my compliments to M. Hoppé, to whom I am greatly obliged for the forwarded letter.[11]

It is impossible to determine whether Gluck was motivated entirely by goodwill towards Mme Laurenti or whether, still dissatisfied with his own *Armide*, he sought an excuse to delay it. Clearly he regarded the production of another *Armide* (by an amateur) in a very different light from the abortive contest over *Roland*.

My dear friend,

I do not know what to think, having received no letter from you by the last courier. I hope you are not angry with me. I have had a letter from M. Berton, in which he tells me he knows the opera by M. Laurenti, but that he does not think it substantial enough to be produced at the Opéra. I shall send you his original letter by the next courier. Meanwhile I am giving you the means to sound out M. Berton himself: it is a bill for 1,000 *livres* which I would ask you to be good enough to cash for me, and keep the money for me till I arrive. Take the opportunity to speak of the poor widow's need; spoken words can often make more of an impression than written ones. I also ask you to do everything possible to progress the [score] of *Alceste*. My wife sends her kindest regards to you and to Herr von Blumendorff, as do I, who also have the honour to be, dear friend, your most devoted servant,

Gluck.

PS   Please forward the enclosed lightweight letters to their addresses.[12]

No more is heard of Laurenti's opera. One of the enclosed 'lightweight letters' was to Arnaud, in which Gluck shows his sensitivity to the parties that were forming for and against him in Paris:

Monsieur,

I have at last divined the reason for your silence towards me. It is the return of the Neapolitan ambassador [Carraccioli] to Paris. You know he is my enemy,

---

[11] Letter to Kruthoffer, Vienna, 30 Sept. 1776, in Kinsky, *Glucks Briefe*, 23. Hoppé was Kruthoffer's colleague at the embassy.

[12] Letter to Kruthoffer, Vienna, 31 Oct. 1776, in Kinsky, *Glucks Briefe*, 25.

for we each have different opinions about music. It suits you, therefore, to prefer the friendship of a titled man to that of a simple musician like me. My feelings for you are no less unchangeable, and you will always remain my hero. I
have read in the journals that you gave an admirable address on the Greek language. If it is printed, I would ask you to send me a copy by the Viennese
diplomatic courier. It is not enough for me that I know you to be a great
man—I would like all Europe to do you homage. On the subject of great men,
the portrait by your M. Duplessis is much admired here by the connoisseurs,
but they are critical of the hands. I should like it if he could amend them, in
order to perfect his reputation in this country: I ask your advice on the matter,
and whether I should bring [the portrait] back to Paris, on the condition, however, that he can finish it quickly. They tell me from Paris that almost everyone is pleased with *Alceste*. I flatter myself that you are, too. Your approbation
means more to me than that of an entire nation.

I remain, monsieur, your most humble and obedient servant,

Gluck.

PS My wife sends you a thousand compliments. The word 'Sussola' that
Chevalier Planelli speaks of means a post-chaise used by ladies in Naples.
They are painted very tastefully, somewhat like your festive coaches.[13]

Arnaud remained true to Gluck, and was shortly to write a long letter to
Martini, defending French opera traditions in comparison with Italian and
extolling Gluck's contribution to 'tragic operas manifesting total continuity, of which each part is intimately connected with every other, each
enhancing and strengthening the rest, and working together reciproc-
ally'.[14]

The Franco-Italian rivalry was the basis of a public exchange between
Gluck and Nicolas Framery. It referred to the charge of plagiarism in connection with *Alceste*, already refuted by Arnaud in 'La Soirée perdue'.[15] In
September 1776, Framery addressed a letter to the *Mercure de France*, alleg-
ing that Sacchini had prior claim to the disputed air from the finale to Act
II, 'Ah! malgré moi, mon faible cœur partage'. Framery argued first that
the prior date of the Italian *Alceste* was irrelevant because it had been given
only in Bologna, 'where it is not the custom to publish scores', and because
in any case 'the music of the French *Alceste* is entirely different from the
Italian and almost all the airs are different'. He then claimed that the air in
question had been composed by Sacchini for Millico in a pastiche version

---

[13] 31 Oct 1776, in L.R., 'Correspondance inédite', 10–11. For Planelli and *Alceste*, see Ch. 16
above and *Mémoires secrets*, ix. 90 (23 Apr. 1776).

[14] Letter dated 1 Dec. 1776: Vienna, Österreichische Nationalbibliothek, 7/1–1. Pub. in Lesure,
Querelle, 240–8 (dated 2 Dec.); and in Schmid, *Gluck*, 475–81, followed by Martini's reply.

[15] See Ch. 16 n. 36.

of *Olimpiade* in 1773, and that Millico had sung the air repeatedly while lodging with Gluck in Paris, even teaching it to Nanette, who also performed it. Framery's argument culminated in the claim that as a composer who had adapted many of Sacchini's airs to French words, he had the expertise to claim that the air was originally made for the Italian words in *Olimpiade*, 'Se cerca, se dice'.[16] The accusation was easy to refute, and Gluck wrote the following reply to the editor of the *Mercure de France*:

There is, in the *Mercure* for the month of September 1776, a letter from a certain S[r] Framery on the subject of M. Sacchini, who would be greatly to be pitied if he needed such a defender to uphold his reputation. Almost everything that M. Framery thinks fit to say about M. Gluck, M. Sacchini, and M. Millico is false. M. Gluck's Italian *Alceste* has never been given in Bologna, nor in any town in Italy, because of the difficulty of performing it when M. Gluck is not present to direct his work.

He has given it only in Vienna in Austria in 1768 [*sic*]. The Sr Millico sang the role of Admetus in the revival of this opera. It is correct that M. Sacchini inserted the passage in question in his air 'Se cerca, se dice', but this musical material had already appeared in M. Gluck's Italian *Alceste* as 'Ah! per questo già stanco mio core', published in Vienna in 1769. We would say in addition that there is another passage at the end of the same air [by Sacchini], which he has taken from the air 'Di [te] scordami' in *Paride ed Elena*, also published in Vienna. M. Framery does not know that an Italian composer is very often forced to accommodate himself to the whims and the voice of the singer, and it was the S[r] Millico who compelled M. Sacchini to insert the phrases in question into his air. M. Gluck himself reproached his friend Millico, because at that time M. Gluck had not yet given his *Alceste* in Paris, although he planned to do so. Someone as talented and as full of fine ideas as M. Sacchini has no need to steal from others. But he was sufficiently accommodating to the singer to borrow these passages, in which the singer believed he shone the brightest. M. Sacchini's reputation has been long established. It is not in need of rescuing. But it could perhaps be harmed if his arias composed for the Italian language were adapted to French words, bearing in mind the difference between the two [national] musical styles and the two prosodies. M. Framery, as a man of letters, ought to do rather better than to confuse the national characteristics of the French and the Italians, and to create a 'hermaphrodite' music by parodying airs which, although tolerated in opéra-comique, are not suitable for tragic opera.[17]

---

[16] *Mercure de France*, Sept. 1776, 181–4. Pub. in Lesure, *Querelle*, i. 96–9.

[17] Vienna, Nov. 1776, pub. in *Mercure de France*, Nov. 1776, 184–5. Pub. in Nohl, *Musiker-Briefe*, 37–8; Lesure, *Querelle*, i. 100–1; Prod'homme, *Écrits*, 409–11.

Gluck's letters to Kruthoffer from this time are once more dominated by concern for the publication of his scores. The following refers obscurely to some new clause in connection with Peters's edition of *Alceste*, relating to the number of free copies allowed to the composer:

My dear friend,

I have safely received your letter of 17 October, in which I learn of M. Peters's request. I shall grant it this time because he is your good friend. A few scores shall be reserved for me, but no precedent is established for future operas relative to these few, which he will give [without payment]. The courier is about to depart. I can write no more to you except to send you and M. de Blumendorff very sincere compliments on behalf of my wife and me. Please send me no more parcels of poems to be made into operas, as I am cruelly bombarded with them. I remain, dear friend, your most devoted servant,

Gluck.[18]

The same contract with Peters was still an issue in the next letter, which also reveals that Gluck had heard of Piccinni's arrival in Paris on 31 December (in exceptionally harsh weather, so that he was said to have exclaimed, 'Does the sun never shine in this country?'):[19]

My dear friend,

Please ask Herr von Blumendorff to give his brother a little reprimand, because after I had enquired of him three times [for letters], each time he told me that nothing had arrived for me. He did not send me the packet until 11 January, and then without offering any plausible explanation for this omission. Consequently I received your letter some thirteen days late. I am sending you the contract, though it is not worth the trouble of drawing up a document for such a bagatelle, and I do not believe that M. Peters will make use of any such clause against me. I also ask you, dear friend, to send me reliable information as to why and on whose account, and for what purpose, Piccinni has been summoned to Paris, and what salary he receives. Entertain me with some news! I hope that the roads will soon be good enough for me to embrace you in person. I remain, dear friend, your most devoted servant,

Gluck.[20]

---

[18] Vienna, 29 Nov. 1776, in Maria Komorn, 'Ein ungedruckter Brief Glucks', *Neue Zeitschrift für Musik*, 99 (1932), 672–5.

[19] Pierre Louis Ginguené, *Notice sur la vie et les ouvrages de Nicolas Piccinni* (Paris, 1801), 25.

[20] Letter to Kruthoffer, Vienna, 15 Jan. 1777, in Kinsky, *Glucks Briefe*, 26. For Blumendorff's brother, see Ch. 24 n. 9.

His next letter, still concerned with Peters, also includes one of many references to his desire to complete his setting of *Hermannsschlacht*.[21] Descriptions of his performance of the poem continue until his last year:

My dear friend,

Your letter had such a flavour of Klopstock about it that it actually gave me the idea of completing *Hermannsschlacht*. You see what power your letters have! The contract with M. Peters requires an explanation, since if I were not to come to Paris again, he would have to pay nothing. It must be understood as referring to the time when I might arrive in Paris. I can write no more to you; I do not know whether or not the courier has already left. My compliments from my wife and me to you and to Herr von Blumendorff. Send me all the news, for [Paris] must be humming with theatrical affairs. Your most devoted servant,

Gluck.[22]

With the arrival of spring, Gluck was able to look forward to his next visit to Paris:

My dear friend,

I am grateful to you for the news you sent me in your letter. I hope, with God's help, to embrace you this year without fail, and perhaps it will be soon, for my informants tell me that they want to revive *Siège de Cythère* again, and that requires my presence. Concerning the Italian *Alceste*, I had almost predicted that Le Marchand would want to play one of his tricks; M. Eberts asked me for twenty-five copies for distribution. He has received them, and I here enclose his own letter about this; it will better inform you [of the circumstances] than if I described them to you. My wife and I send you and Herr von Blumendorff our best compliments, and we hope soon to take many walks with you. Meanwhile I remain, dear friend, your most devoted servant,

Gluck.[23]

Dear friend, this time I can write nothing to you. The courier is leaving overzealously, for he has only just arrived. I hope, with God's help, to embrace you during April or early May. Adieu. Remember me with a little affection! Our compliments to Herr von Blumendorff.[24]

---

[21] See e.g. his letter of 14 Aug. 1773 (Ch. 11 above).

[22] Letter to Kruthoffer, Vienna, 31 Jan. 1777, in Kinsky, *Glucks Briefe*, 27.

[23] Letter to Kruthoffer, Vienna, 3 Mar. 1777, in Kinsky, *Glucks Briefe*, 28. *Cythère* was not revived in 1777. The meaning of the ref. to Le Marchand is not clear; presumably he intended to publish extracts from the Italian *Alceste* in an attempt to spoil Peters's edn. of the French score.

[24] Gluck to Kruthoffer, Vienna, 30 Mar. 1777, in Kinsky, *Glucks Briefe*, 29.

An unusual image of the composer appears in a letter by the writer Heinrich von Bretschneider; the account stems from Bretschneider's friend Riedel, still apparently living in Gluck's household.[25] Whatever the truth of this clearly biased account, it is a reminder that Gluck continued to enjoy the patronage of the Lobkowitz family:

Did you know that the great composer Gluck is a parasite? Would you imagine that he lets himself be used as court jester by a certain Count [Ferdinand Philipp Joseph] Lobkowitz . . . to such an extent that he pulls the wool over this count's eyes and acts as if he suffers all sorts of nonsense from him, and then gets the count to pay him for it? Gluck has already extracted more than 60,000 florins from this count, though to earn it he must not only play the clavier day and night, but also let himself be used on household business. What Gluck is to Lobkowitz, Riedel is to Gluck.[26]

---

[25] See Ch. 14.

[26] Letter to Friedrich Nicolai, 14 Mar. 1777, in Werner (ed.), *Aus dem Josephinischen Wien*, 147.

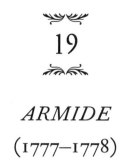

19

ARMIDE
(1777–1778)

GLUCK returned to Paris on 29 May 1777:

Immediately upon his arrival in France, Gluck was admitted to the queen's chamber, and throughout the time he remained there, she did not cease talking to him. One day, she asked him if he was near to finishing his tragic opera *Armide*, and if he was satisfied with it. Gluck answered her very coldly, in his German accent, 'Madame, it will soon be finished, and it will be truly *superb*.' ... People exclaimed greatly over the confidence with which this artist used to talk about one of his own creations. The queen defended him warmly; she argued that he could not be unaware of the merit of his work, that he knew that this opinion was widespread, and that he doubtless feared that the modesty demanded by the rules of etiquette would in him seem only false.[1]

The queen's support of Gluck never wavered, and the composer was apparently ever ready to play the courtier in return:

Gluck composed his Armida in compliment to the personal charms of Maria Antoinette. I never saw her majesty more interested about anything than she was for its success. She became a perfect slave to it. She had the gracious condescension to hear all the pieces through, at Gluck's request, before they were submitted to the stage for rehearsal. Gluck said he always improved his music after he saw the effect it had upon her majesty.

He was coming out of the queen's apartment one day, after he had been performing one of these pieces for her majesty's approbation, when I followed and congratulated him on the increased success he had met with from the whole band of the opera at every rehearsal. 'Oh my dear princess!' cried he, 'it

---

[1] Mme de Campan, *Mémoires sur la vie privée de Marie Antoinette* (Paris, 1822), i. 154. The writer was first woman of the queen's bedchamber.

wants nothing to make it be applauded up to the seven skies, but two such
delightful heads as her majesty's and your own.' 'Oh, if that be all,' answered
I, 'we'll have them painted for you, Mr Gluck!' 'No, no, no! you do not understand me,' replied Gluck, 'I mean real, real heads. My actresses are very ugly,
and Armida and her confidential lady ought to be very handsome.'[2]

Lamballe (or her translator, Hyde) is unreliable on names, stating that Mlle
Saint-Huberti was the first to undertake the role of Armida; perhaps this
was the case in the private rehearsals before the queen, but in the theatre,
the roles of Armida and her two 'confidential ladies' were taken by
Levasseur, Lebourgeois, and Châteauneuf; Saint-Huberti sang Melissa.
She similarly misattributes the ballets to Vestris—they were by Noverre—
but the following anecdote may fairly represent the firm hand with which
Gluck controlled the choreographer's bid to include additional dances, in
the light of the problems caused by Berton's additions to Cythère:

it was at one time feared, that the success of Armida would be endangered,
unless an equal share of the performance were conceded to the dancers. But
Gluck, whose German obstinacy would not give up a note, told [Noverre] he
might compose a ballet in which he would leave him his own way entirely; but
that an artist, whose profession only taught him to reason with his heels,
should not kick about works like Armida at his pleasure. 'My subject,' added
Gluck, 'is taken from the immortal Tasso. My music has been logically composed, and with the ideas of my head; and of course there is very little room
left for capering. If Tasso had thought proper to make Rinaldo a dancer, he
never would have designated him a warrior.'[3]

Gluck was accorded the three-month period of preparation he had
demanded, and the first public rehearsal was given on 5 September.[4]

As usual the work was controversial. Gluck was attacked on two fronts.
In addition to the campaign on behalf of Piccinni—who had yet to produce
an opera in Paris—Gluck met opposition from supporters of Lully's setting, composed almost a century earlier: 'The rehearsals continued to be
followed with passion. However, the party of the Lullists was reawakened,
and they alleged that in many places the Chevalier Gluck did not approach
the noble style and the simple beauty of the recitative in the former opera.'[5]

---

[2] Catherine Hyde (Hyde Govion Broglio Solari), Secret Memoirs of the Court of France . . . from
the Journal, Letters, and Conversations of Princess Lamballe (London, 1826), 191–2.

[3] Ibid. 194–5.

[4] Mémoires secrets, x. 215–16 (6 Sept. 1777).

[5] Ibid. x. 227 (22 Sept. 1777).

The première took place on 23 September. The initial reception, according to Grimm, was cool:

This major event had been long and impatiently awaited by the two parties. It was expected to be decisive, but it decided nothing. The Gluckists and the Piccinnists retained the same antagonisms, the same claims, and the same passion. . . . Almost all the opera was heard with profound indifference; only the end of the first act, and several airs in the fourth, were applauded quite warmly. . . . Apart from the choruses and some grand orchestral effects, there were few scenes in which one was not tempted to regret the easy, natural style of the good Lully.[6]

The Piccinnists enlisted the critic Jean François de La Harpe to publish a detailed attack on *Armide*. La Harpe admired Italian opera, in particular 'the fine arias by Galuppi, Jommelli, Sacchini, and Piccinni, which are sung from one end of Europe to the other', in comparison with which 'the role of Armida is almost entirely a monotonous and fatiguing shriek . . . like Medea, not an enchantress but a sorceress.' He reiterated Rousseau's former position in asserting the primacy of melody ('chant') as the vehicle of expression.[7] He conceded some merit in *Orphée*, but noted that

there is little melody in *Iphigénie*, its airs are feeble and poor. There is still less of it in *Alceste*. Then [Gluck] decided to work upon an old opera, in five acts, full of long monologues, in which there is not a single measured air . . . what can be inferred from this strange enterprise, but that the composer is persuaded that expressive airs—the only kind apt for drama—are by no means necessary to opera, and that recitative, choruses, and harmony are all that are needed to achieve a perfect entertainment?'[8]

Gluck responded with another exposition of his dramatic principles, answering La Harpe teasingly, point by point:

It is impossible, monsieur, for me not to agree with the very judicious observations you have just made on my operas in your *Journal de littérature* of the fifth of this month. I find nothing, absolutely nothing, to refute.

    I was naïve enough till now to believe that music, in common with the other arts, engaged with the whole range of passions, and that it could not please less

---

[6] *Correspondance littéraire*, xi. 537–8 (23 Sept. 1777).

[7] e.g. in Rousseau's *Lettre sur la musique française* (Paris, 1753).

[8] La Harpe, 'Annonce de l'opéra d'*Armide*', *Journal de politique et de littérature*, 5 Oct. 1777; repr. in Lesure (ed.), *Querelle*, i. 259–70.

in expressing the distractions of a madman, or a cry of anguish, than in representing the sighs of love.

> Il n'est point de serpent ni de monstre odieux,
> Qui par l'art imité, ne puisse plaire aux yeaux.[9]

I believed this precept to be as true of music as it is of poetry. I held that melody, when thoroughly imbued with the colour of the feelings it has to express, must take its shape from them, and show as many different shades of feeling as there are different nuances [in the words]; in short that the voice, the instruments, all the sounds, the very silences, must work towards a single aim, that of expression, and that the union between words and music must be so close that the poem is no more made for the music than the music for the poem.

These were not my only errors. I thought I had observed that the French language was unstressed, and did not have the same fixed quantities as the Italian language. I had also been struck by the difference between the singers of the two nations: if I found among one nation soft and flexible voices, the other nation seemed to me to employ more strength and more vigour in its delivery. I deduced from this that Italian melody could not suit the French. Then when I examined the scores of your old operas, despite the ornaments, cadenzas, and other faults which seemed to me to burden their airs, I found enough genuine beauty there to make me think that the French had within themselves their own resources.

These, monsieur, were my thoughts until I read your remarks. Immediately light dawned upon my darkness. I was astounded to see that you had learned more of my art in a few hours of thought than I had after practising it for forty years. You show me, monsieur, that one has only to be a man of letters to be able to pronounce on everything. Now I am quite convinced that the music of the Italian masters is the best music, that it is *music itself*, that if melody is to please, it must have regular phrases, and that even in moments of confusion, when the character singing is moved successively by different emotions, the composer should always retain the same melodic material.

I agree with you that of all my compositions *Orphée* is the only one which is tolerable. I sincerely ask pardon of the god of taste for having *deafened* my listeners by my other operas; the number of performances accorded them and the public's eager acclaim do not prevent me seeing that they are wretched. I am so convinced of this that I want to rewrite them, and as I see that you admire tender music, I want to put into the mouth of a furious Achilles a melody so touching and so sweet that all the audience will be moved to tears.

With regard to *Armide*, I shall not attempt to keep the poem as it is, since, as you judiciously remark, 'Quinault's operas, although full of beauties, are constructed in a manner little favourable to music; these are very fine poems

---

[9] 'There is no serpent or odious monster which, rendered by art, cannot please the eye.'

but very bad operas.' In order to turn them into very bad poems, therefore—
which according to you will unquestionably produce good operas—I beg you
to introduce me to some versifier who can put *Armide* in order, and who will
arrange to have two airs in each scene. We shall between us determine the
quantities and the stresses of the lines; provided the number of syllables is
complete, I shall not bother myself further. I for my part shall work at the
music, from which I shall, as is only right, diligently banish all noisy instruments like the kettledrum and trumpet; I want nothing to be heard in my
orchestra but oboes, flutes, horns, and violins—muted, of course. There will
then be nothing more to do than to fit the words to these airs, which will not
be difficult because we shall have taken our measurements in advance.[10]

Then the role of Armida will no longer be a *monotonous and fatiguing shriek*;
it will no longer be a *sorceress like Medea*, but an *enchantress*; in her despair, I
shall have her sing for you an air with such *regular phrases*, and at the same time
so *tender*, that the most neurotic lady dilettante ['la Petite-Maîtresse la plus
vaporeuse'] might hear it without the least excitement to her nerves.

If some malicious wit thought fit to say to me, 'Take care, monsieur, that
Armida, when mad, does not express herself like Armida when intoxicated
with love', I would reply: 'Monsieur, I have no wish to *alarm the ears* of M. de
La Harpe; I do not want *to imitate nature*, I want to *embellish* it. Instead of making Armida cry out, I want her to *enchant* you.' If he were to persist, and to
point out to me that Sophocles, in the most beautiful of his tragedies, dared
indeed to show the Athenians Oedipus with his bleeding eyes, and that the
recitative, or the kind of inflected declamation, in which was expressed the eloquent grief of this unhappy king, must doubtless have expressed a tone of
deepest sorrow, I repeat by way of answer that M. de La Harpe does not wish
to hear *the cry of a man who suffers*.

Have I not, monsieur, fully mastered the essence of the doctrine laid down
in your comments? I have given several of my friends the pleasure of reading
them. 'You must be grateful,' said one of them as he returned them to me,
'M. de La Harpe gives you excellent advice. He declares his principles in
respect to music; do the same for him. Obtain his poetic and literary works,
and, out of friendship towards him, reveal everything in them that displeases
you. Many people maintain that artistic criticism has no effect but to wound
the artist against whom it is directed, and to prove it, they say that poets have
never had more critics than now, and have never been more mediocre. But
consult the journalists on this subject, and ask them if anything is more useful
to the state than journals. It could be objected that as a musician you have no
right to judge poetry, but is that any more astounding than to see a poet, a man
of letters, pronouncing despotically on music?'

---

[10] Gluck did almost exactly this in crafting *Iphigénie en Tauride* from pre-existing material; see
his letter to Guillard, 17 June 1778, in Ch. 20 below.

This is what my friend said. His arguments seemed to me very soundly based. But despite my gratitude to you, and after much thought, I feel, monsieur, that it is impossible to comply with his advice without incurring the fate of the orator who, in the presence of Hannibal, gave a long discourse on the art of war.[11]

The sustained irony of Gluck's letter irritated an amateur, Fabre, who defended La Harpe's preference for Italian arias in a letter to the *Journal de Paris*.[12] Tired of the controversy, Gluck invited a 'man of letters' to support him, the academician Jean-Baptiste Suard, who took the pseudonym of 'L'Anonyme de Vaugirard':

Monsieur,

When I came to regard music not only as an art to entertain the ears, but as one of the most powerful means of touching the heart and arousing the feelings, I adopted a new approach. I devoted all my attention to the stage; I tried to find a style that was deeply and strongly expressive, and I sought above all to unify all the parts of my works. At first I found the singers, male and female, were against me, together with a great many composers, but I found sufficient compensation in the praise and marks of esteem accorded me by all the intellectuals and men of letters, in Germany and Italy, without exception. In France it has been different; if there are men of letters whose approbation should, in truth, console me for the loss of others, there are also many who have declared themselves against me.

It seems that these gentlemen are more felicitous when they write on other matters, for if I can judge by the welcome the public has been good enough to give my works, this public does not take much account of their expressions and their opinions. But what do you think, monsieur, of the new attack that one of them, M. de La Harpe, has made on me? This M. de La Harpe is a fine pedant! He speaks of music in a manner that would make all the choirboys in Europe shrug their shoulders; he says, *I want* and he says, *my doctrine*,

Et pueri nasum Rhinocerotis habent[13]

Will you not say a few words to him, monsieur, you who have already so effectively defended me against him? Ah, I beg you, if my music has given you some little pleasure, put me in the position of being able to prove to my learned friends in Germany and Italy, that among the men of letters in France there are those who, in speaking of the arts, at least know what they are saying.

[11] *Journal de Paris*, 12 Oct. 1777, 2–3; repr. in Lesure (ed.), *Querelle*, i. 271–5; Nohl, *Musiker-Briefe*, 40–3; Prod'homme, *Écrits*, 414–19. The italicized phrases are quotations from La Harpe's 'Annonce' (see n. 8 above).

[12] 16 Oct. 1777, 2–3; repr. in Lesure (ed.), *Querelle*, i. 276–9.

[13] Literally: 'And boys have a rhinoceros's nose'.

I have the honour to be, monsieur, with the greatest of respect and gratitude, your most humble and obedient servant,

Chevalier Gluck.[14]

Suard, who with his wife Amélie had been among the composer's most
faithful friends and supporters since 1774,[15] responded with a lengthy
defence which reiterates the usual arguments over the nature of melody
and expression.[16]

Meanwhile, Paris enjoyed the dispute as much as the music which
engendered it. It was difficult to avoid taking sides, and Leopold Mozart
warned his son 'to avoid the company of both Gluck and Piccinni as much
as possible' in order to escape making implacable enemies.[17] A few enjoyed
remaining aloof:

Here they are tearing out each others' eyes in support of or against Gluck.
Writing under the name of the *Anonyme de Vaugirard*, Suard took La Harpe to
pieces. Then La Harpe tore him apart. Friends and relations are quarrelling
and falling out over the subject of music. Marmontel preaches, the Abbé
Arnaud hurls epigrams. No one thinks of America any more; melody and harmony are the subject of all the articles. How happy I am, at my own fireside,
without prejudices, without partisan feelings! Peace reigns in my humble her-
mitage.[18]

Gluck expressed his own weariness with the controversy in a long letter of
complaint to his friend Anna von Fries:

I have been so harassed about music, and I am so disgusted with it, that at present I would not write a single note for a louis. You will therefore know,
madame, of the degree of my devotion to you, in bringing myself to arrange
for harp the two songs which I have the honour to send you. There never was
a more terrible battle, or one more fiercely fought, than the one I caused with
my opera *Armide*. The cabals against *Iphigénie*, *Orphée*, and *Alceste* were nothing more than minor skirmishes with slight forces in comparison. In order to
secure a great success for Piccinni's opera [*Roland*], the ambassador of Naples
indefatigably intrigues against me, as much at court as among the nobility. He
persuaded Marmontel, La Harpe, and several academicians to write against

---

[14] *Journal de Paris*, 21 Oct. 1777, 2–3; repr. in Lesure (ed.), *Querelle*, i. 280–1; Nohl, *Musiker-
Briefe*, 48–9; Prod'homme, *Écrits*, 412–14.

[15] See Ch. 13.

[16] *Journal de Paris*, 23 Oct. 1777, 3–5; repr. in Lesure (ed.), *Querelle*, i. 282–313.

[17] Letter to Wolfgang Mozart, 9 Feb. 1778, in Mozart, *Briefe und Aufzeichnungen*, ii. 272.

[18] Marie Riccoboni to Garrick, 9 Oct. 1777, in *Private Correspondence of David Garrick*, ed. James
Boaden (London, 1832), ii. 634. Ricoboni refers to the American War of Independence.

my system of music and my style of composition. The Abbé Arnaud, M. Suard, and some others undertook my defence, and the quarrel became so heated that insults would have led to deeds if mutual friends had not restored order among them. The *Journal de Paris*, which is issued daily, is full of it. The quarrel is making a fortune for the editor, who already has more than 2,500 subscribers in Paris. This, then, is the French revolution in music, carried out with the most resounding ceremony. The enthusiasts tell me, 'You are fortunate, monsieur, to enjoy the honour of being persecuted; all the great geniuses have suffered that.' I would willingly dispatch them and all their fine speeches to the devil. The fact is that the opera which was spoken of as having failed has earned, in seven performances, 37,200 *livres*, not counting the subscribers and the boxes rented by the year. Yesterday, the eighth performance raised 5,767 *livres*. Never before has so enormous a crowd been seen, nor so uninterrupted a silence. The stalls were so full that when a man, who had a hat on his head, was asked by the attendant to remove it, he replied, 'Come and remove it yourself, for I cannot use my arms.' That raised a laugh! I saw people leaving with their hair dishevelled, and their clothes as wet as if they had fallen into a river. You have to be French to pay such a price for your pleasure. There are six places in the opera where the audience are compelled to lose control and to allow themselves to be carried away. Come, madame, and see all this commotion; it will entertain you as much as the opera itself. I despair that I cannot yet leave [Paris] because of the bad roads; my wife is too frightened. I beg you to present my compliments to M. le Baron and to M. Gontard. I remain, madame, with the most perfect esteem, your most humble and obedient servant,

Chevalier Gluck.

PS   My wife sends you a thousand tender compliments.[19]

The Piccinnists for their part were equally harassed by the strife:

I can never think of this terrible Chevalier Gluck without trembling. When I read Ariosto, I feel compelled always to substitute the name of Gluck for that of Ferraù.[20] Your pamphlets for and against music convince me that this Teuton is armed with Hercules' club. Let him batter to death your old French music if he pleases, provided he lets our illustrious friend [Piccinni] live and prosper. For the rest, do not believe that this Gluck is as malicious as the

[19] Paris, 16 Nov. 1777: autograph in New York, Pierpont Morgan Library, Mary Flagler Cary Music Collection. Facsimile in F-Pn, Fac-Sim 147, no. 17. Pub. in D'Escherny, *Mélanges de littérature*, ii. 367–8; Prod'homme, 'Lettres de Gluck', 258; Prod'homme, *Écrits*, 419–21; L.R., 'Correspondance inédite', 12. Anna von Fries was the wife of Gluck's business partner in the Afflisio affair (see Ch. 11) and sister of Count d'Escherny, a Gluckist since 1774 (see Ch. 13). Jacob von Gontard was a Viennese banker and the recipient of a letter from Gluck (see Ch. 22).

[20] A Spanish warrior in Ariosto's *Orlando furioso*.

devils he introduced into his *Orphée* and his *Alceste*. Piccinni himself told me that, when dining with the director Berton, he found himself sitting beside his rival, whereupon the worthy German filled his glass, and said to him in an aside, 'The French are a fine people, but they make me laugh: they want one to write melodies for them but they don't know how to sing.'[21]

Armide gradually won over the unbiased members of the public. In December, Grimm's *Correspondance littéraire* reported that

Armide by the Chevalier Gluck, whose first performances were so poorly received, still dominates the season, with much success. Although of all the subjects M. Gluck could have chosen, this is the one least suited to his style, all are agreed that in this work can be found many difficulties overcome, very beautiful choruses, and several new, if misplaced, ideas; in sum, it is the most unified and the most skilful composition he has ever produced, at least for our stage.[22]

Gluck remained in Paris long enough to see the première of Piccinni's *Roland* in January 1778, with the Gluckist baritone Larrivée in the title role; no existing source suggests that he begrudged the Italian his success.

One last episode from this Paris visit gives further evidence of his magnanimity when not threatened by genuine rivalry. In 1775, the Italian composer Giovanni Giuseppe Cambini had set the final scene of *Armide* for concert performance; it was due to be revived in January 1778, but Cambini, perhaps fearing to incur the wrath of the Gluckists, attempted to withdraw the work. The following exchange, published in the *Journal de Paris*, was designed to do credit to all parties:

We have, monsieur, a scene from *Armide* in our repertory ('Le perfide Renaud me fuit'). For reasons of delicacy, and in deference to the fine treatment of this text in your opera, the composer, M. Cambini, begs us to perform this scene no longer.

You may be assured, monsieur, that we would share M. Cambini's feelings of what is honourable and delicate if it were possible that his scene might damage yours, or yours his. The two scenes, each in their own place, the one in the theatre, the other in the concert-room, have different merits, and each has its own qualities. We hope, monsieur, that you will reply to this letter in such a

[21] Abbé Ferdinand Galiani to Marmontel, Naples, 30 Nov. 1777, in Galiani, *Correspondance inédite* (Paris, 1818), ii. 291–3. The letter is incorrectly dated 1778. The story is repeated, with more evidence of cordiality between the two composers, in Ginguené, *Notice*, 45–6.

[22] xii. 34.

way as to persuade M. Cambini to continue to enjoy the success of his work, which was known at our concerts two years before you wrote your opera.[23]

M. Gluck is very aware of the honourable feelings of both the gentlemen of the Concert des Amateurs and of M. Cambini. He has the privilege of assuring these gentlemen that he will take great pleasure in hearing a performance of the scene from *Armide* by M. Cambini. It would be a tyranny in music to suggest that composers might not perform their compositions. M. Gluck enters into competition with no one, and he will always be pleased to hear music which is better than is own. The only aim should be the advancement of the art.[24]

[23] The Amateurs to Gluck, *Journal de Paris*, 12 Jan. 1778, 47–8; repr. in Lesure (ed.), *Querelle*, i. 404.

[24] Gluck to the Amateurs, *Journal de Paris*, 12 Jan. 1778, 47–8; repr. in Nohl, *Musiker-Briefe*, 50; Prod'homme, *Écrits*, 422; Lesure (ed.), *Querelle*, i. 405.

20

NEGOTIATIONS AT A DISTANCE
(1778)

GLUCK returned to Vienna on 1 March 1778. His letters from this year show his thoughts dominated by the musical scene in Paris, and he continually bombarded his friends with requests for news. The composition and marketing of his last two operas, *Iphigénie en Tauride* and *Écho et Narcisse*, occupied him throughout the year. Kruthoffer continued to act for him in both professional and private transactions:

My dear friend,

We arrived here safely yesterday afternoon, after enduring much hardship on the journey; the coach and its wheels broke and stuck in the snow, and suffered every possible disaster. Moreover I have arrived here at the wrong time; everyone is preparing for war, which it will be difficult to prevent.[1] I am sending you a letter for Mlle Levasseur, together with the ring, which I ask you to give soon to M. Zoller so that he can insert the stone; give him our compliments. When the ring has been cleaned and repaired, please give it to Mlle Levasseur, together with the letter.[2] Tomorrow I intend to go to court, to see what is happening there. Do not forget to write to me with plenty of news, and to send me a few scores of *Armide* if you have not sent them already.[3] My head is still quite muddled from the journey, and I scarcely know what I am writing to you. Our compliments to Herr von Blumendorff, to you, and to all our good friends. Love us as we do you, and think sometimes of your old servant,

Gluck.

PS   Please deal with the enclosed letters.

---

[1] War between Prussia and Austria (the War of the Bavarian Succession) was imminent.
[2] The ring for Levasseur may have been in acknowledgement of her hospitality on Gluck's last visit.
[3] *Armide* had just been issued by Charles Mathon at the Bureau du journal de musique.

PS   I have just received your charming letter of the 17th [February], and read it with great pleasure. You must not send my womenfolk silk lace![4]

A letter from Klopstock to Gluck reverted to the continuously postponed setting of *Hermannsschlacht*. The poet chose the actor Johann Brockmann, apparently one of Gluck's fervent admirers, to deliver his letter:

Brockmann brings you this letter. He is a man who can understand and feel that which you sing to him.

You will certainly not yet have forgotten your beloved little one, and never will, as neither shall I. Perhaps on one of your distant journeys, you might travel to Paris by way of Hamburg? If you were to sing something, we would like to heed you properly, with fresh and undistracted attention, and feast you with old wine. I hear that they want to perform *Hermannsschlacht* in your city. Are you already so far on with the composition? Send me a few words on this. But will not the beautiful, wonderful, magnificent, beneficial war delay this, as so many other projects? The emperor wins my heart more and more. He is making a great mistake if be believes that the old man of Potsdam[5] is grown too old. If it were not the case that in wartime everything languishes, I would repeat my request to you to remind the emperor that he has not kept the promise he made through me to the scholars.[6] But for now—your

Klopstock.[7]

Meanwhile in Paris there was a new director at the Opéra. Anne Pierre Jacques de Vismes de Valgay had taken up his appointment in September 1777, and Gluck sent him belated congratulations:

Monsieur,

I received your kind letter with great pleasure, and was most touched by the marks of friendship and the expressions of kindness you show towards me; I hope that some day the occasion will arise when I may show you the extent of my gratitude. Meanwhile I wish you every success in your new enterprise, in which, my heart tells me, you will not fail, as you have all the qualities needed to succeed in it. It only remains to me to beg you to continue your cherished

---

[4] Letter to Kruthoffer, Vienna, 2 Mar. 1778, in Kinsky, *Glucks Briefe*, 29–30; Tenschert, *Gluck . . . Reformator der Oper*, 204–5.

[5] Frederick the Great of Prussia.

[6] Presumably a ref. to the academy to be established in Vienna; see Gluck's letter of 24 June 1775 (Ch. 15 above).

[7] Hamburg, 16 Mar. 1778: autograph in Graz, Steiermärkisches Landesarchiv, Autographensammlung Handschrift 1506/2. Pub. in Ferdinand Bischoff, 'Ein Brief Klopstocks an Chr. Willibald Gluck', *Neue Musik-Zeitung*, 31 (1909–10), 357–8.

friendship, and to accept the feelings of esteem and regard, with which I have the honour to be, monsieur, your very humble and obedient servant,

Chevalier Gluck.

PS   Please present my compliments to M. de Campan.[8]

Gluck apparently wrote by the same courier to Du Roullet to complain that he had failed to receive any letters from his friends in Paris.[9] In particular, he awaited instalments of the libretto of his *Iphigénie en Tauride*. The authorship of this opera raises questions. At some point between 1775[10] and 1778, authorship of the libretto passed from Du Roullet to Nicolas François Guillard. Whether Guillard took Du Roullet's unfinished poem as his starting-point is unclear, though it can be proved that Guillard originally intended to offer a libretto with this title to Gossec.[11] It emerges from an exchange of letters between Du Roullet and Kruthoffer, however, that the former still took responsibility for keeping Gluck supplied with the developing poem, as it underwent extensive revisions at Gluck's command: '[Gluck] has asked for changes to *Iphigénie*; I am sending them to you so that you might have the goodness to forward them to him by the first courier. There is no time to lose, for as he has given the queen his word to produce an opera before her confinement, *Iphigénie* must be ready for the month of November'[12]—a deadline Gluck failed to meet. Gluck continued to refer to the opera as Du Roullet's.[13]

The only surviving letter from Gluck to Guillard is informative about the composer's role in shaping the libretto, a task forced on him in this instance because of the unprecedentedly extensive reuse of old material:[14]

Your letters reach me very late, my friend; I received your latest yesterday; it took sixteen days, and I thought you must be ill. You wish me to reply to the essential points in your letter? I am ready to do so. To begin with, I must tell

---

[8] Vienna, 1 Apr. 1778: F-Pn, Gluck lettres autographes, no. 1. Pub. in Tiersot, 'Pour le centenaire', 267; id., *Lettres*, i. 52 (pl. IV is a facsimile). De Campan was a *valet de chambre* to the queen, and the husband of Mme de Campan (see Ch. 19).

[9] Letter of 12 Apr. 1778: F-Pn, Du Roullet lettres autographes, no. 2. Pub. in Tiersot, 'Pour le centenaire', 267.

[10] See Gluck to Du Roullet, 1 July 1775 (Ch. 16).

[11] Gossec wrote Guillard a long letter complaining not only of the loss of the *Iphigénie* libretto, but of the many occasions on which his work had been delayed or edged out by Gluck's. See F-Pn, Gossec lettres autographes, no. 7; pub. in Tiersot, *Lettres*, i. 207–10. Le Brisoys de Desnoiresterres attributed this letter to Grétry: see *Gluck et Piccinni: La Musique française au XVIIIe siècle, 1774–1800*, 2nd edn. (Paris, 1875), 254.

[12] Du Roullet to Kruthoffer, 15 May 1778: F-Pn, Du Roullet lettres autographes, no. 3. Pub. in Tiersot, 'Pour le centenaire', 267. The queen's first child was born on 19 Dec.

[13] See his letter of 29 July 1778 (below).

[14] See Hortschansky, *Parodie und Entlehnung*, 202–20.

you that the changes you have made in your fourth act will be simply wasted, because I have already finished the duet between Orestes and Pylades and the air which ends the act, 'Divinité de grandes âmes'. I can make no further changes. Furthermore, in that which you call the fifth act, I think it necessary to cut the third strophe of the hymn, or to write a more interesting one which does not contain the words 'le Scythe fier et sauvage': these words do not contribute to the pathos of the situation. Moreover, the lines must be of the same metrical scheme, four plus four syllables. I have arranged the second strophe thus: 'Dans le Cieux et sur la terre, tout est soumis à ta loi, tout ce que l'Erebe enserre à ton nom pâlit d'effroi.' If you want to write a third strophe, it must go like the second, because while it is being sung, the ceremony takes place to the same music—this is most essential. I would also like Thoas to enter in the fourth scene in a rage, with an air of invective. I should like all the lines to be written so that they can be sung without recitative, right through to the catastrophe. That will give heat to the denouement and a very effective impetus to the soloists and choruses. If you want to act upon this suggestion, do not delay in sending it to me, otherwise I shall keep to the words which are already provided. We come to the air which ends the act during the funeral sacrifices. I would like an air in which the words express both the situation and the music. The meaning should always be completed at the end of a line, not at the beginning, nor half-way through the following line. This is as essential a quality in an air as it is bad in recitative; it constitutes the difference between them; the airs are then better adapted to a flowing melody. We come to the metre of the air I am interested in. I am giving you the Italian words, and where I have placed a sign, that syllable must be long and sonorous; the lines must have ten syllables:

> Se mai senti spirarti sul volto,
> lieve fiato que lento s'aggiri,
> di, son questi gliestremi sospiri,
> del mio fido che muore per me.[15]

I would like the third line to open with a monosyllable, as in the Italian. For example, 'Vois nos peines, entends nos cris perçants'. The last line must if possible be sombre, to match the music. After these four lines—or eight if you wish, provided that they all have the same metre—will come the chorus, 'Contemplez ces tristes apprêts', which seems to me very apt for the situation. I would like the [solo] air here to have roughly the same meaning. After the chorus, either the air will return da capo, or else just the first four lines that you will have written will be sung. I explain myself a little confusedly because my

---

[15] The Italian words are those of Sextus's aria in *La clemenza di Tito*, Act II, on which Gluck based this number.

head is excited by the music. If you do not understand me, leave the matter until I come, then it will be done in an instant. I think everything else may stay as it is. The recitatives can be cut here and there, where they seem repetitious or too long—that will not spoil the work, which in my opinion will have an amazing effect. I do not answer you concerning the terms of my engagement. I shall await your first letter to contain the proposals before I give you my opinion. Meanwhile, arrange matters so that the queen asks to have me for an unspecified period, a few years only, so that I can decently extract myself from here.[16] But let her do this at once, without losing any time, because I am no longer going to travel in winter. I could leave at the beginning of September, but I must know about it a couple of months in advance, in order to be able to sell my property and arrange my affairs. Adieu, my very dear friend; I embrace you and all our acquaintances with my whole heart.

PS   I cannot find *Il prologo*, but in any case Abbé Pezzona can obtain it from Parma. Speak to our dear Abbé about it.

This is how I would like the work to be divided in four acts:[17]

Scene i

Orestes and Pylades in chains; all the remainder of the scene, finishing with the air 'Unis de la plus tendre enfance'.

Scene ii

Orestes, Pylades, the Minster; the five lines remain cut, as they are unnecessary.

Scene iii

Orestes alone.

Scene iv

Orestes, the Eumenides.

Scene v

Iphigenia with Orestes only, without bringing back Pylades. This scene could be effective as a dialogue, and the word 'Agamemnon' which Orestes repeats three times is significant. It will produce a sort of duet between the two principal protagonists; most of what they say to each other may remain. This will give yet more variety to the piece, because Orestes and Pylades are already too often together, and in this scene everything that Pylades says is unimportant and contrived. Orestes is in a strong situation by himself, and Iphigenia tears his words from him, almost by force, consequently he has no need to be

---

[16] Gluck still had in mind his permanent removal to Paris; see Ch. 13.
[17] Guillard had cast his libretto in five acts, ending his Act II with what is now Act II, scene iv, so Gluck's rearrangement in four acts depended on restructuring the second act.

restrained by Pylades. Write this scene as quickly as possible, for I would like the opera to be finished by the end of July.

Scene vi

The scene of the funeral sacrifice, then the act finishes.

In this way the opera can remain in four acts. If it is put in five acts, the end of the second act is weak in my opinion, because the Eumenides only appear to Orestes in a dream and in his imagination: this destroys the idea that in seeing Iphigenia he sees his mother. He must be still immersed in his dream when he says the words 'Ma mère! Ciel!' otherwise they will be of no effect. The act will be a little longer, but no matter; everything in it will be more intense.[18]

Gluck worked on *Iphigénie* and *Écho* throughout the summer. He wrote to Kruthoffer:

My dear friend,

You are very kind with your letters. It is only on your account that I take pleasure in the arrival of the courier. Please continue to write to me at such length. Your letters refresh my head, which at the moment is in a ferment and entirely occupied with two operas, *Iphigénie* and *Narcisse*. This is also why I write to you so laconically, for I am sure that you would not want to hinder me in my work. You say I should not come to Paris at present, but others write to me that I should not let the opportunity pass to present an opera for the queen's confinement[19]—whom should I follow? I shall act prudently and continue with my work. My tenderest compliments to Mlle Levasseur (I write nothing to her for I wish to retain the title she awarded me of 'infernal idiot'); my wife also sends her a thousand tender greetings. For the rest, always think of me kindly. My wife and I send you, Herr von Blumendorff, and all our friends a thousand compliments, and I remain now and for ever, dear friend, your most devoted servant,

Gluck.[20]

Gluck continued to fret at his absence from Paris and to plan an early return. From time to time he referred to the need to obtain the empress's permission for a further visit to Paris, but later documents reveal this to be

---

[18] Gluck to Guillard, Vienna, 17 June 1778: facsimile in *Iphigénie en Tauride*, ed. Fanny Pelletan (Paris, 1874), pp. iii–v. Pub. in Desnoiresterres, *Gluck et Piccinni*, 250–2; Gluck's *Sämtliche Werke*, 1/9, pp. vi–vii. See also 'Der Brief Glucks an Guillard', in Klaus Hortschansky (ed.), *Christoph Willibald Gluck und die Opernreform* (Darmstadt, 1989), 373–89.

[19] See n. 12 above.   [20] Vienna, 28 June 1778, in Kinsky, *Glucks Briefe*, 30.

either an unnecessary scruple or a deliberate stance in his negotiations with De Vismes. Arnaud was one who encouraged Gluck's immediate return to Paris. Gluck responded:

You are quite right, monsieur, I shall not be able to finish my two operas in Vienna. I need to be near the poets, because we do not understand each other well at a distance. I expect to leave here in the month of September, if M. de Vismes can obtain the empress's permission for me to go to Paris. I could not leave without it. M. le Bailli [du Roullet] will tell you why. So I shall probably once again need your redoubtable arm to strike down my enemies this coming winter. Without you, I lack the courage to risk another battle. Meanwhile, muster your troops, persuade our allies, above all Mme de Vaisnes, to whom I entreat you to present my respects, as to all her illustrious circle. Does she still have that beautiful Circassian head? I often conjure up her image when I do not feel sufficiently inspired when working; she must contribute greatly to the success of my operas.[21]

The opera at Bologna was very well attended.[22] The Duke and Duchess of Parma and the Archduke and Archduchess of Milan went to see it. The Italians referred to it widely as 'the great opera of Bologna'. One of my friends who saw it performed in Vienna wrote to me that De Amicis, who played the role of Alcestis, had her head in the clouds, that the singer who took Admetus was too old, and that the ballets were all nonsense: they even danced in the chorus 'Piangi, o Patria, o Tessaglia!' ['Pleure, ô patrie, ô Thessalie!'].[23] You can imagine the rest. My friend referred to an Italian proverb when he wrote, comparing *Alceste* with the world, saying 'il mondo va da se, e non casca, perchè non hà dove cascare'.[24] I must tell you in addition that the other day, when I was with Prince Kaunitz, the envoy from Naples asked me to send him all the operas I had written in France, because he is being asked for them in Naples, where they want to have everything that I have composed—here is a story that will not give much pleasure to His Excellency the ambassador, God bless him![25] My wife sends you a thousand compliments, and I remain as ever, with the greatest admiration for your genius, monsieur, your most humble and obedient servant,

Gluck.

---

[21] Madame de Vaisnes is not mentioned elsewhere as a Gluckist, but was a leading figure in Parisian society: Diderot praises her beauty and intelligence. See Desnoiresterres, *Gluck et Piccinni*, 249 n. 2.

[22] *Alceste* had been given in Bologna on 9 May, with Anna de Amicis as Alcestis, Giuseppe Tibaldi as Admetus, and ballets by Giuseppe Canziani.

[23] Writing to the Abbé in French, Gluck quoted from the French version.

[24] 'The world spins by itself, and does not fall, because it does not know how to'.

[25] Carraccioli, the leading patron of Piccinni.

PS Do not forget to present my compliments to M. the Count de Rochechouart and all his family, also to M. and Mme Suard.[26]

Gluck was eventually persuaded to remain in Vienna. While he worked 'phlegmatically' at his two operas, he took a new guest into his house, Carlo Calin, perhaps replacing Riedel as secretary and companion (and gardener?). His next letters (to Kruthoffer) are full of the Austro-Prussian war:

My dear friend,

Your reminders are like commands to me, so I am sending you the two letters you wanted—please have them dealt with. Your delightful letters always give us much pleasure, especially as I now have M. Calin about the place. He is currently lodging with me. He sends you his best compliments. He now argues even more than before; we have, moreover, more matter to argue about, on account of the present war, in which our army has so far held off the Prussians at every encounter. The presence of the emperor has an incomparable effect. Incidentally, I shall take your advice about my journey to Paris, and also about working phlegmatically. I have undertaken two operas, because I wanted to disappoint neither the Bailli [du Roullet] nor Baron von Tschudi,[27] and one of the two would never have forgiven me. But if M. de Vismes is not successful in securing the empress's permission, than I shall stay at home and think like Goldsmith's boy.[28] Send us plenty of news. Our compliments to you and to all our good friends. I remain ever yours.[29]

My dear friend,

I am sorry that I cannot tell you anything interesting about our war. There are many skirmishes, and we have the upper hand almost all the time—a clear proof of this is that the emperor has already several times promoted officers in the field because they have led their men so well. It is true that General de Vins was surprised by Prince Heinrich's troops, by which we lost some thousand men; on the other hand Lieutenant Nauendorf took 243 provisions wagons

---

[26] Vienna, 15 July 1778, in *L'Amateur d'autographes*, 16 Jan. 1864, 24–5; Desnoiresterres, *Gluck et Piccinni*, 249–50; Prod'homme, 'Lettres de Gluck', 259; Prod'homme, *Écrits*, 423–5. Gluck had asked De Vismes to petition the queen to apply to the empress for his permission to travel. His reputation in Italy grew steadily: in Aug. 1777 he was approached to write an opera for the rebuilt opera-house in Milan, though nothing came of this: see Schmid, *Gluck*, 297.

[27] Baron Ludwig Theodor von Tschudi, Swiss poet, *encyclopédist* and the librettist of *Écho*.

[28] The first German translation of Oliver Goldsmith's *The Vicar of Wakefield*, *Der Landpriester von Wakefield*, tr. Johann Gellius, was pub. in Leipzig in 1767, 2nd edn. 1776. In ch. 6, Moses Primrose says: 'However dark the habitation of the mole to our eyes, yet the animal itself finds the apartment sufficiently lightsome.'

[29] Gluck to Kruthoffer, Vienna, 29 July 1778, in Kinsky, *Glucks Briefe*, 32, with facsimile between pp. 32 and 33.

and thirteen goods wagons together with 600 horses, either taking prisoners or destroying the convoy. Apparently we are not attempting to attack, because [the Prussian] army has so much illness, and so many deserters, that it could well annihilate itself. The king would like to join forces with his brother; only Loudon stands between them. As soon as there is anything new, I shall report it to you. Best wishes to you and Herr von Blumendorff from my wife and from the noisy Calin—you should hear him now, he is shouting like one possessed. Adieu, dear friend.

Please turn over

The news has just come in that the king has tried to attack the Pass of Hohenelbe, just where General Wallis commands a corps of 15,000 men, in order to join forces with Prince Heinrich. He ordered General Anhalt to attack [Wallis], but he has been driven back, and the king must remain in the mountains. General Wunsch has also attacked General Wurmser with three cavalry regiments. Wurmser, with two regiments of Hussars and a batallion of brave Croats, has repelled him. The details are to follow. Meanwhile it has already been agreed that before the end of the campaign, the Prussian army must withdraw from Bohemia, and then it will be our turn to plunder foreign lands. Adieu, I had to open the packet in order to tell you this.[30]

Gluck continued to bargain with De Vismes to obtain the best terms for his new operas. The letters are lost, but it appears that he sought the sum of 20,000 *livres* for *Écho*. The ambassador Mercy-Argenteau intervened through Kruthoffer to try to persuade Gluck to agree to come to Paris, and to bring *Iphigénie* with him:

The ambassador has entrusted me, monsieur, with the honour of communicating with you on his behalf. . . . He believes that at this moment, when not only all the connoisseurs, but a very large sector of the public, acknowledge your talents as never before, and impatiently await this new work, you owe it to your reputation not to reject the offers made by M. de Vismes. His Excellency further authorizes me to point out that he hopes to secure for you, if not the whole sum you have asked for, at least that of 12,000 francs, and he thinks you can easily make up this small difference, because the sixth opera [*Écho*] will bring your pension to 1,000 *écus*.

As for the empress's permission which you feel to be necessary for your journey, His Excellency thinks that, in this time of war and disaster, it would not be becoming for the queen to make a request of her august mother, the sole

[30] Gluck to Kruthoffer, Vienna, 29 Aug. 1778: F-Pn, Fac-Sim 147, no. 18. Pub. in Pereyra, 'Vier Gluck-Briefe', 14–15; L.R., 'Correspondance inédite', 13; Kinsky, *Glucks Briefe*, 33. Prince Heinrich of Prussia was Frederick's brother; Anhalt and Wunsch were Prussian officers; de Vins (Baron von Vins), Nauendorf, Loudon, Wallis, and Wurmser served in the imperial army.

object of which would be to add to her pleasures . . . however, His Excellency believes that a new permission would be superfluous, because the assurance which His Majesty the Emperor gave his august sister last year, to allow you to come to France as often as you might contribute to her entertainment with new works, could be regarded as a general permission. . . .[31]

Gluck's next letter to Kruthoffer is, uniquely in the correspondence between the two compatriots, written in French. It lacks the customary affectionate greeting, and was apparently designed to be shown directly to Mercy-Argenteau, and possibly the directors of the Opéra also:

It was the day before yesterday, the 24th, monsieur, that I received your letter of the fourth of this month, and I would not have received it yet had I not sent my servant to ask if the courier had arrived from Paris. This delay compels me to entreat you, monsieur, to present my most humble compliments to His Excellency the ambassador, and to tell him on my behalf that I find it impossible to make any journey at this time. I would need four weeks to prepare my travelling coach and to make my domestic arrangements. There has been too much delay in informing me. Neither my wife nor I could bear the discomfort of so long a journey at the end of October. I shall postpone my visit to Paris till next spring, provided that M. de Vismes does not try to haggle with me, for he treats me like a man who lives locally, and he does not conceive how much one suffers in making a journey of 700 leagues. At my present age, I am too fond of my comforts. If I were not driven by the desire to see my friends again, I would not leave, even if I could earn the sum he offers me just by enduring the hardships of the journey. For the rest, I am entirely appreciative of the goodness which His Excellency the ambassador has shown me in this instance, and for the interest he takes in all that concerns me. Please assure him of this on my behalf. Accept, monsieur, the feelings of esteem and respect, with which I have the honour to be your most humble and obedient servant,

Chevalier Gluck.

turn over

We have, by God's grace, conducted a most glorious defensive campaign, without giving battle. The Prussians have lost at least 30,000 men; their cavalry and guns are destroyed. Loudon is currently pursuing Prince Heinrich, who flees before him, so that you will soon have news that we have reached Dresden.[32]

---

[31] Kruthoffer to Gluck, Paris, 4 Sept. 1778: F-Pn, Gluck lettres autographes, no. 37. Pub. in Tiersot, 'Pour le centenaire', 274–5.

[32] Vienna, 26 Sept. 1778, in Kinsky, *Glucks Briefe*, 34. De Vismes paid Gluck 2,000 *livres* for the expenses of his journey, see Müller von Asow, *Collected Correspondence*, 162.

Meanwhile in Paris the controversy between French and Italian music continued as hotly as ever. Gluck was irritated by a long letter from Marmontel to the *Mercure de France*[33] which Kruthoffer had forwarded to him:

My dear friend,

I read your letter with great pleasure, but the *Mercure* annoyed me. Henceforth I have decided not to come to Paris until M. de Vismes succeeds in obtaining for me an assurance from the minister that the law will not lay hands on me if I come to crop Marmontel's ears. As the *Journal de Paris* has not been able to make him more modest, he needs a more violent treatment, and this would be the best. Our news is excellent. There is not a single Prussian left in Bohemia. Immediately upon the withdrawal of the king, Loudon was hot upon Prince Heinrich's heels. The latter did not stand his ground, but retreated to Saxony in two columns; Loudon's forward party has already reached them; meanwhile, it is said that in his retreat he abandoned 1,900 prisoners, 3,000 deserters, and 23 guns. You see, dear friend, that the pleasure one can take in this campaign is not unlike that which arises from my operas: at first they are underestimated, but in the end they are judged to be not so bad after all. Adieu, many compliments from me and mine to you, to Herr von Blumendorff, and all our acquaintances. M. Calin send his regards to everyone. There is nothing to be done with him at present; he quarrels and shouts like a firebrand.[34]

Shortly after this, Gluck received news that finally persuaded him to return to Paris. De Vismes was in trouble; a revival of Rameau's *Castor et Pollux* had failed, and in the absence of a production guaranteed to draw full houses, the director was in danger of being displaced: 'De Vismes is in despair lest our friend does not come at all this winter,' wrote Du Roullet to Kruthoffer. 'He does not know what to do or what will happen. He has indeed got what he deserved, and he must realize that if he is brought down, it will be his own fault for having haggled with a man before whom he should have prostrated himself.'[35] The prospect of being able to drive a hard bargain with De Vismes seems suddenly to have removed all difficulties from Gluck's path. He wrote to Kruthoffer:

My dear friend,

The empress has informed me that I might travel to Paris, because this could contribute to the queen's entertainment, especially if a dauphin were to be

---

[33] 15 Sept. 1778, 161–86; answered by Suard on Gluck's behalf in the issue of 5 Oct., 56–69.

[34] Gluck to Kruthoffer, Vienna, 30 Sept. 1778, in Kinsky, *Glucks Briefe*, 37; Treichlinger (ed.), *Briefe*, 59–60.

[35] 17 Oct. 1778: F-Pn, Du Roullet lettres autographes, no. 5. Pub. in Tiersot, 'Pour le centenaire', 274–5.

brought into the world. Thus I have no more excuse for delaying. I therefore ask you to look around as quickly as possible to find a decent lodging for me. Perhaps you will be able to find something with your friends of whom you spoke to me last year. *Nota bene* room, food, and bedlinen included. I expect to arrive about the twentieth. Leave a letter at the city gate, addressed to me, so that I shall know where I can put up. I rejoice with all my heart at the prospect of embracing you soon. With God's help we shall again be able to talk and amuse ourselves to our hearts' content. Adieu, dear friend, till we meet again soon.[36]

Gluck repeated his requirements to Du Roullet, who communicated them to Kruthoffer, observing, 'He does not tell me if he is coming with Mme Gluck, but I presume so, as I do not imagine that they could be separated for so long a time.'[37]

[36] Vienna, 1 Nov. 1778, in Kinsky, *Glucks Briefe*, 38.
[37] 11 Nov. 1778, in Kinsky, *Glucks Briefe*, 38–9.

21

THE LAST YEAR IN PARIS
(1778–1779)

W HILE Gluck was working on *Iphigénie* in Vienna, in Paris, Piccinni was drawn into setting the same subject. Undaunted by Gluck's earlier refusal to compete with *Roland*, de Vismes planned to take advantage of the continuing rivalry among the composers' adherents by staging another operatic confrontation. After Gluck's departure in March 1778, he allegedly summoned Piccinni to a secret conference and offered him a libretto by Alphonse Dubreuil:

'Here is an excellent libretto which I suggest you set to music; it is *Iphigénie en Tauride*. M. Gluck will compose another setting, and it will be for the impartial public to judge between you. Just as in Italy, two composers will be seen to set the same poem—this is a custom I wish to introduce into France.' 'But monsieur, in that case it has to be the same libretto.' 'This is not exactly the same libretto, but it is the same subject. . . .' 'But you cannot be ignorant, monsieur, of the prejudice against me, and even the hatred which I suffer without cause. If M. Gluck's *Iphigénie en Tauride* were heard first, no one would want to hear mine.' 'I give you my word that your work will be produced before his. In return, give me your word that you will speak to no one of this . . . in order that this new contest has the effect I anticipate, no one must have the least suspicion.'[1]

On Gluck's return to Paris in November 1778, all promises were broken, and Piccinni learned his work was to be delayed: it was eventually performed in 1781.

A curious anecdote is attached to the early months of 1779, purporting to portray Gluck at work. If not the literal truth, it concurs with other

[1] Ginguené, *Notice*, 47–9; Desnoiresterres, *Gluck et Piccinni*, 256–7. Dubreuil's libretto was later revised by Piccinni's friend and biographer, Ginguené.

accounts of the physical energy Gluck expended in every aspect of his operas. The narrator is Étienne Nicolas Méhul:

I came to Paris in 1779, possessing nothing but my sixteen years, my fiddle, and my optimism. I had a letter of introduction to Gluck: this was my treasure. To see Gluck, to hear him, to talk to him—such was my only desire when I came to the capital, and the thought of it made me tremble with joy. I could scarcely breathe as I rang the doorbell. His wife admitted me, but said that M. Gluck was working and she could not disturb him. My disappointment must have shown in my distressed expression, which touched the worthy lady. She asked about the purpose of my visit. The letter of which I was the bearer came from a friend. I grew confident, I spoke warmly of her husband's work and of the happiness I would have in merely seeing the great man, and Mme Gluck yielded entirely. Smiling, she suggested I might see her husband at work, but without speaking too him and without making the slightest noise.

She then led me to the door of the study from which issued the sound of a harpsichord which Gluck was striking with all his might. The door was opened and closed again without the illustrious artist suspecting that an uninitiated was entering the sanctuary. Here was I, behind a screen, which by good luck was pierced here and there so that my eye could feast on the least movement or the slightest grimace of my Orpheus. His head was covered with a black velvet cap in the German fashion. He wore slippers, his hose were carelessly drawn in to his nether garments, and his only other item of dress was a sort of cotton nightshirt with wide sleeves, which barely reached his belt. I thought him magnificent in these clothes. All the pomp of Louis XIV's attire could not have filled me with such wonder as Gluck's informal dress.

Suddenly I saw him leap from his chair, seize the seats and armchairs, position them around the room to form the wings [of a stage], return to his harpsichord to sound a note, and here he was, holding a corner of his nightshirt in each hand, humming an *air de ballet*, curtseying like a young dancer, performing *glissades* around his chair, leaping and prancing, adopting the poses, gestures, and all the dainty attitudes of a nymph from the Opéra. Then he seemed to want to direct the *corps de ballet*, and as he had insufficient space, he attempted to enlarge his stage; to this end he struck the first leaf of the screen, which unfolded suddenly, and I was discovered. After an explanation, and further visits, Gluck honoured me with his protection and his friendship.[2]

The 'dainty attitudes' seem more appropriate to *Écho* than to *Iphigénie en Tauride*; Noverre was the choreographer for both works.

Rehearsals for *Iphigénie* proceeded in the usual storm of controversy. The scenes containing the Scythian chorus attracted particular interest,

[2] Cited in Desnoiresterres, *Gluck et Piccinni*, 260–1, from *Le Ménestrel*, 29 May 1836.

and the colourful orchestration was greeted with delight.[3] The final rehearsal on 10 May had to be halted because the theatre was 'so crowded and so noisy that it was impossible to listen to it with the necessary attention'.[4] The première, planned for 11 May, was postponed because of Levasseur's illness. (De Vismes vainly suggested using an understudy, a resource Gluck had expressly rejected in connection with *Armide*.[5]) An extra rehearsal was held on 15 May, the audience restricted to ministers and courtiers. The *Mémoires secrets* claimed, with clear exaggeration, that as 'by common consent the fourth and last act was found to be very inferior to the others, and especially to the third act (the strongest of all), the Chevalier Gluck did not regret the respite, and thoroughly reworked it.'[6] The opera opened on 18 May, with Levasseur in the title role, Larrivée as Orestes, and Le Gros as Pylades. It enjoyed the usual royal support:

Iphigénie en Tauride took place last Tuesday. The queen, who had not appeared in the capital for a long time, honoured the theatre with her presence. . . . The opera was well applauded. It was in a new style. It is a genuine tragedy, a Greek tragedy, declaimed more authentically than in the Théâtre française. There is no overture, no ariette, and only one strongly characterized ballet, but the varied accents of passion, expressed with the greatest energy, imbue it with an interest unknown till now in the lyric theatre. One can only applaud Chevalier Gluck for having discovered the secret of the Ancients, which he will doubtless take further. Some of the audience were seen to weep from beginning to end.[7]

Iphigénie enjoyed the greatest immediate success of any of Gluck's French operas, and its subtleties were quickly recognized:

M. Gluck will show himself to be as great a poet as he has shown himself great painter. After his first fit of madness, Orestes falls prostrate upon a stone bench, and sings these words:

> Le calme rentre dans mon cœur. . . .
> Mes maux ont donc lassé la colère céleste!
> Je touche au terme du malheur.
> Dieux justes! Ciel vengeur!
> Vous laissez respirer le parricide Oreste.

But listen to the instruments; they will tell you that this is exhaustion, not repose. They will tell you that Orestes has lost not the awareness of his

---

[3] *Mémoires secrets*, xiv. 46–7 (10 May 1779).   [4] Ibid. xiv. 52 (15 May 1779).
[5] See his letter to Du Roullet, summer 1776 (Ch. 18 below).
[6] *Mémoires secrets*, xiv. 52 (15 May 1779).   [7] Ibid. xiv. 58 (21 May 1779).

troubles, but the strength to give them voice. Indeed, his melody is more admirable, the more true, in that it extends over a very small range of harmonies, and has no periodic phrasing; his melody is accompanied by the violas, which lash the subdued, remorseful voice, while the violins express a profound agitation, mingled with sighs and tears.[8]

The *Journal de Paris* criticized the descent of Diana in the last act,[9] and the opera was, as usual, found to be too short. Gossec was commissioned to add a final ballet divertissement, which was welcomed in the *Mémoires secrets* on 4 June.

The score was issued during the summer. Gluck entrusted the work to Mathon, who had already published *Armide*:

I the undersigned acknowledge having sold to M. Mathon de la Cour my two scores, *Iphigénie en Tauride* and *Narcisse*, on the express condition that if I do not present *Narcisse* at the Opéra, I will return to him, in money or in bills of exchange, the value of the said opera, agreed between us to be 2,000 *livres*, and that he will be able to claim no further compensation.

Chevalier Gluck.[10]

It was again dedicated to the queen. Gluck's comment on the importance of distinguishing between genres may indicate some unease at the stylistic difference between his classical tragedies and the pastoral *Écho*, which was shortly to appear:

Madame!

In deigning to accept the homage I make bold to offer you, Your Majesty fulfils all my desires. All that was necessary to complete my happiness in publishing my scores has been that the operas, which I have written to contribute to the pleasure of a nation of which Your Majesty constitutes the ornament and the delight, have won the attention and obtained the approbation of an enlightened and perceptive princess, who loves and protects all the arts and who, while applauding all the genres, is careful not to confuse them, and who knows how to accord each the degree of esteem it merits.

I am, with deepest respect, Your Majesty's most humble and most obedient servant.

Chevalier Gluck.[11]

---

[8] *Mercure de France*, 15 June 1779, 172–80, repr. in Lesure, *Querelle*, i. 432–4. This detailed, anonymous appreciation may well have been submitted by Du Roullet or Guillard.

[9] 19 May 1779, 558–9, repr. in Lesure, *Querelle*, i. 427–9.

[10] Letter to Mathon, Paris, 5 May 1779, in Kinsky, *Glucks Briefe*, 40.

[11] Letter to Marie Antoinette, Paris, summer 1779, in *Iphigénie en Tauride* (Paris, 1779), p. iii, repr. in Nohl, *Musiker-Briefe*, 51–2; Prod'homme, *Écrits*, 425.

Several hints in the letters of the late 1770s suggest that Gluck was 'bombarded' with librettos from poets eager to share in his artistic goals.[12] During the summer of 1779, he was apparently seriously considering one such suggestion from Heribert von Dalberg:

Noble Baron,

I had the privilege of receiving your lordship's most honoured letter on the fourteenth of last month. I had already read with great pleasure the poem *Cora*, sent me by Count von Sceau,[13] and the news that you are the author of it has increased its value. I would very much have liked to be able to accept your gracious invitation to Mannheim, but since my business here has already detained me beyond the time appointed for it, as soon as it is completed I shall have to return to Vienna by the shortest route. In connection with the musical setting of the poem, it is of the first importance that I am fully instructed on the intentions of the Count von Sceau concerning the performance of this work, the abilities of the singers engaged for it, and the quality of their voices. On my journey through Munich I shall discuss these points with the count, and with this preliminary information it will be easy to decide upon the proposed amendments and additions which you deem necessary by letter, as the work progresses. I only regret that my present circumstances will deprive me of the advantage of a personal meeting with your lordship. Meanwhile it would give me great pleasure if the fulfilment of your intentions were to bring me into a closer relationship with them, and to afford me more frequent opportunities to express both the esteem due to your merit and the most complete respect, with which I have th honour ever to be your lordship's most obedient and devoted servant,

Chevalier Gluck.[14]

The summer was occupied with tiresome disputes. *Écho* was planned for September, but Gluck continued to haggle over the price. (De Vismes reduced Gluck's initial demand by half, though the sum he paid, 10,000 *livres*, was unprecedented in the history of the Académie.) He also insisted on the casting of his choice, in particular the recruitment of Mlle Beaumesnil for the part of Echo.[15]

Then among the continuing wrangles of the pro-Italian and pro-Gluck parties a new controversy arose over an air Gluck had introduced into

[12] See e.g. his letters to Du Roullet, 1 July 1775 (Ch. 16) and to Wieland, 7 Aug. 1776 (Ch. 17).

[13] Joseph Anton von Sceau was the director of the Munich opera.

[14] Gluck to Dalberg, Paris, 8 June 1779, in Nohl, *Musiker-Briefe*, 52–3; Treichlinger (ed.), *Briefe*, 61–2. Baron Dalberg was a founder-director of the Nationaltheater in Mannheim; he offered his *Cora* both to Mozart and to Anton Schweitzer. It was never set.

[15] *Mémoires secrets*, xiv. 82–3 (15 Jun. 1779).

Orphée five years earlier. An attack on Gluck's Paris operas by Claude-Philibert Coquéau appeared that summer, published anonymously under the title *Entretiens sur l'état actuel de l'Opéra de Paris*; it included the following sentence: 'The very Italianate ariette, 'L'espoir renaît dans mon âme', is very beautiful, but let us not forget that it is by Bertoni'.[16] A writer to the *Journal de Paris* immediately challenged the assertion, asking for chapter and verse.[17] Coquéau responded with a detailed comparative analysis between Gluck's air and Bertoni's 'So' che dal ciel discende', which had just been published in a collection of Italian arias; Coquéau further claimed that Bertoni had written the aria for his *Ifigenia in Tauride* in 1767.[18] The usual course for such controversies was to attempt to establish the earliest use of the material, as happened with Framery's claim on behalf of Sacchini in 1776.[19] In this instance, an anonymous correspondent claimed that Gluck had composed the air for the coronation of the emperor in Frankfurt in 1764, reusing it in *Le feste d'Apollo* in Parma in 1769.[20] Bertoni then undertook his own defence:

I was very surprised to see myself called into question in the letter you did me the honour of writing, and I in no way wish to be compromised in a musical quarrel which, from the heat with which you write, could become of very great importance; your assurance that *fanaticism* is involved is a further reason for me to detach myself from its consequences. I would ask you, therefore, to permit me to answer you simply that the aria 'So' che dal ciel discende' was composed by me at Turin for Sig.ra Girelli; I do not remember in which year and I could not even tell you if I actually wrote it for *Ifigenia in Tauride* as you assure me I did. I rather think it belonged to my opera *Tancredi*, but that does not prevent the aria being mine—it is this that I can and must attest, with all the truth of an honourable man, who is full of respect for all the works of the great masters, but full of tenderness towards his own.[21]

The chronology of the aria material runs as follows: Frankfurt, 1764, saw Gluck's coronation cantata *Enea e Ascanio*, which may have contained the original version of the aria, now lost; in Vienna, 1765, the aria 'In un mar che non ha sponde', closely resembling in its first section 'L'espoir renaît', was sung by Archduchess Maria-Elisabeth-Josepha in Gluck's court enter-

[16] (Amsterdam and Paris, 1779), 66. Repr. in Lesure, *Querelle*, ii. 367–538.

[17] Letter from 'L.C.D.B.', pub. 18 July 1779, 811, repr. in Lesure, *Querelle*, i. 473.

[18] *Journal de Paris*, 27 July 1779, 847.

[19] See Gluck's letter to the *Mercure de France*, Nov. 1776 (Ch. 18 above).

[20] *Journal de Paris*, 28 July 1779, 851.

[21] Letter to Coquéau, quoted in Coquéau, *Suite des entretiens sur l'état actuel de l'Opéra de Paris* (Paris, 1779), 47–8; Desnoiresterres, *Gluck et Piccinni*, 273–4.

tainment *Il Parnaso confuso*; in Turin, 1767, Antonia-Maria Girelli-Aguilar sang 'So' che dal ciel' in Bertoni's *Tancredi*; in Parma, 1769, virtually the same aria appeared in Gluck's *Atto d'Aristeo* in *Le feste d'Apollo*, to the words 'Nocchier che in mezzo all'onde'; the singer was again Girelli-Aguilar. The final appearance of the disputed air was in Paris, 1774, in *Orphée*, sung by Le Gros. In view of these facts, Gluck's claim would seem secure, were it not that the common currency of figures and motifs in mid-eighteenth-century opera weaken any claim to exclusive property of such material. The part played by Girelli-Aguilar appears to mirror that of Millico in connection with Sacchini's 'Se cerca, se dice.'

Another dispute to be followed in the columns of the *Journal de Paris* concerned the singer, who replaced Levasseur in *Iphigénie en Tauride* during the course of the summer:

The Académie royale de musique will give tomorrow the seventeenth representation of *Iphigénie en Tauride*. The role of Iphigenia will be sung by a singer making her début.

Chevalier Gluck, who knows better than anyone how to appraise the abilities appropriate for the performance of his works, wanted very much to train this beginner, and he himself suggested her to the Académie.[22]

Messieurs,

The note that you inserted in yesterday's issue could have given the impression that the actress who is to make her début today in the role of Iphigenia was chosen by me, and that I have trained her. I have not had the time to give her much instruction; I have heard her with pleasure, but without being able to indicate to her my ideas on the manner in which the role should be performed, and I only suggested her in view of the illness of the two actresses who have taken the role till now [Levasseur and Laguerre]. I have the honour to be, etc.

Gluck.[23]

The actress who made her début yesterday in the role of Iphigenia is Mlle Dupuis. She sang formerly at this theatre, from which she retired eight or ten years ago. Her voice seemed fine enough. The applause was very marked in the first two acts, and her superiority in the famous number at the end of the second act, 'O malheureuse Iphigénie', was quite widely acknowledged.

Although it might be unfair to compare a consummate actress with a beginner, it seemed that the public missed the noble and sensitive acting of Mlle Levasseur. They did not applaud Mlle Dupuis in any scene of action. Her voice is true, and the fluency of her performance proves that she is a good

[22] *Journal de Paris*, 26 July 1779, 844.   [23] Ibid. 27 July 1779, 847.

musician. But her excessive obesity will always stand in the way of her employment.[24]

After three performances, Dupuis was dismissed. She complained to Gluck at great length in the columns of the *Journal de Paris*, citing the scarcity of singers suitable for the mature roles of queens and sorceresses, dismissing the younger Levasseur as more suited to princesses:

There are very few women to take the roles of Alcestis, Armida, and Iphigenia. . . . But if, as you have done me the honour of telling me a hundred times, you think you could entrust them to me, will you remain indifferent in a matter which could benefit your operas? Is there anyone in the world who has more right to speak about it than you, monsieur, to whom the Opéra owes both its splendour and the immense profits it has won since you began working for this theatre?[25]

Ever eager to placate in a dispute which did not touch his purse or his principles, Gluck made what amends he could:

When, madame, I introduced you to M. de Vismes, and when he suggested you should sing *Iphigénie en Tauride* two days later, I doubted neither your success nor the eagerness which would be expressed to admit you to the Opéra. Events and public opinion justified my judgement on the first point, and it appears to me that your admission should necessarily follow. I do not know, in view of how very useful you would be there, any reason to exclude you. And I owe you the justice of saying and making public that where voice, method, intelligence, and sensibility are concerned, you lack nothing which could prevent you from deserving and obtaining the greatest applause, to which I will add the particular esteem in which I hold your person and your character, with which I am, madame, your most humble and obedient servant,

Chevalier Gluck.[26]

Earlier in the summer, the *Journal de Paris* had carried more sombre news: 'Last Friday [30 July], the Chevalier Gluck was struck down with a serious illness, the symptoms of which were very alarming. His friends feared for his life. Although he still suffers, he is completely out of danger.'[27] It was his first stroke, and although Gluck was to recover fully on

---

[24] *Journal de Paris*, 28 July 1779, 852.
[25] Ibid. 12 Nov. 1779, 1287–8. Letter undated, but preceding the following.
[26] Paris, 3 Oct. 1779, pub. ibid. 12 Nov. 1779, 1288.
[27] Ibid. 5 Aug. 1779, 875.

this occasion, his famous energy was diminished, and the rehearsals for *Écho* were suspended until 6 September.[28]

During the course of rehearsals, a heated discussion, which Gluck may have anticipated, arose over the genre of *Écho*. Gluck spoke of it as 'un opéra d'été': an opera for the summer season, by implication a lighter work, and more comparable to *Cythère* than to *Iphigénie*.[29] It was later reported as 'not a pastoral but a genuine tragedy'.[30] The confusion accounted for much of the disappointment at the first performance on 24 September 1779:

From the second performance [on 28 September], the balcony, gallery, and circle were empty, so that the opera *Écho et Narcisee* was spoken of as having virtually failed. If it held its own at all, it was on account of the ballets by the Sr Noverre. The Chevalier Gluck did not want any on principle; he claimed that his works had no need of them, and it was not even he who had written the music. His supporters have deserted him, or rather his opera, on this occasion, blaming the failure on Baron von Tschudi's libretto. In truth it would not be possible to read worse words. . . .

As for the Chevalier, he cares nothing for all that. Following his custom, he secured in advance the price of 10,000 francs for his music, and it has been reckoned that together with the other revenues, he will make 22,000 *livres* from it.[31]

Receipts for the Académie were disastrous. Where average takings for *Iphigénie en Tauride* has been between 4,000 and 5,000 *livres* a performance, those for *Écho*, after the première, quickly dropped below 2,000.[32] The loyal *Journal de Paris* tried to sustain the opera with appreciate judgements on the characterization and the choruses.[33] This assessment, so out of step with popular opinion, drew many protests.[34] In his weakened physical state, the failure of *Écho* depressed Gluck more than any other indifferent reception he had experienced. He left Paris on 9 October:

The Chevalier Gluck, whose self-esteem, like that of all talented men, is very acute, disappointed with the little success of *Écho et Narcisse* and on the point

---

[28] *Mémoires secrets*, xiv. 173 (6 Sept. 1779).   [29] Ibid. xiv. 82–3 (15 June 1779).
[30] Ibid. xiv. 185 (20 Sept. 1779).   [31] Ibid. xiv. 191 (30 Sept. 1779).
[32] Martial Teneo, 'Les chefs-d'œuvre du Chevalier Gluck à l'Opéra de Paris', *Revue d'histoire et de critique musicales*, 8 (1908), 109–16. Gluck had, however, raised huge wealth for the Opéra: 'It is calculated that from Easter 1774 to 1 January 1780, the five operas, namely *Iphigénie en Aulide*, *Orphée*, *Alceste*, *Armide*, and *Iphigénie en Tauride* . . . had brought in 1,500,000 *livres*, and since then, as the operas have been given so frequently, a further 100,000 *livres* can be added. There is no other instance which approaches such receipts in a similar period of time.' *Mémoires secrets*, xv. 90 (17 Mar. 1780).
[33] 29 Sept. 1779, 1106–7.   [34] *Mercure de France*, Oct. 1779, 164–72.

of leaving for Vienna, went to receive his orders from the queen. He did not attempt to conceal his distress, and made clear his intention to return no more. The queen, wishing to dissuade him from this plan, made him music master to the royal children, and gave him permission to leave only in order to arrange his affairs, with the injunction to return to establish permanent residence in France.[35]

[35] *Mémoires secrets*, xiv. 204 (9 Oct. 1779).

22

WITHDRAWAL TO VIENNA
(1779–1780)

BACK in Vienna, Gluck's life unfolds mainly through a series of letters to Kruthoffer, to whom he addressed a multiplicity of practical requests: financial management, dealings with publishers, domestic commissions, and repeated demands for news of theatrical life. Although writing no new music, Gluck remained full of plans for activities which never materialized. The production of *Écho* in Vienna was one:

PS   We had the finest journey in the world.

My dear friend,

I am greatly obliged to you for all the trouble I cause you. But neither of us is dead yet, and who knows whether one of us will be able to do the other a favour while still in this world; in the meantime I alone am the debtor. I hope the other changes [to *Écho et Narcisse*] will be made. But please urge M. Mathon to complete the score, and send me a copy at once, as I wish to produce *Écho* here. Write to us with all the theatre news you can scrape together, as it entertains my wife, M. Janson (who sends you his compliments), and me. M. Calin sends his respects, also to Herr von Blumendorff, to which please add my own, and to all our good friends. My wife and I thank M. Le Marchand for the music he sent. The courier is leaving, and I am in a hurry. For now, I remain ever your most devoted friend and servant,

Gluck.[1]

Gluck's impatience to receive the score is partly explained by the fact that he had apparently omitted to take a manuscript copy back with him to Vienna.[2] Meanwhile aspiring librettists continued to send him poems. Nicolas Gersin was one of several to be refused:

[1] Letter to Kruthoffer, Vienna, 31 Oct. 1779, in Kinsky, *Glucks Briefe*, 40.
[2] See his letter of 31 Dec. 1779 (below).

Monsieur,

I am very sensible of the honour you do me in sending me the outline of a tragedy for me to set to music. I judge it very likely to be most effective, but you doubtless do not know that henceforth I shall write no more operas. I have finished my career; my age, and the disappointment I experienced lately at Paris in connection with my opera *Écho et Narcisse*, have deterred me for ever from writing any others. It would, however, be a pity if you were not to finish your work, because you will be sure to find very worthy composers in Paris who would be capable of meeting all your desires. I have the honour to be, with the greatest respect, monsieur, your most humble and obedient servant,

Gluck.[3]

The publication of *Écho* continued to give Gluck problems, as he explained to Kruthoffer:

My dear little Kruthoffer,

You become kinder by the day. My wife, Calin, and I embrace you heartily; we are always glad to read your letters. Remain true to us, and send us all the theatre news. I commend the Mathon affair to your usual efficiency. I really must see if I can help you to get a position here as privy counsellor, then things would go merrily. Please send me, through the courier, on account: two boxes of tablets for the chest from the Sr Archibald, the English doctor, at twenty-four *sous* the box. You can draw either on the next instalment of money due to me from Mathon or from the pension [from the Opéra] for the outlay. The tablets are obtainable from Le Brun, Dépôt général, Marchand Épicier, rue Dauphine aux armes d'Angleterre, and Magazin de Provence et de Montpellier, Hôtel de Morny. Our best regards to Herr von Blumendorff. Adieu, dear friend, I remain ever yours.[4]

In Paris, Von Tschudi worked on revisions to *Écho*. Criticism had been largely directed towards the libretto, and the poet made a number of amendments which he sent to Gluck through Kruthoffer, urging the small amount of work their incorporation would entail. The majority of the changes affected the role of Echo, where Von Tschudi claimed to have written new words expressly designed for a more lyrical setting, to increase the opera's appeal. Complaining of the insolence of Le Gros as Cynire, he considered rewriting the role for Larrivée or Moreau, but the part

[3] Letter to Gersin, Vienna, 30 Nov. 1779: F-Pn, Fac-Sim 147, no. 1. Pub. in *Isographie des hommes célèbres: Collection de facsimile de lettres autographes et de signatures*, ed. Auguste Simon Louis Bérard (Paris, 1837–8), 2; Nohl, *Musiker-Briefe*, 53–4; Prod'homme, *Écrits*, 428.

[4] Vienna, 30 Nov. 1779, in Kinsky, *Glucks Briefe*, 41.

remained for a tenor.[5] The final chorus ('Hymne à l'Amour') had already had some success with the Parisians, however, and Gluck planned to perform it in Vienna. All negotiations passed through Kruthoffer:

My wife, Calin, and I wish you, dear friend, and Herr von Blumendorff, and all our good friends every imaginable happiness for the New Year. But I cannot send the New Year present by this courier, because I have only just received your letter; it will, however, not fail to appear next month, for you deserve it for sending us such a splendid and worthy bundle of news. I have given Herr Bailli du Roullet the task of having the 'Hymne à l'Amour' copied on small paper to be sent without fail by the first courier, as M. Janson needs it for his benefit concert. Please make sure this is done, for if the copy does not come, he will be vexed. Concerning Von Tschudi's *Narcisse*, I am ready to make the amendments, but I must at all costs have the score of it. If he sends me the manuscript through the courier, I shall send it back with the corrections. I must see to the key-relationships,[6] a task I cannot do without the score. Concerning Herr Mathon, you must press for payment in every possible way, as I have assigned this debt to Baron von Fries to have at his disposal in Paris, and I would not for the world have him think me unreliable, so please look closely into this matter. Tell M. de Vismes that I thank him for his communication, and that I shall do so in writing as soon as possible. Your theatre news is most remarkable. Continue to send it; you cannot imagine how grateful my wife is to receive it, for you always write with that certain Attic salt. But I will not over-praise you, but say only that I consider myself happy to be ever your true friend and servant. Adieu, dear friend. In haste.[7]

Baron von Fries continued to be one of Gluck's bankers. Another was Baron Jacob von Gontard, to whom Gluck wrote the following:

Gluck has the honour to advise M. de Gontard that none of his French operas is on sale here in Vienna, only *Alceste* and *Paride ed Elena* in Italian. Your correspondent will easily find the operas he seeks in Paris: *Iphigénie en Aulide*, *Alceste*, and *Orphée* at M. Le Marchand's in the rue Grainell-St-Honoré, and *Iphigénie en Tauride* at M. Mathon's shop, where he will also find *Armide*, perhaps the best of my works, which well deserves to be in your friend's collection.

The same M. Mathon has the rights to engrave *Écho et Narcisse*. He can learn from him whether the opera will soon be ready to be sold to the public.[8]

---

[5] Von Tschudi to Kruthoffer, 6 Dec., 13 Dec., and 29 Dec. 1779 and 4 Jan. 1780, in Kinsky, *Glucks Briefe*, 43–6.

[6] 'Ich muss ja die Übereinstimmung der Tönne regulieren'.

[7] Gluck to Kruthoffer, Vienna, 31 Dec. 1779, in Kinsky, *Glucks Briefe*, 42.

[8] Vienna, end of 1779, in Prod'homme, *Écrits*, 426; id., 'Lettres de Gluck', 260. Gontard is first mentioned in the letter to Anna von Fries, 16 Nov. 1777 (Ch. 19 above).

Gluck apparently continued to consider setting Dalberg's *Cora:*[9]

Your lordship,

I received the letter with which you honoured me. I have read with pleasure the opera you were kind enough to send me, but as I know nothing of the singers who would perform it, I could not undertake to compose the music for it. As soon as the opera I am working on here, of which I had the honour of speaking to you, is finished, I shall give myself the pleasure of sending it to you, and we can talk about the other one.

I have the honour to be, with the greatest respect, your very humble and obedient servant,

Christoph Gluck.[10]

In his next letter to Kruthoffer, Gluck responded to some of Von Tschudi's requests, in particular the anxieties of Caumartin, a Parisian merchant, who was involved in rescuing De Vismes and the Opéra from financial peril. Caumartin was eager that the projected changes to *Écho* should not involve further long rehearsals:[11]

My dear friend,

I am obliged to you for your news of the theatre; do continue to send it. Here is the song you wanted.[12] Please continue to act for me. I shall write nothing to Herr von Caumartin; if they want me to make alterations, they should ask for them. I am completely indifferent to acclaim or criticism in Paris. Concerning the Marmontellian crew, I refer them to M. Palissot's *Dunciade*, in which they will find what their general is worth—he has answered for me for all time.[13] About the Mathon affair, please write to him again yourself to find out whether or not he will pay. Then you can let things take their course, and it will be on his own fault if he suffers misfortune. Good wishes from my wife, Janson, and Calin to you, and to the whole house, and to all our good friends. Do not reproach me for writing so short a letter. I am not at all well. Nevertheless I am, and remain, ever your true friend and servant,

Gluck.[14]

---

[9] See his letter of 8 June 1779 (Ch. 21 above).

[10] Gluck to Dalberg, Vienna, 19 Jan. 1780, in Nohl, *Musiker-Briefe*, 54.

[11] See von Tschudi's letter of 13 Dec. 1779 (n. 5 above).

[12] The identity of the song is not clear.

[13] Charles Palissot's satirical poem *La Dunciade* (Chelsea, 1764), written in imitation of Alexander Pope's poem of the same title, ridicules Marmontel in these words: 'La déité, par un excès d'honneur, | Voulant sur lui signaler sa faveur, | Fait allonger ses superbes oreilles | De son atmet ce magnifique ornement | Donne à ses traits un air plus imposant.' See Gluck's letter of 18 Mar. 1780, below.

[14] Letter to Kruthoffer, Vienna, 31 Jan. 1780, in Kinsky, *Glucks Briefe*, 45.

His next letter responds to a message of sympathy from Grand Duke Carl August of Sachsen-Weimar, presumably on the occasion of his stroke the previous autumn:

Most Serene Duke,

Most Gracious Lord,

At the time when I received Your Serene Highness's gracious letter I had succumbed to a mortal illness. [Your letter] was filled with so many tender and moving expressions that it contributed greatly to my recovery. When I was again in a condition to render Your Highness my deepest thanks, the new spapers informed me that Your Highness was about to set out on a journey. As I have just heard of your safe return, however, I cannot refrain from telling Your Highness that never has music, united to the finest poetry, exerted so powerful an impression on the heart as this precious letter has made on mine.

I am now very old, and have squandered on the French nation most of my mental powers, yet I feel within me an inner compulsion to do something for my [own] nation, which I shall be spurred on to accomplish by the longing to hum something German for Your Highness before I die, and at the same time to express personally to you the profound thanks I owe you for your ever-gracious attitude to me. Until then I beg Your Serene Highness to accept my deepest respect with which I shall ever be, Serene Duke, Your Serene Highness's most humble [servant],

Gluck.[15]

Kruthoffer continued to receive a mixture of personal greetings, business instructions, and domestic commissions:

My dear friend,

Scarcely has the one courier arrived, than the other is despatched again, so I must reply immediately. I am glad that the little song I sent you gave you pleasure.[16] The Klopstock odes will also follow soon. This letter consists of nothing but commissions, for which I beg your forgiveness in advance. 1. Please tell Baron Tschudi that if he wants me to revise his opera, he must send me the score by the next courier, as the words he sends me are the ones I have myself sent him; if I once begin something new, the old matter gets laid aside. 2. Ask M. de la Porte for the poem by M. Millicent, and act as if I had sent it to you

---

[15] Vienna, 10 Feb. 1780, in Erich Hermann Müller von Asow, 'Zwei unveröffentlichte Briefe Glucks an Carl August', *Die Musik* (1923), 652; Treichlinger (ed.), *Briefe*, 64–5.

[16] See Gluck's letter to Kruthoffer, 31 Jan. 1780, above.

from Vienna, and give it to him instead of mine.[17] 3. Ask M. de la Porte for the address of the nuns who make the little candles to burn in the lamp; they cost 24 *sous* a packet. Send them with the next courier. You will earn the present of a little portrait from Mme Gluck, who sends you her best compliments.[18] This is all for the moment. Do not forget about Mathon. Adieu, dear friend; our compliments to Herr von Blumendorff and to all our good friends. I hope for a good reception for [Piccinni's] opera *Atys* so that I may remain undisturbed.[19]

Gluck was unable to forget the Piccinni controversy and the enemies who had tormented him, and he remained grateful to those who had ridiculed them, as the following letter to Palissot reveals:

I can delay no longer, monsieur, in informing you of the very great pleasure I experience in reading your works. I owe a good deal to the Count de Brancas for having introduced me to one of the great geniuses of France. If, during my stay in Paris, I had known of your comedy *Les Philosophes* and your *Dunciade*, what good use could I have made of them against the invective of Marmontel and his party! If ever I return to Paris, your works will serve me as an aegis against the insects of Parnassus. M. Janson, who brings you this letter, is as enchanted by your genius as I am myself, and is very desirous of making your acquaintance; he did not want to leave the country without [this letter], and he will count this occasion as one of the most agreeable in his life. I beg you never to doubt the esteem you have inspired in me. I am, with great respect, monsieur, your most humble and obedient servant,

Gluck.[20]

Meanwhile at the Opéra, financial troubles led to the resignation of De Vismes and the reappointment of Berton. Gluck remained disgusted with the administration. The following letter to Kruthoffer must have been written in the knowledge that four performances—two each of *Iphigénie en Aulide* and *Armide*—given in Paris for the benefit of the singers at the Opéra had raised the huge sum of 40,420 *livres*.[21] Yet it is one of the bitterest he wrote:

[17] The exact nature of the transaction Gluck intended to initiate is unclear. Jean-Baptiste Millicent was the author of a poem on *Alceste*, 'L'œil humide des pleurs que tu m'as fair verser', pub. in Lesure, *Querelle*, 93–5. Abbé Joseph de la Porte was the editor of the *Almanach des spectacles de Paris*.

[18] The little portrait ('ein Bildel'), possibly of Mme Gluck, may be the one mentioned in Gluck's letter of 29 Apr., below. The only known portrait of Mme Gluck is one of a pendant pair by Étienne Aubry, reproduced in *Gluck in Wien*, ed. Croll and Woitas, 165.

[19] Gluck to Kruthoffer, Vienna, 2 Mar. 1780, in Kinsky, *Glucks Briefe*, 48. The successful première of Piccinni's *Atys* was on 22 Feb. 1780.

[20] Vienna, 18 Mar. 1780: F-Pn, Fac-Sim 147, no. 19. Pub. in Desnoiresterres, *Gluck et Piccinni*, 289; L.R., 'Correspondance inédite', 14; Prod'homme, *Écrits*, 431.

[21] *Mémoires secrets*, xv. 90 (17 Mar. 1780).

My dear friend,

I am obliged to you for the little candles and the news: that makes it much easier for me to forget Paris, for I know all that goes on there. Only continue to write to me; a letter can always travel with the courier. I have absolutely no wish to have the gazette by M. de la Blancherie; you must send me no more.[22] If you want to have your expenses paid, you must make a clean sweep of recovering my debts. I have at last received the score of *Écho*, and everything will be finished by the end of April. But as to my coming to Paris again in person, nothing will come of it as long as the words 'Piccinnist' and 'Gluckist' are in use. For, thank God, I am now in good health, and do not wish to spew bile again in Paris. It is hard that the courier has scarcely arrived before he is on the way back again. Adieu, dear friend. Our compliments to Herr von Blumendorff (who has sent me a splendid communication, which I have not yet been able to answer) and to all our good friends.

Your most devoted Gluck.[23]

Work had apparently not even started on the engraving of *Écho*, although Gluck had been asking after it since 31 October 1779. The delay at least ensured that the published score contained Gluck's revisions.[24] Gluck was obviously still under some pressure to make another journey to Paris:

My dear friend,

It is a truly wretched thing that there is scarcely time to read through the letters before the answer must be ready again. One is compelled to be laconic. I am hardly likely to be persuaded into becoming yet again the object of the praise or censure of the French nation, for they are as changeable as weathercocks. If it were to happen, things would have to be made very comfortable, for my only pleasure nowadays is idling.

Wait a little longer until the time Herr Mathon has determined for payment. It is as well that he has not yet had the score engraved, because the work will turn out better in the new version. When someone buys a thing, however, he must know that the agreement has to be adhered to, whether he makes use of it or not.

Because Herr Mathon has failed to pay, I have had to send a bill to Herr Rilliet in order to repay Baron von Fries, from whom I had received the 1,000 *livres* to settle a certain debt.

The matter of the portrait made me very angry. The French seek every

---

[22] De la Blancherie launched *Nouvelles de la république des lettres et des arts* in 1779; it included several attacks on Gluck.

[23] Vienna, 31 Mar. 1780, in Kinsky, *Glucks Briefe*, 49.

[24] Ibid.; cf. Tiersot's introd. to *Écho*, ed. Fanny Pelletan (Paris, 1902), p. xlii.

excuse to torment themselves or other people. The portrait was too big to be put in the bracelet, and too small to hang. The copy we have had made can take its place. It would be a pity if the painting had to be kept in a box. It is now in good hands, and many people will have pleasure in seeing it in a place where the original is loved by the public. I am like the lamb in the fable in this affair. Mme Gluck sends you her best wishes; our compliments to all our good friends. I want no more packages: they contain nothing but poetry. Your entertaining letters are all I desire. Adieu, my dear friend, farewell.[25]

Gluck's intermittent correspondence with Klopstock reverts to a possible means of indicating nuances in performance, first promised by Nanette.[26] And in addition to the often-mentioned *Hermannsschlacht*, the following letter implies there might be another lost setting, that of Klopstock's ode 'Clarissa':

I write to inform you, my dear friend, that Herr Schröter had an excellent reception here, both at the court and from the public, and what is more, he deserved it, for he is truly a very exceptional and very natural actor. I do not doubt that he will be very pleased with Vienna. You always reproach me for not sending you an explanation of how *Alceste* should be performed. I would have done it long ago if I had found it practicable. As far as the vocal line is concerned, it is easy for someone with feeling, who has only to follow the instincts of the heart. But in the accompaniment, the instruments need so many annotations that without my presence nothing can be done. A few notes must be drawn out, others hurried over, these should be played moderately loud, those either louder or softer, not to mention the speed—to play a little too slowly or too quickly can ruin a whole movement. I therefore believe, my dear friend, you will find it much easier to make the Germans accept your new orthography,[27] than I to obtain a performance of an opera in accordance with my method, particularly in your country, where the rules of composition take first place and the power of the imagination is despised and cursed—which is why most of your composers want only to be masons, not architects.

Although you have written nothing on the death of my dear little one, my wish has nevertheless been fulfilled, for your 'Clarissa' so resembles the maiden that you, with all your great genius, could not have written anything better. This is now my favourite ode, and very few hear it without being moved to tears. You do not know why I have hesitated so long over *Hermannsschlacht*: I want to make this the last of my musical compositions, but

---

[25] Gluck to Kruthoffer, Vienna, 29 Apr. 1780, in Kinsky, *Glucks Briefe*, 50. See n. 18 above.

[26] See her letter of 17 Mar. 1775 (Ch. 14 above).

[27] On Klopstock's plans for a new orthography, see Josef Müller-Blattau, 'Gluck und die deutsche Dichtung', *Jahrbuch der Musikbibliothek Peters*, 45 (1938), 30–52.

till now I have not been able to work on its because the French gentlemen have occupied me so much. But although *Hermannschlacht* will be my last work, I believe it will not be the least important of my compositions, because I assembled the principal material for it at a time before age had weakened my creative powers. Farewell; I remain ever your devoted admirer,

Gluck.[28]

In the next few letters to Kruthoffer, Gluck brooded on the wounding treatment he had received in Paris. He continued to refer to the possibility of returning, and it appears that Kruthoffer urged this. Meanwhile the *Mémoires secrets* recorded a rumour that 'it seems settled that we shall not be able to rejoice in the presence of the Chevalier Gluck this year. This great man, hungry for success and piqued that, after having captivated Germany and France, he has not yet succeeded in Italy, plans a new attempt there. He will go to Milan. Bets are being laid here for and against his success.'[29] (Gluck himself did not mention the invitation until 31 October).

My dear friend,

I ask your forgiveness for bothering you over Herr Mathon. You can tell him at once that he should have the opera *Narcisse* engraved, as it has now been corrected; the music is certainly no better, but the piece is more consistent. The Opéra has lost much in Herr Berton, and I regret his death.[30] I wish someone might come who could take my place, and please the public with his music, so that I might be left in peace. I still cannot forget all the chatter about *Narcisse* I was made to listen to from friends and foes alike, nor the pills I had to swallow, all because the French cannot distinguish between a musical eclogue and an epic poem.[31] I am enclosing the corrections of *Narcisse* for Herr Bailli du Roullet; please send them on to him. I send my best wishes to M. Rousseau and to all our good friends; I shall not fail to inform Abbé Pezzana if anything happens about *Iphigénie*.[32] I am glad that the little songs I wrote have been acclaimed by the ambassador.[33] My compliments to Herr von Blumendorff and to Janson—I have written to him, but addressed it to the Faubourg St Germain, as I do not know where he is living. He must go and

---

[28] Letter to Klopstock, Vienna, 10 May 1780, in *Briefe von und an Klopstock*, 293–5; Tenschert, *Gluck . . . Reformator der Oper*, 207–8; Treichlinger (ed.), *Briefe*, 65–6.

[29] xv. 188 (12 June 1780). See Gluck's letters of 31 Oct. and 29 Nov. 1780, below.

[30] Berton died suddenly on 14 May 1780.

[31] The public expected *Écho* to be the latter: cf. *Mémoires secrets*, xiv. 185 (20 Sept. 1779; Ch. 21 above).

[32] M. Rousseau is probably the young tenor who took over roles associated with Le Gros. I have not been able to identify Abbé Pezzana.

[33] Cf. the songs mentioned in letters to Kruthoffer, 31 Jan. and 2 Mar. 1780, above.

get the letter, and answer it, and tell me his address. Tell him that we are well here, and send him best wishes from all my acquaintances, all his good friends, and from Mme Gluck and myself. Adieu, my dear friend. Write to me soon with all the news. I am entirely your own

Gluck.[34]

I thank you heartily for the pains you take in seeing to my affairs. Your last letter was greatly enjoyed here. Only write more often to regale us Viennese with your witty thoughts and enlightened mind, so that we can admire them more frequently. If the stupid arguments in Paris over music and the theatre were to fall out of fashion, I might perhaps resolve to go to Paris again, and whistle something more to them. I no longer trust them—the burnt child fears fire—but it might yet come about to please my friends, among whom you are one of the foremost. Best wishes to all our acquaintances and friends. I am ever yours.

Gluck.[35]

Bravo, my dear friend! Your letter received more acclaim here than all my operas in Paris. If you do not become privy counsellor, you deserve to be one. But who knows what you, with all your qualities, might yet become? *Accidit in puncto quod non contingit in anno.*[36] I am sorry I cannot say a little to you about the new version [of *Écho*], but as soon as I have received the letters, I must in the same instant send the replies, so that I scarcely have the time to acknowledge receipt of them, which is why I remain so laconic. My wife, who sends you her best compliments, cannot understand why you have changed your mind about my return to Paris, you who used always to be so against it. She asks for an explanation of this. I remain now as ever, my dear friend, your utterly devoted servant and friend,

Gluck.

PS   I gradually begin to feel English again.[37]

   Echo et Narcisse was given in its revised version on 8 August. Even in Vienna, Gluck was involved in the usual run of disputes with the Opéra. For reasons which it is not now possible to determine, Du Roullet intervened to have the conductor Louis-Joseph Francœur replaced.[38] The latter complained to Gluck, whose reply was more concerned with his own grievances than with Francœur's:

---

[34] Letter to Kruthoffer, Vienna, 30 May 1780, in Kinsky, *Glucks Briefe*, 51; L.R., 'Correspondance inédite', 15.

[35] Letter to Kruthoffer, Vienna, 30 June 1780, in Kinsky, *Glucks Briefe*, 53.

[36] 'That which has not happened in a year may yet arrive in a moment.'

[37] Letter to Kruthoffer, Vienna, 30 July 1780, in Kinsky, *Glucks Briefe*, 53–4. The postscript apparently refers to Gluck's position in connection with the American War of Independence (1776–83).

[38] Francœur's letter is reproduced in Desnoiresterres, *Gluck et Piccinni*, 291–2.

I am very sorry about the dispute which has arisen between you and the Bailli du Roullet as a result of one of my works. Shall I never be free of the theatrical upheavals of the Paris Opéra, whether on the spot or at a distance? A few days ago I received a little French journal in which it was said that I was opposed to Mlle Beaumesnil playing the role of Echo in this same opera. I am no longer surprised I have so many enemies in Paris, since so many lies are told about me. All this greatly diminishes the desire I had to return to Paris, for I detest these troublesome matters like the plague. Please excuse me, monsieur, if I decide to leave it to the administration at the Opéra to decide the grievance you have with M. Bailli du Roullet, especially as I am not in Paris. If I were in charge, you would have no reason to complain of anyone; I have always had a great regard for your musical talents, and for the loyal friendship you have shown me on several occasions. I hope you will receive justice without delay, and that peace will soon be restored.

I have the honour to be, with the greatest respect, monsieur, your most humble and devoted servant,

Gluck.

Please present my compliments to the members of the orchestra.[39]

The revival of *Écho* was a failure. Gluck's supporters had done their best to make the first performance a success, but the receipts subsequently plummeted: 'There could have been no sadder funeral oration.'[40] Gluck's next letter to Kruthoffer was probably written before he learned of the failure of *Écho*:

My dear friend,

If you continue to write me letters like the last two, I shall make a collection of them and have them printed by subscription: this would bring me in more than the operas I have sold to Mathon! I beg you with all my heart, if he does not pay up at once, to have him, if not hanged, then at least put to street-sweeping. Joking aside, your letters do you much honour, and everyone wants to make your personal acquaintance. Herr Riedel, Calin, I myself, and all our circle always await the courier anxiously, so that we can enjoy your elegant compositions. You are quite right in thinking that my journey to Paris cannot take place so soon, as I have not yet discovered whether anyone has made a request to our court here. My wife sends you many good wishes, and will follow your advice implicitly. If a journey does come about, then shall we eat, drink, and be merry with you, dear friend, and our good acquaintances. Give

---

[39] Letter to Francœur, Vienna, 20 Aug. 1780, ibid. 293. Beaumesnil was replaced by Laguerre after three performances.

[40] *Mémoires secrets*, xv. 264 (15 Aug. 1780).

our kindest regards to Herr von Blumendorff and Janson; I know of nothing to say to him but that I love him and hope that he enjoys life. I remain ever your most devoted friend and servant,

Gluck.[41]

News of the failure of *Écho* caused more disillusion, and Mathon's failure to publish the score continued to worry Gluck for the rest of the year:

My dear friend,

I received your letter today, and must reply *stante pede*[42] if I am not to miss the courier again. The emperor is in Bohemia, which is why the packages arrived so late. I am very much obliged to you for the news you sent, with the sole exception of that which concerns Mathon. I would have thought that as he had delayed for so long, he could be imprisoned in his own vaults, for he deserves no further excuse. Concerning *Écho*, I could not have imagined that the company at the Opéra should treat it so contemptuously, because the profit is all theirs.[43] Now that I see their ill will, my return to Paris will come to nothing, for I can no longer involve myself in such troubles. We shall nevertheless meet, dear friend, on some other occasion. I cannot reply to the letters [you] enclosed because of the shortage of time. Please give my compliments to your whole household, and to our other friends. Many good wishes to you from Mme Gluck. I remain ever your most devoted,

Gluck.[44]

My dear friend,

I am deeply sorry to hear of your indisposition; if you were here, you would be free of your fever at once, for I have a good friend who invariably cures such illnesses within a few days.[45] I am obliged to you for the news, although most of it was already known to us here. I hope within two months to have news for you which will please you greatly.[46] If you see Baron von Tschudi, please ask him whether he received my letter; I wrote one to him addressed: M. le Baron de Tschudi, Envoye du Prince Évêque de Liège; I could not put the street where he lives, because I do not know it. Please pursue the payment from Mathon as best you can, and when you receive the money, take a louis from it to give to M. Corancez for the Rousseau subscription, of which I make

[41] Vienna, 30 Aug. 1780: autograph in New York, Pierpont Morgan Library, Mary Flagler Cary Music Collection. Pub. in Kinsky, *Glucks Briefe*, 54; Treichlinger (ed.), *Briefe*, 67–8.

[42] Literally 'with the foot standing', at once.

[43] A ref. to the benefit performances; see above and n. 21.

[44] Letter to Kruthoffer, Vienna, 30 Sept. 1780, in Kinsky, *Glucks Briefe*, 55.

[45] Kinsky identifies the doctor as Joseph von Quarini.

[46] Gluck's news concerned the invitation to Naples; see above and n. 29.

you a present in advance.[47] My wife sends you her very best wishes, also to Herr von Blumendorff, Rousseau, Thierry, Rollan, and all our good friends. I remain ever, dear friend, your most devoted servant,

Gluck.

I have a headache and cannot write clearly.[48]

Gluck's last letter of 1780 ends the year on a tantalizing note. Despite Maria Theresia's misgivings over his self-control,[49] he had kept secret from Kruthoffer his news of an invitation to Naples, rumoured in the *Mémoires secrets* in June. The commission was arranged by Calzabigi, who had moved to Naples early in 1780, and it is likely that one of the four operas Gluck planned to produce would have been a setting of his *Ipermestra*, which Calzabigi had prepared for him a few years earlier:

In 1778 . . . Gluck entreated me to write a new drama for him. I wrote a *Semiramide* . . . but he thought it would not suit the actors who shone at that time on the operatic stage. . . . I had earlier mentioned an *Ipermestra* to him . . . he was enthusiastic about it; he told me he would have it translated for the Opéra, and that was all he said on the subject.[50]

The invitation was postponed on the death of the empress on 29 November (though *Ipermestra* became *Les Danaïdes* and was eventually set by Salieri with some assistance from Gluck);[51] Gluck's delight at the discomfiture of the anti-Gluckists is pleasing to imagine:

My dear friend,

The confusion and sorrow into which I and all the inhabitants here have been thrown on account of the sad circumstances of Maria Theresia's death prevent me from replying properly to you letter, even although it is of great interest to me. I will do no more than tell you—and this on account of the bee in your bonnet[52]—that I am to go to Naples to present four operas there. I did not want to tell you until I knew whether or not my conditions would be accepted. A droll event for the anti-Gluckists in Paris! I embrace you with all my heart,

Gluck.[53]

---

[47] Olivier de Corancez, editor of the *Journal de Paris*, was preparing an edn. of Rousseau's works. It is typical of Gluck's financial dealings that he asks Kruthoffer to collect a debt, to use part of it to pay a third party, and to accept the goods thus paid for as a present.

[48] Letter to Kruthoffer, Vienna, 31 Oct. 1780, in Kinsky, *Glucks Briefe*, 56. For Rousseau, see n. 32 above; Thierry was Louis XVI's *vallet de chambre*; Rollan was one of the subscribers to Houdon's bust of Gluck.

[49] See Ch. 14.   [50] Calzabigi to the *Mercure de France*, 15 June 1784, pub. 21 Aug. 1784, 129.

[51] See Ch. 24.   [52] The literal translation, 'flea in your ear', bears a different sense.

[53] Letter to Kruthoffer, Vienna, 29 Nov. 1780, in Kinsky, *Glucks Briefe*, 57.

23

A TESTIMONIAL YEAR
(1781)

THE year 1781 opened unpromisingly with the indefinite postponement of
the Naples visit, the prospect of a return to Paris unlikely, and Mathon's
debt still unpaid.[1] Gluck's most positive plans concerned his German version of *Iphigénie* as *Iphigenie auf Tauris*, a substantial revision, with the role
of Orestes recast for a tenor; the libretto had been translated by Johann
Baptist von Alxinger, and the Parisian painter Jean-Michel Moreau was
engaged to produce the designs. Kruthoffer continued to be the principal
recipient of Gluck's correspondence:

Your letters, my dear friend, are so delicious and entertaining as to make us
forget Linguet and his *Annales*.[2] All those I allow to read them are consumed
with the desire to make your acquaintance. You are becoming more famous
here through your letters than I with my operas in Paris. Mme Gluck thoroughly enjoys them; she sends you all good wishes, and asks if you can give
her any information about a certain Doctor of Medicine from these parts,
called Mesmer, whether he is in Paris, and what credit he has gained for his
magnetic cures.[3] The death of the empress has caused my Neapolitan journey
to be postponed. The theatres here will reopen on the twenty-first of this
month. My return to Paris is most unlikely to take place. As you rightly say, a
mature man should have nothing more to do with that rabble, and yet I would
like to see my friends once more. Greet them all heartily from me: Janson,
Rousseau, Moreau, Thierry, etc., and put Herr von Blumendorff at the head

---

[1] Mathon went out of business before the end of 1780. The exact date of the eventual publication
of the score by Des Lauriers is not known. See Hopkinson, *Bibliography*, 63.

[2] Simon Nicolas Henri Linguet, satirical author of *Annales politiques, civiles et littéraires* (Paris,
1777–92).

[3] The celebrated Dr Franz Anton Mesmer, early patron of Mozart, whose practice of 'mes-
merism' (hypnotism by the use of magnets) is parodied in several comic operas of the period,
notably *Così fan tutte*.

of the company for me. Seize Mathon by the ears on my behalf, so that we may finish with him once and for all. If the book on strategy is not very big, please send it me. Farewell, I give you a kiss on your left eye, and remain ever your

Gluck.[4]

The opening 'postscript' of the next letter contradicts a rumour that the ambassador Mercy-Argenteau was to be recalled to Vienna. The change of regime was blamed for many inconveniences in Vienna, but Gluck's complaints about the movements of the courier were nothing new:

PS   Nothing is being said here about the change of post of which the Parisians are thinking.

My dear friend,

M. Blumendorff[5] sends me your package, with the advice that if I should want to send anything to Paris, I should give it him immediately, as the courier is already about to return. How is it now possible to write you a complete letter when I have scarcely had time to read yours? You must be patient until the courier's movements are put in order again, at which time I shall be able to send you news of what is happening here, for at present there is nothing to be heard but sheer gossip. I shall wait for something reliable, which will be more pleasing to you than all the chatter. This much is certain: the emperor works so astonishingly hard that all the counsellors together can barely keep up with him. I look to have M. Moreau's designs by the next courier. please give Mlle Levasseur good wishes from Mme Gluck and me, and explain to her yourself why the courier prevents me from writing to her. We are both assured of your noble heart and true friendship, and you must not doubt the same of us. I am surprised that M. le Bailli has not answered my letter. My respects to the Baron von Tschudi; I cannot reply to him because I have not had time to read and consider the poetry he sent me. Adieu dear friend. I remain ever yours.[6]

Gluck's health was poor throughout the spring and summer:

PS   I had almost forgotten to thank you greatly for the continual trouble I cause you until such time as I can demonstrate my gratitude.

My dear friend,

Although I cannot always reply to your entertaining letters because of the irregular arrival and departure of the couriers, yet I hope that, in your

---

[4] Letter to Kruthoffer, Vienna, 3 Jan. 1781, in Kinsky, *Glucks Briefe*, 58.

[5] This Blumendorff was the brother of Gluck's diplomatic friend in Paris.

[6] Gluck to Kruthoffer, Vienna, 31 Jan. 1781, in Kinsky, *Glucks Briefe*, 59. The poetry sent by von Tschudi may well have been his translation of Calzabigi's *Ipermestra* as *Les Danaïdes*; see Ch. 22 above.

friendship, you will never forget me, but continue to delight me with your news from afar, as before. I have read your very successful translation with great pleasure, and congratulate you on it. Perhaps it will help me to make your abilities known here in Vienna, for such demonstrations are more persuasive than mere speech. Embrace M. Moreau some dozens of times on my behalf. He has completely delighted me with his designs. I am not well. March keeps me indoors, but as soon as I venture out again, I shall make your work known to the High Chamberlain, and inform you of the approval which you are sure to win. If I can contrive to get anything good from him, it will please me even more. Mme Gluck sends you her best compliments, and asks you to send her a few packets of the little night-lights. Try to get Mathon to pay once and for all, so that we can pay you for them. Tell M. le Bailli du Roullet that he should come to Vienna to cure me with his entertaining conversation; I suffer much from melancholy. Please give Mlle Levasseur my best wishes, as also Herr von Blumendorff. Farewell, dear friend. Think of me affectionately.[7]

Gluck's recovery was not helped by news of poor attendances at the Opéra, which confirmed him in a settled disgust for 'the French gentlemen':

My dear friend,

I cannot yet tell you that I am restored to health. I must be patient until the good weather arrives, when I hope to recuperate in my garden. And though I have existed for a long time in a state of inactivity, my *Iphigenie auf Tauris*, which is to be produced at the earliest opportunity, may well get me back in action, and set my blood flowing again. Meanwhile, I am very grateful to you and to all my friends who take an interest in my health. If they [the Opéra] produce all my operas so abominably, is there not the danger that they will be thought to be unbearable everywhere? Their action is, however, the best and only way to establish Italian music in Paris, so we may congratulate the French gentlemen on what they have done. I thank God I am quit of them once and for all. I noticed from the Bailli du Roullet's letters that he is not quite well, because, like me, he writes with an unsteady hand. His company would be most welcome to me. Mme Gluck, who sends you her best wishes, is disappointed that you have not sent her the night-lights—do not forget them, of all things. Our compliments to all our friends. I embrace you heartily,

Gluck.[8]

---

[7] Gluck to Kruthoffer, Vienna, 28 Mar. 1781, in Kinsky, *Glucks Briefe*, 60. The nature of Kruthoffer's translation has not been identified. The High Chamberlain was Franz Xavier, Prince of Orsini and Rosenberg.

[8] Letter to Kruthoffer, Vienna, 1 May 1781, in Kinsky, *Glucks Briefe*, 61; Treichlinger (ed.), *Briefe*, 68–9.

The letter is the last we have in Gluck's own handwriting. The garden in which Gluck hoped to recuperate was that of his country house in St Marx, where Burney had visited him and Riedel laboured with the shovel. Gluck sold this house in the autumn of 1781 and bought a larger estate in Perchtoldsdorf, which was his favoured retreat until he sold it a few months before his death.

Meanwhile his return to Paris was constantly rumoured in the *Mémoires secrets*. Gluck responded with unusual directness:

Do not believe all the rumours you hear about my early return to Paris. Unless orders from on high draw me there, I shall never go to this city until the French are agreed as to the genre of music they want. This fickle people, after having welcomed me in the most flattering manner, seem to have lost all taste for my operas, which they no longer go to see in the same numbers as formerly. Now they give all their attention to *Le Seigneur bienfaisant*. They seem to want to revert to their taste for the popular songs of the Pont-neuf: they must be left to their own devices.[9]

Shortly after, Gluck suffered a second stroke. Calin was put to use as amanuensis:

Highly honoured Sir and dearest friend,

Is it credible that the Chevalier Gluck is compelled to write to you through me? It is nevertheless true, beyond the slightest doubt. A few weeks ago, the fate that ever rules over us rendered his hand powerless. . . . What hurts the Chevalier, in his unfortunate condition, is that for some time he has received no news from his good friends in Paris. He looked for something from you, dear friend, through the courier, but on account of the journey of His Majesty the Emperor, that means is lost . . . His good friend the Bailli du Roullet, who used to be unfailing in his replies, gives rise to the worry whether he has not paid his debt to Nature. . . . Every day he counts on seeing letters from your hand. To rouse him (and also me), tell him of any newsworthy happenings at the Opéra. The war news here begins to diminish. If you have more confidential and reliable news about how things are in America, this would be welcome, but it must not be bad news. If you will undertake a lively correspondence with him, you will receive sufficient thanks when you see how your sympathetic actions bring new strength to the Chevalier's paralysed arm—for he has no one else left.[10]

[9] Letter to the editor of *Mémoires secrets*, Vienna, 11 May, 1781, pub. in xvii, 197–8 (30 May 1781); Prod'homme, *Écrits*, 432. *Le Seigneur bienfaisant* was an opera-ballet by Floquet (see Ch. 18 n. 10 above). The music, comprising a series of undemanding 'pont-neufs', or popular songs, was judged 'aisée, gracieuse et chantante' (*Mémoirs secrets*, xvi. 106 (20 Dec. 1780)).

[10] Calin to Kruthoffer, Vienna, 19 June 1781, in Kinsky, *Glucks Briefe*, 62.

The last sentence can scarcely be true, but there are many gaps in Gluck's correspondence from this time; the composer sent few greetings to the circle of friends in Paris, and his old informal intimacy with Kruthoffer is absent from the dictated letters. There were, however, better prospects in Vienna. Duke Carl August continued to show the composer a friendly concern:

Most Serene Duke,

Gracious Sir,

It has pleased Your Serene Highness in a letter of the eighth of this month to give me a token of your favour and most gracious remembrance; I acknowledge this high favour with my most heartfelt and humble thanks.

The persistent paralysis of my right hand makes it impossible for me to thank Your Serene Highness in my own hand, but I hope that the Baden bath, which I am now taking for the second time, will gradually alleviate this malady, at least in part.

I am heartily sorry that this same illness makes it impossible for me to fulfil Your Serene Highness's gracious intention in regard to the young musician, for although, thank God, my unfortunate accident has had no ill effect on my mental powers, my present circumstances in no way allow that expenditure of effort that would be necessary in such a case.[11] If, nevertheless, Your Serene Highness should wish to let this young man come here, I am certain that his stay will not be without great value, since there will be operas given for the visit of the Tsar, and he can learn more from a single performance than from long study [of the scores].[12] I shall be glad to be of service to him as far as my circumstances permit, and at least attempt to be useful by giving him good advice and by arranging good contacts.

In awaiting Your Serene Highness's further commands, I am, with humble devotion, Serene Duke, Gracious Sir, Your Serene Highness's most humble servant,

Gluck.[13]

Four of Gluck's operas were in rehearsal in Vienna that autumn. In addition to the première of *Iphigenie auf Tauris* on 23 October, revivals of *Alceste* (25 November), *La Rencontre imprévue* (5 December), and *Orfeo* (31 December) were prepared. These prestigious events (and the subse-

[11] Carl August had asked Gluck to undertake the instruction of Philipp Christoph Kayser, a protégé of Goethe's. It is not known whether Kayser came to Vienna on this occasion.

[12] Archduke Paul was not crowned Tsar Paul I till 1796, but was widely referred to by this title in Vienna in the 1780s.

[13] Letter to Carl August von Sachsen-Weimar, Vienna, 21 Aug. 1781, in Müller von Asow, 'Zwei unveröffentlichte Briefe', 653; Treichlinger (ed.), *Briefe*, 70–1.

quent incorporation of the works into the repertoire) constituted a public
testimonial to Gluck's status as musical elder statesman in the imperial capital. But how genuine was Joseph's appreciation? Mozart, far from disinterested in the matter, suggested reluctant support: 'The emperor has with
difficulty been persuaded to have Gluck's *Iphigenie* and *Alceste* performed';
and writing of the engagement of Bernasconi at Gluck's insistence, he suggested 'the emperor is at heart as little impressed with her as he is with
Gluck.'[14] It is clear that Mozart saw Gluck as a stumbling-block to his own
chances:

I think I mentioned recently that Gluck's *Iphigenie* in German and *Alceste* in
Italian are to be performed. If either *Iphigenie* or *Alceste* were to be given, I
would be happy, but it annoys me that it should be both. I will tell you the reason. The man who translated *Iphigenie* into German is an excellent poet. I
would gladly have had him translate my Munich opera [*Idomeneo*]. . . .
Moreover Mme Bernasconi, Adamberger, and Fischer would have been
pleased to sing it, but they now have to study two operas, which are very
demanding ones . . . a third opera would be too much.[15]

Gluck must have been well enough to play an active part in the
rehearsals, according to the testimony of two musicians. First the Irish
tenor Michael Kelly:

A number of foreign Princes, among whom were the Duc de Deux Ponts, the
Elector of Bavaria etc., with great retinues, came to visit the Emperor, who,
upon this occasion, signified his wish to have two grand serious operas, both
the composition of Chevalier Gluck;—*L'Iphigenia in Tauride* [*sic*] and
L'Alceste, produced under the direction of the composer; and gave orders that
no expense should be spared to give them every effect.
   Gluck was then living at Vienna, where he had retired, crowned with professional honours, and a splendid fortune, courted and caressed by all ranks,
and in his seventy-fourth [*recte* sixty-seventh] year.
   L'Iphigenia was the first opera to be produced, and Gluck was to make his
choice of performers in it. Madame Bernasconi was one of the first serious
singers of the day,—to her was appropriated the part of Iphigenia. The celebrated tenor, Adamberger, performed the part of Orestes, finely. To me was
allotted the character of Pylades, which created no small envy among those
performers who thought themselves better entitled to the part than myself,

---

[14] Letter to Leopold Mozart, 29 Aug. 1781, Mozart, *Briefe und Aufzeichnungen*, iii. 152.
[15] Letter to Leopold Mozart, 12 Sept. 1781, ibid. iii. 156. Antonia Bernasconi sang Iphigenia, the
tenor Valentin Adamberger the recast role of Orestes, and the bass Ludwig Fischer the part of
Thoas.

and perhaps they were right;—however, I had it, and also the high gratification of being instructed in the part by the composer himself.

One morning, after I had been singing with him, he said, 'Follow me up stairs, Sir, and I will introduce you to one, whom all my life, I have made my study, and endeavoured to imitate.' I followed him into his bed-room, and, opposite to the head of the bed, saw a full-length picture of Handel in a rich frame. 'There, Sir,' said he, 'is the portrait of the inspired master of our art; when I open my eyes in the morning, I look upon him with reverential awe, and acknowledge him as such, and the highest praise is due to your country for having distinguished and cherished his gigantic genius.'

L'Iphigenia was soon put into rehearsal, and a corps de ballet engaged for the incidental dances belonging to the piece. The ballet master was Monsieur De Camp, the uncle of that excellent actress, and accomplished and deserving woman, Mrs Charles Kemble. Gluck superintended the rehearsals, with his powdered wig, and gold-headed cane; the orchestra and choruses were augmented, and all the parts were filled.[16]

The testimony of the double-bass player Joseph Kämpfer cannot be so certainly associated with the 1781 performances: it mentions the 'wrong' *Iphigénie*[17] and implies a degree of physical vigour which seems unlikely in a man who was from this time able only to dictate his letters. Kelly, however, does not suggest the Gluck was too paralysed to train his singers, nor to move freely about his house. And Kämpfer confirms that Gluck's conduct of rehearsals was no less tempestuous in Vienna than in Paris:

Although in every other circumstance in life he is a kind, good-natured man, as soon as he takes his place as director, he becomes a tyrant, who is roused to the utmost passion by the slightest appearance of an error. He requires the most diligent players in the orchestra, among whom there are acknowledged virtuosi, to repeat passages more than twenty or thirty times, till he obtains the ensemble he requires. He abuses them so much that they often rebel, and are induced to play under his direction only by the persuasion of the emperor: 'You know that is just how he is! He doesn't mean any harm by it!' Moreover they have always to be paid double, and those who would usually receive one ducat for their performance receive two when Gluck is director. In certain passages, no fortissimo can be too loud for him, and no pianissimo too soft. Moreover it is quite unprecedented how, sitting at the keyboard, he represents each emotion, whether fierce, gentle, or tragic, in every expression and gesture. He lives and dies with his heroes, rages with Achilles, weeps with

---

[16] *Reminiscences*, i. 254–6.

[17] A common mistake, however; 'After Easter, Gluck's *Iphigénie en Aulide* will be given in German'. *Deutsches Museum*, 31 Mar. 1781, cited in Gluck's *Sämtliche Werke*, 1/11, p. vii n. 4.

Iphigenia; and in Alcestis's dying aria, at the words, 'manco . . . moreo . . .' etc. he sinks right down and becomes almost a corpse.[18]

Iphigenie was a popular success, as Mozart records: 'The première took place yesterday, but I was not present, for those who wanted to obtain a seat in the stalls had to be at the theatre by four o'clock. . . . Six days earlier, I had tried to reserve a seat in the circle, but they were all taken. However, I attended almost all rehearsals.'[19] Gluck dictated the following account to Kruthoffer:

My dear friend,

I have read the two letters you sent me with great pleasure, especially as I thought from your long silence that you had completely forgotten me. I have again escaped from the jaws of death, even before I was fully recovered from my earlier illness. An inflammation of the lungs, together with a fever, have completely robbed me of what little strength I had. I am now once more a feeble convalescent. I must inform you that *Iphigenie* was produced here on the twenty-third, to great acclaim. The designs by Herr Moreau contributed substantially to the good reception. I am sending you back the sketches [of Moreau's designs], which I wanted to keep; this is a hard sacrifice for me, and only for you have I been able to resolve to deprive myself of them. Congratulate him warmly on them, on behalf of the public here. When I am again in a condition to get out into the world, I shall not fail to try to get something for him from the emperor. All Vienna, including myself, rejoices in the birth of the dauphin, not on account of the French, but on the queen's behalf.[20] I told you not to deal so gently with that scoundrel Mathon, but to hold him to his contract, as his claims have always been based on his own account; he should rather make some reparation because of his long-delayed payment. My wife sends you all good wishes, Calin sends his compliments, and I embrace you, dear friend, with all my heart.[21]

The Tsar and Tsarina arrived in Vienna on 21 November. On the twenty-fifth, *Alceste* was given at Schönbrunn in his honour, 'got up with magnificence and splendour, worthy an Imperial Court.'[22] Reluctant Gluckist or not, the emperor conceded that 'it was very successful'.[23] The

---

[18] In Cramer (ed.), *Magazin der Musik*, 1 (1783), 561–4.

[19] Letter to Leopold Mozart, 24 Oct. 1781, in Mozart, *Briefe und Aufzeichnungen*, iii. 170–1.

[20] The dauphin, Louis Joseph Xavier François, was born on 22 Oct. 1781.

[21] Vienna, 2 Nov. 1781, in Kinsky, *Glucks Briefe*, 63; Tenschert, *Gluck*, 208–9.

[22] Kelly, *Reminiscences*, i. 256.

[23] Letter to Archduke Leopold 26 Nov. 1781, quoted in Kinsky, *Glucks Briefe*, 65. *Alceste* was repeated at the Burgtheater on 3 Dec., and, with *Iphigenie*, *La Rencontre*, and *Orfeo*, was retained in the repertory till the end of the winter season.

Tsar saw *Iphigenia* at the Burgtheater on the twenty-seventh. The following day, he sought out the composer. Gluck recounted the scene to Kruthoffer:

My dear friend,

I read with the greatest pleasure your letter which gave me so much news of the war and the theatre. I regret the loss of the valiant General Koch, and wish that the rumour of my complete recovery were true. News of the success of the German *Iphigenie* is better founded, for the Tsar of Russia was so delighted with it that he visited me the other day, together with the Prince of Württemberg, and expressed a great desire to make my acquaintance.[24] This has caused a great sensation here, and the place where I am staying was completely filled by a crowd of people, all talking about it. He has also heard the Italian *Alceste*, and was particularly struck by the air at the end of the second act, especially at the words 'me déchire le cœur'.[25] There is a particular lesson for Herr Marmontel here, for [the Tsar] paid me the compliment of saying that although he had heard a good deal of music, nothing had touched his heart as closely as mine. I am sending you the German translation [of *Iphigenie*] as you desire. I hope you have received the letter, together with Herr Moreau's sketches, which I sent you by a French courier; if not please tell me at once. Send me no more newspapers from M. de la Blancherie, for it is not worth the bother of reading them.[26] I also wish to hear no more of Mathon; deal with him as you see fit; I can rely on your wisdom and honesty. Mme Gluck sends you all good wishes, and I remain ever your most devoted servant,

Gluck.[27]

Of the two further operas revived this season, *La Rencontre imprévue* was given in German as *Die Pilgrime von Mekka* on 5 December, and on 31 December, *Orfeo* was performed. Gluck wrote to Kruthoffer on the eve the latter revival, but without mentioning the event. Instead his letter concerns the transmission of a portrait, probably a copy of the Duplessis, to the wife of the art-collector La Ferté:

My dear friend,

I ask you to undertake the following commission, namely to give the enclosed letter together with the portrait in the tin box to M. Bailli du Roullet. But

---

[24] Prince Ferdinand of Württemberg was the Tsar's brother-in-law. In the next sentence, Gluck's phrase 'der Platz wo ich logire' (the place where I am staying) suggests that the royal party visited him in his apartment in the Lopresti house in Kärntnerstrasse.

[25] The aria is 'Ah per questo già stanco mio core'.

[26] See Gluck's letter of 31 Mar. 1780 (Ch. 22).

[27] Vienna, 30 Nov. 1781, in Kinsky, *Glucks Briefe*, 64. Only the signature is in Gluck's hand.

please open it and have it stretched on a frame before you hand it over, because it will appear better when stretched. I want him to take both the letter and the portrait to Mme de la Ferté. Should he be absent from Paris, however, please undertake this task yourself. I cannot answer your letter on this occasion, as the room is full of people, so I close by adding that I remain for always your most devoted servant and friend,

Gluck.[28]

[28] Vienna, 30 Nov. 1781, in Kinsky, *Glucks Briefe*, 67.

24

LAST YEARS
(1782–1787)

ONLY one letter survives from 1782. Little is known of the recipient, Valentin, who was director of music to the Duke D'Aiguillon. He appears to have asked Gluck to comment on a score:

I must thank you for your kind letter, which gave me great pleasure. It flatters me, and I read in it both the stamp of an ardent genius, eager to learn, and a fundamentally good nature and excellent character, which do you much credit.

If the state of my health still allowed me to undertake something in the nature of dramatic composition, I would find nothing more immediately appealing than to accept the offer you have made me, and I believe we would both be pleased by the outcome.

I have been ill for several months following the apoplectic stroke I suffered last year. My head is weakened, and my right arm is paralysed. I am incapable of undertaking any work requiring continuous application; I am not allowed, and still less am I able, to apply myself in any way. So, monsieur, you see that I cannot accede to a request which does you credit and honours me. It is against my wishes, but it is impossible to act otherwise.

You are young, monsieur, and full of good intentions. If you apply yourself, I have no doubt that you will make progress, gain advancement, and succeed.

Be bold and determined in your studies, aim to consider the unity of a complete work, and above all seek true expression. All this, combined with the rules of art, will take you far. Let the simplicity of nature and the strength of feeling be your guide above all other considerations. To depart from these precepts is to fall into absurd incongruities, which would confine you to a mediocre status.

These precepts are my masters: make them your own. In this school, and with the necessary natural and acquired abilities, you will take the right path.

Several stray from it for want of observing these rules and following instead the usual practices.

Subject these masters to a thorough investigation; consult and question them. They are gentle with those who seek them out. They will listen to you and respond. They will guide you.

Adieu, monsieur. Accept this piece of advice from an invalid, who is no longer able to do more than advise, and be assured that you have inspired in me those feelings of esteem which you deserve; I have the honour to be, monsieur, your very humble and obedient servant,

Chevalier Gluck.[1]

Brief references in Mozart's letters from this year suggest that Gluck had befriended the younger composer, and was active in promoting his career: 'My opera [*Die Entführung aus dem Serail*] was given another performance yesterday at Gluck's request. He has paid me many compliments about it, and I am dining with him tomorrow.'[2]

The following year found Gluck restless again, toying with more foreign visits, which were invariably vetoed by Mme Gluck. His characteristic niggardliness is shown with regrettable clarity in his burdening of Kruthoffer with numerous domestic commissions, for which the composer, as usual, expected his friend to recompense himself with money extracted from his publishers, promising to square the account through a bequest in his will. There was, however, no bequest to Kruthoffer, and it is unlikely that the diplomat was ever reimbursed for his purchases. (Mme Gluck was still pursuing the money due from Mathon two years after Gluck's death[3]):

My dear friend,

The reason why I have lately failed to keep up a regular correspondence with you is that under the present administration, no one knows whether the courier is coming or going. I would like to spare you the cost of postage, but I have felt a little hurt by the fact that you, who are so gifted in making light of all the tasks that come your way, have managed my affairs with such apathy. Perhaps the new peace with England will make you more active again. To test this, I shall trouble you with a few commissions, the expenses of which you may deduct from the money you receive [from Mathon] together with the interest due on it. My wife, who sends you her warm regards, asks you for some best-quality rouge—two small pots for brunettes and two small pots for

[1] Vienna, 17 Apr. 1782, pub. in Prod'homme, *Écrits*, 432–4; id., 'Lettres de Gluck', 260–1.
[2] Letter to Leopold Mozart, 7 Aug. 1782, in Mozart, *Briefe und Aufzeichnungen*, iii. 218.
[3] See letters from Salieri to Kruthoffer, 4 Feb. 1788, 8 Mar. 1789, and 25 July 1789: F-Pn, Salieri lettres autographes, nos. 29, 30, 32.

fair skins, four pots in all; next, four pounds of brown [hair] powder from Marechal à la Canelle; in addition, some night-lights like the ones you have already sent us; and finally a round box of the white confections, which, when one puts them in the mouth and bites them, make one cool.[4] It is not necessary to send everything at once, but just one thing of each kind, the remainder to follow gradually. Forgive me if I trouble you with new commissions; if one is in need, one turns again to old friends. However, I do not ask for your help without recompense, for I have already decided to include you in my will to recompense your efforts. One thing more: please give my wife's regard to M. Le Gros, and recommend to him a certain M. Fischer, who is an incomparable baritone, and whom he will be able to make good use of in his concerts; he will travel from here to Paris during Lent. Please let me know if Le Gros is willing to be of service to him.[5] My compliments to Herr von Blumendorff and to all other good friends. Perhaps we shall meet again this year, if my wife does not rule it out. I remain ever, dear friend, your most devoted servant,

Gluck.[6]

My dear friend,

We received the night-lights, together with the pastilles, and my wife, who sends you her best wishes, is most grateful to you for them. The cosmetics can come to no more than 12 kreutzer, and 15 kreutzer for the hair powder: please recompense yourself for the outlay from Mathon's payment. My wife wants brown [hair] powder, and the rouge should not be light in colour. I hope to be able to thank you in person for all the inconvenience I cause you, for I am really considering coming once more to enjoy the company of my friends, though not to expose myself to the criticisms of Marmontel and De la Harpe by presenting a new work. Please see to the enclosed package. It came to me from you, so I am returning it again. I have the honour to be, dear friend, your most devoted servant,

Gluck.[7]

My dear friend,

My secretary's illness prevented me from replying to you earlier, to let you know that my wife, who sends you her best wishes, has safely received the hair powder. She hopes also in due course to receive the rouge suitable for a brunette. I would not presume to mention Mathon's debt again—you yourself will arrange that as best you can—but I come to trouble you for a new favour:

---

[4] The following letter reveals the 'brown powder' to be hair powder. The night-lights are a constant request. Kinsky plausibly suggests that the white sweets were peppermints.

[5] Ludwig Fischer had great success as Thoas in the Viennese *Iphigenie* and as Osmin in *Die Entführung*.

[6] Letter to Kruthoffer, Vienna, 22 Feb. 1783, in Kinsky, *Glucks Briefe*, 67–8.

[7] Letter to Kruthoffer, Vienna, 28 Mar. 1783, ibid. 69.

Herr Rilliet has cashed my nine-months' pension, but the exchange rate here is so low that I ask you to receive the money from him (he has already been informed of this) and send it to me in cash [*in Natura*], in instalments, by the guardsman who departs every month. Otherwise I would lose considerably, as the louis d'or is here worth only eight florins and about fifty kreutzer. Forgive me these tedious matters. Why did Heaven appoint you to be my friend? You possess so many fine qualities that, as you already know, I seldom spare you. I remain for all time, your most devoted servant and friend,

Gluck.[8]

My dear friend,

I have received your letter safely from the hands of the guardsman who has just arrived, but not the promised rouge, nor has any package addressed to me arrived at the Customs. I therefore ask you to be so kind as to enquire what accident can have befallen it. To avoid any further difficulties over the dispatch of money, it will surely be best if you send it to Herr von Blumendorff,[9] addressed to me. Concerning the Mathon affair, I heartily deplore the French [nation], because even legal contracts have no power in their land. My idea would be to employ a lawyer so that the thing might once and for all be at an end. I have taken such a dislike to the French that I no longer desire to see them in Paris. Perhaps I shall travel through there one day on the way to London, where I have been invited to produce the Italian operas I have already written. I remain with all respect, dear friend, your most devoted servant,

Gluck.

PS   My wife sends you her best wishes.[10]

The same man who drove a hard bargain where money was concerned, who exploited his friends and fussed over his wife's rouge and nigh-lights, was seen by others in a different light. Gluck was now a hero and an object of pilgrimage. Visiting rulers called upon him; composers valued his approbation; men of letters beat a path to his door. One such was Joseph Martin Kraus:

---

[8] Letter to Kruthoffer, Vienna, 9 July 1783, ibid. 70. Gluck's pension from the Opéra was 6,000 *livres* a year, or 4,500 *livres* (225 louis d'or) for nine months. Exact calculations are impossible, but Gluck certainly suffered under exchange fluctuations.

[9] Brother of the Blumendorff at the Paris embassy; see Gluck's letter of 15 Jan. 1777 in Ch. 18 above.

[10] Letter to Kruthoffer, Vienna, 4 Aug. 1783, in Kinsky, *Glucks Briefe*, 71. Nothing precise is known of an invitation to England, though Kinsky surmises that there might have been one from Robert O'Reilly, director of the King's Theatre. Rumours were rife of a return to Paris: 'All the Gluckist party tremble with joy since they have learned that the Chevalier Gluck is completely cured of his illness, and has decided to set out for France'. *Mémoires secrets*, xxi. 71–2 (24 Aug. 1783).

At last I have met Pan Gluck. No pilgrim approached the relics of the Holy Land more reverently than I approached this great patriarch. . . . His last illness has affected him most severely, with the result that he has difficulty in expressing his thoughts, and is from time to time forced to search for words. . . . His right hand lacks its former suppleness; this was why Salieri had to write down his *Danaïdes* for him, but even this strained him too severely . . . so that he abandoned the opera, and Salieri has been invited to Paris to compose it there in his stead.[11] Gluck thinks the music will have too much of his own ideas in it (Salieri has had plenty of opportunity to hear these) for it to be Salieri's own work, yet he did not have sufficient confidence in the young man's talent to let the music be passed off under his [Gluck's] name. . . . It is an amazing characteristic of this great composer that from time to time he composes several operas in his head, without writing them down, and is able to retain them in his memory for a number of years. In addition to many scenes from Klopstock's bardic poem [*Hermannsschlacht*], I heard him play whole acts from his French and Italian operas, which had been created in this manner. He has an incomparable ability, when he is in his element, to transport himself immediately into any passion he chooses; he sweeps the listener along with him, like a storm, and it is impossible to resist until he finishes. I only wished that Herr Counsellor could hear the scene 'Un seul guerrier' and the chorus 'Poursuivons notre ennemi', from *Armide*: I quite forgot myself, and hunted through the whole room to find a weapon with which to rescue Armida![12]

In the autumn, Gluck was visited by Johann Friedrich Reichardt, who drafted the following account (in the third person) for his autobiography:

For Reichardt, the most valuable aspect of this visit to Vienna was making the personal acquaintance of Gluck, who received him with great kindness and friendship in his country house, a mile from the city[13] . . . He was met by a grand old man, of imposing bearing, dressed elaborately in a grey coat embroidered with silver, and accompanied by his domestic servants; he received the young Kapellmeister [Reichardt], who was in travelling-clothes, with more dignity and display than the latter had expected. They soon sat

---

[11] Calzabigi's opera *Ipermestra*, tr. von Tschudi as *Les Danaïdes*, had been passed on to Salieri: see Ch. 22.

[12] Kraus, *Tagebuch*, ed. Irmgard Leux-Henschen (Stockholm, 1978), 251–4 (15 Apr. 1783). See also Bertil van Boer, 'The Travel Diary of Joseph Martin Kraus: Translation and Commentary', *Journal of Musicology*, 8 (1990), 266–90. The German composer Kraus had lived in Stockholm since 1778.

[13] Gluck received Reichardt at his country house at Perchtoldsdorf (see Ch. 23), see Brauneis, 'Gluck in Wien'. He sold the property a few months before his death to Antonia von Gudenus. The receipt for the sale is reproduced in translation in Müller von Asow, *Collected Correspondence*, 208; I have not been able to locate the original.

down to a well-supplied table, where, however, the strict supervision of his wife caused the hero, weakened by an apoplectic attack, to be more moderate than he seemed to wish. Meanwhile the conversation was cheerful and varied. The highly intelligent and well-informed lady of the house, and a family priest who looked after Gluck's correspondence and accounts—Gluck was always very active in the stock market, investing to enhance his considerable fortune—took a lively part in it. There was first much talk of Klopstock and the Margrave of Baden, at whose house the two great artists came to know, love, and esteem each other. . . . As soon as coffee was drunk and a short walk taken, Gluck sat down at the piano and sang several of those original compositions, with a weak, hoarse voice and palsied tongue, accompanying himself with single chords—to the great delight of Reichardt, who received from the master permission to write down an ode from his dictation.[14] Several times during the songs from *Hermannsschlacht* Gluck imitated the sounds of horns and the cries of the swordsmen from behind their shields; once he interrupted himself to say that he must invent his own instrument for the work. . . . It is surely an irreparable loss that the composer himself did not write down the songs. . . .

The beautiful life-size oil-painting by Duplessis of Paris hung in the room, showing the inspired artist at the piano, all heaven in his eyes and all love and greatness on his lips. No sooner had Reichardt expressed the wish to have a good and faithful copy of this beautiful painting than Gluck promised him one. . . .

When Gluck entertained his guest alone in his study, he told him of his stay in Paris and his work there. He knew Paris and the Parisians through and through, and spoke about them ironically, telling how, after their presumption and prejudice, he had treated them and made use of them in his own grand manner. . . .

During the evening, Gluck had, in a lively moment, promised to go with Reichardt to Vienna next day to dine with him together with the poet Schroder and Kraus from Stockholm, thus forming a small gathering of practising artists. This idea seemed rather to frighten the cautious lady . . . who frustrated the plan.[15]

The character of Mme Gluck emerges more clearly in these years, not only protective of her husband's health, but making an effort to temper his habitual financial prudence:

---

[14] 'Ode an der Tod' was pub. by Reichardt in *Musikalischer Blumenstrauss* (Berlin, 1792). See Josef Liebeskind, *Ergänzungen und Nachträge zu dem Thematischen Verzeichnis von Chr. W. v. Gluck* (Leipzig, 1911), 12.

[15] 'Bruchstücke aus Reichardts Autobiographie', *Allgemeine Musikalische Zeitung*, 13 Oct. 1813, 665–74 *passim*.

My dear friend,

A few days after your departure, I fell prey to rheumatism in the head and catarrh; the latter still torments me, and is the reason why you perhaps received the desired portrait sooner than my answer to your very agreeable letter. I wish for nothing so much as to be able to fulfil your plan next spring, and to be able to spend some time in the pleasant company of Klopstock and yourself. My wife, who sends you her best wishes, is of the same opinion, though we thought differently over your portrait, for she wanted me to bear the costs of this, but I held that one must not buy the applause of a learned musician with presents; I would rather appear rude than corrupt. Adieu, dear friend, your most sincere servant,

Gluck.[16]

A third stroke during the winter of 1783–4 put paid to any thought of ful-filling Reichardt's plan to arrange another meeting with Klopstock.

The following year saw the much-delayed première of *Les Danaïdes*. It was announced in Paris as Gluck's latest work:

Les Danaïdes, the famous opera by Chevalier Gluck, which was announced so long ago, and which has met obstacles on the part of the committee over pay-ment (in that the composer vowed that he had only written the first act), is today in a very happy state: it has been accepted and definitively announced as his masterpiece. Gluck has not however come in person to produce it. He is not in a condition to travel, and it is the Sr Salieri, his pupil, who has under-taken this task.[17]

The première of *Les Danaïdes* will definitely be held tomorrow. This five-act opera has words by the late Baron von Tschudi, revised and corrected by M. le Bailli du Roullet. As for the music, it is announced as being jointly by Chevalier Gluck and M. Salieri, director of music to the emperor and in charge of the theatres of the Viennese court. At the rehearsals, no inconsis-tency was detected which might reveal the difference between the two hands, suggesting that the pupil is worthy of the master. Connoisseurs who are not partisan judge the opera to contain grand tragic effects, but little melody and poor dance airs.[18]

The publication of letters from Gluck and Salieri clarifying the authorship appears to have been manipulated, perhaps by Du Roullet, and delayed until the success of the work was assured:

---

[16] Gluck to Reichardt, Vienna, 11 Nov. 1783, pub. in *Zeitschrift für Musikwissenschaft*, 6 (1924), 351; Treichlinger (ed.), *Briefe*, 73.

[17] *Mémoirs secrets*, xxv. 253–4 (8 Apr. 1784).   [18] Ibid. xxv. 295 (25 Apr. 1784).

I beg you, my friend, to have published in the *Journal de Paris* the declaration I make here: that the music of *Les Danaïdes* is entirely the work of M. Salieri, and that I had no part in it other than the advice that he was eager to take from me, and which my esteem for him and my small experience prompted me to offer.

Chevalier Gluck.[19]

The declaration by M. le Chevalier Gluck which I have just read in your journal is a new favour bestowed on me by this great man, whose friendship reflects a ray of his glory in my direction.

It is true that I alone wrote the music for the opera *Les Danaïdes*, but I wrote it entirely under his direction, guided by his light and instructed by his genius.

The value of musical ideas is too commonplace, and by itself too insignificant to take pride in. It is their deployment, their association with the words, their dramatic pacing that constitutes all the worth and that gives them true merit; and in this respect, all that is good in *Les Danaïdes* I owe to the author of *Iphigénie* . . .[20]

Criticism of the poem in the May issue of the *Mercure de France* provoked a long defence by Calzabigi, who also took the opportunity to claim the credit for Gluck's dramatic strengths.[21] Du Roullet's response supplies a useful detail: in answering Calzabigi's claim that Gluck was unable to pronounce Italian properly, he pointed out that Gluck's spoken French was 'even more inaccurate than his Italian', though this had not prevented him from setting French poems superbly, in particular *Iphigénie en Tauride*, which the author had not even had the opportunity of reading to him.[22]

Hopeful librettists continued to send him their work, apparently content for it to be set by a pupil or follower of Gluck's, if the great man himself were not able to do so:

Monsieur,

I am equally flattered to receive your obliging letter, monsieur, and mortified that my condition and my situation do not allow me to respond to your attentions and to fulfil your wishes.

I am absolutely unable to undertake any work such as this, requiring application; and as to entrusting it to another, under my direction, that is always a tricky and uncertain business, subject to a thousand drawbacks, the more so in

---

[19] Gluck to Du Roullet, Vienna, 26 Apr, 1784, pub. in *Journal de Paris*, 16 May 1784, 597. Repr. in Prod'homme, *Écrits*, 434–5; id., 'Lettres de Gluck', 261.

[20] Salieri to the *Journal de Paris*, Paris, 28 Apr. 1784, pub. 18 May 1784, 609. Repr. in Adolphe Jullien, *La Cour et l'Opéra sous Louis XVI* (Paris, 1878), 183–4.

[21] *Mercure de France*, Aug. 1784, 128–37; extracts in Ch. 8 and Ch. 22 above.

[22] *Mercure de France*, Oct. 1784, 86–90.

that the one I might have in mind is heavily burdened with other work, and could not accept even this commission.

Your work is rich in tableaux and in dramatic moments, and regarding the few small alternations which might be required, we would need to be near each other to arrive at an understanding—it is not possible to undertake this work at a distance, as you can easily appreciate. As *Cora* is your first dramatic work, I can assure you that you have made a very happy beginning, and if you continue to exercise your talents in this sphere, as I advise you, you can hope for considerable success.

I send you many thanks, monsieur, for your gracious expressions towards me, and for thinking so well of me. In the hope that, as I doubt not, you may find some composer who will reinforce by his fine music the beauty of your opera, which I return to you, I have the honour to be, with the highest esteem, monsieur, your most humble and obedient servant,

Chevalier Gluck.[23]

It would be interesting to know on which of his pupils Gluck considered bestowing *Cora*. He had already given Salieri *Les Danaïdes*, and was shortly to propose him to set *Tarare* by Beaumarchais.[24] It was Méhul, never formally a pupil of Gluck's who eventually composed a setting of *Cora*, which was produced with little success in 1791.

Salieri is the source of one of the most vivid accounts of Gluck in his last years:

In the spring of 1786, Salieri was pressingly invited to Paris. After he had obtained permission from his imperial master, he prepared himself for the journey. Before departing, he bade an affectionate farewell to his friend Gluck, to whom he owed the greater part of the fame and fortune awaiting him, for despite his talents, he would scarcely have attained so splendid a destination without the recommendation of one so highly esteemed in France. Gluck, whose mother tongue was Bohemian, had to struggle to express himself in German, and even more so in French and Italian, and this difficulty only increased in his last years on account of his paralysis. In conversing, he customarily mixed several languages, so that his farewell to his beloved protégé ran as follows: '*Ainsi . . . mon cher ami . . . lei parte domani per Parigi . . . Je vous souhaite . . . di cuore un bon voyage . . . Sie gehen in eine Stadt, wo man schätzet*

---

[23] Letter to Valadier, Vienna, 1 May 1785: F-Pn, Gluck lettres autographes, no. 40. Pub. in Tiersot, *Lettres*, 35; id., 'Pour le centenaire', 274; L.R., 'Correspondance inédite', 14–15.

[24] 'Beaumarchais sent his opera to Gluck. The grandeur of the scheme delighted him, and it seemed worthy of his genius; he told him, however, that his age no longer allowed him the strength to undertake so vast an enterprise. He entrusted the work to M. Salieri, the wisest of his disciples.' Philippe Gudin, *Œuvres complètes de Pierre-Augustin Caron de Beaumarchais* (Paris, 1809), vii. 287.

... die fremden Künstler ... e lei si farà onore ... ich zweifele nicht.' Embracing him, he added, '*ci scriva mais bien souvent.*'[25]

Gluck made his will this year, a curious document acknowledging only his immense debt to his wife:

Though nothing is more sure than death, the hour of it is uncertain, therefore I the undersigned, being of sound mind, have made my last will and testament as follows:

1. I commend my soul to the infinite mercy of God and my body to be consigned to the earth in accordance with Christian Catholic custom.
2. I leave twenty-four florins for fifty high masses.
3. I bequeath one florin to the Poorhouse, one florin to the general hospital, one florin to the town hospital, one florin to the elementary school fund, in all four florins.
4. To each of the servants in my employ at the time of my death, I leave a year's wages.
5. I rely completely on the discretion of my sole heiress whether or not she wishes to give something to my brothers and sisters; and
6. As it is essential to any will that a sole heir should be appointed, I here name as my one sole heiress my beloved wife Maria Anna von Gluck, née Bergin. And so that no doubts may arise concerning the silver and jewellery, whether it is my property or that of my wife's, I here declare that everything by way of silver and jewellery is the sole property of my wife, and does not belong in my bequest. Should these my last requests not be valid as a will, I wish them to be accepted as a codicil or such.

Finally I name my highly esteemed cousin, Herr Joseph von Holbein, imperial privy counsellor, as executor of this my will, and leave him a snuffbox as a memento. To confirm this document, in the presence of witnesses, I append my name and seal.

Christoph von Gluck.[26]

Gluck's retirement gave rise to several premature reports of his death. The rumour had been formally contradicted in a 'life certificate', which declared Gluck to be resident in Vienna at his Kärntnerstrasse lodging in

---

[25] 'Thus ... my dear friend ... you leave tomorrow for Paris ... I wish you ... with all my heart, a good journey ... You are going to a city where foreign artists are held in high regard ... and you will do yourself credit ... I do not doubt ... write often.' Mosel, *Über das Leben*, 93.

[26] Vienna, 2 Apr. 1786, in Schmid, *Gluck*, 473; Nohl, *Musiker-Briefe*, 55–6; Tenschert, *Gluck ... Reformator der Oper*, 212–13.

the parish of St Stephen on 8 October 1785.[27] Two years later, his acknowledgement of the dedication of Johann Christian Vogel's opera *La Toison
d'or* was accepted as another such proof, the *Mémoires secrets* remarking
that 'the continued existence of the Chevalier Gluck, who for some years
has several times been spoken of as dead, is proved by a letter he has written to M. Vogel, thanking him for the dedication this composer has made
him of the score of *La Toison d'or*.'[28] This is Gluck's last letter to survive:

Monsieur,

I have received through M. Salieri a copy of your first opera, *La Toison d'or*,
which you wished to do me the honour of dedicating to me. As my eyes no
longer allow me to read, M. Salieri gave me the pleasure of letting me hear this
music on the harpsichord; I find it worthy of the praise it has won you in Paris.
A talent for the dramatic illuminates all the other qualities, and I congratulate
you on this with my whole heart. It is a talent all the more rare in that you have
not obtained it through experience, but from instinct. The same M. Salieri has
also told me that he has heard your second work [*Démophoön*]; may it add to
your reputation to the extent that I would wish, and may it make you the most
celebrated of artists. It is with the expression of these sentiments that I beg you
to believe me to be your etc.,

Gluck.[29]

[27] Pub. in Schmid, *Gluck*, 462–3. Gluck seems to have moved between several town houses in
these years. In 1783 he was registered as living in the Michaelerplatz in a house belonging to Antonia
von Gudenus (see n. 13 above). In 1784 he bought his last house in the suburb Auf der Wieden, a
sizeable property with large garden and summer-house (Brauneis, 'Gluck in Wien', 48–52). Gluck
could not have received Kelly here in 1781, as Brauneis suggests.

[28] xxxvi. 68 (3 Oct. 1787).

[29] Letter to Vogel, Vienna, 3 Aug. 1787, pub. in *Journal de Paris*, 13 Oct. 1787, 1193.

25

DEATH
(1787)

GLUCK died on 15 November 1787. Schmid provides several details, many quoted without source, which can only originate with the unidentified guests in the following episode, or with a servant in Gluck's household:

[On the fourteenth of November], Gluck entertained two friends, recently arrived from Paris, in his house in the Wieden. On his doctor's advice, Gluck regularly went out in his carriage after dining, to enjoy the benefit of fresh air and moderate exercise. After the meal, coffee and liqueurs were served, and after dispensing drinks to the two guests, Gluck's wife left to order the carriage. In her absence, one of the guests refused his proffered drink. Gluck, who had always been fond of wine, but who was now strictly forbidden alcohol on account of its inflammatory effect, urged his friend to empty the glass, and when the latter excused himself, he feigned anger at the refusal, gulped down the drink, and quickly wiped his mouth, asking his guests, with a jest, not to betray him to his wife. She returned. The carriage was ready. She bade the guests amuse themselves in the garden for half an hour, till she and her husband returned. The guests accompanied the couple to the carriage. 'Au revoir! Adieu!' rang out from both sides. This farewell was Gluck's last. Barely a quarter of an hour later, he suffered another stroke.[1]

Mme Gluck related that on returning home, 'he was bled, and then seemed to make a complete recovery.'[2] The fullest account of the next hours is given in a letter from Salieri, who was present for the last of them:

[1] *Gluck*, 397–8.
[2] Letter to François Antoine de Lasalle, 18 Nov. 1787: autograph in Vienna, Wiener Stadt- und Landesbibliothek, HIN 1.337; it contains an impassioned plea for Gluck's pension from the Opéra to be transferred to his widow.

You will surely have heard of the death of Chevalier Gluck, which took place on the fifteenth of last month. After dinner on the day before his death, the poor man went for a ride in his carriage with Mme Gluck. She told me that he had been very well that day, that he had dined well, and that on going out of the house he had joked with his servant. Half an hour later, while in the carriage, he suffered an apoplectic attack. It was four o'clock. He was taken home, and at ten o'clock he suffered another stroke, despite which he was still able to speak and was fully rational. The next day, at five in the morning, he suffered a third stroke. At nine o'clock the same morning, Mme Gluck informed me of this disaster. As you might expect, I hastened to his house. I held him, and, with tears in my eyes, I kissed his right hand, which he still moved a little, but he no longer recognized anyone, and at seven in the evening, he expired. He had almost foretold the day of his death. Two weeks before the tragedy, I showed him my new chorus . . . with the title 'The Last Judgement'. I had written two melodies for the moment when the voice of God is heard, and in recommending me to choose one rather than the other, he spoke these exact words: 'I think this one is more appropriate than the other, because it is further removed from the common tone of men, and consequently it is more apt for the idea we can have of divine majesty. If, however, you are not convinced by my argument, wait a few days, and I shall give you news from the next world.'[3]

Gluck's setting of the 'De profundis', which dates from the last years, speaks persuasively of his intuitions. Directed by Salieri, it was performed at the funeral, on 17 November in the cemetry at Matzleinsdorf.[4]

The death was briefly but warmly noted in the Viennese press:

Those who know his name know also his reputation, and will appreciate the extent of the loss which the art of music has suffered in the death of this man, who, through his own efforts, raised it to the highest level. Wherever this is felt, there will be those to mourn the loss. But in Vienna, where for many years he enjoyed both the favour of [Maria] Theresia and Joseph, and also widespread respect, there will also be shed tears of friendship for this good, honest, modest man.[5]

---

[3] Vienna, 5 Dec. 1787: F-Pn, Salieri lettres autographes, no. 1. Pub. in Prod'homme, 'Lettres de Gluck', 262–3; Tiersot, 'Pour la centenaire', 274–5. The identity of the recipient is not known.

[4] Certification of the death and burial was transcribed for Schmid in 1844 by the priest of the Wieden parish; pub. in Schmid, *Gluck*, 463–4; Tenschert, *Gluck . . . Reformator der Oper*, 213.

[5] *Wiener Zeitung*, 21 Nov. 1787. The *Wienerisches Diarium* had been renamed the *Wiener Zeitung* earlier in 1787. The obituary is reproduced in Schmid, *Gluck*, 401, which corrects the date of Gluck's death, incorrectly given as 17 Nov. in the *Wiener Zeitung*.

The red marble gravestone carried this inscription: 'Here rests an honest German. A zealous Christian. A faithful husband. Christoph Ritter Gluck. Great master of the sublime art of music. He died on 15 November 1787.'[6] 'An act of homage more durable than marble' was proposed in Paris by Piccinni: 'An annual concert, to take place on the anniversary of his death . . . at which his music alone would be performed.'[7] The plan failed, 'whether through the jealousy of rivals, who opposed it, or whether the extravagant tone of the appeal was held to be bizarre . . . might the queen have disapproved?'[8]

The last portrait contains the most sustained of all the records purporting to represent Gluck's own spoken words. Olivier de Corancez, editor of the *Journal de Paris*, captured in a string of anecdotes a portrayal of Gluck at his most articulate; his ready defence of his principles and practice, elsewhere well attested,[9] is illustrated here with convincing consistency.

I have been waiting for some time for you to fulfil, with respect to Chevalier Gluck, the kind of tribute you have undertaken to provide for all famous men, whether in the Sciences, Letters, or Arts. I presume you have held back only because of the difficulty of establishing the principal achievements of his life. You doubtless thought that his works, which continue to dominate the lyric stage with total success, testify to his genius more completely than anything you could say. I respect your reticence. I, too, shall refrain from praising him. But there are certain incidents, known to me personally, which I have for some time been asked to communicate to your readers. They have in common the ability to reveal the spirit in which he wrote his operas, and I feel they may be useful both to those who attend the performances of the masterpieces he has left us, and to composers who intend to follow the same path. . . .

My acquaintance with Gluck arose through my collaboration with the immortal Rousseau of Geneva.[10] On his arrival in Paris, Gluck had the keenest desire to be introduced to Rousseau . . . and he was advised to consult me. I suggested the meeting to Rousseau, who agreed. . . . Rousseau said to me one day (it was before the first performance of [*Iphigénie en Aulide*]), 'I have seen the scores of many Italian composers which contain fine dramatic numbers. But M. Gluck alone seems to me to have made the attempt to give each of his characters their own individual style; and what I find even more admirable is that this style, once established, never varies. His scrupulosity in this regard has even led him into committing an anachronism in his opera *Paride ed*

---

[6] Reproduced in Schmid, *Gluck*, 399.

[7] *Journal de Paris*, 15 Dec. 1787, 1501–2.

[8] *Mémoires secrets*, xxxvi. 313 (24 Dec. 1787).

[9] 'He defended his system of opera very ably.' D'Escherny, *Mélanges*, ii. 366 (see Ch. 13 above).

[10] Corancez made an edn. of Rousseau's works: see Ch. 22 and n. 47.

Elena'. Astonished at this, I asked him to explain. 'M. Gluck,' he continued, 'endowed the role of Paris with all the superficial brilliance and all the effeteness of which music is capable. By way of contrast, he gave Helen music with a certain austerity which characterizes her throughout, even when she expresses her passion for Paris. This distinction doubtless arose from the fact that Paris was Phrygian and Helen Spartan. But he has not considered the fact that Sparta acquired the severity of its customs and language only under the laws of Lycurgus, and Lycurgus lived much later than Helen.' I repeated this observation to M. Gluck. 'How happy I would be,' he replied, 'if a few more of my audience could understand me and perceive my intentions in this spirit. Please tell M. Rousseau that I am grateful to him for the attention he has paid to my work. But tell him that I have not committed the anachronism of which he accuses me. If I have given Helen a severe style, it is not because she is Spartan, but because she has this same character in Homer. Tell him, in a word, that she is admired by Hector.'

All Paris saw this same Rousseau, who had for some time shunned the theatre, attend every performance of *Orphée* without fail. It was at a performance of this work that he declared publicly that M. Gluck had just proved him wrong when he had previously said that there could be no good music written to French words.[11] 'I am far from sharing the opinion that M. Gluck is devoid of melody,' he told me one day; 'on the contrary, I find that he exudes melody from all his pores.'

On another occasion, he said to me: 'What I find admirable and truly extraordinary in the music of M. Gluck is not so much the superior beauties, of which there are plenty, but rather his moderation and restraint. I can find no more perfect example of this decorum than the scene in *Orphée*, set in the Elysian Fields. Everything rejoices in a pure and calm happiness, but the expression is so consistent that there is no gesture, either in the singing or in the dance airs, which in any way oversteps the proper mark.' So judicious a word of praise from the mouth of one such as Rousseau seemed to me too flattering to withhold from Chevalier Gluck. 'I was instructed', he replied, 'by the description Eurydice makes of the abode of the Blessed:

> Rien ici n'enflamme l'âme,
> Une douce ivresse laisse
> Un calme heureux dans tous les sens.[12]

The happiness of the Blessed Spirits', he added, 'consists chiefly in their continuity, and consequently in their consistency. That is why what we call "pleasure" has no place there. Pleasure is susceptible to degrees of difference; besides, it becomes tedious, and dulls the palette.'

---

[11] In *Lettre sur la musique française*.
[12] *Orphée*, II. i. In the pub. score, Eurydice sings 'Nul objet n'enflamme . . .'.

I asked him one day why, not being a musician, I became so bound up in his works that I could not tolerate the least distraction during their performance, and why, in contrast, all the operas given before he came seemed to me cold and monotonous, and why in these operas, all the melodies seemed to me to resemble one another. 'That arises from just one cause, a thing crucial to truth,' he told me. 'Before I begin, my greatest concern is to forget I am a musician. I even forget myself in order that I shall see only my characters. The attempt to do otherwise is poisoning all the Arts which aspire to the imitation of Nature. The poet who does not try (or does not want) to forget himself will compose tirades which are not, to speak true, devoid of beauty, but which hold up the action because they work against it; the painter who thinks to embellish Nature becomes inaccurate; the actor who rants becomes incapable of expression; the musician who tries to impress produces satiety and disgust. The passages of music which you believe to resemble each other have in fact nothing in common. If you were a musician, you would not reproach them with this; you would see not only very distinct differences, but also beauties which might make you tolerant of them, despite yourself. That does not prevent your observation from being devastating, for they seem the same to you only because they are all equally ineffective.'[13]

One day at my house, someone sang the scene from *Iphigénie en Aulide*, 'Peuvent-ils ordonner qu'un père'.[14] I noticed that on the first occasion when the line 'Je n'obéira point à cet ordre inhumain' is sung, there is a long note on the word 'je', but when it is repeated the same 'je' takes only a short note. I mentioned to M. Gluck that I found this long note spoilt the melody, and that I was all the more surprised that he had used it on the first occasion in that by discarding it on the second occasion, he apparently attached no importance to it.

'This long note,' he responded, 'which offended you so much in your own home—did it offend you equally in the theatre?' I replied in the negative. 'Well then,' he returned, 'your answer satisfies me. And as you will not always have me on hand, I would ask you to apply the same test in all similar situations. If I succeed in the theatre, I shall have achieved my aim, and it ought to matter little to me—and I swear to you that it matters little indeed—to be judged pleasing either in a salon or in a concert setting. If you have often been in the position to notice that good concert music makes no effect in the theatre, it follows that good theatre music will rarely succeed in a concert. Your question is like that of a man who, from the high gallery of the Dôme des Invalides, calls out to the painter below, "Monsieur, what have you tried to do up here? Is this a nose? Is it an arm? It is like neither the one nor the other!" The painter

---

[13] 'Lettre sur le Chevalier Gluck', *Journal de Paris*, 18 Aug. 1788, 997–9.
[14] *Iphigénie en Aulide*, I. iii.

shouts to him in his turn, and with much justification, "Monsieur, come down, look, and judge for yourself."

'I must tell you, however, that I had a strong reason not only for putting a long note on the "je" the first time Agamemnon sings it, but also for suppressing it at every repetition. Consider: the prince stands between the two strongest opposing forces, Nature and religion. Nature wins in the end, but before pronouncing this terrible statement of disobedience towards the gods, he needs must hesitate, and my long note represents the hesitation. But once he has uttered this word, however often he repeats it there is no more hesitation, and the long note would be no more than a fault of prosody.'

I also complained to M. Gluck that, in the same opera *Iphigénie*, the chorus of soldiers, who come forward so many times to demand loudly that the victim must be given up to them,[15] not only offers nothing outstanding from the point of view of the melody, but is also constantly repeated, note for note, even though variety is so desirable a quality.

'These soldiers', he told me, 'have left all they hold most dear, their country, their wives, and their children, in the sole hope of attacking Troy. They are becalmed in the middle of their journey, and forced to remain in the port at Aulis. A contrary wind would be less disastrous for them, because at least it would enable them to return home. Suppose', he added, 'that a large province experienced a terrible famine. The citizens assembled in large numbers, and went in search of the ruler of the province, who addressed them from his balcony: "My children, what do you want?" All would reply together, "Bread." "But is that how . . ." "Bread." "My friends, we're going to provide . . ." "Bread, bread!" To every speech, they reply "bread"; not only do they pronounce nothing but the one laconic word, but they say it always on the same note, because great emotions have but one accent. Here, the soldiers ask for the victim; all the circumstances are as nothing to their eyes; they see only Troy, or a return home. They can only utter the same words and always with the same accent. I could doubtless have composed a musically more beautiful chorus, and gratified the ears by varying it. But then I would have been only a musician, and I would have departed from Nature, which I must never do. Do not believe, however, that you would at least have gained the pleasure of hearing a beautiful piece of music; on the contrary, I assure you that you would have lost by it, for a beauty out of place has not only the disadvantage of losing most of its effect, but it harms the spectator's judgement, by destroying his inclination to take an interest in the unfolding of the drama.'

M. Gluck was not repelled by my total ignorance of the art of music. I did not fear to question him, especially when it concerned the refutation of some apparent fault. His replies had always an air of simplicity and truth, which did nothing but increase my personal esteem for him, day by day.

---

[15] *Iphigénie en Aulide*, III. i–viii: 'Non, non, nous ne souffrirons pas'.

I asked him to explain why the movement representing the anger of Achilles, in the same opera *Iphigénie*, usually roused me to a passion, and put me, so to speak, in the same situation as the hero himself, even though if I sang it by myself, far from finding anything terrible and threatening in the melody, I found nothing but a march, pleasing to the ear.[16]

'You must realize, before all else,' he told me, 'that music is a very limited art, and it is particularly so in the aspect called melody. You might search in vain through the combination of notes which make up a vocal line for a method by which to identify certain passions—there is no such method. The composer has the resource of harmony, but often even that is insufficient. In the movement you speak of, all my magic is wrought during the music which precedes it and in the choice of instruments which accompany it. For some time, you have heard nothing but Iphigenia's tender regrets and her farewells to Achilles; the most important part here is played by the flutes and the lugubrious timbre of the horns. It is no miracle if your ears, first lulled in this way, then suddenly struck by the piercing sound of the ensemble of military instruments, cause you an extraordinary reaction—a reaction which it is, in truth, my duty to make you feel, but which, however, derives not the least of its strength from a purely physical effect.'

. . . One day, he played on his piano the movement in *Iphigénie en Tauride* where Orestes, alone in prison, after experiencing the agitation to be expected, throws himself on a bench, saying that the calm has returned to his heart.[17] The melody which follows the outburst of madness expresses the subsequent calm, but an attentive listener noticed that Gluck's left hand did not cease from playing a shuddering figure and prolonging the previous agitation. He remarked to M. Gluck that he thought he perceived a contradiction in the left hand, with respect not only to the melody, but to the situation and the words, for, he added, 'Orestes is at peace, and says so.' 'He lies,' exclaimed M. Gluck, 'he mistakes his weakness for calm, but the madness is always there,' (striking his chest). 'He has killed his mother.'

The ability he had to see dramatic situations in their true light enabled him easily to grasp the same implications in the works of others. Someone criticized in his presence the chorus from the second act of Rameau's *Castor et Pollux* as being too close to church music. 'Beware,' said Gluck, 'this is no metaphorical ceremony—the body is there!'[18]

I was present at the first rehearsal of the opera *Alceste*. I thought myself alone in the ampitheatre, which was unlit. At the performance of the March of the Priestesses[19] I gave some visible sign of approbation. Unknown to me, M. Gluck was close by my side. 'You seem to like this march,' he said, as he

---

[16] Ibid. III. iii: 'Calchas, d'un trait mortel'.   [17] II. iii: 'Le calme rentre dans mon cœur'.

[18] Corancez, 'Lettre sur le Chevalier Gluck', *Journal de Paris*, 21 Aug. 1788, 1009–11.

[19] *Alceste*, I. iv.

approached. 'Yes indeed,' I replied, 'I find it has a religious tone which both pleases and amazes me.' 'I shall explain it to you,' he said. 'I noticed that all the Greek poets who wrote hymns for temple scenes followed the rule of making a certain metre predominate in their odes. I concluded that this metre must have an intrinsic character appropriate to things sacred and religious. When I wrote my march, I observed the same sequence of long and short quantities, and now I see I was not wrong to do so. These Greeks were fine men!' he added, slapping me on the shoulder. I saw from his air of hilarity that he took no credit for the success of his march, and that he gave the Greeks all the honour. . . .

The première of *Alceste* was a failure. I joined M. Gluck in the corridors, where I found him more preoccupied with seeking the cause of an event he found so extraordinary than affected by the lack of success. 'It would be singular', he said, 'if this work failed. That would constitute a landmark in the history of your country's taste. I allow that a work composed exclusively in accordance with the rules of music might succeed or fail: that will depend on the very unpredictable taste of the audience. I even allow that a work of this sort might enjoy a major success at first, and fail later even with those who admired it originally. But that I should see the failure of a work founded entirely upon the truth of Nature, in which all the passions are accurately expressed, troubles me, I confess. *Alceste*', he added proudly, 'ought not to please only at present, while it is new. It is not the work for a single moment in time; I declare that it will please as much two hundred years hence, if the French language has not changed, for I have grounded it in Nature, which is not subject to fashion.' This incident proved the confidence of this extraordinary man in the truth of his principles.

The chorus of the underworld gods[20] aroused in me the greatest terror, but I could not understand what had led M. Gluck to have four lines sung on a single note. He told me: 'It is not possible to imitate the language of supernatural creatures, because we have never heard them. But we must strive to get close to the ideas we have of the functions they undertake. Demons, for example, have a well-known and well-defined conventional character, and their portrayal should be dominated by an excess of rage and fury. But the underworld gods are not demons; we think of them as the agents of fate; they are subject to no emotion; they are impassive. They are indifferent to Alcestis and Admetus; the only necessity is that their destiny is fulfilled. To represent this impassivity, which is their particular characteristic, I thought I could do no better than to deprive them of all inflexion, reserving for my orchestra the task of painting all that is terrible in their words.'

. . . He had a method of composing which I believe was unique to him. He often told me—these are his very words—that he began by giving careful

---

[20] *Alceste*, III. iii.

consideration to each act; then he did the same for the entire work, always imagining himself viewing it from the middle of the stalls; once his opera was assembled in this way, and its individual components characterized, he considered his work as finished, even though he had not yet written a note. But this preparation usually cost him a complete year of the most exacting labour, and as often a severe illness, too—and that is what many people call 'writing songs'!

I affirm, messieurs, all the facts I have related; they are all personally known to me.[21]

---

[21] Corancez, 'Lettre sur le Chevalier Gluck', *Journal de Paris*, 24 Aug. 1788, 1021–3.

LIST OF
PRINCIPAL DOCUMENTS CITED

CHAPTER 1

date of event

Baptismal record	4 July 1714
Matriculation record	1731

Additional sources from Burney, Mannlich, Reichardt, and Schmid.

CHAPTER 2

Review of *Demofoonte* (*Gazetta di Milano*)	9 Jan. 1743
Review of *Ippolito* (*Gazetta di Milano*)	10 Mar. 1745

Additional sources from Carpani, Reichardt, Schmid, and *Gazetta di Milano*.

CHAPTER 3

Review of *La caduta de' giganti* (Burney)	7 Jan. 1746
Review of *Artamene* (Burney)	4 Mar. 1746
Walpole to Mann	28 Mar. 1746

Additional sources from Burney, Reichardt, and *General Advertiser*.

CHAPTER 4

Record of Gluck as singer in Mingotti's troupe	15 Sept. 1747
Review of *Semiramide* (Khevenhüller)	14 May 1748
Metastasio to Pasquini	29 June 1748
Record of Gluck as director of troupe	3 Oct. 1748
Gluck to Franz Pirker	Sept. 1748
Gluck to Franz Pirker	Jan. 1749
Review of concert in Copenhagen	Apr. 1749

Additional sources from Franz and Marianne Pirker.

CHAPTER 5

Marriage contract	3 Sept. 1750
Marriage certificate	15 Sept. 1750

CHAPTER 6

Le cinesi (Ditters)	24 Sept. 1754
Review of *L'innocenza giustificata* (*Journal encyclopédique*)	8 Dec. 1755
Metastasio to D'Argenvillières	19 Feb. 1756
Review of *Il rè pastore* (*Journal encyclopédique*)	8 Dec. 1756
Metastasio to Farinelli	8 Dec. 1756
Additional sources from Ditters, Khevenhüller, Metastasio, Leopold Mozart, Reichardt, and Tufarelli.	

CHAPTER 7

Durazzo to Maria Theresia	21 Jan. 1763
Durazzo to Favart	20 Dec. 1759
Angiolini	1761
Dancourt to Favart	25 Apr. 1762
Additional sources from Angiolini, Burney, Ditters, Favart, Khevenhüller, Metastasio, Zinzendorf, *Journal encyclopédique*, and *Journal étranger*.	

CHAPTER 8

Calzabigi to *Mercure* (15 June 1784)	1762
Reviews of *Orfeo* (Zinzendorf, *Wienerisches Diarium*)	5 Oct. 1762
Favart to Durazzo	10 Nov. 1760
Favart to Durazzo	28 Jan. 1763
Favart to Durazzo	19 Apr. 1763
Durazzo to Favart	6 May 1763
Favart to Gluck	June 1763
Dancourt to Favart	5 July 1763
Additional sources from Burney, Casanova, Favart, Grimm, Wille, Zinzendorf, *Journal encyclopédique*, and *Journal étranger*.	

CHAPTER 9

Bevilacqua to Preti	16 Oct. 1762
Ditters on *Il trionfo di Clelia*	14 May 1763

Review of *Ezio* (*Wienerisches Diarium*)   26 Dec. 1763
Durazzo to Favart   19 Nov. 1763
Review of *Il Parnaso confuso* (Khevenhüller)   24 Jan. 1765
Van Swieten to Cobenzl   16 Feb. 1765
Archduke Leopold to Franz Thurn-Valsassina   20 May 1765
Additional sources from Bevilacqua, Burney, Ditters,
    Favart, Khevenhüller, Zinzendorf, *Journal*
    encyclopédique, and *Wienerisches Diarium*.

CHAPTER 10

Calzabigi to Kaunitz   6 Mar. 1767
Review of *Alceste* (Sonnenfels)   26 Dec. 1767
Calzabigi to Greppi   12 Dec. 1768
Gluck to Archduke Leopold   1769
Review of *Alceste* score (Forkel)   1771
Additional sources from Calzabigi, Khevenhüller,
    Metastasio, Leopold Mozart, and Rousseau.

CHAPTER 11

Gluck to Crommer   16 Jan. 1769
Anon to ?   15 May 1769
Salieri   winter 1769
Gluck to Kaunitz   31 Dec. 1769
Gluck to Caroli   26 Jan. 1770
Gluck to Caroli   22 Feb. 1770
Gluck to Caroli   1 Mar. 1770
Gluck to Caroli   19 Mar. 1770
Gluck to Martini   14 July 1770
Gluck to Duke Giovanni of Braganza   1770
Burney   Sept. 1772
Gluck to Klopstock   14 Aug. 1773
Additional sources from Kelly, Khevenhüller,
    Reichardt, and *Wienerisches Diarium*.

CHAPTER 12

Du Roullet to Antoine d'Auvergne   1 Aug. 1772
Gluck to *Mercure de France*   1 Feb. 1773
Gluck to Martini   26 Oct. 1773
Mannlich   1774
Du Roullet, preface to *Iphigénie en Aulide*   1774
Review of *Iphigénie en Aulide* (*Mémoires secrets*)   19 Apr. 1774

Maria Antoinette to Marie Christine   26 Apr. 1774
Gluck to Louis XVI, dedication of *Iphigénie*   1774
Additional sources from Salieri, Arnaud, Forkel, Grimm,
    and *Mémoires secrets*.

CHAPTER 13

Gluck to Le Marchand   10 July 1774
Gluck to Marie Antoinette, dedication of *Orphée*   1774
Gluck to Mercy-Argenteau   11 Aug. 1774
Gluck to Mercy-Argenteau   16 Aug. 1774
Gluck to Académie royale   Oct. 1774
Additional sources from Mme du Deffant,
    François-Louis d'Escherny, Dominique-Joseph Garat,
    Stéphanie Brulart de Genlis, Sara Goudar, Grimm,
    Rousseau, Amélie Suard, Voltaire, *Journal des
    Beaux-Arts*, and *Mercure de France*.

CHAPTER 14

Herder to Gluck   5 Nov. 1774
Riedel to Ring   10 Dec. 1774
Petersen to Merck   Nov. 1774
Mercy-Argenteau to Maria Theresia   19 Jan. 1775
Maria Theresia to Mercy-Argenteau   4 Feb. 1775
Mercy-Argenteau to Maria Theresia   20 Feb. 1775
Gluck to Kruthoffer   9 Mar. 1775
Nanette Gluck to Klopstock   17 Mar. 1775
Additional sources from Cramer, Gebler, and
    Maria Theresia.

CHAPTER 15

Kruthoffer to Peters   28 Mar. 1775
Kruthoffer to Gluck   31 Mar. 1775
Gluck to Kruthoffer   15 Apr. 1775
Gluck to Le Marchand   15 Apr. 1775
Kruthoffer to Du Roullet   *c.*30 Apr. 1775
Gluck to Arnaud   12 May 1775
Gluck to Kruthoffer   30 May 1775
Gluck to Klopstock   24 June 1775
Additional sources from Kruthoffer and Peters.

CHAPTER 16

Gluck to Du Roullet	1 July 1775
Gluck to Kruthoffer	31 July 1775
Gluck to Du Roullet	14 Oct. 1775
Gluck to Du Roullet	22 Nov. 1775
Gluck to Kruthoffer	29 Nov. 1775
Gluck to Du Roullet	2 Dec. 1775
Gluck to Du Roullet	13 Dec. 1775
Gluck to Kruthoffer	31 Dec. 1775
Gluck to Arnaud	31 Jan. 1776
Gluck to Kruthoffer	30 June 1776

Additional sources from Arnaud, Du Roullet, Grimm, Kruthoffer, Peters, *Journal de Paris*, and *Mémoires secrets*.

CHAPTER 17

Gluck to Klopstock	10 May 1776
Wieland to Gluck	13 July 1776
Duke Carl August to Gluck	July 1776
Gluck to Wieland	7 Aug. 1776

Additional sources from Gerber.

CHAPTER 18

Gluck to Du Roullet	summer 1776
Gluck to the musicians in the orchestra at the Opéra	14 Aug. 1776
Gluck to Kruthoffer	29 Aug. 1776
Gluck to Kruthoffer	30 Sept. 1776
Gluck to Kruthoffer	31 Oct. 1776
Gluck to Arnaud	31 Oct. 1776
Gluck to *Mercure de France*	Nov. 1776
Gluck to Kruthoffer	29 Nov. 1776
Gluck to Kruthoffer	15 Jan. 1777
Gluck to Kruthoffer	31 Jan. 1777
Gluck to Kruthoffer	3 Mar. 1777
Gluck to Kruthoffer	30 Mar. 1777

Additional sources from Arnaud, Bretschneider, Framery, Martini, Piccinni, and *Mémoires secrets*.

CHAPTER 19

Princess de Lamballe	summer 1777
La Harpe to *Journal de politique et de littérature*	5 Oct. 1777

Gluck to Kruthoffer	31 Dec. 1779
Gluck to Jacob von Gontard	end 1779
Gluck to Von Dalberg	19 Jan. 1780
Gluck to Kruthoffer	31 Jan. 1780
Gluck to Duke Carl August	10 Feb. 1780
Gluck to Kruthoffer	2 Mar. 1780
Gluck to Charles Palissot	18 Mar. 1780
Gluck to Kruthoffer	31 Mar. 1780
Gluck to Kruthoffer	29 Apr. 1780
Gluck to Klopstock	10 May 1780
Gluck to Kruthoffer	30 May 1780
Gluck to Kruthoffer	30 June 1780
Gluck to Kruthoffer	30 July 1780
Gluck to Louis-Joseph Francœur	20 Aug. 1780
Gluck to Kruthoffer	30 Aug. 1780
Gluck to Kruthoffer	30 Sept. 1780
Gluck to Kruthoffer	31 Oct. 1780
Gluck to Kruthoffer	29 Nov. 1780

Additional sources from Calzabigi and *Mémoires secrets*.

CHAPTER 23

Gluck to Kruthoffer	3 Jan. 1781
Gluck to Kruthoffer	31 Jan. 1781
Gluck to Kruthoffer	28 Mar. 1781
Gluck to Kruthoffer	1 May 1781
Gluck to *Mémoires secrets*	11 May 1781
Carlo Calin to Kruthoffer	19 June 1781
Gluck to Duke Carl August	21 Aug. 1781
Kelly	1781
Joseph Kämpfer	?1781
Gluck to Kruthoffer	2 Nov. 1781
Gluck to Kruthoffer	30 Nov. 1781
Gluck to Kruthoffer	30 Dec. 1781

Additional sources from Joseph II and Mozart.

CHAPTER 24

Gluck to Valentin	17 Apr. 1782
Gluck to Kruthoffer	22 Feb. 1783
Gluck to Kruthoffer	28 Mar. 1783
Gluck to Kruthoffer	9 July 1783
Gluck to Kruthoffer	4 Aug. 1783

CHAPTER 25

BIBLIOGRAPHY

ABERT, HERMANN (ed.), *Gluck-Jahrbuch*, 1 (1913), 2 (1915), 3 (1917), 4 (1918).

ALCARI, CESARE, 'La cartella no. 88', *Musica d'oggi*, 14 (1932), 257–60.

ALGAROTTI, FRANCESCO, *Saggio sopra l'opera in musica*, 2nd edn. (Livorno, 1763).

ANGERMÜLLER, RUDOLPH, 'Opernreform im Lichte der wirtschaftlichen Verhältnis an der Académie royale de Musique', *Die Musikforschung*, 25 (1972), 267–91.

ANGIOLINI, GASPARO, *Dissertation sur les ballets pantomimes des anciens* (Vienna, 1765, repr. Milan, 1956).

—— *Lettere di Gasparo Angiolini a Monsieur Noverre sopra i balli pantomimi* (Milan, 1773).

—— *Riflessioni di Gasparo Angiolini sopra l'uso dei programmi nei balli pantomimi* ([Milan], 1775).

BACHAUMONT, LOUIS, PETIT DE. See *Mémoires secrets*.

BARTHÉLEMY, MAURICE, 'Les Règlements de 1776 et l'Académie royale de musique', *Recherches sur la musique française classique*, 4 (1964), 239–48.

BÉRARD, AUGUSTE SIMON LOUIS (ed.), *Isographie des hommes célèbres: Collection de facsimile de lettres autographes et de signatures* (Paris, 1837–8).

BRAUNEIS, WALTHER, 'Gluck in Wien: Seine Gedenkstätten, Wohnungen und Aufführungsorte', *Gluck in Wien*, ed. Gerhard Croll and Monika Woitas (Kassel, 1989), 42–61.

BROWN, BRUCE ALAN, 'Christoph Willibald Gluck and Opéra-Comique in Vienna, 1754–1764', Ph.D. thesis (Univ. of California, Berkeley, 1986).

—— 'Durazzo, Duni, and the Frontispiece to *Orfeo ed Euridice*', *Studies in Eighteenth-Century Culture*, 19 (1989), 71–97.

—— *Gluck and the French Theatre in Vienna* (Oxford, 1991).

BURNEY, CHARLES, *A General History of Music* (London, 1786–9); ed. Frank Mercer (London and New York, 1935, repr. New York, 1957).

—— *The Present State of Music in Germany, the Netherlands, and United Provinces*, 2nd edn. (London, 1775; repr. New York, 1969).

BUSCHMEIER, GABRIELE, '*Ezio* in Prag und Wien: Bemerkungen zu den beiden Fassungen', *Gluck in Wien*, ed. Gerhard Croll and Monika Woitas (Kassel, 1989), 85–8.

CAMPAN, MME DE, *Mémoires sur la vie privée de Marie Antoinette* (Paris, 1822).

CASANOVA DE SEINGALT, JACQUES, *Histoire de ma vie*, ed. Fritz Brockhaus (Paris, 1960–2).

CAUCHIE, MAURICE, 'Gluck et ses éditeurs parisiens', *Le Ménestrel*, 28 (1927), 309–11.

CHURGIN, BATHIA, 'Alterations in Gluck's Borrowings from Sammartini', *Studies in Music*, 9 (1980), 117–34.

CORANCEZ, OLIVIER DE, 'Lettre sur le Chevalier Gluck', *Journal de Paris*, 18 Aug. 1788, 997–9; 21 Aug. 1788, 1009–11; 24 Aug. 1788, 1021–3.

CRAMER, CARL FRIEDRICH, *Magazin der Musik* (Hamburg, 1783–6).

CROCE, BENEDETTO, *I teatri di Napoli, secolo XV–XVIII* (Naples, 1891).

CROLL, GERHARD, 'Ein unbekannte tragisches Ballett von Gluck', *Mitteilung der Gesellschaft für Salzburger Landeskunde*, 109 (1969), 275–7.

—— 'Glucks Debut am Burgtheater', *Österreichische Musikzeitschrift*, 31 (1976), 194–202.

—— ' "Il mio ritratto fatto a Roma . . .": Ein neues "fruhes" Gluck-Bild', *Österreichisches Musikzeitschrift*, 42 (1987), 505–17.

—— and DEAN, WINTON, 'Gluck, Christoph Willibald', *The New Grove Dictionary of Music and Musicians*, ed. Stanley Sadie (London, 1980), viii. 455–75.

—— and WOITAS, MONIKA (eds.), *Gluck in Wien: Kongressbericht Wien 1987* (Kassel, 1989).

D'ESCHERNY, FRANÇOIS-LOUIS, *Mélanges de littérature, d'histoire, de morale, et de philosophie* (Paris, 1811).

DESNOIRESTERRES, LE BRISOYS DE, *Gluck et Piccinni: La Musique française au XVIIIe siècle, 1774–1800*, 2nd edn. (Paris, 1875).

DEUTSCH, OTTO ERICH, 'Gluck im Redoutensaal', *Österreichische Musikzeitschrift*, 21 (1966), 521–5.

—— 'Höfische Theaterbilder aus Schönbrunn', *Österreichische Musikzeitschrift*, 22 (1967), 577–84.

DITTERS VON DITTERSDORF, CARL, *Lebensbeschreibung* (Leipzig, 1801, repr. Munich, 1967).

EINSTEIN, ALFRED, *Gluck*, tr. Eric Blom, 2nd edn. (London, 1964).

FAVART, CHARLES-SIMON, *Mémoires et correspondances littéraires, dramatiques et anecdotiques* (Paris, 1808).

FORKEL, JOHANN NICOLAUS, *Musikalisch-kritische Bibliothek* (Gotha, 1778–9).

—— 'Schreiben, woraus ein Componist lernen kann, auf welche Weise man den Direktoren der Académie royale de Musique in Paris Lust zu einer neuen Oper machen müsse', *Musikalischer Almanach für Deutschland*, 4 (1789), 151–63.

FÜRSTENAU, MORITZ, *Zur Geschichte der Musik und des Theaters am Hofe der Kurfürsten von Sachsen und Königen von Polen* (Dresden, 1861–2).

—— 'Das Festspiel *Il Parnaso confuso* von Gluck', *Berliner Musik-Zeitung Echo*, 19 (1869), 205–8.

GARAT, DOMINIQUE-JOSEPH, *Mémoires historiques sur la vie de M. Suard, sur ses écrits, et sur le XVIIIe siècle* (Paris, 1820).

GENLIS, STÉPHANIE FÉLICITÉ DUCREST DE SAINT AUBIN BRULART DE, *Mémoires inédits de Mme la Comtesse de Genlis pour servir à l'historie des dix-huitième et dix-neuvième siècles* (Paris, 1825–6).

GERBER, ERNST LUDWIG, 'Christoph von Gluck', *Historisch-biographisches Lexicon der Tonkünstler* (Leipzig, 1790–2), i. 514–18.

GINGUENÉ, PIERRE LOUIS, *Notice sur la vie et les ouvrages de Nicolas Piccinni* (Paris, 1801).

GOTTO, TITO, 'Bologna musicale del 1700 e Cristoforo Gluck', *Due secoli di vita musicale: Storia del Teatro Communale di Bologna*, ed. Lamberto Trezzini (Bologna, 1966).

GRÉTRY, ANDRÉ MODESTE, *Mémoires, ou essais sur la musique*, 2nd edn. (Paris, 1797).

GRIMM, MELCHIOR (ed.), *Correspondance littéraire, philosophique et critique* (1813), 3rd edn., ed. Maurice Tourneux (Paris, 1877–82).

HAAS, ROBERT, *Gluck und Durazzo im Burgtheater* (Vienna, 1925).

—— 'Von dem Wienerischen Geschmack in der Musik', *Festschrift Johannes Biehle zum 60. Geburtstage*, ed. Erich Müller (Leipzig, 1930), 59–65.

—— 'Der Wiener Bühnetanz von 1740 bis 1767', *Jahrbuch der Musikbibliothek Peters*, 44 (1937), 77–93.

HAMMELMANN, HANS, and ROSE, MICHAEL, 'New Light on Calzabigi and Gluck', *Musical Times*, 110 (1969), 609–11.

HEARTZ, DANIEL, 'Haydn und Gluck im Burgtheater um 1760: *Der neue krumme Teufel*, *Le Diable à quatre*, und die Sinfonie "Le Soir" ', *Bericht über den Internationalen Musikwissenschaftlichen Kongress, Bayreuth 1981*, ed. Christoph-Helmut Mahling and Sigrid Wiesmann (Kassel, 1983), 120–35.

—— 'Coming of Age in Bohemia: The Musical Apprenticeships of Benda and Gluck', *Journal of Musicology*, 6 (1988), 510–27.

HOPKINSON, CECIL, *A Bibliography of the Printed Works of C. W. von Gluck 1714–1787*, 2nd edn. (New York, 1967).

HORTSCHANSKY, KLAUS, 'Gluck und Lampugnani in Italien: Zum Pasticcio *Arsace*', *Analecta musicolgica*, 3 (1966), 49–64.

—— 'Glucks Sendungsbewusstsein: Dargestellt an einem unbekannten Gluck-Brief', *Die Musikforschung*, 21 (1968), 30–5.

—— 'Unbekannte Aufführungesberichte zu Glucks Opern der Jahre 1748 bis 1765', *Jahrbuch de Staatliches Institutes für Musikforschung Preussischer Kulturbesitz 1969* (Berlin, 1970), 19–37.

—— 'Gluck nella *Gazetta di Milano* 1742–1745', *Nuova rivista musicale italiana*, 6 (1972), 512–25.

—— *Parodie und Entlehnung im Schaffen Christoph Willibald Glucks* (Cologne, 1973).

HOWARD, PATRICIA, *Christoph Willibald Gluck: A Guide to Research* (New York, 1987).

HYDE, CATHERINE (Hyde Govion Broglio Solari), *Secret Memoirs of the Court of France . . . from the Journal, Letters, and Conversations of Princess Lamballe* (London, 1826).

JULLIEN, ADOLPHE, *La Cour et l'Opéra sous Louis XVI* (Paris, 1878).

KAPLAN, JAMES MAURICE, 'Eine Ergänzung zu Glucks Korrespondenz', *Die Musikforschung*, 31 (1978), 314–17.

KELLY, MICHAEL, *Reminiscences* (London, 1826).

KHEVENHÜLLER-METSCH, JOHANN JOSEF, *Aus der Zeit Maria Theresias: Tagebuch des Fürsten Johann Josef Khevenhüller-Metsch, kaiserlichen Obersthofmeisters*, pub. in 8 unnumbered vols.: 1742–4, 1745–9, 1752–5, 1956–7, 1758–9, 1764–7, 1770–3, ed. Rudolph Khevenhüller-Metsch and Hans Schlitter (Vienna, 1907–25); 1774–80, ed. Maria Breunlich-Pawlik and Hans Wagner (Vienna, 1972).

KINSKY, GEORG, *Glucks Briefe an Franz Kruthoffer* (Vienna, Prague, and Leipzig, 1927).

KLOPSTOCK, FRIEDRICH GOTTLOB, *Auswahl aus Klopstocks nachgelassenen Briefwechsel*, ed. Christian August Heinrich Clodius (Leipzig, 1821).

——— *Briefe von und an Klopstock*, ed. Johann Martin Lappenberg (Brunswick, 1867).

KOMORN, MARIA, 'Ein ungedruckter Brief Glucks', *Neue Zeitschrift für Musik*, 99 (1932), 672–5.

L.R., 'Correspondance inédite de Gluck', *La Revue musicale*, 10 (1914), 1–16.

LE BLOND, GASPARD MICHEL, *Mémoires pour servir à l'histoire de la révolution operée dans la musique par M. le chevalier Gluck* (Paris, 1781).

LESURE, FRANÇOIS (ed.), *Querelle des Gluckistes et des Piccinnistes* (Geneva, 1984).

LEUX-HENSCHEN, IRMGARD, *Joseph Martin Kraus in seinen Briefen* (Stockholm, 1978).

LIEBESKIND, JOSEF, *Ergänzungen und Nachträge zu dem Thematischen Verzeichnis der Werke von Chr. W. v. Gluck* (Leipzig, 1911). See Wotquenne.

MANNLICH, JOHANN CHRISTIAN VON, *Ein deutscher Maler und Hofmann: Lebenserinnerungen 1741–1822*, tr. Eugen Stollreither (Berlin, 1910).

——— 'Histoire de ma vie', MS in Munich, Bayerische Staatsbibliothek, Codex Gallicus 616–19; excerpted in Henriette Weiss von Trostprugg, ed., 'Mémoires sur la musique à Paris à la fin du régne de Louis XV', *La Revue musicale*, 15 (July–Aug. 1934), 111–19; (Sept.–Oct. 1934), 161–71; (Nov. 1934), 252–62.

MARIA THERESIA, *Correspondance secrète entre Marie Thérèse et la Comte de Mercy-Argenteau*, ed. Alfred von Arneth and Mathieu August Geffroy (Paris, 1874).

MARIE ANTOINETTE, *Correspondance inédite de Marie Antoinette*, ed. Paul Vogt de Hunolstein (Paris, 1864).

MARX, ADOLF BERNARD, *Gluck und die Oper* (Berlin, 1863, repr. Hildesheim, 1980).

Mémoires secrets pour servir à l'histoire de la république des lettres en France depuis MDCCLXII jusqu'à nos jours (London, 1777–89), ed. Louis Petit de Bachaumont, Mathieu François Pidansat de Mairobert, *et al.*: vols. i–v ed. Bachaumont; entries relevant to Gluck begin at vol. vii, ed. Pidansat.

METASTASIO, PIETRO, *Tutte le opere*, ed. Bruno Brunelli (Milan, 1947–54).

MOSEL, IGNAZ FRANZ EDLEN VON, *Über das Leben und die Werke des Anton Salieri* (Vienna, 1827).

MOSER, HANS JOACHIM, *Christoph Willibald Gluck: Die Leistung, der Mann, das Vermächtnis* (Stuttgart, 1940).

MOZART, WOLFGANG AMADEUS, *Briefe und Aufzeichnungen*, ed. Wilhelm Bauer, Otto Erich Deutsch, and Joseph Heinz Eibl (Kassel 1962–75).

MÜLLER VON ASOW, ERICH HERMANN, *Angelo und Pietro Mingotti* (Dresden, 1917).

—— 'Zwei unveröffentliche Briefe Glucks an Carl August', *Die Musik* (1923), 652.

—— and MÜLLER VON ASOW, HEDWIG, *The Collected Correspondence and Papers of Christoph Willibald Gluck* (London, 1962).

NICOLAI, FRIEDRICH, *Beschreibung einer Reise durch Deutschland und die Schweiz, im Jahre 1781* (Berlin and Stettin, 1783–96).

NOHL, LUDWIG, *Musiker-Briefe. Eine Sammlung Briefe von C. W. von Gluck, Ph. E. Bach, J. Haydn, C. M. von Weber und F. Mendelssohn-Bartholdy* (Leipzig, 1867).

NOVERRE, JEAN-GEORGES, *Lettres sur la danse, et sur les ballets* (Stuttgart and Lyons, 1760).

—— *Lettres sur les arts imitateurs en général et sur la danse en particulier*, 2nd edn. (Paris, 1807).

PAGLICCI BROZZI, ANTONIO, *Il Regio Ducal Teatro di Milano nel secolo XVIII* (Milan, 1894).

PEREYRA, MARIE LOUISE, 'Vier Gluck-Briefe', *Die Musik*, 13 (1913–14), 10–15.

PLANELLI, ANTONIO, *Dell'opera in musica* (Naples, 1772).

PROD'HOMME, JACQUES-GABRIEL, *Écrits de musiciens* (Paris, 1912).

—— 'Lettres de Gluck et à propos de Gluck', *Zeitschrift der Internationalen Musikgesellschaft*, 13 (1912), 257–65.

—— *Christoph-Willibald Gluck*, 2nd edn., rev. Joël-Marie Fauquet (Paris, 1985).

REICHARDT, JOHANN FRIEDRICH, *Briefe eines aufmerksamen Reisenden die Musik betreffend* (Frankfurt and Leipzig, 1774–6).

—— 'Fortsetzung der Berichtigungen und Zusätze zum Gerberschen Lexicon der Tonkünstler', *Musikalische Monatschrift*, 3 (Sept. 1792), 72–4.

—— 'Bruchstücke aus Reichardts Autobiographie', *Allgemeine musikalische Zeitung* (13 Oct. 1813), 665–74.

RICCI, CORRADO, *I teatri di bologna nei secoli XVII e XVIII* (Bologna, 1888).

RIEDEL, FRIEDRICH JUSTUS (ed.), *Ueber die Musik des Ritters Christoph von Gluck* (Vienna, 1775).

ROUSSEAU, JEAN-JACQUES, *Lettre sur la musique française* (Paris, 1753).

—— *Traités sur la musique* (Geneva, 1781).

RUSHTON, JULIAN, 'Music and Drama at the Académie Royale de Musique (Paris) 1774–1789', D.Phil. thesis (Oxford, 1969).

—— '*Iphigénie en Tauride*: The operas of Gluck and Piccinni', *Music and Letters*, 53 (1972), 411–30.

—— 'From Vienna to Paris: Gluck and the French Opera', *Chigiana*, 9–10 (1972–3), 283–98.

SCHMID, ANTON, *Christoph Willibald Ritter von Gluck* (Leipzig, 1854).

SCHMITT, JOSEPH, 'Zur Familiengeschichte des berühmten Oberpfälzers Christoph Willibald Ritter von Gluck', *Verhandlung des Historischen Vereins für Oberpfalz und Regensburg*, 95 (1954), 215–25.

SONNENFELS, JOSEPH VON, 'Nach der zweiten Vorstellung der *Iphigenie in Tauris*', *Deutsches Museum* (Leipzig, 1782), 400–16.

—— 'Briefe über die Wienerische Schaubühne', *Gesammelte Schriften* (Vienna, 1784), v. 131–392.

SPULAK, ROSWITHA, 'Ein unbekanntes Schriftstück Christoph Willibald Glucks', *Die Musikforschung*, 40 (1987), 345–9.

SQUIRE, WILLIAM BARCLAY, 'Gluck's London Operas', *Musical Quarterly*, 1 (1915), 397–409.

STRAUSS, DAVID FREIDRICH, 'Klopstock und der Markgraf Karl Friedrich von Baden', *Kleine Schriften* (Leipzig, 1862), 23–67.

SUARD, AMÉLIE, *Essais de mémoires sur M. Suard* (Paris, 1820).

TENSCHERT, ROLAND, *Christoph Willibald Gluck: Sein Leben in Bildern* (Leipzig, 1938).

—— *Christoph Willibald Gluck: Der grosse Reformator der Oper* (Olten and Freiburg, 1951).

TIERSOT, JULIEN, 'Pour le centenaire de Gluck: Lettres et documents inédits', *Le Ménestrel*, 23–35 (1914), 214–15, 221–2, 236–7, 243–5, 246, 251–3, 261–2, 266–7, 274–5.

—— *Lettres de musiciens* (Paris, 1924).

TREICHLINGER, WILHELM M. (ed.), *Christoph Willibald Gluck: Briefe* (Zurich, 1951).

VATIELLI, FRANCESCO, 'Riflessi della lotta Gluckista in Italia', *Rivista musicale italiana*, 21 (1914), 639–74.

VOLTAIRE, FRANÇOIS-MARIE AROUET DE, *Œuvres complètes* (Kehl, 1785–9).

WERNER, RICHARD MARIA, *Aus dem Josephinischen Wien: Geblers und Nicolais Briefwechsel während der Jahre 1771–1786* (Berlin, 1888).

WIELAND, CHRISTOPH MARTIN, *Auswahl denkwürdiger Briefe*, ed. Ludwig Wieland (Vienna, 1815).

WILLE, JEAN-GEORGES, *Mémoires et journal de J.-G. Wille Graveur du Roi*, ed. Georges Duplessis (Paris, 1857).

WOTQUENNE, ALFRED, *Ch. W. v. Gluck: Thematisches Verzeichnis seiner Werke*, tr. Josef Liebeskind (Leipzig, 1904). See Liebeskind.

ZECHMEISTER, GUSTAV, *Die Wiener Theater nächst der Burg und nächst dem Kärntnertor von 1747 bis 1776* (Vienna, 1971).

INDEX